DRAGON BLOODED

BOOK ONE: THE HIDDEN HERITAGE SERIES

DAN KENNER

Akewnon Books

For Mom and Dad and how you raised me to be bold and do what sings to my heart.

For Mom and Dad and how you raised me to be bold and do what sings to my heart.

CONTENTS

FLAMING HANDS AND FLAMING HAIR

I press the tip of the pencil to my thumb, the point of the graphite impressing on my skin. When I pull it away, it leaves a small spot—the only evidence of my boredom in this class. Mr. Rogers is talking about something dull in US History again. I hear him mention Abraham Lincoln at one point, but I'm not paying attention.

Instead, I'm staring out the window at the shining sun. I wouldn't normally be so consumed with the outside, but I'd stayed up too late the night before with my football buddies. I was having a hard time staying awake.

"Mr. Smith, what year did Lincoln issue the Emancipation Proclamation?"

My mouth goes dry the moment I hear my name.

"Uh . . ." I glance around the room. At least half of my classmates are staring at me. This is something I should know. It's also something I've neglected to even try to remember. I'm not terrible in school, and history doesn't always bore me, but my mind has been way too focused on tonight's homecoming game.

I open my mouth but snap it shut when nothing comes to mind. There's no point in pretending to know the answer. Instead, I shrug and put on a wry smile.

"Your silence is not encouraging me, young man," Mr. Rogers says, clearing his throat. "I know you have the big game this evening, but can you at least *try* not to drool while staring out the window?"

I stifle a laugh. The class doesn't stifle theirs. It doesn't bother me though. The comment was pretty funny.

"Easier said than done, but sure, I'll give that a go." I put my hands behind my head and grin.

Mr. Rogers folds his arms, a look of mock frustration on his face. His dark hair is well-kept, gelled into place, and subtly swept to the right side of his head. I can tell he's just pretending to be annoyed with me. I am one of his favorites, after all. He doesn't have to say it, I just know.

"Remember that you'll have to pass the final exam this semester if you want to keep playing," he says, his head shifting side to side. He's still smiling, even if it's slight.

"Yes, sir," I answer with an exaggerated tone. I salute him as if he were a commander in the army.

He sighs, shakes his head again, then continues the lesson.

"Bro, you're gonna fail out of this class someday," the boy to my left whispers.

Amir Sharma. He's been my best friend ever since we moved to this small town. His dark eyes watch me under thick eyebrows. He styles his hair similarly to Mr. Rogers. It's almost uncanny. I've joked with him about it before, but he doesn't care. It's all about looking professional—that's what he says at least.

"I'll keep trying my luck. They know they can't take me out of the game, not with how well I've been playing this season." I wink at him.

He rolls his eyes, then points to the front of the classroom.

Amir is the sole reason I'm passing any of my classes. He's not only a genius, but he's also very, *very* good at explaining things that don't make sense coming from a boring teacher. We didn't register for all the same classes, but I tried to match as many of them as I could.

My dad hired Amir to tutor me back in the eighth grade. Our parents worked together for their jobs. I didn't ask much about it because I was too grumpy about the tutoring. Geometry was a beast. At first, I hated the idea, but I did not expect to genuinely like my tutor. Amir's a nerd, but I learned that he's a pretty cool guy, in his own way.

A few of the other teens watch me for a moment longer before they turn to listen to Mr. Rogers. I don't know all of their names, but they look familiar. Even if I don't know them, they know me.

That's something my dad is still not thrilled about. I'm supposed to stay low key, hide under the radar, not draw attention to myself.

That's not really a strength of mine.

See, I'm half dragon. That's not the type of thing that small-town Shelbyville, Kentucky, could wrap their minds around.

Heck, I can't even wrap my mind around it some days, and I've been living this way my whole life.

The bell rings, and I gather up my notebook and pen. Taking a quick look at my phone, I see a text from Monica. She wants to hang out after the game tonight. A smile tugs at the edges of my mouth. There's nothing I would rather do than spend time with my girlfriend after the game. We've been dating for a week now. She didn't have to text me to ask to hang out. It's kind of a given, after all. Still, the fact that she did text makes me happy.

"So, did you actually do your Pre-Calc homework this time? Or are you still hoping to barely hang above a C- in that class?" Amir asks, standing up and peering at me over my phone.

"I did it! But—I'm guessing you assumed I didn't," I say, flashing my teeth at him.

He shakes his head. "Actually, yeah, I guessed you hadn't. You treat your math homework like you do taking out the trash. You wait until it's piled up so high that your whole life is stinking."

I laugh but don't deny it. Math isn't my thing. But Amir? Everything is his thing. Not that I hate math. Really, it's a fine subject. I kind of like the idea of solving problems. It just takes too much time. Give me a calculator and I'll be fine. Derivatives? Are they actually going to save my life someday?

My heritage makes that thought even more humorous than it ought to be. I can almost feel my palm heating as I think about the other half of my family. The half I don't know much about, the half I almost didn't believe existed. Some days, I'm convinced my dad is lying to me, telling me I'm something I'm truly not, but that wouldn't explain the fire.

Yup, that's right. The fire. I can create fire out of nowhere or control a flame that's already lit. I remember the first time I accidentally started a house fire. I was working on my throw, trying to put the right spin on the ball. I was eight, and my dad hadn't bothered trying to teach me anything related to football, so I'd done a lot of research. Well, the ball went wide—so wide that it fell in our pond. I was so angry that I stomped my foot, threw my hands out, and shouted.

And then fire shot out of my palms.

We never replaced some parts of the burned trim. It was too expensive to fix, and I swear my dad left it there as a reminder that I should be careful with my temper.

"Well, today, the math homework is done. Is it correct? I couldn't say. I tried your tricks to solve the problems quickly, but I just don't have the heart to show all my work."

Amir chuckles. "You'd be fine with a C-? How do you do that? How do you not care?"

I wiggle my eyebrows at him.

"It's a skill that would do you some good, Mr. Sharma," I say, taking on the mature tone of a teacher.

He scoffs and punches me in the arm. It hurts more than I expect, but I pretend that the pain is unbearable. This awards me with yet another set of rolled eyes before he slaps my shoulder. "Hey, I have to run to the bathroom. See you in class?"

I nod. "Sure thing."

Amir disappears down the busy hall of high school students.

I stand there for a moment, watching the hustle and bustle. Kids walk in groups or alone, laughing and shouting, shoulders bumping—the air filled with normal conversation. What would my life be like if I wasn't here? What if I never made it to this world? I was only a baby when Dad brought me to earth. No, I'm not an alien. I'm just not from this realm. Or, at least, that's the story I've been told.

It's been a while since I've thought about this. All at once, doubts and troubles crash down on me like a full bench press bar. I don't technically belong here. We started out in Seattle for some of my earlier years, but after too many fire incidents and way too much attention coming our way in the big city, ended up leaving. We jumped from one place to the next, but each had its own problems, so we moved again. Fifteen times. That's how many moves I'd had. My dad brought me to Kentucky as a last resort because it was "out of the way." It's supposed to be "in the boonies" enough not to draw attention to myself. I'm half dragon, as I said before, but I didn't get into why. My mom, a dragon herself, sent me away with my dad to protect the bloodline. The *royal* bloodline. That's right, she's the queen, or so I'm told.

It all sounds like a fantasy book, to be honest, but I don't dwell on that too much. I don't like to read. When my dad told me about all of this at the ripe age of seven, I laughed so hard that I almost peed. That was, until I lit the house on fire. To be honest, it still sounds odd. Dragons existing? A kingdom full of large, fire-breathing creatures somewhere in a different place? Yet, I can't deny what I can do. Or the letter from my mother.

I don't know what they're protecting me from, but it sounds bad. Whenever I try to get into detail, my dad shuts down the conversation. Apparently, it's not a Kentucky-worthy conversation.

"Hey, Davy!" a boy shouts to me from down the hall. It's my fellow teammate. He imitates throwing me a ball, and I pretend to catch it. He laughs, then shouts, "Looking forward to you bringing it home tonight!"

"If you can keep your throws straight!" I shout back.

Chuck is the quarterback for our team. I'm the wide receiver, and I'm dang good at it. Is it because I have mystical blood running through my veins? Most likely. But that's not something I can tell someone. I'm sure I'd get put in a mental institution for saying it out loud. I stop at a drinking fountain close by and press the button with my thumb. It resists a bit too much, so I press harder, my fingertip aching from the pressure.

As I begin to drink, a wave of electric energy washes over me, and I freeze, the cold water dripping from my lips. My hand falls to my side, and my fingers rub together. Then heat explodes across my fingertips. I level my breathing, looking around. A set of hardened blue-green eyes lock on to mine.

There's a girl standing twenty feet down the hall. She wears an enormous hoodie. And when I say enormous, I mean it had to be at least 5XL. Her hair, crimson to a ridiculous degree, runs over her shoulders wildly. Her brows are painted thickly with black makeup.

I've never seen this girl before. She isn't pretty, at least not in a beautiful, popular kind of way, but she isn't unfortunate looking. Her eyes bore holes in my chest as she stares me down. I watch her warily, then her gaze flickers to my hand—the one I am working up a flame with. Movement next to her draws my attention to another teen standing there. It's a boy, blond hair buzzed close to his head. He's huge. Not the fat kind of huge, but the naturally-massive-from-genes kind of huge.

I stare back at them, blink, and they're gone.

What was that about?

"Fire! David's on fire!" a student shouts.

I snap back to reality, and then I smell it. Smoke curls in the air around me and I feel heat in my arm. When I look down, I notice my jacket sleeve has caught on fire. Cursing, I smack it until it goes out. A few of the teens around me stare, their mouths agape.

"Drinking fountain is acting up. The electrical pieces must have malfunctioned and lit me on fire," I say, feeling awkward at my dumb explanation. "It's just the universe knowing that I'm going to be flaming tonight on the field."

I say it with exaggeration and pop both thumbs up. The kids closest to me shake their heads. One laughs at my cheesy joke. And though I know they won't forget about what they saw, I think I've diffused the situation for now.

If my dad finds out about this, he's going to kill me. I'm not supposed to use my abilities away from home. For the most part, I've been good about that. Unfortunately, I'm a sixteen-year-old boy and have wild emotions. It sometimes does me good on the field, but anywhere else? Let's just say I've had more than one close call. This has been the worst by far.

Fiddling with the charred edges of the bottom of my shirt, I wonder if I should tuck away the blackened pieces. But that would make me look like a goon. Not today, Captain.

I sigh and walk to my next classroom as quickly as possible, hoping that Amir will be there when I arrive. Part of the reason he's my best friend is that he's coolheaded. He can stay calm in the most strenuous of situations—unless it's a pop quiz about something he's only spent four hours studying for instead of his standard fifteen.

My math classroom isn't far from where the incident happened. Still, most of the witnesses have parted ways with me. Either these kids didn't see my flaming outburst or they forgot about it. I bite my lip. No kid will ever forget that: star wide receiver with his hand and shirt aflame.

I'm distracted when I push the door open, and I almost walk straight into the teacher. Ms. Connolly gasps and steps back, her hand on her chest.

"David, please watch where you are walking. Not all of us are as light on our feet as you are." Her brow furrows, and she folds her arms, but the twinkle in her eyes tells me she's not actually mad.

No one gets mad at the star player.

"Sorry, Ms. Connolly, had a problem with the drinking fountain and—" I trail off, fingering the seam of my blackened shirt again.

Her expression melts into something confused and one of her brows raises in a silent question. It's one of her dominant gestures. If you get the look from Ms. Connolly, you best be prepared to answer the question. I can slack off in history. Math? Not so much.

"Nevermind, I'm fine," I reply, even though my mind is still spinning from that girl's creepy stare.

She breathes out, "Just get your act together before the game tonight. It would be bad timing on your part to choke." She moves to the side and opens her hand in a wide gesture.

I grin, then head to my desk. Amir sits next to me, and his eyes immediately flick down to my shirt. He notices everything. There have been times I've tried to surprise him for his birthday, or even scare him from around the corner. He never really gets surprised. Amir tells me he's not an extraordinary person, but I know he's like a teenage Sherlock Holmes.

"What did you do? Pick up smoking and use the lighter on your clothes instead?" He snickers at his own joke.

I scowl at him. "Hilarious. No, the drinking fountain had an electrical short and caught my shirt on fire. I'm good though."

He narrows his eyes. "An electrical short? That sounds *very* possible."

The sarcasm in his voice tells me he doesn't believe it. I ignore him and turn forward, prepared for the lesson. I can feel his eyes boring into the side of my head, but he won't pry once class starts. With any luck, he'll forget about it.

"You can tell me the truth, you kno—"

Amir stops mid-sentence. His eyes are wide, his mouth hangs open, and a loose strand of black hair has fallen out of his styled do, hanging down the middle of his forehead like a thick spider web. The fact that he doesn't fix it right away is the first evidence that something is wrong. The second is that he's shrinking back in his seat.

"What?" I ask.

He shakes his head, then nods to the other side of the room. I turn that way, and my body grows cold.

Blue eyes, veiled by black brows. Red hair, just like the flames I'd accidentally called up in the hallway.

The strange girl is in my math class.

AN ARSENAL FOR WHAT ARMY?

For a moment, I can't look away, even though my brain is screaming at me to avert my eyes. It might not be so bad if she weren't staring back at me with unwavering intensity. Panic floods me before I press it away.

I don't know why I'm nervous. She's not even doing anything. Her makeup is weird, sure, and her eyes are intense. She's a little freaky, but she's not as tall as me, and it doesn't seem like she could take me in a fight.

I chuckle internally. Why would I go straight to that? She's just some miffed girl who I've never seen before.

Of all the thoughts in my mind, this I was sure of: I'd never seen this girl *or* the boy who stands with her. His blond hair looks well kept, and he seems nervous about something. He keeps glancing at me, but I pay him no mind. I'm fixated on this girl. I don't know why I keep gazing at her like we're in some odd staring contest, but I can't tear my attention away. The only thing that forces us to end the eye contact is her companion grabbing her shoulder and shaking it. My eyes finally switch to him, and I can see that he's averted his gaze now.

"Class, we have a set of new students today! They just moved from—oh goodness, where did you say from?" Ms. Connolly says.

"Seattle," the girl says. Her voice is higher pitched than I would have expected. I have no idea what I was expecting. It's probably my subconscious impressions of her intensity put to practice.

Seattle? What are the chances of that? A strange familiarity rings in my bones, but I am sure I've never seen these two before. Even if I had seen them when I was still there, I would have been too young to really remember much.

"Why don't you and your brother stand up and tell us your names?" Ms. Connolly suggests. "And something unique about you."

She shuffles forward, her oversized hoodie falling around her like a massive tent. If it's a style, it's a strange one. I never understood why girls wore bigger clothes. This 5XL hoodie looks ridiculous. She's wearing larger sweatpants, too. I wonder if maybe she lost weight and didn't bother getting new clothes.

"Krista, and I collect knives," she says coolly before taking her seat.

The islander boy behind her waves. He is larger than his sister. He's wearing a standard button-down plaid shirt and jeans. He's definitely taller than me. Built large, like a beast.

"I'm her brother, Jared□and I have fifteen pets," he says, sitting down.

I cock my head slightly. How could these two possibly be siblings? He seems so much more approachable despite his physique, and they look nothing alike. At least one of them is adopted, if not both.

Jared looks awkward in his desk. Not like it's too small for him but like he doesn't feel comfortable in it. I think for a moment he might be a good recruit for the football team. His wide shoulders and heavy frame would do well on the defense team. I'm not the captain, but I could put in a good word.

Jared laughs, looking down at his desk, as if he'd just heard a ridiculous joke. Krista has said nothing, and none of the surrounding kids seem interested in talking to him. What was he laughing at?

"Well, welcome to Shelby County High. I'm sure you'll like it here. It's smaller than Seattle, and you will get used to the farm smell," Ms. Connolly jokes. "All right, class, we are back to derivatives."

She moves to the white board and picks up a blue marker. I hardly recognize any of the things that she writes. I don't like this subject, and I've found that I'm pretty terrible at it. I tilt my head toward Amir. He still looks nervous.

What is her problem? he mouths to me.

I don't know. She seems crazy, I mouth back.

He shakes his head and messes with his backpack, pulling out his thick math book. I do the same, glancing at my charred shirt hem for a moment before sitting up. Whoever this girl is, she'd ruffled my feathers enough that I literally lit myself on fire. Something like this hasn't happened since middle school. At that time, it was easier to play off. Once, I'd been in beginning chemistry and a chemical reaction startled me. Let's just say the desk catching on fire was easier pegged as a burner malfunction.

Dad worked with me for *days* to control my abilities and disconnect them from my emotions. I hated the practice, and I don't think I'll ever be more tired in my whole life than I was at that moment, but my dad insisted it would be for my safety. To this day, I'm unsure what he's trying to keep me safe from. Our lives have been uneventful, yet he still insists on moving from place to place. Since nothing has happened, I convinced him to stay here. We've been here for six years now. That is a record for my life.

Ms. Connolly calls names for answers to the most recent homework assignment, and I sit forward, trying to forget about the girl. I still spare glances in her direction, but it's like she's forgotten me. The boy, her supposed brother, appears uncomfortable—nervous, even. I still can't get over the fact that they don't look *or* act like siblings.

"David, what did you get for number thirty-four?" Ms. Connolly asks.

I bite my lip, flipping to page three of the packet and reading my sloppy writing.

"Thirty-nine point two meters per second."

"Good work." She moves to the next question, which goes to Amir.

He seems to have forgotten the odd pair, for which I'm jealous. As much as I wish I could ignore them, I'm too unsettled. It isn't just the way she stared at me with some hidden hatred; it's also the oddity of them as a whole. Of the two, I'd peg the larger boy as hostile. But that's not the case. It's the girl with the dark makeup and flaming hair who makes me nervous.

I won't survive this math class with the two newbies as a distraction . . .

The bell rings, and I snap back to reality.

"You okay over there? Did Monica text you and say she wants to break up?" Amir says this with a smirk on his face.

I scoff at his comment. "No, we're fine. I'm distracted by—you know—the weird girl over there."

Amir flashes a grin, then looks over his shoulder. "Maybe she's already discovered your infamy as the best football player at Shelby County High." He gives an exaggerated "quotation" motion with his fingers. Twerp.

I shake my head. "And what? She's jealous? That expression has fire in it—if you know what I mean."

My stomach clenches at the mention of fire and the reminder of what happened right before class.

Amir waves his hand in the air. "She'll get used to you. I mean, *I* had to. Took some time, but you aren't too bad anymore."

I make a disgusted face in jest and punch his shoulder. He winces and punches back.

As I gather my things and stand, I peer back over at their desks. A few of the other kids are talking to Jared. One of them is a girl trying to get a date with him. The girl is standing there with a half smile on her face and her arms folded. Krista says something to the group of kids around them, and one girl steps back. Krista's face doesn't look *hostile*, but there seems to be something dangerous there.

The group disperses, and her eyes fall on me again. A shot of electric fear rushes through my body, and I feel my palms heat again, an instant reaction to the growing unease in my gut. Her half smile grows to full size, and she raises her hand upward to wave at me.

I blink in surprise, but before I can react, she turns away and walks out the door.

My back is sweating now, drips falling down my spine.

"That was odd," Amir says, shivering. Then he shrugs. "Guess she doesn't hate you after all!"

He claps me on the back. "See you tonight. I'll have my book so that way there's no chance of me losing my mind."

I mumble something in return, but I doubt he hears it.

The image of Krista waving is stuck in my mind. I could have sworn her waving hand was bigger than normal, as if it grew a few sizes while she waved.

My mouth tastes sour, and I clear my throat, flipping my backpack on my shoulder and walking out the door.

***

My car rattles across the country road, the sun shining high above. The big game is tonight, and a bunch of other football players stick around for the afternoon until the game starts. I would, but I want to tell my dad what happened today. It would be better if he heard it from me and not through the grapevine.

Palms sweaty from nerves, I take the last turn into a broad field. The neighbors must have recently harvested because their heavy machinery sits in the middle. It's dormant, but the smell of fresh greens assaults my nose.

I take a deep breath, absorbing it in.

The mansion I drive by still astounds me. We live on a horse farm on the outskirts of town. It's not a terrible drive when it's nice out, but when it gets cold, it's far less fun. Today, I'm merely appreciating the view. The large house must have at least fifteen bedrooms and an equal number of bathrooms—or more, I'm not sure. It houses the family that hired my dad.

I've only been inside it a few times. The family isn't rude. They invite us over often, but Dad tells them we like to keep to ourselves. He's terrified they'll find out what I really am.

I forget about it most days.

Except not on a day like this.

I drive a quarter mile past the house into the fields where I can see the beautiful coats of the horses, bred to perfection. Most of them are milling about, doing nothing in particular, but a couple have riders. I guess it's the owners' children. They tend to come a few times a week to ride their prized horses.

When I get to my house, the nerves almost take over. We live in a small home: two bedrooms and one bathroom, right next to the large horse barn. It's small and quaint but filled with nice things. As I walk to the door of the house, I take a moment to appreciate the newness of everything. The floors, the counters, the light fixtures . . . everything was installed within the last two years. I'm not sure why, but the owner who is swimming in wealth from his horse farm business makes sure to update everything inside the house every two years at a minimum.

Seems like a waste of money to me, but I can't complain. The house is extravagant.

I traipse through the door. My dad is putting away food in the fridge. He doesn't eat much during the day, opting for a larger lunch after he finishes his morning work.

"Hey, Dave, how was school?" he shouts from behind the refrigerator door.

"Uh—fine, yeah. Not too bad. Just looking forward to the game tonight." A lump forms in my throat, preventing me from telling him what happened.

"Ah yes, the homecoming game, your pride and joy. I—"

His words trail off as he stands up and looks at me. His eyes lock on the burned part of my shirt. He closes the fridge and moves to me so fast that I almost stumble backward. He grabs the hem of my shirt.

"What happened? Did you get attacked? Is the school compromised? Do we need to move?"

His questions are coming so fast that my mind is spinning.

"Dad, stop it. I wasn't attacked. I still don't have any idea *what* would attack me. You should be more open about that," I say, not able to keep the small bit of anger out of my voice.

He ignores my comment. "What happened to your shirt?"

I drag out a breath. It won't help to keep it to myself since he'll find out from someone. "My emotions got the better of me, and I lit myself on fire."

Dad's mouth falls open, and he narrows his eyes. "You—lost your temper? And—lit yourself—on fire."

I can see he's not buying my excuse. He closes his mouth, letting my shirt fall out of his hands.

"It's been years since you had an incident like that. Did something change? You don't just *light things on fire* when you're upset anymore."

"I know. I know. There was this weird new girl and her brother. They were staring at me—well, *she* was staring at me, and she looked angry. It made me nervous for some reason."

It was more than that. The fear I felt from her was almost—primal, unnatural. For a moment, I wonder if I've imagined the whole thing, but I push the thought away. That girl, Krista, was very real, and the hostility in her eyes was no joke.

His eyes shoot open, and he grabs my arm, yanking me through the house like I'm a child again. I could pull away and express the frustration burning in my chest, but I'm too surprised to do so. Dad doesn't ever act this way. It's concerning.

"What's going on? Where you are you taking me?" I demand, but he grunts, not answering my question.

We reach the door to the basement, and he stops, reaching for the handle. My heart skips. He told me never to go into the basement. No matter where we've lived—here, Sacramento, Salt Lake, Boise—there has always been a place I'm not allowed to go. An extra bedroom, a cellar, an outdoor shed. He always said the time wasn't right for me to go inside.

No matter how many times I'd tried, despite his warnings, I could never get the doors to budge. Even now that I'm a somewhat-fit sixteen-year-old, the door would never open. I'm sure he figured I had tried. He wasn't dumb, but he never scolded me for it. In fact, we'd never talked about it much.

Dad holds his hand on the doorknob, then studies me.

"I hope you're ready for this." He turns back and whispers something near the door. It sounds like "macaroni," which might be hilarious if he weren't acting so strange.

Red lettering appears out of nowhere on the handle. It flickers like the embers in a fire before moving off the knob, up the side of the door, and into the doorjamb.

Then an excessively loud click issues from the seam.

"Dad—are you—letting me go in there?" My voice is shaking. This is serious. I'd given up hope of ever seeing what's down there, but now that he's opening it up and ushering me inside, I have a bad feeling.

Like, terrible.

"Yes. As much as I don't want to, I think it's time to show you." He grasps my shoulder and pulls me through the doorway.

Too many horror movies flash through my mind at seeing the darkened wood-framed stairs. They don't appear old or rickety. The stairs are new, as if they have never been used before. Still, I swallow hard, trying not to imagine ghosts or other terrors.

I hear another click behind me, and a few single bulbs light up along the ceiling. It's meant to make it seem less creepy, but it manages the opposite. Working my jaw to deal with the fear, I step gingerly down the stairs.

I'm unsure of what I'll find when I get to the bottom, but anything normal is absolutely out of the question.

Every wall is covered with mounted brackets. Each bracket is filled with a weapon. Swords, bows, maces, spears, shields, and other things I've never seen before. All of them are sitting there as if they were a perfectly normal decoration for a modern home.

A laugh escapes my mouth, and I hold my belly, trying to prevent myself from bending over and laughing harder.

"Dad, I didn't realize you were into LARPing. If you liked DnD, you didn't have to be so afraid to tell me."

Except for the fact that the door was locked by an ethereal red light that was impenetrable except by whispering every child's favorite meal. This fact I promptly ignore, trying to find some level of comfort in this odd experience.

Do I think the idea of my dad playing DnD sounds ridiculous? Absolutely. But hey, I'd respect the guy for his passion. As long as he didn't make me play along.

I turn toward him. He's frowning at me.

"This isn't my stuff," he replies. There's a hardness in his cool blue eyes. His hair is cut in a professional style, black as night, the gel reflecting in the basement lighting. The button-up blue plaid shirt he wears, one of the many variations that flood his closet, bulges at his biceps and chest. He works out way more than I do, and I've never understood why. It seems like he was trying to prove something.

He continues, "Everything in this room is yours. Except that bit in the corner over there."

A slight nod of his head draws my attention to an enormous sword grasped in a full set of armor.

"Mine?" I repeat. For a moment, I think he's pulling my leg, but he looks dead serious. Oh—my—gosh. He's been carting these weapons around everywhere we went my whole life? All I can think of is how he kept these hidden for so long. "From my mom, I'm guessing?"

He nods, then turns his head down to look at the floor.

"And you waited to tell me until now because—"

I trail off, seeing him wince, as if I'd thrown a punch at him.

"Frankly, I didn't want you to have to deal with the knowledge. I was supposed to teach you how to fight with a sword, how to shoot a bow, how to command an army to lay siege on a castle." He runs a hand through his black hair. When he pulls it away, the gel holds it in place in large spikes shooting up from his scalp. "Things to help you prepare for battle."

My mouth tastes sour.

"As in, actual battle?" I ask, turning and pointing to the armor. "Like . . . wear that, yell a battle shout, and run into battle, *battle*?"

Even as I say it, I recognize how ludicrous it sounds.

"Your mother would be so angry if she learned I'd neglected to teach you," he says, strolling over to "his corner" and grasping the handle of the sword.

"Dad, you realize how insane you sound right now? What is all this, really? Is this about Mom? Because I know you've worked the 'Mom is a dragon' angle, but it's okay to admit I'm a vat-born freak. It's okay if I'm not actually your son."

My chest hurts as I say the words, as if I'm opening up a deep wound that has been there for years. Ever since we'd started training my fire abilities, tying them to my emotions and tearing them away for control, I've taken it for granted. I'm not sure I ever bought the "Mom dragon queen" story, but it was easier than thinking she just left us. That was too painful.

I hear a low growl from his throat, and he shouts, tearing the sword from the wall and spinning ferociously with it. I yelp and fall backward, my back hitting the wall and knocking down a heavy-looking shield. It clangs to the ground, barely missing my hand, and I curse. I watch with a combination of horror and awe as he takes steps forward, maneuvering the sword as if it were a part of him. He's moving so fluidly, it's obvious he's trained with the blade. I swallow, my hands shaking as I press against the wall for fear of being sliced to bits.

Then he stops.

"I assure you, son, I haven't lied to you. And now that you've seen this stuff, it's time to come clean."

I GET A MESSAGE FROM A DRAGON

We sit on the floor, Dad fingering the blade as if it weren't something sharp that could literally lob off a man's head. He's treating it like it's some sort of baby.

"Okay, then, spill," I say, folding my arms.

He sighs and sets the sword aside. After giving it a couple gentle pats, he turns to me.

"Your mother's name is Ellistra. And yes, she is literally the queen of dragons. That is . . . if she's still alive."

A name. He's never even given me that much. The letter she left for me telling me that she loved me and that she sent me away with Christian—my dad—to keep me safe, enters my mind. I used to read the letter hundreds of times each year. Currently, it sits in my nightstand drawer, ignored. Now he's telling me that she might not be alive.

A lump forms in my throat. I want to swallow it, forget about the room full of weapons, and walk away. But my brain wants more.

"Okay, so why did she really send me away?" I ask, my tone harder than I intended.

He winces, then clicks his tongue, looking directly at me.

"It's not a lie, what the letter said. Other kingdoms from the darker parts of our homeland were invading her kingdom. They were after her and the rest of the bloodline. She did send you away with me through a portal to the human realm. We assumed they couldn't reach us, and that may very well be true, but after hearing about the girl—"

Krista. So that's what this is about.

"Where is she from? The dragon world? Is she one of these things trying to kill me?" I laugh again, though my stomach is twisting. A silent testament that I'm not feeling okay with all this. A reminder of the uncomfortable terror coming from that girl's hard gaze sends a shiver up my spine.

"I don't know! All right? I just . . . the moment you told me about her, I had a feeling in my gut that you had to see this."

He stands quickly and walks to the wall. There's a metal door with a built-in safe sitting just below chest level. I didn't even see it at first. Another teen might see a safe built into the wall and think it was the strangest thing. Now it seems like the most normal part of this basement.

He reaches toward the handle and says the macaroni word again. Glowing red script wriggles on the handle and the lock disengages. I shift uncomfortably at what appears to be magic. When he reaches in, he pauses, then nods, pulling out an ornate box.

It looks like a literal treasure chest. Like, deep-in-the-sea, covered-in-barnacles, the-lost-booty-of-a-pirate-captain-status treasure chest. Of course, it isn't covered in grime or seaweed; it just looks really expensive with jewels on the top and sides. Before I can ask if it's real and why we haven't sold it yet, he plops back down on the ground and slides it to me.

"From your mother," he says.

I look from him to the box and back again.

"You want me to open the strange pirate box?"

He nods, then folds his arms. He clearly isn't keen on my joking at the moment. For some reason, this freaks me out even more.

I clear my throat, pressing my hands to the lid and trying to lift it upward. Nothing happens.

"Uh, seems like Ma forgot to leave the key," I say sarcastically. I guess I can't keep humor out of this awkward conversation. My words sound darker and more brooding than I intended them to. Give me credit, I'm struggling to process all this strangeness.

"Oh yeah, about that." He licks his lips, then pulls a dagger out from behind his back.

I freeze. I don't feel threatened, but the fact that he is brandishing a knife to solve this problem doesn't bode well. It wouldn't have been my first solution of choice to a locked box. Not in any of the scenarios that fly through my head, at least.

He sees the expression on my face and smiles a little.

"No, it's not for sacrificing you or anything. It just needs blood—dragon blood, to be specific. It's a lock, see, just there?"

Dad reaches over and puts a finger on the top of the box. A dragon figure is carved into the wood. When I look closely, it's way more ornate than I expected something like this to be. He holds the dagger closer to me and raises his eyebrows. I'm waiting for him to bust up laughing, give up the gag, and tell me that I'm a radioactive mutant hidden from the world because of mistreatment.

It's an odd world when being an X-Man is less weird than being the son of a dragon.

He doesn't say anything like that though. He just stares at me.

"Wait, you're completely serious?" I say, frowning now.

He nods.

"No way! I'm not going to cut myself. That's—that's—gotta be unsanitary. What about infection or something?"

The argument sounds weak, even to me. He grits his teeth, moves closer to me, and leans forward to look in my eyes. Suddenly his hand has mine locked down in a vice grip. I gasp in pain. The dagger is only a flash of reflected bulb light before I feel stinging on my palm. I stare at it in shock, my brain not processing what it's seeing. A few drops of my blood land on the wood of the box, and it glows almost instantly.

It sounds like an egg is cracking, and for a moment, I think he's unleashed a dragon on the world, waking it up to consume not only us but the rest of the humans on this earth. The tension I feel throughout my body makes my brain want to jest its way out of this situation, but I've seen plenty of movies with dragons in them.

The stories don't end well.

Intense heat seeps into my palm, and I drop the box, the wood slamming to the ground. It springs open. I'm not sure if it's my sports instincts or what, but I fling my foot outward for a decisive kick. The box flies away from me and hits the wall with a thud before turning over, a few things clattering to the ground.

I can't breathe. When nothing happens right away, I let the images of a dragon chasing me and Dad down to eat us dissipate from my mind.

"That was more theatric than necessary," he comments, giving me a strange sideways glance. "Did you think I was going to cut your arm off or something?"

I stare at him before pressing my fingers to the gash in my right palm. It's shallow. I can tell that much from the injuries I'd sustained from years of football practice, but for some reason, the sight of this blood—and knowing what the cut did—makes me nauseous.

"Dads have a chance of losing their minds, too. Have you watched the news?"

I squeeze my palm a little more, waiting for the stinging to stop. It doesn't immediately, so I just hold tight for a bit longer.

"If I didn't know what kind of dad you were, I'd be a lot angrier that you just sliced me open without asking," I say, unable to keep the hardness out of my tone.

He frowns and shrugs, a small apologetic gesture, then moves across the room to where the box lays. It isn't glowing anymore—something that probably should make me feel a little better, but it doesn't.

"I never got to see what your mother put in here. I have to say, it's a little disappointing." He crouches down in a squat.

It's obvious he doesn't want to come in contact with anything, which makes my stomach squirm into even tighter knots. If he's not willing to touch it, he sure as heck better not expect me to either.

He waves me over with his left hand, letting his right hover over what looks like a ring on the floor. When I don't come right away, he looks up at me. Is that a trace of annoyance in his eyes?

"Don't you want to see what your mom sent you here with? Or are you going to let it sit on the ground for eternity?"

I stare back at him, my mouth hanging slightly open, searching for words, but I can't think of what to say. He raises an eyebrow as if to ask, "Are you ever going to come over here?" I sigh. Pushing my bleeding palm into my pant leg—probably not the wisest decision, but I'll figure out how to deal with the jean bloodstain later—I walk over and crouch down next to him. I frown, realizing then that my palm doesn't sting any longer. Glancing at the cut, I gasp quietly.

There's no cut at all. Blood stains my palm around the area, but where I was previously cut is perfectly healed skin. If there weren't bloodstains on my skin, I would think I'd imagined the whole thing.

I hold it up questioningly to my dad, who just raises his eyebrows and nods a little. He's not even the least bit surprised.

"H—how is that even possible?"

He shakes his head. "Later. Focus on this now."

He's pointing down to the pile of random things again.

On the floor, there's a piece of yellowing paper, a ring with a massive ruby in the brackets, and a long wooden thing with holes in it. I blink, inspecting it, and then I reach out for the stick of wood. It's a flute or a whistle of some sort.

"Okay. The great dragon queen didn't say anything in her letter about this box or the basement full of weapons," I say. "Which, by the way, how did you hide all this from me? I'm pretty sure if the cops came here to find all these weapons, they'd think we were in a cult."

The look he gives me is all too clear: stop procrastinating and get on with it.

I sigh again. "Fine. I get it. Later."

I'm not sure if we actually will get to it later, but for some reason, I feel better telling him that I intend to bring it up again. I shake my head. This is a terrible time for all of this. The big homecoming game is tonight, and my dad is throwing too many wide passes for my liking. Gritting my teeth at the swell of anger roiling in my chest, I reach out slowly and let my hand hover over the ring. There's a slight tingling in my hand, and for a moment, I want to pull away, but I hold it there.

"Why does it feel like my hand is asleep?" I ask, holding still.

Dad chuckles, then rubs a hand down his face.

"Considering who your mother is, do you really think she wouldn't leave you some magic infused things?"

Magic. Well, at least he admitted it. Seeing the clearly magic-locked door and box wasn't enough to convince me. Him even saying the words causes my shoulder to relax downward. I look at the ring, annoyed. "I'm a sixteen-year-old boy playing high school football. Excuse me if the thought has never crossed my mind. Besides, you know I have a hard time believing anything about Mom." I pause, still scrutinizing the ring. "How confident are you that this isn't a booby trap or something?"

He shrugs. "Don't know, to be honest. But your blood worked on the box like she told me it would, so I'm guessing it won't kill you."

I pull my hand back from the ring.

"This is going to have to wait until after the game," I say. The idea makes my whole body wash in coolness, a relief after the high adrenaline.

Dad looks at me with an exasperated expression. I stare back, preparing to counter him, when he locks his jaw and throws his hand out toward mine. I barely have time to start a shout of surprise when his hand hits my wrist and he presses my forearm down onto the ring.

Everything goes black.

My breath catches in my throat. I try to scream, but I can't move. A wash of color blurs all around me, appearing out of nowhere. It all coalesces into images, into things that look familiar. I'm sitting on a mountain cliff looking out across a vast forest landscape. Cool winds blow across my face and ruffle my light brown hair. It feels cold pressing against the sweat on my brow.

Did I just teleport somewhere? A nervous chuckle leaves my throat.

The idea is so stupid, but I swear I can feel everything. The rocky ground beneath my knees hurts where my weight is focused. I can smell the pine trees. It all feels so real.

When I look down, my throat completely closes. The ground is thousands of feet below me. I'm only inches from the ledge. Vertigo takes me and the world spins. Bile rises in my esophagus, and I choke it back. I fall backward, silently sending thanks to God that I didn't fall forward.

Rock slams into my back, but the sensation is distant. Then, I'm back in my brain.

Heights. I can't do heights.

For initiation into the football team, it's tradition to go to the top of the bleachers and take a zipline down in nothing but your underwear. I passed out at the top of the seats before I could even get a hold of the handlebars.

The football team still ridicules me to no end about that.

I'm staring through a thin canopy of trees, the blue sky above, when I hear flapping wings. It sounds like a massive bird. Like—this bird has to be the size of an airplane because the whooshing is so loud. Slipping my bare elbows beneath me and wincing at the pain of the pebble-covered stone on my flesh, I push myself up to look at the ledge I was just standing on.

Something huge is flying toward me, and I shout in alarm, rolling to my stomach and pushing myself to my feet. I try to run down the hill, but I'm met with resistance. It doesn't feel like a solid wall so much as ropes tying every inch of my body down and pulling me backward. I fight it, but I can't break free from the sensation.

I spin around as the flapping wings get so loud that I can't hear anything else. I gape at the sight before me. It's not a bird. It's a dragon—and it's massive. Red scales shine in the sunlight, hidden from my view below the tree canopy. Gold spikes protrude from the dragon's head, lining its back. Sharp talons glint momentarily before the shade of the trees hides them from the sun. It lands on the ledge of the cliff. I can feel its hot breath. I'm shouting now, but I can't even hear myself.

All of a sudden, the dragon starts to glow, the edges of the creature blurring before it's awash in light. I flinch at the brightness, but the light is gone in moments. I keep my eyes closed for good measure.

"Daviron, my son. You are finally here," a woman's voice sounds.

My real name, the one only Dad knows . . . I'd almost forgotten about it but hearing it now makes me shiver.

My neck prickles at the sound, and I peek open my eyes. A woman stands before me where the dragon had been moments before. She wears a crown of small branches woven together into a circlet. Her eyes are piercing green, and her hair is light brown. Her voice twinges something in my memory, as if someone were whispering the secret of who she is in my ear.

"M-mom?" I stammer, almost not believing the word itself.

She smiles brightly, then throws her arms open in a grand gesture, striding over to me.

"My son, I can't believe it's taken all these years before I could see you like this."

Like a stranger walking toward me, my body reacts, pushing back toward the trees and the decline of the steep hill, but the invisible ropes pull me back, preventing me from escaping. She stops, frowning, then looks behind me.

"You can't go anywhere, unfortunately. This is a memory, a message I created for you when you were first born. It's restricted to this area, I'm afraid. This is Qotan, our land," she says.

Her tone makes it sound like something normal, but my brain is not computing what's happening.

"No hug, then. I understand. This is a memory, as I said before. I'm not truly here, and neither are you."

She turns, walking back to the cliff. When she gets there, she gestures for me to follow.

I still don't move.

Her expression changes, and her brow crinkles like she's worried.

"Oh heartstring, did we create a deaf dragonling? That will really make this memory less meaningful for you. If I'd have known, I would've changed the message to account for that."

For a moment, I think it might be better to pretend I am deaf. Maybe she'll leave me alone.

She sighs. "I am not equipped with that type of message, so I will tell you what I've been given. Daviron, my son, I've sent you to Earth to keep you safe from the war. Our lands are troubled by battle and darkness. In an effort to keep you and the bloodline safe, you were sent, along with others, to the world of humans. It's a place I cannot venture, and if you were a full dragon, you wouldn't either. Thus, the human in you keeps you grounded there. It keeps you safe."

There are so many words that I'm having a hard time understanding them. My mind is still stuck on the massive man-eating dragon and the hot, acrid breath on my face from moments before.

My mom narrows her eyes, but when I don't speak, she continues.

"I do not know how long this war will last, but I trust that your father will have prepared you for anything. He promised to get you ready for battle, should we need to call on you, but I hope it doesn't come to that soon. Until we can push away the darkness, you will have to stay in the human world. Your father was instructed to train you with steel and with your dragon abilities. When you come of age, we will call on your strength. If we have need of you before then, it will be from pure desperation. Until such time, train hard and know that I love you. I hope to see you again someday."

My mouth is dry. She said this is a memory and that she's not really here, but this feels real. The burning scent of the pine trees and the rush of fresh wind tempt me to close my eyes and revel in nature surrounding us. I swear, I can feel the air. I could smell and feel the heat of her dragon breath.

"What does that mean? What darkness? What does it mean to 'come of age'? I don't understand any of this," I say, the questions pouring out.

There's a deep sorrow in her eyes, and when I look closer, I see that they aren't fully human. Her pupils are a slit down the center, the irises a stark green like the seas.

She sighs, a hand coming to her chest as she looks at me with a loving gaze.

"Oh heartstring bless. You aren't deaf. Don't get me wrong, I'd love you still the same, but it is good to know this message won't fail to reach you."

She turns and lifts both hands out in a grand gesture.

"Urothar, the Orc king, needs you for the curse to come to fruition. He must not have you. Once you are of age, you can properly defend yourself and the others until such time. Live well, my son."

Others? What are these others she's talked about over and over?

She stalks closer to me, and I shy back, not because I'm scared of her, but because I still have so many questions that she hasn't answered. I don't know what I thought it would be like meeting my mom for the first time, but it wasn't this. Until I'd seen the dragon flying down on me, my dad's story about her seemed like a hoax, like something from a fantasy book that nerds read.

But here she is. Her hand reaches out for my cheek. If this were just a message—a memory—then how could she possibly know where I would be standing? I lift my hand to touch hers, wondering if it will feel hot like mine does when I summon the flames. Before we can touch one another, she and the surrounding forest burst into dust, like the pixels of a computer screen exploding apart on a broken monitor.

I let out a desperate cry. None of my questions were answered. But she's gone, and all I see is blackness.

THE UNUSUAL GAME
SPECTATORS

As my basement slowly forms back in my vision, I'm left panting, as if I can't draw enough air into my lungs no matter how deeply I breathe.

"What happened?" Dad asks. He's leaning over me, eyebrows furrowed in concern.

I'm staring at the joists under the main floor. We never finished the basement. Dad said it wasn't a priority financially—plus he didn't think we needed the space. I remember our landlord thought he was strange for not wanting it done because he would've paid for the whole thing.

I know the real reason now. It was to hide everything that was down here.

I blink quickly, trying to bring myself back to reality. The musty air smells more potent in my nostrils than it did before, the fresh forest air having spoiled my senses. Even the colors of the basement are dulled compared to the beauty of Qotan.

"You fell over the moment you touched the ring," he says, his voice quivering slightly. "Are you okay?"

"You never told me!" I say, gasping through my ragged breaths.

His mouth falls open slightly. That is not the answer he was hoping for.

"I never told you what? About the weapons? About the box? It wasn't time for that. You weren't old enough. Or—I never felt right about telling you."

I hold up a hand. It's enough to make him stop talking. I want him to stop trying to explain it away. I don't understand why he kept it hidden, but I'm sure he'll tell me soon enough. The weapons are creepy beyond belief. Knowing that I've slept on top of a medieval arsenal all my life freaks me out.

But that's not why I'm mad.

"First, you cut open my hand, *then* you shove my hand on a ring that could have been booby trapped. And now I find out that you were supposed to train me to *fight*? You never told me you were supposed to train me," I say. My tongue feels scratchy from how long it's been since I've had a proper drink.

His quizzical look melts away and is replaced by something apologetic—pensive.

"Oh. Did you see something? Was it a message from your mother?" he asks.

I toss the ring to the side, the metal pinging against the cement floor and rolling to a stop under a table. My fists ball so tightly that I can feel my fingernails digging into my palms.

"I'm being *hunted* by the Orc king? What else is hunting me? Why didn't you tell me the real reason you brought me here? All you've ever said was that it's not safe for humans in Qotan. You never said anything about me being hunted."

I almost say the phrase "that world" as I have for my whole life. Until now, I had never heard the name of the place. Dad told me he brought me here to keep me safe from the dangers of the "other realm." He said that humans weren't meant to live there and that he'd almost died dozens of times from the few years he spent there.

Now I know that wasn't true—at least not completely.

Dad's jaw locks up. He's probably trying to come up with some excuse for not telling me. I'm sure, given different circumstances, I could probably accept what he would say to me. But not anymore. Not with all this new information swimming in my ill-prepared brain.

The silence reaches a very uncomfortable level, like the level of awkwardness when your date tells a dumb joke that isn't funny and it's so bad that you can't even laugh at it.

I speak from experience. Except it wasn't a date that said the awkward thing. It was me.

Secondhand embarrassment washes over me at the memory, but I press it away, drawing on the heat in my chest. Dad's not going to get away with telling me nothing useful again.

He sighs, his shoulder slumping. "I didn't think I needed to tell you more. Creatures from the other"—he pauses, considering me through slits for eyes—"from Qotan can't come here to earth. It's not in their nature. If they try, they just fall apart, melting into nothing. That's how it's always been. Did your mother tell you that much?"

I can feel my face flush at the comment. To be fair, no, Mom didn't say any of that. I try not to let my anger seep toward her or the glimmer of the memory of her from that strange vision, but I don't know how long I can keep it at bay.

"Did she need to? *You're* the one who brought me here. *You're* the one who was supposed to 'train me with steel.'" I put my fingers up and air quote grandly, a dramatic gesture that hopefully captures what I'm feeling adequately. Dad's eyes follow the gesture, and he frowns. "But you didn't even do *that*. Why? Why didn't you at least tell me anything?"

Even as the words leave my mouth, they sound ludicrous. I'm a junior in high school—a runner on the football team, nothing more. I don't even read books, but I feel like I've been thrown into one. And somehow, I have a regret for not liking to read. Amir loves to read. He's always trying to get me to buddy-read something with him, but I just can't. I don't have time. I don't have the mental capacity for it. I don't—

I pull myself together from losing it to frustration.

"I've been to Qotan, David. I know what creatures exist there. I also know that they can't get you here. The orcs, the goblins, the trolls—all of them. They can't come here because if they try, they are reduced to a pile of black sludge. That is why your mother secured the dragon bloodline in a human form. *You* can live here, you *have* lived here, and you've been safe. In the sixteen years we've been here, there has not been one moment of danger. There's no need for all of this," he says, gesturing around him.

"Then, why bother bringing it with us? Why show me at all?" I say, my voice hard. "And what would happen when I 'come of age' as Dragon-Mom said I would?"

His eyes widen at the remarks, and he shoves his jaw forward. I got him with that one. I can't even revel in my cleverness because my mind is moving without me.

"Because I could never be sure. If there had been an attack, even though that's impossible, I'd have been there to keep you safe. I didn't see a need to help you learn to fight. Besides, you have fire. In a pinch, it would protect you well enough—and why am I explaining myself to you? I'm your father, and I know what's best. Let's move on and you can tell me what your mother said."

He appears wistful, and the look gives me pause. I may be just a teenager, but I've seen enough acting in movies to know when someone is moon-eyed. This guy is lost for the dragon lady.

I wince internally at the crass definition of the very woman—creature—thing—who created me. My mind begins to wander to the possibility of it and how strange it all is when I shake my head. He doesn't get anything from me. Not right now. Chest burning from the recent mistakes of my father, I glare back at him.

"I—don't—have—time—for—this!" I say, punctuating every word with anger. "I have a game tonight, and I can't choke. This was easily the *worst* timing for you to show me all of this. Come to the game if you want to—or don't."

I stand in a huff and walk quickly to the wooden staircase. Dad calls after me, and my brain screams at me to turn around and talk to him like an adult, but I can't do it. The combination of satisfaction and guilt mesh inside, and I feel sick from it. To this day, we've never had a fight. Not like this.

But the fire still swells within me. My palms burn. I could call up fire and just light the whole place up. It would be easy. For a moment, I think I might do just that, but logic gets the better of me and I clench my hands to stave off the temptation.

When I get to my beat-up truck, I turn to check if he's followed me. He hasn't. I can't tell if I'm relieved or bothered by this, but I don't have time to think much about it before I close the door and drive away. Our house disappears quickly in the rearview mirror. Just before it's too small for me to see, the front door opens and Dad rushes out.

Way too late, old man.

My hands tremble on the steering wheel as I squeeze it entirely too hard, but I'm only thinking about what I said to him. He's never missed a game. In terms of dads, he's about as perfect as they come.

Some of the other kids can't get their parents to acknowledge they're in a sport, let alone come to an actual game. Dad's always been there.

Now I'm irrationally terrified that I hurt him too much and he won't come. I almost turn around, but then I see the time.

"Oh, freak, I'm late," I mutter. Coach is *not* going to be thrilled about that.

Fortunately, living in the country, I don't run into any traffic going into the town. I park in an available front parking spot and yank up the parking brake. It's old and requires a lot of "elbow grease" to make work. Still, I can't complain. I have a real car, something that I can take places on my own.

I rush through the school doors and to the locker room. When I get there, I'm relieved to see a few other members still getting their gear on.

"Cutting it close, Smith, don't you think?" Jonny, the kicker for our team, says.

He's scrawny and lightweight. I could easily take him in my tall and broad form. I think idly for a moment about the name Smith. Dad did say he picked something generic to blend in with the society of earth, but hearing it now just sounds ridiculous. The son of a dragon—a terrifyingly large and red dragon woman—has the last name Smith.

I'm a joke.

"Yeah, well, my dad had some things to get off his chest. Took longer than I expected," I reply, throwing open my locker and yanking off my shirt and pants.

"Ah, you two okay, then?" he asks with a measured tone. Even if Dad and I had been fighting, Jonny wouldn't really care. He doesn't like to talk. Not like Amir. Don't get me wrong, I like Jonny, just like I like the other guys on the team, but they aren't my buddies. They're more like army brothers, or at least the way I think army brothers would feel.

"We're fine. It's not worth talking about," I say flatly, pulling my shoulder pads on and setting them right.

Jonny's tight expression melts, and he lets out a heavy breath. "Cool. How about I stick around until you're done? Coach doesn't like it when we get ready slowly, but I'll save you from taking the heat alone. It would be best if he didn't try to bench our receiver because he was *late*."

I want to turn Jonny down and get ready by myself, but my mind doesn't let me. I guess I'm starving for some human attention, even if it's just Jonny trying to keep me from getting into trouble.

"Thanks, man."

I get ready in record time. In fact, I'm sure I could be in some record book for how quickly I affixed my football gear. Jonny stands next to me and makes some offhand comments about something Phil, one of our defenders, said before I made it to the locker room. I'm not listening, so when he busts up laughing at his own joke, I give him a half smile and slam my locker shut.

The cool air rushes through my shaggy brown hair, and I let out a sigh. I didn't notice how hot and muggy the locker room was, but now that I'm out of it, I feel like my mind is getting a hit of clarity—a clarity I could really use right now because we *cannot* lose this game.

"Smith, tell me why you find it appropriate to be *late* to warm-ups for your *first* homecoming game. Do you want me to bench you for the first half?" Coach Sanders says, raising one of his thick eyebrows.

I grit my teeth, then shake my head in response. Coach isn't a rude person, but when he's mad about something, it's best to keep your mouth shut. Anything I say will sound like a dumb excuse anyway. Even if the real reason I'm a bit off my rocker is because my *dragon* mother from *another dimension* left me a secret memory locked inside a ring.

Wow, I sound like I need to be put in an asylum. The thought makes me chuckle, and Coach gives me a confused look.

"Anyway, I won't do that because you weren't technically the only one late. Finnegan, I don't care why you were late, get on the line and start drills!" Coach shouts at Jonny.

Jonny gives me a knowing look as if to say, "You really owe me for this bud." I nod in appreciation. That seems to be my favorite gesture this awkward evening.

I lean into the drills. They aren't hard or fast, just the right movement to get our bodies hot and our minds sharp. Coach wouldn't tire us out before the big game. Still, my shuffling feet and quick passes fill me with exuberance. It's enough to push the memory of my mother away. All the sensations, the confusion, the anger, and the sadness pressed away by some simple exercises.

Man, I'm grateful I made the team. It was actually pretty easy to do it. Dad says my reflexes are quicker and my stamina is higher than a normal human. It's a dragon thing. On days Coach slays us with practice, I don't feel stronger, but my catches are consistent, and I can speed across the field easily.

Dragon or not, I'm pretty dang good at football.

"All right, that's it!" Coach shouts, blowing his whistle.

The other team has come out of their locker room and is doing stretches and warm-ups. Their yellow jerseys practically shine from the overhead lighting, and I think idly for a minute that I'm glad we don't have pee-colored jerseys.

I know, I know. It's a childish thought, but I can't help it.

"Get some water. Rest up for a minute. Game's about to start!" Coach shouts, then blows his whistle once again before pulling it off his neck and pocketing it.

He's gotten in trouble with the refs more than once for accidentally blowing it during the game. Assistant Coach Tracy Hone had to take over a game once because he got booted. Coach Sanders can't afford to slip up for this one.

I'm stretching my arms behind my back when I see her. The red-headed girl. My insides go cold instantly, and I shift on my feet. Her eyes bore into me from the stands, her larger and almost terrified-looking brother standing by her. She wears the same baggy sweatshirt and sweats. For some reason, it feels like she's literally looking into my soul. I hate it so much, but I can't look away. An inexplicable cold terror worms through my chest, making my limbs shiver and my head scream at me to run away. It's there for a moment, freezing me in place, when all of a sudden, it's gone. I frown, staring back at her.

Until I see the movement next to her.

Dad is waving at me frantically, his arms looking like those blow up guys that furniture stores have on the side of the road, only a little less chaotic. I growl quietly in my throat, then tell Coach I'll be right back. I have no desire to talk. I'd be fine waiting until after the post-game party, but it doesn't look like he has the same idea. My only solace is seeing that Amir is with him. I can't see his face because he's reading his math textbook like a nerd. The fact that he has a book tells me it's him. No other spectator has a book, let alone a *school* book.

"Hey," I say to Dad, my eyes flicking to the weird girl, who miraculously isn't staring at me anymore.

"Dave, I'm sorry about earlier. I didn't mean to keep those things from you."

He glances at Amir and the other girl.

"It's fine. I just want to win this game and move on," I say.

Dad licks his lips, clearly considering what else to say, then he pockets his hands and shrugs.

"Well, yeah, that's a good idea," he says, apparently deciding to hold back on more words. "In any case, I met your friends here. Krista and Jared?"

He turns to the red-haired girl and my skin prickles. Dad literally just called this goth-looking girl my friend. She's looking at me again with the same piercing blue eyes, but she's grinning now. I can't tell if it looks good or more scary considering who she is.

"Hey, Dave. Your dad's pretty awesome. Funny how we ended up sitting next to each other. What a coincidence," she says.

I swallow hard, then plaster a false smile on my face. "Yeah. Yeah, that's great."

"And Jared, her brother. And their parents, Bob and Stacey."

I clear my throat, trying not to laugh at their very generic names. I've seen too many commercials with "Bobs" and "Staceys," so it seems so ironic that such normal-named people could be the parents of this girl.

Krista. Her name is Krista. I repeat this to myself so I don't accidentally call her a terror or a monster.

"Hey, young man. I hear you're the star of the team this year. Looking forward to seeing you play," Bob says.

So that's where Jared gets his size: his dad. Bob's skin is a rich brown color, and he has some wicked cool tattoos all along his neck and down one of his arms. They look like those amazing Islander tattoos that the buff guys have. He must be Samoan, or Tongan, or something like that. Because when I say he's big, I mean he's a *big* man. If he wasn't flashing a smile at me, I'd probably feel intimidated.

"We love coming to the football games. We're trying to get Jared to try out, but we've had no success yet," Stacey says. Her hair is deep brown, and her eyes are the same piercing blue as Krista's. How did these two people produce those two teens? Jared has the same brown skin as his dad, but his hair is blond. Krista has her mom's eyes, but where did that red hair come from?

"Yeah, the games are pretty fun. We'll make sure to give you a good show," I say.

"Go give them heck!" Dad says, and the discomfort I feel from the odd family disappears momentarily. My anger diffuses at his cheer. I smile broadly and pump my fist in the air, letting out a whoop.

A part of me wonders why Jared and Krista's parents really came to the game. I mean, they did say that it's fun for them, but it still seems strange. Neither one of their kids play. And Krista's not on the cheer squad. Before I can think much more about it, Coach blows the whistle for us to come in.

I shudder at the thought of Krista's eyes boring into me constantly from beyond the field. Chancing one more glance, electricity runs through my veins. She's staring again. Her arms are folded now, and she looks meaner than ever. Fear locks my throat and causes me to almost freeze, but I turn away and shake off the feeling.

"Smith! You done with your love fest over there?" Coach Sanders jokes.

The heat that rushes through my face makes me want to hide in a hole, but I puff out my chest and nod.

"That girl wants nothing but for me to burn in a bonfire," I reply. A couple of my teammates laugh, but most of them ignore me. It's not a great assumption. But what else could those looks from her mean?

"Let's get it, boys! Bring home the big W!" Coach Sanders calls out.

We shout our team name, then move to the field.

This game is going to be epic.

A GAME TO REMEMBER

The game goes *perfectly*. And when I say it goes perfectly, I'm not joking. Halftime hits, and we're up by two touchdowns. Our opponents manage to get one, but that's mainly because their receiver is about as slippery as me.

Only *about* as slippery.

Two of the touchdowns are seamless. I catch the ball and weave in and out of their defenders like it's open season and the deer is smarter than the hunter. The third one isn't my doing, which I am a little bitter about. It's dumb, but I love the idea of being the sole person responsible for winning the game. That thought is soon sucked away by the elation of victory. Unless things go really bad for us in the fourth quarter, we aren't going to lose.

The cheer squad is dancing in their standard blue outfits, the color and logo matching our jerseys perfectly. Thoughts of Krista waltz through my mind again, and I can't help the disgusted look that creeps across on my face.

"You okay over there, Dave? Looks like you're about to be sick," Moses says.

I narrow my eyes at him.

"Just sick at how we're going to completely obliterate the other team," I reply, throwing my hands up in a wide V.

He rolls his eyes and throws his water bottle at me. It's supposed to hit my chest, but I snatch it out of the air with ease. His smile turns to a scowl, and he holds out his hand for me to give it back. I don't at first. Messing with him is too much fun.

Halftime ends quickly. A couple of the team members groan at the thought of having to push ourselves out there again, but all I feel is the rush of adrenaline. I don't tire easily. That's how it's been since I was a kid. It's also part of why it's challenging to make friends. When I was younger, I'd play tag or race, and because I would win without even huffing a small breath, most kids got annoyed. I guess they didn't love losing all the time.

Amir's different. He's pretty fit himself. For a hot second last year, he was on the swim team, but he decided he should prepare for college rather than compete. It was a shame because that kid could swim like a dolphin.

"Get out there! Win us the game so we can call it a night!" Coach Sanders shouts.

We rush onto the field and get into position. It only takes one down to get past the scrimmage line. We repeat. Two downs. Now that we've made it twenty yards down the field, the quarterback gives me the nod.

Oh, the *nod*. It's my favorite play. I know he's going to lob that ball so far that the opposing team won't even think about it. He'll fake left, spin around, fake a throw, jump back, and then really throw it.

I ready myself to sprint through their defense. The center calls out the play, looking left and right, then shoves the ball back to the quarterback. I'm gone in a flash, zipping through them like they aren't even there. It's like my mind funnels forward, all distractions gone in an instant.

When I spin around, I'm only ten yards away from the end zone. The ball has already started to fly toward me. I see it coming, distinct against the black sky. I look at the stands where my dad is. I don't know why I do it, probably to show off as I catch the ball.

And Krista.

She's staring me down again, but now she's holding up her hand—and it's *huge*. When I say huge, I mean, it's at least three times what her hand should be. It looks like a balloon, though without the pudginess. They are the hands of a giant. Thick purple veins course up and down, making her skin look even paler.

I blink, my mind not processing what I'm seeing. Then I feel the ball land in my palm, and I pull it to my chest.

What I don't see is the opposing team member boring down on me from the left. He slams into me, and I grunt, the air leaving my lungs. We both fall. The ground tilts sideways until my helmet bounces off the turf. It doesn't hurt that bad—okay, my leg actually hurts a bit—but then I feel the ball slip away. My insides squirm.

I hear cheers from the wrong side of the stadium as one of the opposing team members picks up the ball and rushes down the field.

I fumbled the ball. I've not fumbled the ball since I started playing, not even in practices. But here I am, empty-handed and under a large defender.

And Krista's hand grew three freaking sizes.

I push myself up. Coach Sanders is yelling frantically at the top of his lungs. He's going to give me a large load of crap for that fumble. The interceptor is running through my team, and for a moment, I think he'll touchdown, but he's tackled just before our line. About where I was when I went down—only he doesn't fumble. My team wasn't expecting to have to chase anyone. Dave Smith never fumbles a ball.

I'm still trying to process what happened, what I saw, and how I dropped the ball. None of it seems to make sense in my brain. Then I hear my name, and it's not with a voice I recognize.

"David! Behind you!" a deep voice shouts.

I look up, my flustered mind trying to process the voice which yelled the warning, but it's Krista, and she is running right at me. Frowning, I crouch low instinctively as if preparing for her to bowl right into me. She's not that large, but she's coming fast, and if she hits, it could be with force.

Then she starts to grow.

My eyes widen as the redheaded girl expands at least a foot and a half in height, the rest of her body following the shift. Her arms fill the loose gray sweater and matching pants. Her fingers change to the size of sausages, and her face develops what looks like purple stretch marks. Rounded black horns sprout through her red hair and shoot toward the sky.

The "terror" is truly a terror.

I lick my dry lips. My whole mouth turns to ash. Krista is now taller and bigger than me, and she's coming right at me, the same angry look on her face.

"Behind you!" she bellows, her voice much deeper than before.

I'm stuck in a mental block. I hear her words, but I think she wants to distract me so she can kill me. She could probably squeeze my head off now. Against my brain's warning, I turn to see what she's referring to.

Two men with green faces and cloaks jump from the bleachers. Their bottom canines protrude above their upper lip like a strange backward walrus, though with smaller teeth. They rush at me, dropping their cloaks to the ground to reveal chain mail and swords. They point their weapons right at me.

I take a few steps back, and my stomach drops. Green is *not* a normal skin color. They are both taller and much bigger than me. I'm about to be kabobbed.

A roar from behind reminds me that Krista is coming, too, but she doesn't hit me. She rushes past me right at the two green men. They shout in surprise and swing their swords at her. For a moment, I think these men must be LARPers gone wild, but when one of their blades cuts the hood off of Krista's hoody while she spins, I know they're not carrying fake swords.

Krista dodges one of the blades and throws a fist into the nearest green man's face. His head snaps back at a sickening angle, then he melts into black tar-like liquid. The other man manages to get his sword righted and slices at Krista's stomach. It connects, and the blade squelches through her flesh. Purple blood flicks from his blade and splatters on the ground.

Blood is not supposed to be that color.

Krista roars again, the voice not her own, but something deeper and more terrifying. The cut must not have been bad, for she swings her other fist, and the second green man melts to black tar, like the first.

She spins on me, a wild look in her eyes. It is by far the most terrifying thing I've ever seen. And before this game, I had been confronted by my mother—a full-sized dragon.

I'm locked in place, unsure of what's going on. My mind cannot make the mental leap from fumbling the ball to watching Krista, thick and muscley, melt two green-skinned men. Blinking slowly I check the scoreboard to see that the opposing team didn't, in fact, score a touchdown.

Something hard grips my upper arm, and I react, throwing my free arm to the side in a wild swing. It connects with whatever has me, but instead of doing anything, it bounces off, and I howl in pain.

"You're attacking the wrong side, *Davey*." Krista's now lowered voice sounds close to me.

Looking up into her face, my stomach convulses. Her eyes have gone all black, as if the pupils grew to consume the rest of the color of her irises. It looks like her skin split in a few lines on her face, something red and all too fleshy peeking out from behind.

"There's more, you idiot! Grab a weapon—do *something*," she says. She uses the grip she has on my upper arm to spin me around.

I'm facing a bunch of cloaked figures, some with thick torsos and arms, sickly green skin, and red eyes. Others are huge and bulky— and at least five feet taller than me. Their skin glows various shades of blue. Thin tusks poke out of their bottom lips, pushing as high as their noses. One of them mumbles something I can't understand and electricity crackles between his palms. He shouts and throws his hands outward, the blue energy flickering in the air. Hair stands up across my whole body. I'm thrown backward, my body convulsing and my tongue lolling to the side. When I hit the ground, I can barely feel it.

I groan and try to roll over, but it's much harder than I expected. There is screaming now, and I try to focus on where it's coming from. Everyone in the bleachers is panicking, running left and right, slamming into each other and knocking each other over. Pressing my palm firmly over my face, I rub it roughly, trying to bring some awareness to my brain and my limbs.

Another grip snatches my arm, and I'm hoisted upward. Before I can even shout in protest, my dad's face is right before me.

Confusion melts away to relief as he pulls me into a tight hug.

"I really regret not teaching you how to fight," he says quickly in my ear. "Stay here and try not to get killed. Worst case, use your fire."

He shoves me away and gives me a look of pity before spinning around and throwing open the trench coat he's wearing. Did he just *invite* me to use fire? My dad, the most protective human in all the world, just told me to do the thing he's warned me against for years and years.

Wait, how did I *not* notice that he's wearing a trench coat? I guess Krista was really distracting.

He rips two swords from sheaths hidden underneath the coat and stands next to Krista. He gives her a curt nod, and she returns it. I gape at the two of them. The girl who has given me nothing but death glares has somehow managed to save me from—I don't know what, to be honest—and now she's standing next to my dad like some DnD spectacle. If I hadn't just been shocked by that freaky creature, I would think this is all a dream.

Krista and my dad rush forward, him with his blades and her with her fists. She doesn't even seem bothered by where the sword sliced into her midsection. She's acting like she wasn't hit at all.

"Lucky that dragon son fell into our laps," a grisly voice croons.

I spin on my heels, looking around frantically for the source of the voice, but I see nothing.

"Tall fools don't know where the real danger lies," another low and scratchy voice says.

I follow the sound and see two—children? No, that can't be right. I blink rapidly, trying to make sense of it. The two figures in front of me barely make it to my waist. They are green-skinned, but their hair is brightly colored. One's hair is so red that it reminds me of Christmas; the other is a bright pink.

They both brandish daggers and advance on me, sharp teeth visible in the bright stadium lights. I gasp, taking a few steps back rapidly.

"Now, now, no need to give us trouble. King will be happy that we could snatch you away. You'll be sleeping in a bit, so don't worry about that," the red-haired creature says.

He pounces then, swiping the dagger through the air, and I jump backward, the sharp edge barely missing me. The thing spins around and prepares to attack again, but a bulldog jumps out of nowhere and tackles him, teeth tearing into the flesh of his arm.

The pink-haired thing is running at me now.

Worst case, use your fire.

As if coming home from a long trip and feeling the familiar sensation and smell of the house, my palms heat up rapidly. I let them reach peak hotness and flames burst to life up my forearms. The pink-haired thing hesitates, but only slightly. She or he—the pink hair is really throwing me—lunges at me and dodges the fireball I throw. I duck out of the way and thrust my hand upward. This fireball misses it, like the first, but it comes close enough that its cloak lights on fire.

"Grumbles and grime!" it curses, spinning around to pull off the piece of cloth.

Before it can make progress, I shift my hand decisively and lob another flame. This connects with it directly in the chest and explodes. I flinch at the brightness and the heat even though flames don't hurt me, and when it clears, there is nothing but a pool of tar.

My mouth falls open, but I hear struggling still. I spin around, expecting to see the bulldog, but it's gone. It's now a lion, mane tossing to and fro as it pounces and swipes at the creature.

A smudge of black appears out of thin air, and two more of the green creatures come out of it like a portal, their faces determined and their daggers flashing. I try to shout a warning at the lion, but my voice is caught in my throat. The lion stretches and grows after pouncing toward the creature. Its fur melts away into thick, wrinkly gray skin, the paws flatten, and its face transforms into a long trunk.

The elephant lands on the creature, which lets out a terrified scream before melting into the same tar.

"I'm going insane. I'm simply going insane," I chant to myself. I launch a fireball at the two creatures coming up behind the elephant. "Watch out, more behind you!"

The elephant looks at me, a surprisingly human expression, then shrinks rapidly into a bulldog again. It spins around and growls at the creatures. They leap toward it, which then lunges back at them, teeth snapping. In midair, it shifts again, its body growing longer and its fur turning a spotted yellow. The leopard pounces on one of the creatures and bites down on its neck.

More tar.

In the throng, the other creature must have seen and anticipated the shift, for it spins around and slices the side of the leopard. Blood flies in the air as the animal roars in shock and pain. I cry out in shock, but the leopard turns on the creature, teeth bared. It jumps forward and swipes the creature in the face, knocking it to the ground.

Just as it stands on its hind legs, tall and lithe, the animal's eyes roll back in its head and it falls heavily to the ground. The leopard shifts once more, fur turning into skin and clothing.

Jared. The leopard is Jared.

Before I have time to process this, a desperate voice calls out his name as the creature bores down on him. With a determined grunt, I lob a flaming ball at it. My aim is true, and because it's distracted by the unconscious boy, the fire slams right into its face.

The tar splashes on an unconscious Jared. I retch at the sight but stumble over to him. His eyes flutter behind his eyelids, so I know he's not dead, but blood oozes from a gash on the side of his chest, saturating his polo shirt.

"Blasted goblins! How are they here?" a man shouts.

I don't recognize the voice, but when I look, I see it's Jared's dad, huge and looming over his son.

"I'm sorry, I didn't know what to do—" I try to explain.

"There's no time for that. We have to get out of here. We have a van, enough for the six of us. Get to the parking lot and we'll be fine," Bob says. He scoops up the large form of his son and slings him over his shoulder with ease.

"Okay, yeah—that seems smart," I say.

We rush away. There is a lot of tar on the ground, but more and more creatures seem to be coming from everywhere. Dad's splattered with the stuff, and I try *not* to think about how that was a living green or blue thing. I put a hand on my stomach, trying to hold the sick at bay.

He battles back to back with Krista, whose arms are almost completely black from the substance. Stacey, Bob's wife, nocks an arrow on a bow and lets it fly, the sharp edge piercing the shoulder of one of the bulky green creatures. She nocks another but doesn't have the chance to let it fly before she's punched in the back of the head. She crumbles to the ground.

"Mom!" Krista screams. She lunges toward her fallen mother and slams a heavy fist into the chest of the huge blue creature that knocked her down. It flies twenty feet back and hits the ground hard. I note that it *does not* melt to tar.

"There's too many of them!" Bob shouts from my side. "Get to the car! Krista, take your brother!"

I watch with awe as he literally tosses the large boy through the air. She catches him in her beefy arms with a grunt. Bob rushes to his unconscious wife's side and lifts her carefully into his arms. He joins up with us as we move.

We run as a group, Dad swiping his sword sideways to fend off creatures. Bob has a large hammer now, and I have no idea where it came from. He carries the small form of Stacey over his other shoulder.

My heart is thrumming loudly and adrenaline is coursing through me. The bleachers are near empty, and I can only imagine what the spectators are thinking. They came for the most epic homecoming game of the school's history, and they got a freaking LARP battle.

Except this is not a game. We could die.

The thought hits me like a semitruck and I stumble, almost losing my footing. It's enough to slow me down, the others reaching the bleachers first and darting around them.

"Got him!" a deep, slurred voice sounds from behind me. A bulky green warrior grips my jersey, his blade pointed at me. I call fire to my palm, feeling it burst to life, but I'm too slow.

His sword slams into my chest, the blow knocking the wind out of me. Heat washes over the area, and for a minute, I think it's my blood pouring down. I stumble backward, my shoulder connecting with the bleacher bench at that level. My jersey and pads are cut clean through. There's red there.

But it's not a wet red; it's a textured red. Like what I saw in the vision of my mother.

Confused, I touch my bare chest with my hand, feeling the roughness there. They feel like—

"Scales?" the creature grunts in disbelief. He lets out a roar of anger and swings his sword at my arm. I instinctively throw my hand up, and his weapon connects. My arm rattles and pain shoots up it. But the blade doesn't cut me.

More red scales have grown on my bare skin out of nowhere.

"Grimin' half dragon!" the creature curses, and he tries yet again.

I'm still too distracted to even look at him, but this time, his sword clangs against another weapon.

"Leave—my—son—*alone*!" Dad's voice growls next to me.

With a quick instep and swing of his second blade, the creature melts into tar.

"No time to stand there, son, we—"

He stops and examines my arm, eyes wide. Then he locks his jaw and tugs me along. So he didn't know about the scales either. For some reason, that comforts me. One less thing he's lied to me about. Movement from my right makes my whole body tense, but it's a familiar face.

"Amir?!" I exclaim, relieved. "What are you doing here?"

He looks at me like I'm insane, then gives me an extremely Amir answer.

"Dude, I come to these games for *you*, not because I think it's fun." He glances behind me and grimaces. "I did *not* expect it to become a real-life DnD game. This isn't a dream, right?"

I open my mouth to tell him I have no idea what's going on when Dad grabs both our arms.

"Amir, son, this is really not a good time for this conversation," he says. He pulls us along.

Amir's sputtering something that sounds like a complaint, but Dad doesn't listen.

We run full tilt until we come upon the rest of our group. They're up against a few more creatures.

Krista lets Jared's body fall with a thump, and I can't help but wince at the sound. Poor guy's going to hurt a lot when he wakes up. *If* he wakes up.

The thought makes me bite my tongue to ward off the despair.

All but one of the creatures is tar now. The last is a small one, white hair hanging down over his brow.

"The king will reward our people greatly for this!" it shouts with a voice that sounds like shards of glass.

The three of us rush up to Krista, and I bend down to check if Jared is still breathing. Abruptly Bob runs directly at the creature, hammer swinging wildly. Just before his weapon connects, the thing throws a rock that flickers with an odd, wispy red light. It falls in slow motion toward the five of us.

Bob's hammer crushes the creature, and it melts to tar, but I'm focused on the rock, which lands on the pavement right in front of me. When it does, it explodes outward, red light and an eerie darkness spreading across the grass so rapidly that I can't even react.

The ground disappears beneath my feet, and a scream locks in my throat as I fall into darkness.

WE FALL TO OUR DEATHS, OR SOMETHING LIKE THAT

I'm aware of noises, things that both terrify me and intrigue me. Along with an insanely loud whooshing sound like a tornado—or at least what I imagine a tornado would sound like. Everyone is screaming.

My stomach is in my throat, my whole body reeling at the sensation of falling at a breakneck speed. All of a sudden, I halt in midair. Confused, I open my eyes. Everything around me is pitch-black.

Come home, son. Come home to me, a deep rumbling voice sounds from somewhere around me.

Before I can even process what I'm hearing, I'm falling again, and this time, a scream escapes my lips, tearing through the darkness. With a sickening thud, my back hits something both soft and hard. I think I'm about to pass out.

I'm not sure what happens next because I fall into a dream . . .

I'm back home, staring at the walls full of weapons in the basement. I'm a different person, or at least I feel different. I reach up and pull one of the swords down. This one is particularly large. I feel the weight of the weapon in my palm, and a grin spreads on my face. Before I can even think, I'm spinning through the room, swinging the blade with surprising ease and concise movements. When I finish, my heart thrums in my chest in a satisfying way.

It feels like I've been holding a weapon like this my whole life, and the confidence that bursts within feels both foreign and familiar all at once. When I turn to the stairs, Dad is watching me. He's wearing freaky clothes. His normal jeans and T-shirt are not there, but instead, he has on leather pants and—is that chain mail?

"You're ready. Your mother will be glad to have you by her side in battle," he says.

Another smile spreads on my face, and I reply, "The Orc king is not ready for me, that's for sure."

As if to punctuate my comment, I swing the broadsword through the air, the swish both dangerous and profound in the small space of the basement.

"You really should wake up though," Dad says.

I furrow my brow. "What are you talking about?"

He smiles, and when he speaks, it sounds more frantic, more afraid. "Wake up, David. Wake up! Daviron!"

I frown at hearing my real name. Another thing that feels foreign and familiar.

I snap awake suddenly. Dad is leaning over me, and I'm flat on the ground. My head hurts. My back hurts. Heck, everything hurts.

"What the—?" I say, shielding my face as a bright light shines directly on me.

As I blink away the burning in my vision, my dad starts laughing. It's a desperate, terrified noise. My thoughts are validated when I can finally see his face. Tears stream down his cheeks, and he uses the back of his hand to wipe them away.

"I thought—I thought you were gone. I couldn't get you to wake up," he explains.

I'm struck by a combination of things: the fact that I was out long enough for him to think I was dead, and the fact that he's crying. I've never seen him cry before. After a minute, his face hardens again like the man I know.

His show of emotion seems meaningful, like profoundly meaningful, but my head still hurts too badly for me to focus on it.

I break my sight away from Dad to survey our surroundings. My heart stops.

The stadium is gone. The people are gone. Our small town in Kentucky is gone.

I'm confronted with an environment that looks so different that I can't describe it properly. We're sitting at the bottom of a huge mountain with a waterfall about ten paces to my left. The rock beneath me—I'm assuming it's rock, though I can't tell for sure—is completely covered in thick green moss. It feels both soft and hard under my hands.

Also wet. I flinch and lift up my hands, instinctively wiping them on my football jersey.

The events of the past hour come crashing back over me. The game. We were winning the game, but then I was attacked by some freaky green and blue creatures, small and large, and then one of them threw a rock at us and—

"Amir!" I exclaim, looking at Dad, "Where's Amir?"

He grimaces. "I don't know. I woke up five minutes ago. I haven't been able to find anyone else."

The roaring waterfall consumes most of my senses. I rub my eyes and shake my head a few times, worrying that Amir is gone, lost in another part of this strange place. Dad gives me an apologetic look, but I can tell he's still coming off the fear of me being dead. An image of Amir unconscious at the bottom of the river strikes me, and I gasp.

"Dad! Did you check the river for—" I start to say before I'm interrupted.

"Hoy! What the heck is happening?" someone shouts.

Warmth spreads through my whole body. I jump to my feet, wincing at the sudden jolt through my head. Amir is swimming toward us in the river, and he's dragging something heavy alongside him. It's Jared. I try to take a few steps forward, but I suck in a sharp breath and fall back down.

"You stay. I'll help," Dad says. He rushes to Amir, slipping his hands under the giant teen's armpits and hoisting him out of the water. Amir lets out a relieved sigh and flops on the moss-covered stone next to me.

"Dude, did you just lifeguard that massive kid out of the water?" I say, impressed.

"I mean, he was out cold when we fell into the water. Everything was black, then it wasn't, and I was underwater. Lucky thing I'm a dang good swimmer, no? Poor guy hasn't woken up. I think he's taken on water." Amir swallows hard.

Dad curses and leans over Jared, trying to hear a breath. He puts his lips to Jared's, and I can't help but gag. I turn away, knowing full well that Dad is just performing CPR, but it's still disgusting. I try to tune out the desperate grunts of Dad pressing on his chest and the heavy breaths that accompany them. After a minute, there's a choke and cough, followed by the sound of water spilling on the rocks.

I spin back toward them to see Jared sputtering back to consciousness.

"That—is—free—zing!" Jared says between coughs.

Dad is slapping him on the back.

Bloodstains cover the side of Jared's shirt where he'd been gashed by the goblin. My stomach roils, and my eyes widen. Dad follows my gaze and curses, ripping Jared's shirt up. Underneath the shirt is a slash about six inches long, blood trickling down. Cursing, Dad uses the sword he somehow still has to cut off the sleeve of his trench coat. He ties it tightly around Jared's chest to staunch the bleeding.

I remember the attack and how he'd been stabbed. He was a leopard then. I blink slowly, trying to take it in. And an elephant and—

"Who are you?" I find myself saying.

Jared focuses on me, his face pale and clammy.

"I'm like you," he says, coughing a few times again. "My mother is from here—"

I glare at him, my chest burning.

"You're half dragon, too?" I furrow my brow. "I thought it was just me—"

"Not half dragon." He pauses, taking some deep breaths. "My mother is the fairy queen. She's not from our realm either."

"Are fairies notorious for shifting into animals?" I ask with derision. I don't know why I'm so mad, but this is all messed up. First off, Miss Red-Hair glares at me and scares the crap out of me, he tags along, and suddenly I'm attacked by monsters? Nothing makes sense. "And what's Krista? Some child of a demon?"

The last part is dripping with so much sarcasm that it's sickening. I eye Amir, but he seems dead to the world. He is lying on his back with his eyes closed, not listening to us.

Jared frowns. "Yeah, how did you know?"

My mouth falls open, but before I can react, his pupils shrink in horror.

"Where's Krista? Did she land in the water, too?" He glances around.

I tense. I have no idea where she might have ended up. All anger and frustration in me shifts to concern.

"I haven't seen her—" I begin, but the thundering waterfall masks what I'm saying.

"We have to find her. She's probably unconscious like I was! If she's in the water—" Jared says, panicked.

"She's not," Amir says. He sounds groggy, like he just woke up from an extended nap. I bite my lip, hoping he didn't hear the bit about me being half dragon. "When I saw you and snagged you, I looked for anyone else. The water is as clear as the Pacific Ocean. I would have seen her floating if she were there."

I spin, wincing once more, and scan the bottom of the cliff. It's all moss covered for about twenty more feet before it turns into slate-gray stone. My eyes search the area when I see a flash of red.

Red.

"On the ground! There!" I shout, launching to my feet way too quickly. The world fuzzes, and I feel like I might pass out. Vertigo takes hold of me as my body regulates from my fall. When I recover, I see that Dad has already started running toward her. I shamble after him, holding my head and closing one eye to try and alleviate some of the throbbing.

"She's alive," Dad says, listening over her chest.

Suddenly her eyes snap open and she punches him right in the jaw. He falls backward, cursing.

"What in the—"

"Don't touch me like that!" she snarls. Then her eyes fall closed, and she's out again.

Jared and Amir are close behind. Amir collapses on the ground next to me, putting a hand on my shoulder and squeezing. Jared moves more slowly, his arm crossing his chest and resting on the gash in his side.

"Thank the light, you're not dead," Jared says, leaning over her.

He pauses then, considering something. "Our parents didn't get pulled in with us."

My skin chills. "Do you think they're—"

I don't want to say the word "dead," but I don't have to. Jared fills it in as if he stole the words from my mouth.

"Dead? No. They taught us all that we know about fighting. Besides, we took out most of them before we were drawn here."

Krista groans, rolls over, and throws a punch at Jared. "Stop talking! My head is pounding like a construction site."

Jared looks up at Dad apologetically. "I should have warned you that she gets like this after she shifts into her demon form. She gets really angry for a while after."

I narrow my eyes at Jared.

"Did you just say . . . *demon* form? Is that what she was in? She grew twice my size," I say, remembering how she filled out the gray sweats that now again lay loose on her unconscious form.

Jared looks at me, then at Dad, a perplexed look on his face.

"You didn't tell him? That there's more than just him?"

Dad locks his jaw. "I didn't think it was relevant."

Jared laughs deeply, then winces, his hand gripping his abdomen. "Not relevant? He has dragon blood in his veins. Don't you think that he'd feel less alone if he knew?"

Amir sits bolt upright, looking at the three of us in turn. "Woah, woah, woah. What in the blazes are you talking about? Dragon? Demon?" He looks at me. "Did you start a role-playing group without telling me?" His worried expression turns into an amused one. "Dang, man, I'm impressed. That's a pretty geeky thing to play and keep to yourself. Your teammates would have a field day, no pun intended."

I grimace, both at the joke and at the insinuation that I play a dorky game like that.

"No, man, I'm literally—oh man, it sounds so much cheesier saying it out loud." I put my head in my hands. "I'm part dragon. My mom is a dragon, or so Dad says and—"

I look up at Dad, silently asking for help. To my relief, he chimes in.

"I don't think that beating around the bush is going to be worth anyone's time right now. Yes, Amir, David is half dragon, as 'cheesy' as it might sound. It's the truth, and it's why we were attacked in the football stadium." He scratches his chin, staring directly at me. "What I don't understand is why they came now, of all times. I brought you to the human realm when you were days old. Not once has anything come looking for you."

As before, I have more questions than answers, and I find myself feeling dizzy. I lean back heavily on my heels and close my eyes. A cool wind presses against the back of my neck, along with the slight wisps of the waterfall spray.

"We're wasting our time," Krista says.

My eyes snap open, and I glare at her.

"We all know the real reason why we were attacked. It's the first time three royal-blooded kids were in the same place at once. It's not rocket science. Besides, we thought we might have been followed for the past week since we moved to Kentucky. I guess our theory was right. Now, stop jabbering and let me have some quiet," she says, one of her hands moving to her forehead.

I stare at her in disbelief. A rush of heat swirls through me as I prepare a retort to her unnecessary outburst. Before I can say anything, Jared waves his hands in front of my face, gesturing me to follow him. Anger burns within me, but I resign myself to his silent request.

Dad and Amir follow us, too. We walk about twenty paces along the side of the mountain, angling close enough that the bright sun from above is blocked by the large mountain wall to our left. A shiver runs up my back. It's not particularly cold, but I'm still more wet than I would like to be. Who knows how long I'd been unconscious next to the waterfall.

I eye Amir and Jared. Their clothes are far more sopping than mine. They probably feel the chill also.

Jared stops next to a massive pine jutting out from the stone wall at a steep angle. I have no idea how such a large tree could have grown from the side of a steep rock cliff like that, but I push the thought aside.

"She's not herself," Jared explains, raising his hands in a surrendering fashion. "She always gets like this when she calls on her demon side. It's an unfortunate side effect. I suggest we let her rest for a bit before we try and move anywhere else. If you bother her too much, she'll literally try to rip your head off."

I chuckle at the comment, but when he looks at me seriously, my mouth drops in a frown.

"Bro, did you just say *demon* side? What is even going on?" Amir demands, folding his arms across his chest.

When neither Jared nor I answer him, the three of us look sideways at Dad.

"Oh, Ellistra, what did you get us into?" He looks up at the blue sky for a minute.

After a ridiculously large sigh, he points to me.

"Qotan, which is where I'm assuming we are right now, is another realm. It's where David's dragon heritage is from. Nearly seventeen years ago, I was living in peace in the kingdom when the war and unrest between the races of light and the races of darkness reached a peak. Your mom"—he wiggles his finger at me—"told me that to save our land from a curse, we were to preserve the dragon bloodline in you."

My mouth goes dry. I try to open it to ask questions, but it feels stuck together.

Dad continues. "She told me to take you through one of the three open portals to the human world. She couldn't take you herself because, well—the races here can't come to earth without melting. She also couldn't leave her subjects. So I took you, and we've lived in the human world since."

Amir whistles softly, then turns to me, a look of appreciation and admiration in his face. It's awkward and makes me want to squirm out of my skin and hide somewhere. I'm not a stranger to attention, being the skilled football player that I am, but this feels wrong on so many levels. It's a secret I've never believed and therefore never wanted to share with anyone. Jared stands there with a blank expression, his gaze affixed somewhere behind my dad.

"That's wild, man," Amir says. "How is it that *I'm* the fantasy nerd, and I didn't end up the son of a dragon? Life is cruel."

I don't know what's more surprising, the fact that Amir didn't question anything Dad said or the fact that he looks genuinely annoyed at me for being born.

Amir raises an eyebrow at Jared. "Based on your entire lack of reaction, I'm guessing you have ties to this Qotan place yourself?"

The silence that follows makes my skin crawl. I try to be patient, focusing on the breeze and the thundering waterfall. I spot movement on the side of the mountain looming behind my dad. It's a family of deer, a single stag with massive horns leading them. It might be a nice sight if it were in a recognizable location—like, you know, *earth*.

Jared sighs. "Like I said, I'm half fairy. My dad was given the same order from the fairy queen."

Amir's cheeks puff out, and his face turns red. He eyes the massive form of the Samoan teen before us and then booms out a laugh.

"You—are half—*what*? I thought fairies were supposed to be, you know . . ."

Amir holds up his finger and thumb, creating space that's only a couple inches wide.

Jared flushes. "I get my genes from my dad. I think that's pretty obvious. But to be fair, I have no idea how that works or why I look the way I do. My fae blood is unmistakable, and it saved *your* life."

He jabs a finger at me. I don't know why I feel guilty all of a sudden.

"Uh, yeah. Thanks for that, by the way," I say, putting my hands behind my back and watching the deer family behind Dad disappear down the rocky slope. "So, you can turn into animals?"

He nods. "And read minds. So there's no point in keeping secrets from me."

Amir's mouth falls open. "Wait, you can't be serious. What am I thinking now?" He wiggles his eyebrows at Jared and squeezes his lips closed.

"No, I'm not related to her. Tinkerbell is from a movie. She is not a real fairy," Jared says, shaking his head.

"Woah! That's just freaky," Amir comments.

Jared shrugs. "It's just a part of my life. I don't intentionally sift through thoughts, but I hear them without trying."

He winces, looking over to where Krista is lying.

"She's mad that I told you about my powers," Jared whispers.

"Keep your mouth shut, Jared! You're always the reason we have to move because you blabber everything away to anyone who gives you a hug!" Krista shouts.

"I can create flames with my hands," I offer, holding my hand up and summoning a flame. "I have extra stamina, I don't tire easily, and I'm quick on my feet. I also can apparently grow scales, though that's new to me."

I'm not sure why I burst into the admission, but it feels important, like I need to even out the information so they know I'm not a threat to them.

"The fairy kingdom preserved their bloodline, but so did five other races," Dad says distantly. "And they are most likely being hunted by the orcs, too."

Jared nods. "Like you, we'd not been attacked before the last month or so. Goblins tried to gut me while I was leisure reading in the high school library about three weeks ago."

Amir claps his hand on Jared's arm. "Wait, you *read*? Like *for fun*? Dude, what's your favorite book?"

Jared beams and they launch into some dorky conversation about popular fantasy books and their favorite authors. I've only heard some of the titles, the ones that Amir won't stop talking about even though he knows I don't like to read. The most baffling thing about it all is that Jared just admitted to being nearly gutted and Amir is focused on his love for reading.

I close my eyes and shake my head slowly.

Dad reaches out and puts a hand on their shoulders. "I'm glad you have something in common, but we need to figure out what to do from here. I think it's safe to assume that we are in Qotan. Whatever stone that goblin threw at the ground transported us here. I've never heard of something like this before, but the fact that they didn't follow right after us suggests that it was a Hail Mary for that last goblin."

I shift from side to side, trying to imagine what it could all mean. Even before Dad said this was Qotan, it already felt familiar. It's hard to explain, but there's a tingling in my whole body, slight and unnoticeable until I focus on it more closely.

"It feels familiar here. Like I've just come home from a really long trip," I say.

Jared looks thoughtful and gives a doleful nod in response. "For me, too. But another part of me feels like this is all wrong, like I don't belong here."

I furrow my brow. I feel that part, too. I think of home, of the football stadium, and of Monica. We were about to start hanging out more. A tug in my gut comes so quickly and heavily that I double over, gasping. All thoughts of home disappear immediately, and I can only focus on the hard stone ground.

"David! What happened?" Dad puts his hand on my back.

There's the sound of metal scraping against something hard, and I wince. Dad has pulled out his sword, his eyes darting around us.

"I wasn't attacked," I gasp out, taking a moment to catch my breath. "I just . . . feel homesick, I think."

It sounds really dumb, and I can feel my face start to flush, but Dad grunts, pulling any attention from me.

"Oh. Well, okay," he says, frowning. "I have a feeling we shouldn't stay here long. If *they* find out that you are here, I suspect our enemies will come quickly."

I'm a teen football player—with *enemies*. What has my life turned into?

I stand straight, clenching my abs and letting them go to get a feel for whether the tugging sensation is still there. It seems to have gone as quickly as it came. Turning to follow Dad's gaze over the low valley beneath us, my breath is taken away by the vastness of it. You'd think that if you were sent to a different realm where mystical creatures are real, it would be more beautiful.

It looks like an awful desert. Even now, as the sun stretches overhead, sweat is beading in my neck and brow. A few droplets break free from the confines of my skin and roll downward. A strange chill runs through my body and I shiver. Tall peaks of the mountain range backing us tower high, pines, shrubs, and other vegetation covering the sides. Along the bottoms of the mountain range is a clear line when the plants end and the desert begins.

"We can't stay here. It's best if we follow the river until we find someone to talk to," Dad says, sizing me up. "If we can find out where we are, I can guide us to the portal I've used before. If we can get there, we can get back to earth."

He pauses, looks me up and down once more, then grimaces. "We also need to get you all new clothes. I haven't been here in sixteen years, but I don't think Qotan fashion will have progressed much."

"I will not be getting any new clothes. These stay on. I don't care what these dumb creatures think of it," Krista snaps.

We all turn in unison. She's hobbling toward us as if she's broken both of her legs and is having a hard time moving with them. Jared joins her side and puts an arm around her shoulder. I balk as she literally growls at him, fury evident in her gaze. Her brother seems completely unfazed.

"Unless you can't travel," Dad says. He sounds disappointed, or maybe just worried.

"I am just fine—don't baby me like—"

"I'll carry her," Jared offers. And with that, he reaches down and scoops up the small red-haired girl. She curses and slams her fists into his back, but it doesn't seem like there is strength behind the blows. She's just mad. He doesn't last long before he winces and lets her down.

"Or maybe I should wait until my wound heals up a bit," he admits.

She glares at him, throwing another punch. "If anything, I should be carrying *you*."

Amir looks at me skeptically and I shrug at him. She's a firecracker, red hair to boot.

"We need to stay by the river. Climbing the mountains is impractical, and we don't know what's on the other side. It's going to get hot as we leave the range, and we need a source of water until we find civilization. After that, we need to make our way to Dranith. There should be a way back to earth near there—at least, there was almost seventeen years ago when I brought you as a baby," Dad says, giving me a knowing look.

It's the type of look that doesn't offer comfort. I still have so many questions, but the way Dad's acting makes me feel like we're about to get ambushed any moment. My back tingles as I imagine an arrow slipping through my spine. I shake the thought away, knowing it's completely ridiculous. Or, at least hoping it's ridiculous.

"Okay. Dranith is—what again?" I ask, folding my arms and leaning to one side.

"The dragon city. It's your original home. And the place where your mother lives."

My face falls. I don't mean for it to happen, but the idea of seeing my mother makes my insides writhe. That is, if we aren't attacked by something first. The prospect doesn't seem encouraging.

Dad squeezes my shoulder once more before making his way down the rocky, steep edge next to the quick moving river.

I let Amir go next, then Jared with the trailing, cursing girl. I'm not sure why I don't want them behind me. Do I think Jared will try to kill me? No. But Krista on the other hand . . .

I bring up the rear, hoping the imagined arrow in my spine stays an imagination.

7

I LEARN HOW UNCOOL DESERTS ARE

It's hot.

And when I say hot, I mean like melt-your-face-off-if-it-touches-any-surface-of-the-ground-or-metal hot. I've not vacationed much in my life, but I hear about places like Arizona and Texas, and I know those places are not for me. Kentucky has its moments, but it's nothing like this place. As we walk, I wish we could just swim the whole way to this Dranith city. I even suggest it more than once, but Dad shakes his head and gestures forward. Something about staying in a defensible position or whatever.

"Dude, this is intense," Amir admits, his voice sounding over the gurgling river. I suspect he's speaking plenty loud, but the heat has scrambled my mind, and I'm having a hard time keeping track of anything.

Krista says something rude and thumps Jared's back. He's apparently walking too close to her and it's bugging her. The rage fix after being all demon-y is lasting a while. It distracts me enough that when Dad talks, I jump.

"This is not my favorite part of Qotan. I would have dropped us in the Ruflin Forest if I had a choice. I never frequented this desert. Most of the light races avoid it; at least, they did when I lived here."

I'm not sure if it's the heat or the fact that I've had to listen to Krista complain about her brother for the past hour, but I finally snap.

"You keep saying 'light races' or 'dark races' like we're supposed to know what you mean! What are you talking about? As far as a guardian goes, you've done a pretty crappy job of it, *Dad*."

I regret the words almost as soon as they leave my mouth.

He stops and turns slowly, his eyes cast downward and his lips pressed into a thin line.

"I am sorry about that, Dave. I didn't think it would ever come to this. I thought we were safe in the human realm, but—" He pauses, standing up straight and looking me in the eyes. "But what's done is done. We're here now, and you have to learn about this place."

He nods to me, then looks at Jared quizzically. "How long are the aftereffects of her abilities?"

Jared shrugs, talking about her like she's not two paces away. "She's nearly there."

He reaches back and puts a heavy hand on her shoulder. She glares at him, pauses, then takes a deep breath.

"The rage is working its way out of my system finally," she huffs. "Might have been faster if you didn't treat me like a child."

Jared winces. "Hey, I can guarantee you *won't* stab me. Them? Well, that would be a bad way to start an alliance."

To my surprise, she doesn't yell at him. Instead, she adjusts her hoodie over her arms and twists her sweatpants back into place. Just looking at her wearing those clothes is making me sweat more. I look past her to the wide river, swirling and moving at a fast pace to our left.

I'd love to get in, to swim for a minute and cool down, but I suspect it's as hot in the water as it is out here.

Alliance. Just earlier today, this girl seemed like she'd be a high school nemesis. Now we're apparently allies.

Can life get any more ironic at this moment?

"Can we get in for a few minutes to cool off?" I ask.

Dad pauses, considering the water.

Past the river, there is nothing in sight, save for sagebrush plants and the occasional malformed cactus, with a lizard here and there. Sand blows in the hot breeze through the rocks and shrubs. It hits my sweaty body, but it doesn't help. The air has no coolness to it. It's dry and arid.

"Are you going to answer his question?" Krista says, eyeing Dad.

He sighs, then gestures to the river. "Might as well let you all take a dip."

"Thank goodness," Amir breathes, his hair matted and soaked from sweat. He lifts his shirt over his head, tossing it to the side, and leaps into the water. His head goes below the water for only a second before he scrambles out of the river, shouting curses in a language I don't understand. His parents speak Arabic at home, so I suspect it's that.

"Th—th—that w—w—wa—water is fr—free—freezing!" he cries, holding his arms around his chest and shaking.

Dad gives him an odd look, then walks over to the river, reaching down to dip his hand in. Air hisses through his teeth, and he pulls his hand back.

"Well, that explains how it isn't dried up in the wild heat. It's probably magic, enchanted to keep temperature from the top of that mountain and the snow runoff," he says, pointing upward.

Amir shakes his head. "But it was way warmer up by the waterfall."

Dad puts a hand to his chin. "It's not something I'm familiar with. I didn't frequent any desert-like parts of Qotan when I lived here."

Krista folds her arms. "And he's hedging again. No wonder he didn't tell you anything about this realm. It would take him years to explain how to make a sandwich."

Jared snickers at this, then bites his lip, carefully peeling back his tee and moving to the water.

Dad shakes his head and gives a hard look at Krista.

"I take it you get your disposition from your father," he says.

This must have struck a chord with Krista, for she narrows her eyes and shifts her jaw side to side. Her fists are clenched by her sides, and for a moment, it seems like she might hit Dad, but she steps back toward the river instead.

"Yes, unfortunately. The anger lasts longer after I've—grown my body—but it sticks around almost all the time." Her tone is unnecessarily cold.

"Part demon, you said?" He chuckles. "When they betrayed the other dark races all those years ago, many of us didn't believe their allegiance had changed. But you were one of the halflings sent to earth, so it must be true."

They both stare at each other for an uncomfortably long time before I clear my throat.

"Halflings? Races? What do you mean, light and dark races?" I push the issue again.

Dad shakes his head, pulling himself from the odd staring contest. He gestures to the river, and we all take a seat, my eyes locked on him.

"Light races, the creatures for good. Dragons, fairies, dwarves, elves, brownies, and so on and so forth. There are probably more, but I just can't think of them," he replies.

I can't help but let out a single burst of laughter. It all sounds ridiculous, even before he said "elves." He literally said "elves" like it was a completely normal thing. How is he not laughing at his own joke?

He furrows his brow. "You know, I won't bother answering your questions if you won't listen."

I choke down my next bout of laughter, licking my lips and looking away sheepishly. It seems odd that I feel embarrassed about my dad talking about creatures like they're real. But here I am, embarrassed.

"The demons," he continues, "aligned with the dark races. Orcs, goblins, trolls, sirens, and the others who waged a war on the light races. Until about twenty years ago. The demon king, Krell, came to the dragon queen and swore loyalty to the light races and to Qotan. That was right before the war came to a head. The sirens, apparently being inspired by the shift, swore loyalty soon after."

I glance at Krista. Dad just said her bloodline, the demons, were the bad guys. She doesn't seem affected by it.

"They were a fierce addition to the light race army, but it wasn't enough. Clearly . . ." Dad says, trailing off. "I guess Urothar, the orc king, still has power here."

The silence between us three teens grows awkward quickly. It's broken by a yelp and a shout from Jared and Amir as they splash each other and complain about the freezing temperature of the water.

"What about the halflings?" I ask. "You said something about halflings."

Dad licks his teeth. "A somewhat derogatory term for half-bloods." He pauses and points to me and Krista. "I don't know all the details, but your births are important. Dave, I was told to take you to the human realm to get away. There was news of the other halfling children being taken, too, but I wasn't sure where they went."

He eyes Krista uncomfortably, but she seems as gruff as ever.

"How did you find us?" Dad asks her.

Krista shrugs, then points a thumb over her shoulder toward Jared.

"Luck. Bob works remotely. Sometimes he has to travel for his job, and sometimes he brings us. We were just passing through Kentucky when we stopped for gas. Jared, being the busy body he is, overheard thoughts of dragon blood. And—well, Bob and my mom decided to move there within the month. It wasn't hard to find you again after that. Dragon boy can't stop thinking about his dragon half."

I flush, though I really don't have any reason to. I squirm to even think what *else* I might have been thinking about when he'd overheard me. Suddenly every embarrassing moment or thought flips through my mind as I try *not* to think about them with Jared close by.

Dad grunts. "That's a particularly useful power."

He looks at Krista and raises his eyebrow as if to ask her what she can do. She folds her arms and sneers at him. But then she sighs and speaks up.

"I can grow my body to incredible sizes. It makes me strong," she says. "I can heal quickly. And—I can intimidate people."

I stare at her, unsure how to respond

She scowls. "What are you looking at? Did you want to fight?"

I frown, then shake my head. I'm not intimidated by her despite her claim that she can do exactly that. Not that she's not a bit of a weirdo. I mean, she's been staring at me with a creepily terrifying set of eyes for the past day, but she's smaller than me. Sure, I saw how big she could grow, and I watched her take out a lot of green- and blue-skinned creatures, but she's small right now.

"What do you mean 'intimidate people'?" I ask.

She doesn't stop looking at me. Something rushes from my head to my toes. It's the same electrically charged fear that flowed through me when I'd melted my sleeve at the drinking fountain. It makes me want to run away. Then, the sensation is gone as quickly as it had come.

"Woah" is all I can say at first. I rub my temples. "That's what you did to me at school."

She grins, and I have to admit, it looks—nice, on her face.

"Yeah, I couldn't help but humble you a bit. Jared told me about your cocky thoughts, and I wanted to wipe them up."

I glare at her, but rather than getting angry, I decide it's my turn to share.

"I can create fire. I'm also pretty fast, and I heal quickly, too. And scales appear over my skin to make me impervious to damage."

That last part is kind of an assumption. I didn't know I could do that until a few hours ago. But based on all the attacks that came at me, and based on all the movies I've seen about dragon scales, it makes sense.

"Yeah, you said that already," she says, waving a hand dismissively.

I clench my fists at her nonchalance.

Jared pulls himself from the water and makes his way over to sit next to Krista. I give him a half smile as he settles in.

"Sounds handy, dragon boy. Too bad you suck at fighting," she comments.

Her comment is pointed, and I know it's intended to get under my skin. And it *does* get under my skin.

"Hey, that's not my fault. I'm just a regular teenager. How was I supposed to know I needed to use a *sword* someday? It's not like someone warned me that I'd get attacked at the homecoming game." There's venom in my tone even though I didn't mean for there to be. Dad slumps his shoulders, and I feel a tiny stab of guilt, but then I let it wash away.

To be fair, he did drop the ball on that one.

"Yeah—"

"Keep that thought to yourself, Kris," Jared warns, interrupting her.

I scowl as the two siblings pass some message silently between themselves. Jared can read minds, so more than likely she's saying something to him mentally, but more impressive is Jared's ability to respond using only facial expressions. It seems like a thing married couples would be good at.

I hold back a gag. These two are siblings. They can't be married.

"No, David, we aren't siblings. Not even a little bit," Jared says in response to my thoughts. I squirm where I'm sitting, feeling exposed. "We don't even share one parent. My dad and her mom just got married out of convenience. They really do love there—Qotan mates."

Krista rolls her eyes. "Sheesh, Jared. You make them sound like animals."

They have another exchange of silent communication.

"So, like, how did you find out you could grow? That's not something you just figure out during puberty," Amir chimes in.

I hold back a chuckle and bite my lip to prevent it from turning into a smile. Krista is the type of person you probably don't want to provoke.

"My mom knew what to expect. Or at least what demons are like. I don't get the red hair from her, but I'm sure you gathered that," she says.

Her tone is surprisingly chill, like she isn't bothered by Amir's question. She glances over at me, and the fire returns to her eyes. Wait, is she really mad at *me*? What did I do to her?

"Dad warned her about what my abilities might be like. He did not warn her enough about the anger," Krista admits.

She holds out her hands, and the sun reflects off the sweat droplets. Seeing it makes my whole body prickle and feel wet.

"I can't help it. I wish it was something I could suppress, but the rage consumes me. Everything pisses me off, and I want to tear the head off of anyone near me," she explains, putting her hand down on her lap.

She looks out distantly, and we all fall silent. The subject has taken an awkward turn and none of us want to poke the bear. Following her gaze, I look out over the desert plain. It's all pockmarked with rocks and shrubs, nothing green in sight. My brain freaks out a bit because a river that's this full should produce at least *some* green plants, but it's like the landscape won't drink it in, as if the water is poisoned.

My heart skips a beat at the thought, and I spin on Amir, half expecting him to have blue skin or be mutated into one of the goblins or trolls.

Amir grins.

Jared, clearly hearing my thoughts, looks at his hands and frowns. He feels his pulse, checking to see if he is dying. I'm never going to get used to him knowing what I'm thinking.

"I have to say, this is by far the last thing I expected when I came to your football game, David," Amir admits. "My parents . . ." His face falls. "Oh no. My mom and dad didn't even want me to go to the game. They think it's a waste of time, and now I'm not going to make it back for dinner. That, and we have a math test tomorrow. It's worth a fourth of our final grade this quarter!"

I'm incapable of following the logical route his mind just took. To be fair, I didn't think about the implications for his family because, well, my only family member is here with me. Also, school? All I need is passing grades. Amir's parents are pretty intense. They're kind, to be sure, but they have a way of intimidating you if they think you're not living up to your potential. I've seen how they push Amir.

Amir has pulled his backpack in front of him. He's extracting notebooks and papers, his still-wet hair dripping bits of water everywhere. He's muttering something, but I can't understand the words. Something about "wet notes" and "ruined textbooks." Everything he pulls out is water damaged.

Jared smirks at him. "We're stranded in the middle of a desert in another realm, and you're worried about a math test? You need a new hobby."

Dad has wandered off a little ways, but I can still see his back. He's shed his jacket and has it hanging over his shoulder. Underneath, he's wearing a white T-shirt, but it's saturated like he's dipped it in the water and put it back on. I'm struck by how buff he is. I know he works out. He's always spent time at the gym, but now that I've witnessed him cutting things down with a sword, his muscles seem more pronounced. And suddenly I feel scrawny.

I'm *not* scrawny, being a football player and all, but I'm more lanky, with thin muscle tone. Nothing bulky. Without meaning to, I think about what it would've been like if I'd actually trained to fight. Attempting not to feel bad about myself, I change the subject.

"Jared, how long have you been training?" I ask.

He smiles. "Ever since we could walk. It wasn't always with weapons; there's a lot of exercising and sparring with our fists. There's also the trials with our abilities," Jared continues. "Those can be pretty rough sometimes."

Krista huffs. "Speak for yourself. You never had to go through healing exercises."

Jared's smile melts, and he shivers.

Amir and I exchange quick glances. Of course, Amir—being the loudmouth that he is—asks the question we're all thinking.

"How *did* you train that part of your abilities?"

A wicked-looking grin spreads on her face, and she looks at me right in the eye.

"I'll spare you the details since I don't want you getting sick from them. Let's just say sharp instruments and my flesh are well acquainted."

I wish I could say images of Krista getting cut didn't immediately flow through my mind. Unfortunately, I've seen too many horror movies to avoid those thoughts altogether.

"Gosh, Dave. You have some pretty dark ideas," Jared complains.

"I—oh man . . . you saw those?"

He nods, and Amir scrunches his nose.

"Sheesh, I wish I had some magic powers or something. I'm feeling pretty lame right about now," Amir says.

Before I can console him, Dad calls to us.

"I can see buildings up ahead. Hard to say what it is, but we'd best see if we can make it there before dark. Gather your things and let's move."

I know he's told me that Dranith isn't in the desert, but still, the news that there are buildings gives me hope. Maybe we're closer to home than I thought about three hours ago when we started this trek.

Before we go, I yank off my jersey and pull apart my pads. I let out a sigh of relief, the collected heat from underneath my gear dissipating and the hot breeze tickling my sweat-covered skin. I have no idea why I didn't do this before. The feeling doesn't last long as I put my jersey back on. When we start walking, I grimace. My legs are chafing from the heat, but there's not much I can do about that. Even if I wanted to change my clothes, I couldn't. One, because Krista is with us and there is no privacy here, and two, I didn't bring anything else.

Great, it's a strange world when my priority has to do with another girl. I think of Monica and how we just started dating a week ago. She would *not* handle knowing that I was hanging out with Krista, even if it was by force.

We walk for another hour, and the sun dips alarmingly fast into the horizon to our right. I can feel the temperature dropping rapidly. At first, I think it's a good thing because my body is finally getting reprieve from the heat, but then I'm shivering. It's getting entirely *too* cold.

"No way!" Amir says. "My phone actually made it through that splash. And I still have forty-five percent left of my battery."

He thumbs the screen, and some rock music starts playing. It sounds tiny and quiet in the expanse of the wide open air.

"Oooooh yeah, I downloaded a bunch of things a few weeks ago."

He puts his thumb and pinky up and throws his hand in the air, rocking to the beat.

I shake my head.

"You do realize we're in the middle of a desert *not on earth*, and you are playing music on a *smartphone*, right?" I laugh. "You really are the one and only Amir."

He beams at me, and the two of us start singing the words like dorks. Jared stifles his own smile, and Krista glares daggers at us. I make a mental note that I want to challenge myself to get her to smile just once. And not the creepy, mischievous grin she flashed earlier. There's something about impossible tasks that make me want to succeed even more.

Our reverie in the music, however uplifting and freeing it is, comes to an abrupt end when Dad turns back to us and puts a finger to his lips.

"We're going to be within range of that small village in about an hour. Our timing is perfect; the sun should be going down right as we get close enough for someone to see us. They haven't sent anyone out to stop us, so either they haven't spotted us or they don't know we are human yet," he says.

Krista raises a hand. "We aren't human. Only you and Amir are."

Dad frowns. "Yes, I know, but that's not what I mean. This is *goblin* country. If they see anything resembling a human, it's going to be bad for us."

My stomach clenches. "Wait, you mean, you've known this the whole time and you are *just* now telling us? That village"—I nod my head toward the squat collection of buildings still far off—"is full of those green- and blue-skinned things?"

"Just the small green ones. The big, bulky ones aren't from there. That's not to say they won't be there, but—"

Krista speaks up. "Seriously? We were dropped in the middle of a desert that happens to be right in the middle of our ambusher? Why did you think it was smart to go *toward* where they are?"

For once, I find myself agreeing with the girl, a fact I'm not sure I'm thrilled about. Dad looks at us each in turn, but there's no regret in his eyes.

"It was either that or wander away from the river and die from thirst and hunger," he says. "Besides, let's not forget that I'm not the only one here who knew about it."

He turns on Jared, who pales slightly in the waning light.

"They were your thoughts. It's not my place to bring them up. I was raised right, you know," he says in defense.

Dad gives us a half smile, then gestures us to follow.

"We're here now, so no point in trying something different. Just—here," he reaches under his shirt and lifts something attached to his belt. It's a silver-bladed dagger with a black hilt and fat, round pommel. I stare at it for a moment before he waves it before me.

"I know you have no training with this, but it would be better for you to have something rather than nothing."

I frown. "Amir would be better off with that. Can't I just burn them?"

Dad's smile falters. He shakes his head. "Goblins have somewhat of a resistance to fire, so no, that won't work. Plus, I have one for Amir as well."

Sure enough, he reaches into the other side of his jeans and pulls out another blade.

"Sheesh, you got a whole armory in there. Where's the broadsword?" Krista asks.

With a completely deadpan expression, Dad says, "It wouldn't fit under my trench coat."

He turns on his heels and keeps walking.

I quietly run my thumb perpendicular to the blade to feel how sharp it is. The idea of using a weapon like this against a person makes my throat tighten up, so I force those thoughts away. Unsure what to do with it, I let my hand fall to the side, my already sweaty palm gripping the hard metal.

Something tells me the next time I see the color green, it's not going to be enjoyable.

8

WE'RE ALMOST KILLED BY HARD ROCK

I'm surprised by how accurate Dad is with the arrival time. I don't have my smart watch on. I left it in my locker at the stadium, but Amir has his analog watch. In less than an hour, we are moving quietly next to the burbling river just outside the town. The flow has gotten a bit louder here. Heavy rocks litter the inside of the river, causing foaming rapids. The speed has somehow increased, though I'm unsure how considering the terrain has been flat.

I shake my head. It's easier to say that magic exists here and that because it's not earth, things just work differently.

The sun has pretty much dipped behind the horizon, and we've been plunged into darkness. There's a steady glow over the horizon, a kind of greenish-blue light that Dad says is the late-rising moon. As we walk, I find myself stumbling on the rough edges of the ground and tripping on shrubs.

It's gotten very cold. Not like middle-of-winter cold, but I'm pretty sure the air has dropped at least fifty degrees. My sweat-soaked football uniform presses against my skin, picking up the coolness of the air and passing it onto my body. A shiver rocks through me, and I grit my teeth to ward it off. Sucking in a deep breath through my nose, I try to focus instead on how fresh the air is. Gone is the hot, stifling smell of the desert air and sweaty bodies. It now reminds me of the country air of home, minus the grass and plants.

As we move closer to the small village, we fall silent. It seems like the smart thing to do. Amir is walking really close to me, and at first, I'm a little annoyed. How does he expect me to walk without tripping over him? I hear him muttering the answers to simple math problems, which tells me he's terrified because that's what he always does when he's anxious.

The protective part of me takes over, and I forget about the annoyances. I have to keep him safe, even if I'm not likely to be the person who'd *best* keep him safe, especially with Jared, Krista, and Dad here. I only needed to see the three of them fight once to know that they would be *way* better than me in a scuffle. Still, I have my fire, so I can't discount that.

Light flickers between the buildings. It washes over us as we get closer. From what I can tell, they are heavy torches, full with flames and bursting with light. I don't know what I was expecting, but seeing the lighting feels archaic, like I've stepped into a history book. The moon rises, it's blue hue lighting the backs of the buildings enough so I can make out what they are made of. Thin gray stones are stacked haphazardly on one another, the cracks filled with clay and mud.

It seems like they dug up thin stones from the desert ground and stacked them up. It must have taken a lot of time to build one of the buildings.

"Dude, that's wild, how—" Amir's whispers are cut off as Jared presses his hand over his mouth.

Amir's wide eyes are visible in the flickering light, but it makes him look terrifying, like something from a horror movie. I turn briefly to look at the rising moon. It's a full moon, or so Dad said it would be.

He'd told us earlier that the moon is always full and that the cycles of this world don't behave the same as the cycles on earth. Seeing it is a different story altogether. This moon is at least four times the size of ours in the sky.

It explains why the small sliver is casting so much light already.

"Crackle the bundle, right nice-like," a gravelly voice echoes from the building closest to us.

I bite my tongue, holding back the alarmed sound that almost bursts from my mouth.

"Leave me be, I know the work. Built a house before, I have," a slightly higher but equally gravelly voice responds.

"Keep your grump to yourself," the first says.

There's a loud crack and thump, followed by a shout and another crack. This time, there are consecutive thuds and shouts.

I furrow my brow and look around at my companions. Dad's eyes are trained on me, as well as Jared's. Amir looks confused, and Krista looks as angry and frustrated, as usual. Raising an eyebrow to me, Dad approaches and puts his face close to my ear. He whispers so quietly that I can barely hear him, the loud grumbles and conversations of the village overshadowing it.

"Did they spot us?" he asks.

I pull back and shake my head. Why is he asking me like I should know?

He looks relieved, then holds up a finger. *Wait.*

I nod, and he disappears around the corner. My back is sweating from the nerves despite the cold. A droplet moves steadily down the part where my jersey isn't stuck to my back.

Amir grabs my hand and squeezes it, his breath catching in his throat. I look at him and see wide eyes. He's looking over my shoulder. Hand trembling, he points to something, and I turn slowly. There, a few buildings down, a goblin man is standing and staring at the moon. I hear the sound of trickling water and realize he's taking a pee.

I grit my teeth. Gross.

The goblin stands there, moving side to side like he's swaying with the sea. We're all holding our breath now. He hasn't seen us yet, which is a huge miracle. When he finishes, he turns and walks between the buildings.

I let out my breath, and my companions do the same.

Dad reappears and he looks excited. He points to where the goblin man was and starts moving that direction. I want to tell him we saw someone there and that we might get caught, but I can't do it without being loud. So I follow him, grasping his sleeve and tugging. At first, he doesn't get it, but he finally stops and looks at me.

I point and gesticulate my hands to try to pass the message.

He nods. Okay, so he knows about the goblin. After waving his hands in a disarming way, we follow him again.

When we get to a space between the buildings, Dad peeks around and leaps forward to the shadow of the next building. He looks again, then gestures us over. We do this twice more before we get behind an even larger building. It's not tall, but the wall is wide and long and at least three times what the others are.

He points to me, then leans in close.

"No alarm yet. If you hear anything that suggests they know we're here, tell me. Even if you can't whisper. At that point, there would be no use trying to be quiet, and escaping would be our priority."

I nod, though I'm more confused now. Why does he keep asking *me* to watch out for what they say? I almost ask when Dad holds a finger to his lips again.

A wash of frustration flows through my whole being. The tension of the situation is really getting to me. Something hard grips my shoulder, and I flinch. Jared is looking right at me. His expression seems to say, "I know how you feel, but try to stay calm."

Then I remember he can hear all of the embarrassing cursing and grumbling that is going on in my head. I suddenly feel like my whole private life has been played out, all the hidden things and forgotten moments now visible to this large teen. Jared flinches and shakes his head as if to say "No, that's not true," then nudges me to follow my dad.

I can feel my face reddening and immediately curse myself mentally for thinking about blushing. Now Jared knows it, too. Amir rushes out into the open space, and he almost runs right into Dad, who carefully and gently sets him aside like a small child. Krista runs next and she's so fast that I hardly even see her when she becomes a black smudge in my vision. She reappears behind both of them.

Jared's nudging me to go next, but before I can, I hear the voices explode in a loud flurry.

"Eat it!"

"Kill him before he gets away!"

"Success!"

The voices are various levels of gravelly and hard, some higher pitched than others, but they all sound like they're celebrating something. They're jubilant, kind of like when a group of people cheer watching the Super Bowl because their team started winning.

Except they are talking about killing and eating something. My heart thunders in my chest, my breath coming in rapid gasps. Dad's looking at me confused, probably because he heard the same commotion, but I don't understand why he doesn't look worried. He gestures to me wildly to run, and I finally gather the courage to do it. I'm faster than Amir and more coordinated so I run right at him, spinning at the last second and coming to a halt at his side. Jared runs immediately after me, fearless.

"What did you hear? What are they talking about?" Dad whispers to me.

I stare at him with narrowed eyes. "Can't you hear what they are saying?"

He shakes his head, and with a serious tone he says, "I can't understand Goblish. You can."

My mouth falls open. "Dad, please tell me you aren't serious."

He presses his hand over my mouth, and I tense.

"Don't raise your voice unless you want them to hear us," he hisses.

We fall silent, listening to the clanking and shouting, the reverie of the small green people.

Dad finally relaxes and takes his hand away.

"It's a dragon thing. Your mother could understand any of the languages. Based on your face, I can tell you inherited that trait," he says, then he peers behind us along the long wall.

I focus in on the voices, marveling that they sound just like they're speaking English with a strange accent.

"What are they saying?" he asks me.

I'm stunned by the fact that my brain is multilingual in fantasy character languages. The information is still being processed in my mind, so I don't answer him right away.

Instead, Jared does. "They're playing a game of some sort. I think they're eating creatures or animals. It's keeping them distracted."

Dad looks confused for a beat before he closes his eyes and nods, pointing to his head. "You can hear them translated through David's mind?"

Jared nods in confirmation.

"That's handy. At least two of us won't feel completely in the dark. We need to move. They should have stables somewhere. If we can get mounts, we can slip out of here before they—"

Music erupts from behind Dad, who spins to check what's causing it. Amir's pocket glows, the screen of his phone shining through his jeans.

It is the very song we were rocking to earlier.

Amir scrambles to pull it out but struggles with pausing it. We're crouched down low, and it tightens the space too much for him to extract it quickly. My jaw clenches and my whole body chills. The goblins have gone dead silent.

"Dad—" I start to say, ready to warn him, when garbled shouts erupt from all around us.

There's a thud to my left. One of the small green creatures has landed there. I suspect this one is a female, for she has long, stringent silvery hair, and her lips are massive—like, suck-the-life-out-of-you-horror-movie massive.

"Well, what do we have here?" she says, her scratchy voice higher than the others.

Dad shouts something and swings his sword at her. She jumps backward, her small legs proving surprisingly powerful. She lands on the ground ten paces away. Three more goblins skid into the space, but between Dad, Krista and Jared, they fall dead quickly. Dad shouts for us to follow him. He vaults forward in the direction we were planning to go. All the while, Amir's music plays, now somewhat quiet against the snarling of the creatures.

I chance a look behind me and regret it instantly. At least fifteen goblins hobble quickly toward us. They wear crude brown rags that hang off their small forms.

When I turn back to see where Dad is going, my face collides directly with his upper back. We both tumble to the ground in a heap, my elbow slamming into a rock followed by the side of my head. A flash of sharp pain rushes through my skull, and I feel my teeth crunch against each other.

"Darts! Drop them quickly!" the female goblin shouts.

I hear a series of strange sounds, like small puffs of air. I scramble to my feet, spinning just in time to see Amir struck in the neck with a long, thin projectile. His eyes roll back in his head, and he slumps to the ground. Jared is hit soon after, his large body sinking next to my friend. Dad somehow manages to dodge a few of the darts, slashing his sword side to side. There's a few heaps of clothing with green poking out, and I realize he's killed a few of the goblins.

Something hard and long hits me on the cheek, and I flinch, ready for whatever poison is on them to take me down, but nothing happens. My cheek feels hot. Just then, another dart hits me on my forearm. It doesn't pierce me because a set of red scales has sprouted of its own accord.

"Krista, David, you take the goblins behind us, and I'll—augh!" Dad's words are cut short as he's hit in the side by a few darts. I wince as he falls to the ground. Hard. All the while, Amir's music plays in the background.

A few more darts try to prick my skin, but they fail as more scales appear. It's cool that my body has a self-defense system, but I don't have time to dwell on it. I spin around to see four goblins holding jagged iron swords. They slash at me, and I jump back, two of them sparking on the stone wall of the building to my left. The other two connect but glance off new scales that grow on my skin.

There's a blur of motion, and the four creatures are squished against the wall, a heavy and thick body squeezing them before letting go. They fall in a pile.

Before me is a beast. It has bright red hair, pure black eyes, and veiny purple streaks running all along its face and arms. Its mouth is huge, jagged sharp teeth interlocking with each other as it glares at me. It has a few darts poking out of its face and neck, but it doesn't seem bothered by these.

My eyes widen. *Krista.*

"Do something, you idiot! Don't just stand there!" she roars before turning and rushing to the next set of goblins who scream out in fear and try to run away.

The darts are coming faster now, but they can't penetrate my skin. Flares of heat sprout up all over me as the goblins try time and time again to knock me out.

Throwing my hands upward, I summon flames to my palms and they explode outward, responding to my thoughts. Goblins shriek and scream as the hot flames douse over them, many of them lighting on fire. Okay, so they must not be *completely* immune to fire. They whistle and cry out in pain, batting their clothes to get the flames to go out.

Two goblins come at me quickly, their swords raised, but I toss flames at them and they scamper away.

"Halt!" the original goblin says.

Amir's phone blares the fast-paced rock music, and a few goblins surround it cautiously.

Krista is still moving like a storm, if that storm was a gigantic beast with nothing but fury. She throws the creatures left and right, waving her arm that has grown at least four sizes. I glance at my unconscious friends. I can't do much to defend them from where I stand. I press toward Krista until I'm next to her. My confidence grows as more darts fail to drop me.

"Back to back," she says, and I comply.

Despite the terrified warnings in my head that I'm about to touch her, I lean back. Her back is surprisingly springy and soft. One of the goblins staring at Amir's phone stomps downward, and the music finally stops.

"I said *halt*!" the voice says again.

This time, the goblins stop, and they jump away from us. Krista's breathing is heavy and labored, a slight whistling sound coming from her mouth, probably because of the small space between her sharp teeth. She swings her arms left and right but slows down when she sees they've stopped.

Right, she can't understand the goblin woman. I push my elbow back and nudge her, but I have no idea if she feels it.

A shiver slips up my spine, and I have the urge to run away from her, but I shake my head. The goblins are the threat, not her.

"Come at us!" Krista says breathlessly.

The goblin woman approaches us, and the rest of them amass and surround us at an alarming rate. So far, my scales have protected me, but I wonder now how long that will last. There are at least a hundred of these small green goblins, and I know the writing on the wall.

We aren't winning this fight.

As if to validate my thoughts, Krista's body goes limp behind me, and I hear a large thud. She's finally gone down with at least twenty darts in her flesh.

"Dragon kin, are you?" the goblin woman says slowly. She takes a few steps toward me, but I raise my hand in a threatening manner, a fireball appearing there.

"Don't come any closer, or I'll fry you."

She pauses, eyeing me critically. She probably can't understand what I'm saying. Dad said I was multilingual or whatever, but did he just mean for hearing? Or was it for speaking, too?

"Don't come any closer!" I warn.

This time, I know she understands, for she stops eight paces away from me and holds her hands out. A smile spreads on her face, as if she's a cat who just caught her mouse.

"You *are* dragon kin; I can hear it in your accent. Your speech abilities may make you sound like a goblin, but you don't have the true tone of it," she says, looking me up and down with derision on her face. "But you look so young. Why do you choose such a weak-looking visage form? I would think you would choose something more regal. And you are traveling with a demon girl and—"

The goblin pauses, her eyes going wide.

"A half demon," she says in almost a whisper, gaping as Krista's body shrinks rapidly until she's the fiery redheaded girl wearing the oversized sweats.

The goblin's eyes focus back on me, and I suck in a shuddering breath. Her eyes are a bloodred color. Eyes that color only exist in horror stories. A small part of my brain wants to see if the other goblins have similar eyes, but I'm too afraid to check.

"You are half dragon, aren't you?" Her mouth twitches upward in a mischievous smile.

I don't respond, opting to hold my hands up in front of me in fists. It looks silly, I'm sure—a teenage kid standing amongst his passed out companions with his hands raised like he plans to punch the goblins in the face. Bullies would see my reaction and probably fall over laughing. Interestingly, the goblins are still keeping their distance. The one in front of me looks confident, but even she is shifting side to side.

They think I'm dangerous. That has to be why they aren't attacking me. My heart races, and my head feels slightly foggy, but I stare confidently back at her, thinking about what I could say that would intimidate her.

"My mother is the dragon queen. It would be unwise for you to attack one of her blood-borne sons," I say, putting a weight behind my voice. Blood-borne? It sounds dumb, but I'm positive I heard Amir say it once in reference to one of his books.

Her smile changes from a sideways half one into a full out grin.

"A gift, just for me. And it's not even my name day," she says. "What a perfect catch for this deserving goblin tribe leader."

Apparently, my words are exactly the *wrong* thing to say.

I hear my dad yelling in my head about how I should keep my identity hidden. Now I've gone and blurted out who I was to these goblins, and they seem far more antsy than they were before. I let my eyes flicker between the leader and possible escape routes. I could make a break for it, rush through them, and bound into the vast desert. These goblins have short legs. Surely they wouldn't be able to catch me, not with my dragon blood and the physical enhancements they give me.

However, one look at my unconscious companions robs me of that hope. My self-preservation instincts are not as strong as my protective ones. My gaze lands on Amir, his face serene like he is having the best dream of his life.

I won't leave them, and I won't give up.

The goblin leader makes a terrifying guttural trilling sound at the back of her throat. It raises the hairs on the back of my neck. The moment she starts, the masses of green-skinned creatures press in on me, the assault fast and deliberate. Pinpricks of heat flicker on my face and bare arms as they launch volleys of poisoned darts at me.

None of them are hitting. Instead, they glance off of the red scales that appear out of nowhere each time one connects with my skin. A few darts hit their goblin companions, making them collapse to the ground. This makes me smile. So *they* are prone to the poison. I lock this away as something that might be useful later.

They can't hurt me. If I had known before that I'm an indestructible shield, I wouldn't have been so scared in the first fight.

To be fair, I don't know how long the defense will last, so I decide to not press my luck. I throw out my hands, a spout of flames exploding forward and making the goblin leader scream in fear. I hit the two goblins next to her as well. I don't stop pushing out the heat, the flames coming like a torrent, a sideways bonfire with unlimited fuel.

I'm forced to stop when a short sword slams into my forearm and my arm is knocked downward by the blow. The scales stop the sharp edge from cutting into my flesh, but I feel the vibration in my bone. Clenching my teeth, I point my other hand toward the attacker and blast him away. Before I move, another metal sword hits me in the back.

I shout in pain, trying to turn that direction, but not before another sword hits me in the back of the head. My vision blurs and I fall to my knees, panic rising in my chest. All the while at least a dozen goblins pelt me with their poisonous darts. None of them bite into my skin.

With one last look at Amir, I feel the inevitable blow to the top of my head and fall forward. The pain is blunt and heavy, and it makes my head throb. I don't see any blood around me, and I don't feel it on my skin, so the scales must have saved me, but I can't move.

Someone is groaning, and it takes me a minute to realize that it's me.

"Tie him up," another gravelly voice says, deeper this time. "He'll answer for his crimes and the death of our tribe leader. Take them to the stables like the crelotins they are."

I'm barely aware as my hands are shoved behind my back and tied tightly. I expect the ropes to bite into my skin more, but the scales protect me from the sensation.

At least that's one less pain to worry about.

More goblins work on the others. They comment on the strange style of our clothing or how we smell. A lot of them complain about how Amir and Dad smell. They murmur things like "full human" and "dirty mortal." I'm surprised they aren't commenting about me, considering I just played half a game of football before walking for hours in the hot desert.

I smell like death incarnate.

A light chuckle escapes my mouth. The fact that I'm thinking about how I smell when I'm being led to my death is somewhat hilarious. Fortunately, none of them hear me. Instead, they half drag, half carry me into the collection of buildings.

Something instinctual tells me to observe my surroundings, to see where they take us, and try and devise an escape plan. It's hard to focus. Still, I see a pit in the center of the ring of buildings, a bonfire burning brightly. It's not wood that's burning, but it appears to be rocks. A red hue surrounds each of them as they burn. My head hurts too bad to try to comprehend this. My vision is still a bit blurred from the blow to the head. Without that sense, my brain starts to catch up to me. My throat constricts, and shock worms its way in now that the fighting is over.

At one point I pitch forward, my face landing hard on the ground, which is composed of broken up stones and large pieces of gravel. The goblins haul me to my feet and pull me to a squat. We face the broad building across the clearing and over the fire. Smoke burns my eyes and nose as I try to take deep breaths.

"Should we throw them to the fire?" one goblin asks, holding up Amir's hand as a reference.

My skin chills.

"No—human blood is too useful. Urothar will reward us for all of them, especially the three halflings."

There's that word again. So they figured out who Jared is, too.

I can't think much more about this before they drag us to the building, and two goblins work together to draw open massive bay doors. With a hard shove, I stumble inside and fall on my stomach. It's warmer in here. Opening my eyes, I glance up at the ceiling of the hut, and I almost pass out.

I'm face-to-face with a monster.

AN UNLIKELY ALLY

Words cannot properly express what I'm seeing. My brain tries to define it in logical terms—the thing that stands before me—but it's drawing a blank. It looks like a huge crab-horse thing.

The creature is the size of a horse, but it has an insect-like face with four waving tentacles that move like they are underwater. Two thick arms with crab-like pincers come from its long neck, which is then connected to a horse body with six legs beneath it. And it's completely covered in a thick red exoskeleton.

The goblins chatter and shout in joy all around me as they shove my friends into the stables next to me.

I want to scream in terror, but I can't get my mouth to open. It's locked tight. My eyes turn from my unconscious friends to the beast above me. To my surprise, it isn't looking at me. It chews on something lazily and continues to watch the goblins that threw me in here. Even though I can't get my heart or breathing to slow, it's apparent that whatever this thing is, it's not going to eat me or maul me to death. At least not right away.

Another goblin—this one with a much older wrinkly face and bigger nose—comes to the bay door and looks in on me.

"I must say thanks, I suppose, for making me the tribe leader by rights. I've been trying to take her place for many moons, but you've done the work for me, dragonling. The orc king will be thrilled about our catch. Relish the last days you have before you're in the ground," he says, his wide grin flashing a double row of sharp, pointed teeth.

He shoves the doors closed with a thud. A sense of doom washes over me, but I do my best to sit up. A soft groan to my left makes me spin that way, sharp pain shooting up into my head and down my neck. I cry out and close my eyes, waiting for the throbbing to stop. When I open them, I see Krista's eyes fluttering. She moans.

"Krista!" I hiss, trying to keep my voice low even though it's pointless. The goblins already caught us. It is all because Amir's phone decided to have a mind of its own. The irony of a technological glitch in a fantasy world is not lost on me.

My reality sounds like an immense joke. I wiggle my wrists, and after working the ropes for a minute, I'm able to slip out of them. Good thing these goblins aren't good with knots, or I don't know what I would've done.

"They used some type of poison to knock you out," I explain, but she throws a hand up to silence me.

Heat rushes to my face and I open my mouth to say something rude, but then she changes her open hand to a finger, and I pause.

Oh, right, she just woke up from being chemically knocked out. She probably isn't in a chatty mood.

I stare at her for a moment longer before looking away. I inspect the others who are still out cold. Amir lays closest to me, and I reach out to touch his neck. I'm not a doctor, but that seems to be how they always check to see if someone is alive in movies. Sure enough, there is a subtle pulse. I'm relieved.

"Dang, that stuff is powerful," Krista says groggily.

She tries to get up but slumps back down with a mutter of something obscene.

"They hit you with at least two dozen darts. Why did it take that many for you to get knocked out? The others got one, and they are still out," I say, scooting over so I can feel my dad's neck.

He's alive, too.

"Half demon, remember?"

As if I could forget. I imagine her, thinking of her engorged body and pulsing purple veins. Even though she's returned to her slight redheaded version of herself, I can't get her demon form out of my mind. I vaguely remember at this moment that she mentioned being able to heal quickly. "Yeah, still not used to that. Sorry to say it, but you're terrifying when you turn into that thing," I say, moving to Jared last.

He also has a pulse.

"Well, you're not a looker yourself with your red scales," Krista bites back. "Besides, you're still worthless in a fight. You stood there like an idiot when I took most of them out."

I glare at her.

"Woah, are you serious? I killed like half a dozen in seconds before they whacked me in the head with a sword. You were already down-and-out, so you didn't see it."

Krista scoffs. "Oh, come off it. You're making it up. You didn't do anything, I bet. You probably cried on their shoulders while they laughed and flicked you to unconsciousness with their thick fingers."

The rage that comes up inside of me is completely unexpected. I feel it rush forward, and the next thing I know, I'm throwing a fist at her face. Her small palm and fingers wrap around my fist, and she shoves it away.

"Too slow," she says in a mock tone.

"Why are you such a jerk?" I growl.

"Stop it," a weak voice sounds to my left.

We both spin in that direction. An electric energy runs through my limbs, and I stand with my fists up, like in defense.

It's Jared. He's still lying on the ground, but his eyes are open now, and he's watching me carefully.

"It's the cooldown period of her ability. She's not herself," he says, then tries to push himself up.

My anger disappears as I see his struggle. I shuffle over to him, putting my arm around his thick torso and under his armpit. I heave upward as much as I can, feeling his weight pull at me, but I'm not a weakling. I've had to help up injured defenders on my team before—and they aren't lightweight either.

"Where are we?" he asks.

I look around, the dim room becoming visible as my eyes adjust. A bit of flickering light filters in from a large window at the top of the wall. It's too high for me to jump up and climb into, but if we stacked on each other, we might be able to get out of here. My eyes wander downward until they land on the aisle in the middle of about twenty stalls.

I freeze, skin chilling.

There are dozens of pairs of beady black eyes staring back at me.

I want to back away, maybe even turn around and run as fast as possible, but I can't move.

"David, where are we?" Jared repeats himself.

"Don't bother trying to ask him questions. He doesn't know anything. He's worthless," Krista says as she moves up beside me. She pauses. "What the—"

Pure, shiny black eyes bore into us as if they were looking into our souls. The strange creatures stand there, unmoving save for the tentacles that writhe and wave. They watch us as if we might become their next meal. Though I'm terrified and want to look away, I can't. I'm paralyzed.

Krista has gone silent, which scares me because I don't get the sense that her post-demon rampage has a "quiet mode."

Finally, the paralyzing feeling that took over my body falls away. I gasp and slump to the side directly into Krista. I feel her shoulder press up against mine. A small bit of heat rushes to my face at the physical contact, but it soon disappears as she speaks.

"Sheesh, that was horrible," she says. "Is that what my intimidation aura feels like to you?"

The harshness is completely gone from her tone. She sounds peaceful and not scared at all. I feel it, too—almost light and free. Not happy but content, like I've just had a large dose of something nostalgic and it left me satisfied. We both clear our throats and push away from each other. She runs a finger over her ear, brushing a thick strand of red hair behind it.

"Um—what did you say? Intimidation aura?" I say, my voice strained.

She smiles genuinely, and it feels unnatural.

"Another demon ability, my intimidation," she explains.

I stare at her, blinking a few times before I respond.

"Right. That." I shift my gaze from Krista to Jared. "I think we're in the stables," I say, finally answering his question. I point my thumb to the side. "With these—um—crab-horse things."

I glance around. Just over half the stalls have the creatures in them. They don't make any sound. Instead, they simply watch us.

"Crelotins, actually," Dad says down at my feet.

"Dad! Are you okay?" I reach down to help him up. Amir still hasn't moved.

"Amir won't wake up for a little bit," he says, apparently reading my expression and body language. "He's a smaller kid, and the goblins used *a lot* of the helix flower poison."

I blink at his words. At first, I'm confused by how he knows all this, then I remember he used to live in this place.

"Crelotins? They have a name?" Krista says derisively. "That makes them less scary, doesn't it?"

Her words drip with sarcasm.

"They are harmless despite their—um—somewhat terrifying appearance," Dad says. "Chosen vessels for most of the dark races. I've never ridden one personally, and I don't plan to."

"Dad, is Amir going to be okay? He's holding pretty still," I say.

Dad groans and puts a hand behind his neck, squeezing it between his fingers.

"I'm sure. It's a potent neurotoxin, but it won't kill him. It's harmless if you touch it with your skin, but when it enters your blood, it's lights out," he says. "And it looks like it only took one for each of us, so they must have been laced thickly."

My mouth falls open, my eyes asking the question my mouth can't figure out how to speak.

He sighs when he sees me. "Yes, I've used the same poison. It's very useful."

"Wow, you're really inspiring trust with your Qotan background," Krista says. She leans into one hip and folds her arms, sizing Dad up.

Naturally, we all ignore her comment. I shove a thumb toward Krista, lacing my voice with something between derision and admiration.

"It took like a dozen before she went out, so there's that," I say.

Dad's eyes widen, and he looks her up and down, impressed. "Okay. Demon blood is a better healing agent than I expected. I'm glad you're on our side."

She rolls her eyes. "The losing side, apparently. We're trapped in a goblin stable with gross alien creatures."

"They are surprisingly empathetic," Jared comments.

We all turn toward him. He has his hand on one of the thing's necks.

"Bro, do you really want to be touching one of those? It looks like it could snap your hand right off," I say.

Dad shakes his head. "No, Jared's right. They are harmless. Crelotins are docile, but they have a way of making you feel artificial emotions. One look in their eyes and they can paralyze you with fear if they think that you are a danger to them, at least. They must have decided we aren't a danger."

"Oh, that's what that was," I murmur. "Creepy."

"They want us to pet them. In fact, that's pretty much what they are all thinking," Jared says.

"Woah, woah, wait. Can you *hear* what they are thinking?" I ask in awe.

He gives me a forced smile, then nods. "I can't normally understand animals. Mostly it's just humans or humanoids. I can hear the goblins' thoughts, but I can't decipher their words. Only if I hear through your head, David."

The reminder of my apparent translating ability makes me blink and shake my head to come back to it. Even as he says it, I realize I can understand the muffled voices of the goblins through the thick stone door. I can't hear every word, but a phrase here, a single word there. It sounds like they are talking about a slaughter of some kind.

I decide it's better to *not* listen in on them.

"Why can I understand them?" I ask, but I know the answer.

"Your dragon blood. It's part of your ability. It's why dragons are the high nobility of the light races. What better race to rule over the others than one that can inherently speak and understand any language?"

I frown. It makes sense logically, but that would mean I'm a high prince. I know my mother is the dragon queen, but this is the first time I've applied that meaning to myself.

I hate the idea so much that I have to hold back a gag. It sounds so corny, and while the attention would be kind of fun, I'm embarrassed at the same time.

"Okay, this is great and all, but how are we going to break out of here? These goblins aren't going to let us out," Krista says. She points up to the window. "I suppose you could launch me up there, and I can go out swinging, but the poison is going to be a problem."

One of the crelotins moves close to me and nuzzles my face. I recoil, a shiver running through my whole body. Its carapace is hard and very cold. It felt like ice when it touched my skin.

Krista's barbaric suggestion is lost on the group with my reaction.

"It's not going to hurt you, Dave," Jared says, reading my thoughts. "And they warm up when they feel loved."

I shake my head. "Don't call me Dave. I don't even know you."

He shrinks inward, a surprisingly odd movement for someone so large.

"I hate to say it, but Krista is right. We need to get out of here. They plan to hand us over to the orc king, at least that's what their leader said," I explain.

Dad curses. "That's probably why they hit us with that teleportation stone at the football game. They knew it would bring us to the middle of the desert region. The orc king's palace is somewhere in the desert. He's probably not far from here."

Jared flinches, and I look at him, confused. He shakes his head, continuing to pet one of the crelotins.

"We'll *have* to fight our way out of here," Krista says. It's hard to tell in the dim, flickering light from above, but I swear she starts to grow slightly as she speaks. The memory of her purple-streaked face under her wild, fiery hair makes me shudder. I push the thought away. My mouth is dry and sticky, and this room is so hot that it's making me weary. It has to be at least a hundred degrees even though it was colder outside. Shouldn't it smell like manure in here? I've been in stalls. They don't smell great.

I decide I'm just going to be grateful that crelotins have scentless poop.

Dad moves to it and pushes against it with his shoulder. It creaks but doesn't move. "It's too heavy to move easily. If we break out of here through the door, they'll just down us with the toxin again. We can't burst out and surprise them even if we could get it open. Going above will produce the same results, though I appreciate the confidence in your plan."

He nods toward Krista, who grunts and shakes her head, a slight eye-roll joining the reactionary montage.

A groan from below draws all our attention there. Amir is stirring now, his hands on his head.

"Oh my . . . I feel like I've been hit by a—*what in the name of—what is that thing?*" He screams, his eyes flying open wide. He scrambles backward until his back hits another stall, which makes him turn around in surprise, only to let out another wail.

"Amir! It won't hurt you!" I say, but the kid is beside himself.

I worry that the goblins will hear him and come back in here with more poison darts.

"Amir, calm down!" I hiss.

After a few moments, we're able to calm him down and we explain what's happening.

"This is the strangest realistic dream I've ever had." He puffs up his chest, looking at me with a regal expression. "So, Prince David. What's the plan?"

I scowl at him. Krista scoffs, her hands on her hips. I know he's joking, but at the same time, learning about the dragons and their status as high rulers makes me feel like I have a massive weight on my shoulders. Shouldn't I have a plan? Shouldn't I know what I'm doing? Dad didn't prepare me for any of this like he was supposed to.

My eyes flick upward to the big window at the top of the roof. I think that if we stood on the backs of the creatures, we could probably reach it easily. Krista wouldn't have to go alone; we could all head out. I glance at her, fully aware that this was her plan first and that by suggesting it, I'm affirming her. It stings, but really, it's probably the best we have.

"We break out up there and attack from high up, like Krista said," I admit. "But not just *her*. All of us can go."

It sounds bullheaded, and somewhat crazy, but I'm surprised when the group agrees.

"I don't like it," Dad says, moving to the door and pounding a fist on it. "But it doesn't look like we have many other options."

"They seem pretty distracted out there," Jared adds. "But there are a lot more of them than us. It only takes one of those darts before we're down."

Krista sighs, as if she's exhausted having to remind us of her greatness. "It actually took a lot more to knock me out."

Jared grimaces. "Well, not all of us were given the ability to heal rapidly. Our bodies can't just burn off the poison over and over."

His hand lifts to where he'd been sliced by the sword back in the human realm. It isn't healed fully and probably won't be for weeks. He sounds bitter about it. I don't have any siblings, but I've been friends with plenty enough to know that there's a rivalry between them. These two haven't fought much since we've been traveling, but this is clearly a brother-sister spat.

"No, he has a point as well," Dad says. "The smallest of us should climb up the backs of one of the crelotins, jump down from the roof as quietly as possible, and unlock the bay doors."

We all stop talking and look slowly at Amir. He's not that much smaller than the rest of us, but he's clearly the shortest and lightest. His eyes grow wide, and he starts waving his hands.

"Woah, I'm like the only one here who doesn't have mystical blood or a creepy skill with swords," he says, nodding toward my dad. "You really think sending the fully human boy to the goblins will have any outcome besides me becoming dinner?"

"They don't eat humans," Dad points out. "Apparently, they taste bad."

"Okay, well, whatever! I'm not climbing up one of those monsters, *Christian*," he says with a shudder, emphasizing my dad's name like he's a concerned parent.

I frown, thinking of ways to convince him to do it when I happen to look at Jared. He's studying the window, his hands wringing in front of him. I remember how he shifted into a bulldog and an elephant. Excitement seizes me.

"Wait, can't you just turn into a bird and fly out of here?" I ask.

Jared bites his lip, then nods hesitantly.

"I don't like the idea of going out there, especially since I'm pretty sure they'd notice a bird. I haven't seen any signs of birds the entire time we've been in this realm," he says.

"A lizard, then," Dad suggests. "Those are common enough. I saw a few scrambling about while we traveled."

Hope blossoms in my chest. I reach for my belt, remembering that Dad gave me a dagger. But it's not there. The goblins must have stripped me of that when they dragged me here. Dad is apparently thinking the same thing, for he walks over to the wall where there are short metal poles strapped up. He pulls one free and gives it a calculated swing, the metal whooshing through the air.

"Since they took our weapons, we'll have to improvise. Here," he says, ripping another one free and tossing it to me.

I catch it, grunting softly as I feel its weight. It isn't terribly heavy, but even my toned arms would be slow to bring it around if I were going to be sword fighting anyone. Krista strides forward, a fiery something in her eyes, and tears two more down from the wall. She spins them, then tries a few swings herself. The look on her face suggests that she also thinks these poles are impractical to use in a fight. Still, she closes her eyes for a moment before her arms expand outward, purple veins running up and down her skin. The fire intensifies in her eyes, and she manages to swing the poles around wildly fast.

"And with that, I see no reason to wait," Dad says, turning to Jared.

The teen's face pales, but he nods his assent. We move into a group before the wide stone bay doors and ready ourselves for a scuffle.

"Krista, you should be at the front," Dad suggests. "If they start tossing darts, it would be better for you to get hit rather than us. Sorry about that, but it's true."

She nods and stands in front of the rest of us. Jared, seeing us in position, lets out a sigh and we watch his large frame shrink rapidly.

When he changed into the various animals during the fight, I was confused because I didn't understand what was happening. But now it makes sense. Even so, watching him makes my stomach churn and my heart race. It's wild to see his face grow long and sharp, a beak appearing where his nose should be. His eyes go all wide, then shrink into tiny ones. His arms grow flat and feathery. It takes only ten seconds before Jared is gone and a small pigeon hops on the ground before us.

"That is insane," Amir breathes. "Do you know how useful it would be if I could just *fly* to school in the morning? It would save me so much time."

I smile at his comment, but my face goes serious quickly after that. The pigeon flaps its wings and flies up to the edge of the open space. I breathe a sigh of relief, glad the window doesn't have glass covering it. That's probably why the goblins are so easy to hear from inside these stables. Did they think this place was truly secure?

I hold up three fingers to get Jared's attention. He's since shifted to a lizard, small spines going from his head to his tail. I put the fingers down one at a time. Before I can drop the last one, a gravelly voice shouts from the darkness of the stables.

"Stop! You'll get killed easy-like if you go out there like that!"

My heart skips a beat, and I spin toward the sound. Krista is at my side in a heartbeat, her arm brushing up against mine. I recoil when I feel how cold her skin is.

"Who's there?" I say, holding my rod in front of me.

Dad moves over to my other side, Amir cowering behind us.

"Put down the rods. They aren't proper weapons in the least," the voice sounds again. I see the small form of a goblin. He's holding something heavy and grunting as he takes a couple more steps closer to us in the dimly lit room.

"What's it saying?" Dad whispers quietly.

Right, they can't understand goblins.

I don't answer him right away. The flickering firelight from the window above is enough for me to see his outline. He's at least five inches smaller than the others that we confronted earlier, and his hair is reflecting the light at us. It looks like shimmering silver. His bloodred eyes watch me as he walks slowly toward us. He grunts, carrying his heavy load.

"Are you the dragon blood kin?" he asks, looking at me. I don't even have time to answer before he points a gnarled green finger at Krista. "Demon blood kin, and fairy as well? Are you . . . the ones from the prophecy?"

I translate the words quietly for my friends. I look at Dad, and he shrugs. Then I glance at Krista. My face flushes, and I have to look up a whole foot to meet her eyes. They are black as night, and she has a wicked grin on her face. She leans forward and my instincts tell me to stop her. I throw my hand out and grab her thick arm, my chest constricting. Her head snaps in my direction, her black eyes boring into me.

"Not yet," I whisper. "There is only one of him and a lot of us."

The goblin, apparently hearing my words, steps back a couple paces, his mouth opening wide.

"Please, I don't mean disrespect or harm. I just didn't know that you half human rulers' offspring actually existed. I thought it was just a rumor! Please! I brought your weapons for peace."

He shoves his arms outward, and there's a clattering of metal, the swords Dad brought and the dagger he gave me.

"Dave," Dad whispers to me again. "Did he just . . . drop our weapons? What is he saying to you?"

I have to wave my hand to the side to tell Dad to be quiet while I figure out what to do.

"Are you hoping to take us to the orc king yourself? To get the reward?" I ask. "Are you trying to trick us to believe you?"

"Oh no—no—no, nothing like that. I want to know so I can *help* you," he replies, nudging the swords with his toe.

That's confusing. I open my mouth to respond but feel Krista's weight pulling on my grip. I'm still holding her upper arm, and she's trying to break free.

"Dave—"

"Not now, Dad, I'm talking to him. Give me a minute." I'm not annoyed; I'm just worried about taking too long. Still, my tone shuts him up quickly.

"Why should we trust you?" I ask.

The goblin wrings his hands, a forked tongue flicking out of his mouth to lick his large lips.

"Well—I don't know. Not much else you can do, I suppose. I may be a goblin, but these aren't my people. Not anymore. Our tribe leader is—was—a brute. I like the rule of the light races. Cursed I am for being born into a dark one," he says, muttering the last part so quietly that I have to strain to hear him.

"What do you suggest we do, then?" I say. "You must have heard our plan. Are you going to warn your friends?"

The goblin's eyes widen, and he shakes his head vigorously. "No! No, never! I would never betray the actual legends, the half humans of the songs. I can see you are set on leaving, and I wanted to warn you that you will fail."

My stomach sinks. "That's unhelpful."

"Bro, you sound so weird right now," Amir says quietly behind me.

I don't have time to figure out what he means, so I ignore the comment.

"I only mean that—oh, gobbledart! I only mean that you can't go out on foot. Ride the crelotins. They are fast and true. And their hides protect them from our poison darts."

I swallow hard, finally looking away from the goblin to the crelotins. The goblin reaches up and feeds the one nearest to him something. I can't tell what it is, not in this dim lighting, but the creature makes a low-pitched whining sound that increases until it's louder and higher.

"There are plenty of crelotins for you to take. They move swiftly and will overwhelm the others. Quick! Mount them before it's too late!"

My gaze wanders to the creature closest to me, and my mouth goes dry. The thing's beady eyes watch me. As I look directly at it, a feeling of strange satisfaction and contentment washes over me. I shudder, recognizing it's not my own.

"The creatures want to help, like me. Quick, get up on them now!"

One of the crelotins shuffles its feet next to me, and I shy away. Considering the looks on my friends' faces, they aren't going to take this advice well. But it's the best way out.

10

THE TERROR RIDE

"He wants us to ride the crelotins," I tell the others.

A few things happen at once. Amirs says something like "Oh cool," then jabbers about how they look like something from one of his DnD sessions. Jared, having shifted back into a bird, chirps incessantly, and Krista protests angrily. Dad frowns, looking between me and the goblin a couple times. His gaze finally stops on me.

"Will you all be quiet, please?" Dad asks, and when the three of them stop making noise, he continues. "What else did he say? You were grunting and clicking for way too long for him to just have only said that."

"Wait, what? I was speaking English to him," I say.

Amir lets out a small laugh. "Nah, man, you sounded like a crazy person. We only understood you when you told your dad to wait."

I frown, realizing that what sounded like English to me did not to them. Perhaps that's why my throat is sore and my tongue aches from being worked in a new way. The goblin moves toward us with his hands waving. Krista lets out a low and feral growl, holding up her fist like she's going to slam into the top of his head. I pull her back.

"I think we can trust him," I say.

To be honest, I don't know if we can truly trust him. In fact, I don't have a clear opinion about what he's telling me. Logically, riding an animal, or monster, or horse—whatever it is—would be much faster than walking. Plus, he's like three feet tall. If he tries to kill us, I'm sure Krista could pop his head off.

Her body starts to shrink, and she looks more herself almost as quickly as she had changed.

"Are you *kidding me*? That's a goblin, and you want to do what it says? You're a crap leader if you think he'll not stab us in the back and—"

"Krista," I say to stop her. My heart thuds in my chest, a nervous energy taking over as her fiery eyes lock on me. There's a small moment where I'm sure she's going to tear out my throat, but she doesn't. She just glares at me.

"If he tries to, just rip his head off," I suggest.

I give her a small smile, hoping that she'll laugh it off, but instead, she looks at the goblin and nods. "It looks easy enough. I still think you're an idiot for not letting me kill him, but fine, we'll do it your way first."

I don't know what scares me more: the fact that she said it would be easy to rip the goblin's head off, or the fact that she agreed with something I said.

"Jared, come down here," I say.

"No!" the goblin says. "We need someone to open doors. I will help you get on the crelotin. He'll open door."

I nod. "On second thought, stay up there."

Jared has already flapped his way down, but he turns around and goes back up.

The goblin moves along the stalls housing the crelotins, flicking the latches upward. The stall doors swing open on their own. I half expect the mutants to rush out and try to escape, but they stand there as if they are waiting for something.

"Five of you, five crelotins. You can hold ropes for his," the goblin says, pointing to me, then up at Jared. He's shifted to a lizard once more. His body is scaled and sinewy, and I can't help but think he looks adorable.

The lizard wags its tail and chirps. I grin up at him.

The goblin hobbles to the end of the row where there is an empty stall and grabs a bunch of thick ropes. They aren't long, and they have circled bits in the center. The goblin waddles up to one of the crelotins and tosses the rope up toward the thing's nose. To my shock, the tentacles on the sides of the creature's face reach out and snag the rope, pulling it along its snout.

Amir shudders next to me. "That is—slightly disturbing. Do they actually like to wear those things? I thought horses hate wearing bits."

Dad laughs. "Not all horses hate them, though some do, yes. You can train them to let you ride without them, but it's not as easy to direct the horse where you want it to go."

Krista stares at him. "Why do you know so much about horses?"

Dad and I exchange looks and laugh. Then he answers her. "I'm realizing how much we don't know about each other. It's what I've been doing for work for almost a decade now." He studies the nearest crelotin. "I'm hoping these ropes lend us some aid in riding these things."

I stare at the goblin, who stares back without blinking. He raises his silver eyebrows in confusion. I translate quickly, feeling like I'm being redundant.

"No, no," the goblin man says down at my feet. "You won't use ropes for direction; you'll use them for holding on. If not, you might fall. And then you might die."

The others are watching me expectantly.

"He said the ropes are so we can hold on and not fall off and die."

Amir presses his lips into a thin line.

"What? That's literally what he said. I'm just repeating him," I say, trying to justify my blunt response.

The goblin tosses the last rope, and the crelotin wraps it around its nose.

"Climb up first, then pull on the rope here," the goblin says, pointing to one end of the rope.

I hesitate, looking down at him.

"Are you sure? That thing looks like it'll bite my head off," I reply.

As if to validate my words, the crelotin bares its teeth, flashing the sharp, pointed white things. I shiver and back away. A wave of amusement washes over me, and I almost double over in surprise. It feels so unnatural and yet so right at the same time.

Amir mutters something to my dad and Krista, but I'm focused now, a warming comfort flowing through my chest and limbs. There's fear in the back of my mind, but it's like it's drowned out by the strength of this other emotion. I move up to the beast. Its back is at the level of my neck. With a sigh, I grip one of the ropes and pull myself up.

I yelp when I feel the carapace. It's not smooth like it looks. Seeing it from afar, I guessed it was smooth and slippery, like a crab's shell looks. When I touch it, however, my skin and clothing sticks to it. It's textured, almost rough like sandpaper. I can't help but shiver yet again at the unpleasant feeling.

"Well, Dave's not dead, so I guess we're good?" Amir says.

"He says to get on," I reply. "And, yes, we're good."

After some quiet consent from the others, and a few moments for each of them to get on their mounts—I had to dismount to help Amir;

poor guy could not figure out how to pull himself up—we all look at each other from the height of the crelotins' backs. Jared's mount sits empty, and I squint at it.

"What about his? How will we lead it if he's not on top?"

Gobby waves his hand. "It will follow without help. That's the least of your worries. Go through the door as fast as you can. Don't look back. Leave here and run south along the river. Don't stop until the forest," the goblin—I decide to call him Gobby—says.

"How far away is that?" I ask.

His red eyes widen like he's terrified by something, but I've seen him do that before. They are wide for a count of three before they go back to normal. To test it, I ask another question.

"What's in the forest? Will there be someone there for us?"

His eyes open again, then shrink back.

I believe that is the equivalent of a shrug.

"I don't know, but it's fairy land. They are a light race and can help you," he says.

I sense movement from above and glance upward to where Jared is still perched. He's shifting on his little lizard feet. He is hearing my thoughts, and he's most likely responding to the fact that we're being sent to his mother's land. If he's like me, he's only heard obtuse messages from her, and he probably doesn't feel like she's real.

"Okay, what about you?" I ask.

I've seen enough movies to know what happens to the betrayer. He'll probably try and hide what he did, and he may even get away with it, but if they ever found out what he did for us, they'll kill him.

His eyes open wide, then go back to normal.

He doesn't know.

"Not important, you must leave. Get free, then we'll see about me," he replies.

I take a deep breath. Before we do anything, I explain what Gobby and I talked about, even sharing what I learned about how they shrug. I'm honestly impressed at how they waited patiently with understanding. I'm pretty sure if it were me, I'd lose my mind.

"How many goblins are out there?" Krista asks. "Do I need to call on my demon side?"

I shrug, then look at Gobby, who is watching me with a confused expression.

Oh boy, this is getting annoying. Don't they have someone that speaks human? I relay the message and Gobby shakes his head wildly.

"No one speaks human. Also no, do not change until right as the door opens. If you use your blood gifts too much, they'll sense something is wrong," he replies.

I frown, looking up at Jared.

"He's using his gift, and they aren't panicking," I point out.

Gobby shakes his head.

"They already know—listen," he says.

I cock my head. At first, I can't hear anything but garbled grunting and shouting. It all sounds like a raucous party with clanging and the sounds of fighting. But when I focus, my brain translates what they're saying.

"We will kill the fairyling!"

"Dinner, dinner, we're so hungry!"

"Come here, lizard!"

I shudder. Jared, still in lizard form, shudders, too.

"They think he's afraid. They think he won't leave. They will not expect him to unlock the door for you," Gobby explains.

I stare up at Jared. He's hopping from side to side now, a motion that looks unmistakably human. He's probably terrified they'll snatch him up and eat him in one bite. I'm so glad I'm not him right now.

"Are you okay with that, Jared?" I shout over the growing noise outside.

The lizard hops side to side again and turns around to nibble on its tail.

"Umm, okay?" I reply. "I guess because you didn't come back down here and turn human again you are at least kind of okay with it."

Krista grunts. "You suck as a translator, dragon boy."

I glare at her, ready to tell them about the risk that Jared must take to get us free, but I decide against it. There isn't anything they can do to change it. Plus, we could all be on a cooking spit if this fails, so no point in telling them of the danger he's in. We'll all be under fire soon enough.

"Ready?" Gobby says.

"Yes." I look to the others. "I'll count to three. Jared will rush out and unlock the door. We'll burst through with our—crelotins, and we need to rush south along the river."

Amir swallows hard, then puts on a fake smile. Krista doesn't look scared, but she doesn't look confident either. Her flat expression and hard eyes tell me that she's angry we are even here.

Dad grips his ropes in determination. "If I get hit with one of those darts again, I'm going to be miffed. I just got over the headache from the last one."

I can't help but laugh. It somehow lightens the mood. Amir smiles for real and relaxes on the crelotin's back. Krista's face softens a little, and she gives a half smile, but then it's gone quickly.

"On the count of three," I say, looking at Gobby.

The goblin waves at me, then moves behind my crelotin with a little shuffling gait. My hands shake as they hold on to the reins. Even though I know my dragon skin will protect me, Dad's comment reminds me that one dart can take *them* down. I can't leave anyone behind, so we all have to make it out.

"One," I say before I can stop myself. "Two."

Amir is mouthing the numbers with me silently, his eyes trained on the door.

I've ridden horses before, but I've never ridden one of these. My stomach drops at the thought that Jared might throw open the doors and we'll just stand there, our crelotin sitting without moving. We'd be caught quickly, and all this would be for nothing. I don't know how to get this thing to run. Jared could be caught, skewered, and cooked in minutes—or eaten alive, for all I know.

It doesn't matter, though, for my mouth continues the count while my brain panics.

"Three!"

Jared's gone in a flash, his green little body disappearing below the window.

Gobby lets out a growling shout, something that makes my muscles lock up in fear. Then I hear a smack that's so loud that it almost makes my ears ring. Before I can even understand what I've heard, the crelotin jumps to life under me. A scream rips out of my throat as it bolts forward, and my hands strain on the reins as it heads for the closed door.

"Wait—wait—wait you're going to slam into the—"

Before I can finish the phrase, the crelotin's head bashes into the stone door, and I'm hit with a wave of cold breeze and the smell of sweaty bodies. Flashing fires and hundreds of red eyes land on me, and I swear they're glowing. A flutter of wings above draws my attention. It's Jared, now a bird, and he's flying back over the roof of the stable. Clomping hooves sound behind me, and I can only hope my friends' mounts are following.

The goblins jump to action. The one nearest to me pulls its dart blower, but it can't act fast enough before it's trodden underneath the feet of my crelotin. A frantic excitement and nervousness flows through me. The feelings come from the beast beneath my legs. Another goblin pulls out a wicked-looking curved edge blade and prepares to slash upward at me. The feeling of excitement melts into terror. I freeze, my throat tightening up. I can't breathe. I want to run, to get away from this place, to escape and hide in a hole somewhere.

That's when I notice the goblins in front of me have frozen, too. Their bloodied eyes are wide, and they stand there, shaking just enough that they no longer look like statues in a museum.

The crelotin rears up, my fear-locked fingers holding me in place as it rushes toward one of the large fires. It pushes off with its powerful legs and we vault through the air over the flames. I feel it on my feet and skin, but only for a moment before scales cover me up to protect me.

We land, and the crelotin barrels right out of the clearing into the desert. Relief washes over me, and the feeling of terror disappears.

Amir whoops to my left. He's got a wide grin on his face. Dad laughs, too, as we ride away. Krista has a real smile on even though it's more like a smirk. We press on, my white-knuckled hands aching from how hard I hold the ropes.

I hear an agonized cry from behind us. It's not human. It's deep and grating.

My triumph turns to fear once more as the crelotin stops, somehow responding to my feelings. The others rush on, but mine turns around. There's a gathering of goblins on the outskirts of the crude stone village. The leader stands there, his red eyes boring into me, reflecting the light of the moon above. In his hands, he holds Gobby.

"No!" I shout. Instinctively I spur the crelotin into motion, but my foot hitting its hard hide shoots pain up my leg. I wince, but it doesn't matter, for the creature responds to me and rushes back toward the town.

"David! Stop!" my dad cries.

I feel a tingling in my shoulder. *A dart*. It bounces off my shirt as if it didn't even hit me. The warmth that comes with my scales slowly dissipates from the area. Another strikes my face and I grit my teeth, grateful for my new ability. A few more darts hit me, but by this time, I'm nearly twenty feet away. Something strikes me in the left shoulder and my whole body pitches that direction, my hand wrenching from the rope and my body twisting dangerously. I shake my head as a full-sized arrow clatters to the stony ground.

I don't have time to process what I'm seeing before my gut is assaulted with another blow. A dull thud announces it bouncing off me, but I still feel the wind rush out of my lungs. Gasping for air, I pull the ropes with the only hand I have still holding on, and the crelotin slows.

Another arrow hits my head. My neck nearly overextends from the force. A splitting headache radiates in my brain, and I hear galloping behind me.

"David, get out of here!" Dad yells.

The sound of his voice is both comforting and alarming. He shouldn't have followed me. He has no defense mechanism like my scales.

"Dad—" I try to yell at him, but he's gone, his crelotin running past me at full tilt.

A couple more arrows barely miss me. The sound of them whooshing by makes my whole body lock up. Turning to see where Dad went, his crelotin dances side to side, avoiding the arrows like a deadly game of dodgeball. I close my eyes momentarily and breathe deeply, trying to get my head to stop pounding. When I open them, Dad has spun around and runs right at me. The arrows still fly, but the creature below him somehow manages to avoid them all.

Dang . . . I've got a defective crelotin.

The wildness in Dad's eyes as he races toward me is enough of a message for me to hightail it out of here. He still shouts at me to move. My whole body aches, but I grab the rope and yank on it, sending a mental message to the crelotin to get me to safety. It responds easily, and we barrel away, arrows zipping overhead.

"Gobby—" I try to say, but the word comes out garbled and veiled in emotion. I bite my lip, forcing back tears. I can't cry. Why would I? Gobby wasn't even a friend; he was just a goblin. Technically, he was the enemy. He isn't real; he was just a dream.

No matter what I tell myself, I can't stop the tightness in my throat.

I chance a look backward, afraid of what I'll see. It's just in time to see one of the goblins slam the hilt of a sword on the back of Gobby's head. I cough, nausea overcoming me at my failure—at my dad's failure. Another goblin raises his sword, tip down, ready to plunge it into the goblin's chest. A black blur comes from nowhere, and suddenly Gobby is gone.

Blinking, I search left and right, looking for where our unexpected friend went. I can't find him anywhere. What's more, the goblin that was about to kill him strikes downward as if he were still there. When his sword hits the stone harmlessly, he and the others look around frantically.

"What—?" I say, but I don't have time to think before Dad shouts at me again.

"Get a move on, son! They aren't following us!"

Sure enough, the group of goblins is too preoccupied by Gobby's disappearance. We press forward as hard as we can for about five minutes before I see glinting red carapaces about a hundred feet ahead of us. Dad sighs and slows his mount. I haven't given the command or pulled on the ropes, but my crelotin slows as well, keeping pace with Dad's. It's truly responding to my emotions and thoughts.

The first thing I notice is the fiery glare of Krista. Her mouth is pressed into a thin line, and she looks like she's ready to yank my head off.

The second thing I notice is that Jared's crelotin is empty still.

I feel the blood drain from my face.

"Where's Jared?"

Somehow, I know the answer. They have him. They managed to capture him before he could get out. They'll torture him, probably find out all they can about us, and then kill him.

"He followed you when you went back, you idiot!" Krista practically spits. "He had just turned human again when you rushed back into the fight. I couldn't stop him from following you. All because you had to save the stupid enemy. Did you even use your brain? Jared's gone now, all because *you* couldn't stay put!"

Heat flares in my chest, and I hold up a fist. I don't know why I do it—I feel a little ridiculous—but I don't care. I'm too angry. But not at her, more at myself.

What *was* I thinking?

I gaze up at her furious stare and something in me snaps. Walls start going up to protect my ego, but I can't let her step all over me, even if I made a mistake. Pushing all thoughts of Jared aside for a moment, I stab a finger at her.

"I don't give a crap about what you think. Gobby *helped* us, and you were willing to let him kick the bucket for it. Don't you have a soul? Plus, Jared went off on his *own*. I didn't order him to!"

My cheek feels wet, a tear having slipped free. Despite my ego, Jared's gone, and it's my fault. No matter how I try to spin it, he went back because of me. That stings.

"Kids," Dad says.

"*He* knew what he was doing," Krista says, referring to Gobby. "He knew he was putting himself in danger. That's not our fault. We are more important!"

"Why? Because our lame parents gave us their blood and then sent us away? How does that make us more important?" I shout back.

"*Kids!* You need to stop it! Now!" Dad yells louder than I've ever heard him before.

This manages to shut both of us up, but my heart still races, the anger boiling just below the surface. Every part of me wants to lunge at Krista and beat the snideness out of her. Of course, I can't do that. I can't hit a girl. Though, I can't help but wonder if my dragon scales could win out against her demon form.

A piercing screech from up above diffuses my anger. I look up, raising both hands over my head to fend off an attack, but instead, I gasp in surprise.

Gobby is descending on us like a green-skinned angel.

I shake my head and rub my eyes.

No, he's being carried by a bird. A massive black bird has the small goblin in its talons. I laugh out loud, waving up at the bird. Jared wasn't caught. I look over at Krista, who tries to covertly wipe a tear from her eye, but I see it. I'm too elated to care that she showed something other than ferocity.

The bird deposits Gobby on the ground, and I practically leap off my mount. By the time I get to him, he's already stirring, and Jared is back to his massive half-Samoan self. He looks like he's about to pass out.

"Not—healed—fully—yet," he says breathlessly.

I can't help but beam at him. Moving to his side, I slam him on the back in the old football player way and tell him thanks. He winces and I grimace, a muttered apology coming with it.

"Don't—mention—it. Just—lucky I'm—not—goblin food," he huffs.

Looking to Gobby, I'm almost too afraid to ask if he'll be okay, but Jared once again beats me to the punch.

"He'll be—fine."

"That's weird, Jared. I get that reading my thoughts saves you time, but you could at least let me ask the question first," I say.

He shrugs, then slumps to the ground. It's not long before Krista is rushing at him, her body partially expanded. Musings of purple veins tickle the sides of her eyes and mouth as if she were in the process of changing but stopped it. She reminds me of Mr. Hyde.

She slams into him, he grunts, and the strangest wrestle hug of all history ensues. It doesn't last long though. When Krista pulls away, there's a genuine smile on her face.

Don't worry, it's gone before I can say a word about it. She throws a demon-enhanced punch at her brother, who winces in pain.

"You had to go half demon mode, did you? Those punches *hurt*, Kris, even if I'm way bigger than you," Jared says.

"I don't give a flying crap about that. Don't you ever run off like that again, you idiot," she scolds.

There is an edge to her tone—enough to make me tense up—but she doesn't attack him anymore. Gobby stirs on the ground next to me, and I move over to him, flipping him so he's on his back.

"So, you just swooped in and—" Amir questions.

"And picked him up, yeah," Jared finishes. "Figured if Dave was going back for him, he was important."

He called me Dave again. This time, it actually feels appropriate, given the things we've been through.

Amir presses his lips together and folds his arms, clearly sulking. "And I'm just the human kid with no powers or any use at all."

"You can be our team mascot," Krista offers, which only makes him scowl more.

Gobby's eyelids flutter and he looks up at me. I would be lying if I said the bloodred eyes reflecting the moonlight high above didn't make me shiver, but at the same time, I'm relieved.

"Am I—alive?" he asks in a croaky tone.

Despite the discomfort of his eyes on me, I laugh. "Yeah, Jared saved you."

The goblin looks confused, then follows my gaze to where Jared sits.

"You're welcome, I guess," Jared says.

Gobby's mouth stretches out with a toothy smile. Sharp teeth glint back at me, and I instinctively look away. He pushes himself up, his head only coming up to my knees while he sits.

"I am forever in your debt. I will always be grateful. Thank you, thank you," he says.

I look to Jared, ready to translate, but then remember he can understand through my brain.

"Yeah, don't sweat it," he says.

Gobby looks at me, and I sigh.

"He says you're welcome," I translate.

"This is not the time for a feel-good moment. They will follow us soon," Dad urges.

We don't disagree, rushing to our mounts. Once again, I feel a wave of comfort and peace. It's manufactured outside of my brain, but it's strong enough that it meshes with my actual feelings of relief. There was some discussion about where the goblin should ride—some fighting, really. Despite his size, Gobby is shockingly dense. Because of that, it makes sense, at least in my mind, for him to ride with the smallest person. That's Krista.

Yeah, that doesn't go well. Whatever happiness she felt before is replaced by her post-demon anger. I feel lucky I still have all my limbs. I tell them I would feel fine if Gobby rode with me, but I'm not the smallest. Amir is the next smallest, so he, with a very uncomfortable look on his face, sits with the small goblin in front of him.

"Follow me!" Gobby shouts, spurring Amir's crelotin into motion.

We follow along the river, the path dark except for the light of the full moon above. After today, I'm not sure things can go much worse.

I have a history of being wrong.

I'M NOT RELIEVED THAT ELVES ARE REAL

I've lived the past eight years on a horse farm. I've ridden so many times on horseback that I feel comfortable—like I could ride for days. In fact, Dad and I did multiple weeklong trips to close-by areas. They were great experiences. I know I'll remember those for the rest of my life.

That's when I first learned about saddle soreness.

What I'm experiencing now is exactly that except about ten times worse.

I wince every time the crelotin takes a galloping step, which, with six legs, is a lot.

We've been riding hard for hours. The sky starts to get brighter, the sun right on the horizon. A chill bites at my bare arms, but it's not frosty, so I'm dealing with it. As much as I wish I could say the ride seems fast, it most definitely does not. When I'm not consumed by the pain of riding the crelotin, I'm busy beating myself up for my catastrophic failure back at the goblin encampment. I made the conscious decision to turn back and save Gobby. I put myself and the others in danger all because I thought I could stand up to a group of small goblins. That was a dumb move.

My attempt might not have been so embarrassing if I had pulled it off. But no, Dad had to swoop in and save me. And then Jared did exactly what I hoped to do.

I glance over at him. He's staring at me, a grimace on his face. He gives me a face-reddening look of pity.

I hate that he can pick up on everything in my head.

Cursing internally, I force my mind to think of something else—the galloping of the crelotins, the whooshing of the dry air on my face, anything. I peer up at the sky to inspect the stars as we ride, but I can't do that for long before vertigo starts to take over me. The sky is massive here. I'm sure it's about the same size as the earth, but it *appears* huge. Even when a massive green-covered mountain range comes into view in the distance, the sky doesn't seem to shrink at all. The stars glimmer high above, and I can't help but wonder if the constellations are the same or not.

I never was into astronomy.

I could ask Amir, and for a moment, I think I might, but one glimpse at him changes my mind. He's all stiff, clearly trying to keep his distance from Gobby, who rides the crelotin without even holding on. His silver-gray hair flows backward, plastering itself against Amir's chest. This is definitely not what my friend signed up for, but he's probably glad Gobby is short and the hair isn't flapping in his face or mouth.

We're lucky the goblins didn't pursue us. At least, that's what we thought. It wasn't until we rode a little farther that we found out they *did* follow. Another fun fact about goblins: they have magic.

Go figure. Everything has to have magic in this place, doesn't it? A true fantasy-book fairytale. Except the princess in this story isn't a damsel in distress. She's a red-haired force of nature who can level a whole building with a punch.

Jared chuckles behind me. I pointedly ignore him. Instead, I glance at Krista, whose mouth moves subtly as she talks to herself.

After we started riding, Gobby told us that if we hadn't saved him, thus confusing the goblins, they would have been after us faster. As it was, our commotion distracted them long enough for us to get a head start. Gobby took care of the rest.

Goblins have illusory magic, but Gobby is particularly skilled with it. He wasn't the most popular goblin in his—what did he call it, tribal clan? Gobby told us that he learned all his magic from years and years of practice. And, of course, when he shared the information, I had to translate this to everyone. When I got tired of relaying the words, however, Jared was able to pick it up, plucking the translation from my brain and communicating to the others.

The moment Gobby was with us, he'd begun weaving the spell. I hadn't even detected it, but his illusion had to be the reason we didn't have goblins bearing down. He told us that he'd hidden us from view, making it seem like we disappeared into thin air. The other goblins would see through the illusion eventually, and they had, but it distracted them for a time. As we traveled, he also told us that he would change our tracks to appear like they veered off away from the river.

All in all, his tactics must be working.

Dad rides his crelotin at the head of the group, the rest of us running alongside each other. There's plenty of space, given that the desert is massive and rocky. It all looks the same. Suddenly he raises his hand above his head, and we all slow.

"It's hard to be sure in this lighting, but I think I spot a tree line ahead," Dad says. "Let's take a pause for a minute."

Groans and gasps of relief come from each of us as we dismount. I practically throw myself from the creoltin's back to give my legs and crotch a rest. The moment I do, it's like I'm taking off a pair of stiff shoes that I've worn for years.

"Are you sure we're safe enough to stop?" Krista asks. "They could be right behind us."

I glance at Gobby, asking him the question with my eyes. He stares at me blankly. I close my eyes and repeat her words for him.

"They do not follow close, I am sure. Goblin magic works on our own kind. Some can detect the illusions, but it's difficult to diffuse. They followed the wrong path for hours," he says. "But the fake trail will die soon. We should hurry. Though, we can rest first."

Dad's gaze is measured as I share the message, but his shoulders slump in relief. That many hours of riding has taken more out of me than I care to admit.

"Get some water. I bet you're all dehydrated," Dad says.

Krista doesn't move from her crelotin. She's sitting atop it with a flat expression. I observe her as she scrutinizes Gobby for a long moment. I walk up to her and wave my arms in front of her face.

"Hey there, aren't you sore from sitting? Hop down. Gobby's not lying to us," I say.

She scowls at me.

"Glad you have so much confidence in something with red eyes," she retorts, then slips off her horse.

I shake my head, then move to Gobby, who is standing below the crelotin, trying to coax Amir down.

"I can't—I hurt—way too bad. Plus, this thing is *huge*," Amir complains.

I laugh at his reaction. He's ridden a horse at our ranch only once. It did not go well. He was on for about two seconds when something spooked the horse, and it ran away with him screaming in the saddle. To be fair, it was my fault. I hadn't been holding the horse's reins properly, and I kind of put him on a relatively inexperienced horse. I still feel bad about it. Regardless, he's not been much for horseback riding since.

"Here, just give me your hand," I say, offering him my palm.

He glares at me, a very clear friend-to-friend message of "This is all your fault I'm stuck up here and scared to get down." I naturally reply with a look of "You know I still feel bad about that. I'm sorry."

Amir grips my hand and leans into it. He basically falls off the crelotin, but it's all right because he ends up landing on my shoulder in a firefighter carry. I pitch forward to place him on his feet, and he gives me a thankful look.

Gobby gazes up at me from knee level, throwing his hands up in the air.

"That fool of a human looks like a kid goblin. He's like a big baby. He looks unfit to ride a crelotin." He hobbles away to the river to get water for himself.

"What did he say?" Amir asks.

"Oh, don't worry about it. He's just thirsty."

Jared stifles a laugh next to us.

"How close is that forest, did you say?" Amir asks, changing the subject.

"Probably about an hour away, if I'm right," Dad says, then looks to Gobby. "Is that enough time for us to make it?"

This time, Jared translates to our companion, and I stare at him, aghast. What comes out of his mouth is a series of grunts and growls, like a dog that's eaten something bad. It doesn't last long, though, before my brain processes it and it becomes normal English.

Jared grins. "I think, if I focus hard enough, I can grab the translation to Goblish from your head, too."

Gobby looks at Jared thoughtfully, giving the answer, but also commenting on Jared's weird pronunciation for Goblish. Jared nibbles on his lip in embarrassment.

"He says they'll be lost for days, so we're good," I translate.

Dad looks relieved. "Well, let's not spend too much time. Grab the water you need, and we'll get going."

I walk to the river, stopping dead in my tracks when I see Krista has taken off her gray sweatshirt. Underneath, she is wearing a baggy tank top. It hangs off her like she was a larger girl who'd just lost a lot of weight. She's dousing her outer layer in the clear, cold water and wringing it out. I move to the other side of her, cup my hands, and slip them in. It feels like literal ice. My fingers go numb almost instantly. When it goes down my throat, however, I welcome the freshness even if it does give me a brain freeze.

"So," I say, glancing at Krista for a moment, then turning away to where Gobby is lounging inside the ice water. "What's with the big clothes?"

She stares at me. "Is it not obvious?"

I gape at her. "Oh, um, well . . . yeah, it's obvious."

I grimace at the dumb question.

"It's when I grow. I can't go around naked after I expand my size, can I?" she says, then pulls her soaking-wet sweater back on her body. She shivers, then sighs contentedly.

"That would be—different, wouldn't it?" I say.

I have no idea how I should have responded to that..

And apparently, she has nothing else to say either. She turns her back on me and joins the others. Somehow, I feel bad and angry at the same time. I apparently can't have a pleasant interaction with this girl. She needs to chill out.

My stomach growls so loud that I flush. It's been a long time since I've eaten anything, and I'm starting to feel it. When we first were stuck in this hot place, it was all about water. Now that I've had plenty of that, my other needs are coming out.

Everyone is watching Gobby in the cold water.

"He looks so comfortable in that," Amir marvels. "What's he made of?"

No one answers. Probably because none of us knows.

"Does anyone have any food? I'm starving out of my mind," I say.

Dad scratches his chin. "I was just thinking that myself. There isn't any vegetation nearby. We could ask Gobby if he knows—"

"Oh, please don't tell me *you* are going to get on board with calling the goblin that. He's *the literal enemy*. We can't be naming him like a pet," Krista complains.

Dad gives her a harsh look. "He hasn't tried to kill us, so I doubt he will. David came up with the name, and I'm using it for convenience. If you don't like it, you're welcome to stay in the desert, but he's coming with us."

I feel a bit of pride at Dad's reaction but soon forget the pride as my stomach growls again.

"As I was saying, we could ask Gobby if he knows where food is. He is from this area, after all," Dad says.

We all agree that we don't have any other options, so I head to retrieve our little green friend. As I walk up to him, his red eyes fix on me, and he looks angry. I pause, wondering if he's turned on some primal goblin instinct to rip my heart out, but then he waves at me to invite me over.

"So . . . we're pretty hungry. Do you know where we could get some food?" I ask.

Gobby licks his lips to reveal his split snakelike tongue. I shift uncomfortably on my feet.

"Yes, there is food all around. See? Look there," he says, pointing behind me.

I turn to look. Even though it's still early morning, the light from the rising sun is steady and displays the landscape as if it were a darker noon day. I only see what we've seen for the past few hours: flat, rocky, shrubby, and dry nothing. There is absolutely no food in sight.

"I don't see what you mean. It's just rocks."

Gobby grunts and pulls himself out of the river. Without his rough brown shirt on, his green-skinned back is exposed to the rising sunlight. Jagged, puffed up skin lines his body. He must have been whipped by something. Sympathy pain tingles through me, and I inadvertently gasp, which draws his attention.

"You good?" Gobby asks.

Now doesn't seem like the right time to ask him about the scars, so I simply nod.

He grunts again, then moves about ten feet away from the rest of us. He kneels down, fingers something on the hard, dirt-packed ground and lifts up a stone, showing it to us.

"This is food," he says, then pops the rock into his mouth.

My stomach turns as I listen to him crunch the rock between his sharp teeth.

"Dude, we can't eat *rocks*. We'd die," I say.

He frowns, which forces his bottom shark-like teeth to pop up over his lip. It looks both comical and terrifying.

"Humans don't like rock? All right, no problem. There are other things," he says. He trudges farther away, stopping at a shrub. It's all gray and wilted with short, stemlike leaves that are also gray.

"Eat this. It smells gross but is good for the body. Better than starving to death." He rips a branch free and hands it to me.

I grit my teeth, then take it from him.

"Are you sure about this?" I ask.

I'm aware that the others are watching, but I'm not looking at them. Amir is whispering something, probably about how crazy it is that Gobby just devoured a rock, but I can't hear him.

"Just try a bite, it's good!" Gobby says before picking up more rocks. He tosses them into his mouth without hesitation, the crunching sound both loud and muffled by the wide desert.

I watch him chew for a minute, my stomach growling once more. It's like my mind can't comprehend the fact that he's eating rocks. All it can process is that he's chewing something crunchy.

Eyeing the shrubbery, I lift it to my nose and smell it.

That is a terrible mistake. Something sharp and distinctly rotting assaults my sinuses, and I throw my arm away from my face as quickly as possible.

My stomach churns as I imagine dead and rotting animal corpses. Just last week, one of Dad's traps caught a stupid mouse from the surrounding fields. It was small, but dang, that thing had a stench.

The branch smells like that mouse.

Gobby watches me curiously. "Bad flavor?"

I shake my head. "It smells awful! How can you eat this?"

His eyes do the "I don't know" widening and narrowing before he replies, "You don't smell it, just eat it."

Before I can prepare my tongue to give a nasty retort on *that* idea, Jared clears his throat.

"Okay, your thoughts passed the smell sensation to me, and even secondhand that was awful," he replies.

Amir, watching the whole thing next to Krista and my dad, scowls and tromps up to me. He snatches the plant out of my hand and takes a big bite.

"Woah," he says, staggering a little. "That is . . . weird. It's like I'm eating a piece of mint gum and meat at the same time."

I raise an eyebrow. "You can't be serious."

He hands the stalk back to me. "Try it."

I stare at it with hesitation, then close my nose and eyes and take a bite.

The first thing I notice is the menthol-type feeling. It's cool, sharp, and feels a lot like mint gum, but then the salty meat-like flavor hits me. I chance a breath through my nose, but not before holding the branch in my hand as far from my face as possible. The rotten stench is still there, but it's not as bad.

When I swallow, it's like the floodgates of hunger open and I can't stop myself. I devour the branch and grab two more, careful not to smell them.

It doesn't take much to convince Dad and Krista that it's edible. Could Gobby be trying to kill us? Entirely possible, but my hunger prevents me from making proper judgments. Jared requires more convincing, especially because of the secondhand rot experience of the branches from reading my brain.

When I've had my fill, I lean back on one of the larger and flatter rocks that sits on the ground. It doesn't feel great to lie on a stone slab, but right now, my full stomach protests the idea of even moving an inch.

We lapse into silence. I suspect the sated hunger has something to do with it. I get lost in my thoughts. I recall everything that's happened over the past day: how we almost died from hunger, dehydration, and goblin captivity. I think about my failed rescue, but that sets me onto something else. If it wasn't for Dad, I'd have been skewered by one of the goblin swords.

"Wait," I say, turning to Dad. "How did you guide the crelotin so well? Back when the goblins were about to take me out."

He sighs. "I've ridden something like these before. When I was last here, living in this land, I had a horse—an actual horse. They do exist here."

Dad responds to the look of awe on my face.

"Anyway, it behaved similarly. It didn't have the same appearance as these things, but he did connect with my mind. Man, I loved that horse," he says wistfully.

"What happened to him?" Amir asks.

Dad looks sad. "Honestly, I don't know. When I left your mother and the realm of the dragons, I gave him to the stable hands. I wasn't ready to risk bringing him to the human world, not if it meant he'd lose himself. You saw what happens to creatures that come to earth without human blood in them."

I blink slowly, thinking back to the creatures who attacked us at the football stadium. When they died, they melted into a pool of tar. It was both disgusting and kind of relieving. Sure, I'm a teenage boy, but blood and guts don't really jive with my stomach.

Dad continues. "He was old then, and it's been sixteen years. He's either too old to function or died in battle."

He casts his eyes downward and I squirm where I sit, unsure of how to help him with the emotions. Those kinds of things make me uncomfortable.

"The moment I touched the crelotin, it was like waking up from a dream. I could feel him, and I knew he could feel me. It reminded me instantly of my horse," he says, taking another bite of shrubbery and grimacing a little.

A light breeze comes from out of nowhere and picks up my hair. It's sq sudden that I perk up, looking in the direction it came from, which is the forest tree line we are heading to. Ever since we've been traveling in this blasted desert, there has been stagnant air, and if there was wind, it was weak and pointless. The air that hits me now is so fresh and humid that it feels like a dream.

"Blessed day, wind that actually feels like something fresh in this awful furnace," Krista comments, turning away from the conversation and facing the breeze. She holds out her hands, reveling in the weather.

"We really should go," Dad says, pushing himself up with his legs and moving to his crelotin.

There isn't a single complaint from anyone. Before, Amir or Jared might have claimed that the break was too short, but now they climb atop their mounts with no question. I sigh, standing up with more difficulty than I expected. My legs are still sore and achy from the night's ride, but I try not to show it on my face. I can't give Krista the satisfaction of knowing that I'm suffering. She'd get too much of a kick out of it. As it is, she doesn't say anything. She just lifts herself easily up onto her crelotin.

We fall back into formation. Everyone is so full and content that conversations take a lull. We've been up all night, and I can already feel my eyes struggling to stay open. I want to lean forward on the crelotin and sleep, but one quick glance at the ground reminds me that sleeping here is probably not a good call. I would fall off and make a fool of myself.

After looking at nothing but desert landscape for so long, it's refreshing to see the forest line. Tall pine trees create a natural wall that spans both left and right as far as the eye can see. The river along which we follow passes right into the forest, melding with the landscape.

The sun has barely risen, and the large moon still hangs overhead. I know we've come to a new—oh, what did Dad call it?—realm, or something like that, but shouldn't the moon be moving away from us? I open my mouth to ask Dad, but Gobby says something first.

"You look scared. Scared of the moon? Yes? Why are you scared?"

Instead of answering, I glance at Amir. He has apparently become comfortable with our small friend and has his hands threaded under the goblin's armpits. It looks altogether *wrong*, as if a father put his child on a horse in front of him, only to let the child hold the reins while he grips the waist of the kid.

"Why is it so large? I feel like it's going to come out of the sky and smash into the ground," I say with a shiver.

Gobby stares at me, then blinks a few times. "What a strange idea. Why would it do that?"

I wave off his question, unwilling to even try to explain where I'm coming from.

The ride moves more quickly than I expect it to. Amir manages to fall asleep on the back of his crelotin, his head drooping forward and leaning on the top of Gobby's, who doesn't seem to notice. It makes me wonder if goblins don't have a sense of feeling in the tops of their heads. The perceived comfort of the tree line comes to light as the sun rises above the horizon, casting odd shadows through the trunks as if the night were preserved deep within the branches.

"Bad day, bad day!" Gobby shouts out suddenly.

I tense, turning to look at him. His red eyes are as wide as saucers and his face turns from a dark green to lighter. He almost looks like a leaf changing from green to yellow in the middle of fall back on earth.

In any case, it looks bad.

"What?" I shout over the sound of the pounding hooves.

"Goblins! They're coming! And coming fast!" His gravelly voice carries over the noise. I crane my neck around, trying to see behind us, but nothing seems amiss. It's all just fog. Wait, no, that's dust. It looks like a sandstorm.

In a place with nearly no wind.

"Oh no . . ."

I'm not an avid movie watcher, but I've seen enough country westerns to know what dust looks like when it's been kicked up by horses. The kicked up dust from our little group hasn't been too terrible, especially since we've been traveling in a tight pack this whole time.

What's happening far behind us is *not* a little bit of dust. From the side of the river, at least half a mile away, a wall is coming right at us—and the little pinpricks of darkness must be the crelotins and goblin riders.

"I thought you said they wouldn't find our trail!" I shout, unable to keep the frustration from my voice.

Gobby wails in despair. "I know! I was wrong. Very wrong. They're coming fast!"

My head snaps back to the line of trees. It's coming closer and closer, but when I look backward again, the approaching riders are coming even faster. In fact, I can even see that the dark blots are clearly a red base with a green rider. Avoiding the temptation of making some snarky comment about Christmas following us, I yell over to Dad.

"We have to hurry!"

He doesn't hear me.

Gobby tries this time, but Dad doesn't respond to him either. I'm struck again with the realization that he can't understand our goblin companion.

"DAD!" I shout.

This time, he perks up, his head swinging around to look at me. His eyes don't stay on me long before they focus on what's happening behind us. His jaw tenses. Without a word, he spins back and leans forward. The crelotin beneath him responds, and he barrels toward the trees at an impossible pace.

"What's happening?" Krista shouts. "Why did he speed up like—oh, come on!"

She turns around in her saddle and bares her teeth at the approaching riders. Then she starts to grow, her body expanding right before my eyes. It's like watching a marshmallow grow inside a microwave, expanding rapidly until it gets too big and flops over. Purple veins appear like invisible ink being revealed. Her crelotin lets out a cry of surprise, its powerful legs struggling to hold up her weight. I feel the despair of the creature and the pain in its back.

"Don't get too big. Your crelotin can't hold you!" I cry.

She glares at me with fire in her eyes, and the expanding stops. In fact, she even shrinks a little, but not much. All the while, the army behind us advances. By the time I look forward again, I'm not prepared for how close we are to the trees. I watch in horror as Dad, who's pulled at least a hundred feet ahead of us, plunges into the darkness at full speed. My mouth goes dry at the sight of the thick branches and leaves that sit a little higher up on the trees. Atop a mount, we might just hit them.

"Amir, wake *up*!"

My friend snaps awake. I have no idea how he managed to hold on to Gobby while sleeping, but he's alert now.

"What is going—"

He doesn't get to finish his sentence before we fly into the trees. I don't know what being whipped feels like, but I imagine it's something like what I feel on my face and hands at this moment. Stinging erupts everywhere. I open my mouth to say, "Ow" but regret that instantly as leaves and sticks fill it up. I cough, leaning forward toward the neck of my crelotin. Suddenly the crelotin stops, and I almost fly off of its back.

Exclamations around me tell me the others are having a similar experience.

I gasp. The base of emotions from the crelotin is missing from my chest. It feels wrong after having felt it all night. I was just getting used to it, and now it's gone.

"Is everyone all right?" I say, turning in the thick darkness toward where Amir and Gobby should be.

There is only a barebacked crelotin there. I frown, turning to see that Jared's and Krista's are empty, too.

Before I can call out for them, strong hands wrap around my arms and mouth. I scream, but it's muffled, suppressed by a calloused hand. I'm wrenched from the crelotin so roughly that my back twinges. All the pain from my inevitably cut arms and face is whisked away by the terror I feel now.

Whatever holds me forces me to go back into the light near the edge of the trees. My eyes widen as I watch the approaching goblins on their mounts. We're going to die because some idiotic people are holding us hostage and forcing us in front of the very creatures we just escaped. It's unfair, really. I struggle to get out of their grip but to no success.

"Watch. They will leave us," a wizened voice says. It sounds ancient, like a man who's experienced a lot of life.

I do watch, but only because I have no other choice. Whoever has me holds my head in a vice grip, forcing me to stare at the oncoming goblin army. One of the goblins sprouts a thick shafted arrow from his chest and falls off his crelotin. His body rolls to a stop, his crelotin leaving him behind.

Then another three are hit by arrows coming from somewhere near me. More rain down around the mounts, missing their marks entirely. It only takes a moment before the pack leader—the grumpy one who almost ordered us eaten—pulls his mount around and shouts the order to retreat. They disappear into the dust storm kicked up from their crelotins.

"Pesky goblin magic," another voice says, this one female, yet still as old as the first voice. "Can never see them when you need to. Right as I nocked my arrow they started flickering something awful."

"Peace, Gyrwyn. They are gone; that is what matters," the ancient man says. "Now, about the matter of this human."

I struggle but to no avail. I'm pinned against the chest of a very tall person with *blue* skin. It looks like the sky; it's so bright. I think back to the trolls that attacked me during the game, and my throat constricts. I strain against the hands holding my head to peer at the other person. It's clearly a female on account of her—umm, chest. I can't hold the blush back from my face.

"Let—me go—*now*," I manage, still muffled by the hand pressed over my face.

The hand around me tightens, and I scream through it. Whether I'm just a fool or desperate, I let my hand ignite, a ball of flame exploding to life and heating my palm as well as the side of my body.

"Nature bless! What is *that*?" the female voice says, and immediately the grip on the left side of my body is released. I take advantage of that, igniting my left hand and thrusting it outward. I hear her curse, trees rustling as she jumps away. Feeling a bit satisfied that it worked to push her away, I swing my hand over the front of my body, intending to slam it into the other troll. It doesn't make it far before another strong hand grips my wrist. It moves from my waist upward so fast that I can't track it. My feet leave the ground and I squeal a bit unceremoniously.

"Put him down," the wizened voice says.

I grit my teeth, pushing against the hand, trying to force the fire into his chest, but he's too strong. Right as I'm about to light my captive hand on flame, I feel a prick on my neck. It's a small thing, but the moment I feel it, my whole body goes numb. A mumbled set of confusing words escapes my lips before I see the world tilt sideways. My head hits the ground.

I can't feel anything. Panic erupts in my mind, and I'm sure my body is responding to the fight-or-flight reflex, but there's no sensation. It's like I've fallen asleep, paralysis taking over, but I'm not actually asleep.

"He's not human," the older voice says. "Though he looks like it. That was dragon's fire."

"You don't think that it's *him*, do you?" the female asks.

My field of vision shifts so suddenly that I swear I'd feel dizzy if I could feel anything at all. A face is right in front of me. It's blue, like the body that I spied before I was paralyzed. Silver irises stare at me from under deep blue eyebrows. The face has wrinkles, but it also appears youthful with boundless energy. I don't know where my friends are, but I hear a scuffle and some shouts to my left.

Krista, no doubt.

"I believe it could be him," the man says right in my face. I smell his breath, hot and sweet. I would shudder if everything wasn't numb. "Welcome to the realm of elves."

UNUSUAL TREATMENT

I'm being dragged by my armpits through a dark forest like a rag doll. It's humiliating and beyond frustrating. For the first bit, I focus on my body, trying to get my hands and feet to respond. At one point, I manage to ignite a fire on my limp palm, but I only surprise the elves. No actual damage is done. I light a tree aflame, which causes them to scold me for a time, but that doesn't last long either.

After I realize I won't be able to move anytime soon, I force myself to relax. I still can't feel anything. Using what senses I have, I try to appreciate the forest. Everything smells earthy and damp, like after a fresh rain back home. It's an incredible thing to smell after having traversed a wicked, boring, and arid desert. The green landscape becomes more visible now that my eyes are adjusting to the dim, so I examine what I can.

The old-looking elf walks in front of me, though I can't easily watch him with my head lolling from side to side while they drag me along. I know it's him because he keeps telling me random things about the forest and their city.

"The hwifoo tree is a friendly one, capable of growing fruit, which sates one's whole hunger and thirst with one bite. A common tree, yet the crop is rare. It only bursts forth when a traveler is pure of heart and in dire need."

How helpful, I think sarcastically, *if I could move anything.*

"Every tree has dryads inhabiting them who send messages to each other. They listen, they watch. It's very effective for sending word to your allies."

I can't entirely appreciate the cool things he's telling me because of my current state. Right as I have this thought, I feel a sharp pain in the tips of my fingers and on the tip of my nose.

Wait, I feel something.

"Your friends are safe, like you," the leader says. His voice is louder, so I suspect he's turned to talk to me. The elves holding my armpits stop, the moving ground halting beneath my limited vision. It shifts again in a blur and suddenly I'm staring right at him.

"I am sorry for this. We did not realize who you were when you first came into our domain," he explains.

He lifts his fingers and touches my face in a few places. A shudder is just out of reach from within my paralyzed form.

"Elder Yon, are you certain he understands the speech?" the female elf to my left asks. "He is mortal. I've yet to meet any human who can truly speak our tongue."

The old elf smiles, the wrinkles on the sides of his eyes and forehead becoming canyons.

"Yes, he is dragon-blooded. That much is clear. He bears the gift of language, as all dragons do."

It is unfair that he knows this much about me. All I did was try to burn their faces off, and I revealed enough about myself to feel exposed. When I made the joke the day before about being thrown into a real-life role playing game, I didn't expect it would get any worse than seeing the goblins. Now I'm being dragged by a bunch of tall elves. The pain in my fingers intensifies, and I try to wince, but to no avail.

Wait, the pain is growing. It's a burning tingle that crawls up my hands toward my elbows. My cheeks also burn, the sensation flowing from the tip of my nose. I attempt to move my mouth and manage to do it, though the process makes it hurt worse. I can't believe the scales failed me. The goblin poison never touched my blood, but whatever these elves did to me got past my defense mechanism.

"Wh—why?" I say.

The elf's smile deepens.

"I am sorry about this. The toxin in your blood is quite painful as it leaves your body, but it will pass swiftly," he says, turning forward and walking again.

"Let go of me *now*!" I hear Krista shout from somewhere to the left. There is a loud roar as Krista's voice is enhanced by her demon form. She's gone all big, I know it. There's the sound of surprised elves, their tone different in my ears somehow, and a series of thumps.

"Hold her down, don't let her—*augh*!"

Another grunt and thud.

"Don't you dare stick me with that poison again—"

More shouts and thuds.

"Shoot—her—"

"Toxin—"

"Not working—"

The tingling has reached my neck and elbows, and I work my tongue in my mouth, the pain bringing a lucidity back to my brain.

"Let—me—talk to—her," I say.

The old elf regards me with a curious expression, as if he didn't expect me to speak for quite some time.

"Very well," he gestures to the elves holding me, and they snap into action. I can feel the air on my face as the elf on my right lets go of me. I'm tossed over the female's shoulder. Everything bounces up and down, my head and hands slamming continually into her back. In only a few seconds, she slings me backward and spins me until I'm looking at a hulking monster. The sunlight filters through the trees over the massive form of Krista swinging her arms from side to side.

Man, she's terrifying.

"Krista!" I croak, my voice not at full capacity. This makes me cough, and I swear I'm going to hack up a lung. My chest burns like it's on fire.

Demon Krista spins on me with a wild expression in her eyes.

"They're friends, they won't hurt us," I say, though I could be wrong. I have no idea if these elves can be trusted. But Dad said something about light and dark races. Elves are generally good in stories, right? Aren't they on the good side? I hope I'm right. It must have some truth, I figure, because we're not dead yet.

Krista's eyes are all black, and she growls in a low tone. "They poisoned me. That's the work of an enemy."

"They would have killed us already if they wanted to," I reason.

It sounds weak. Still, it gives her enough of a pause that she stops swinging her massive limbs around. The half a dozen elves surrounding her move in toward her with their arms outstretched as if they were corralling a pig.

"Stop that! Do you want to get yourselves killed?" I shout at them. A few of the elves pause and turn toward me, a look of awe in their eyes.

"Oh good, the freak dragon boy can speak *their* language, too. What are you goading them on about? Telling them to skewer me?" Krista's deep tone spits.

The burning is all over my body now, and I hate every bit of it, but I can almost move. I tug on my arm until the elf woman loosens her grip on me. She hesitates and her hand lingers momentarily before she withdraws it.

The pain makes me wince.

"Don't be dumb, Krista. You'll heal from the toxin. You're already recovered enough to fight," I say, inching closer to her.

Have you ever moved toward a rabid dog and watched as it snaps its foaming jaws at you, ready to pounce and tear into your arm? Yeah, neither have I. But that's what it feels like as I move toward the towering and fuming half demon.

"If you kill me, I don't get the sense that this realm will take it well," I say. "Especially the dragon queen."

Krista's face falls. I can tell she understands.

"I'm not the one who did this to you, but I figure the ones who *did* have no intention of hurting us." Once again, the words taste bitter on my tongue. I have a suspicion that if an all-out battle ensues because of her temper, we'll all end up dead.

I shuffle over to her, my hand dabbing her forearm. My fingers feel like they are resting on a block of ice. I didn't expect that Krista in demon form would feel like Antarctica.

"Sheesh!" I exclaim. "How are you so cold?"

She eyes me, her rabid gaze fixing on me for only a moment before she looks over my shoulder. Krista lets out a growl and flicks her thick arm over my head. I duck instinctively, guessing she's going to knock my head clean off, but she shouts instead.

"The friendly *elves* keep attacking us!"

I examine her arm and see she has a dagger buried in it. Blood pours from the wound. I don't know why, but I'm surprised the blood is purple. Her eyes droop for a moment before they snap open, and she whips the dagger out, ready to throw it.

I wish I could say that the squelching sound of the dagger coming out of her arm doesn't make me lightheaded, but it definitely does. I blame the toxin working its way out of my system.

I chance a look at the advancing elves. One of them twirls another dagger through the air, tossing and catching it over and over.

"Stop it!" I say in a commanding tone.

To my utter shock, he does.

"We are half bloods. You can see we aren't here to fight you. The goblins, a dark race, wanted to kill us. Don't you realize that puts us on your side?" I ask.

A bit of a reach, but the "An enemy of my enemy is my friend" mantra seems like a good place to be right now. It seems to work because the lead elf sheathes his knife in a quick motion.

"I'm not happy that the demons have joined the pact of the light races. You will never be welcome in our realm, but I will not kill you this day," the elf says. His silver irises glow in the shaded forest, reflecting the light they pick. I shiver under his gaze. He has deep black hair worn long over his shoulders with leaves woven throughout it. Even without his dark and heated stare, seeing the dude's arms and muscled chest tells me I wouldn't do well in a fight against him. Especially since my scaley defense is evidently broken.

The ancient-looking elf—the one with the long white hair and deep blue eyes—strides up to me.

"Peace, for now. The demon will turn human before we continue," he says, not so much as an order, but more of a cogent question.

"She will," I affirm, knowing that I now have to convince her to do so.

The elf scrutinizes me with a measured expression, and I know he's sizing me up. It's the same look that the other football team gives us when we walk out onto the field. They watch us—decide how much of a threat we are. I puff up my chest, wishing that I still had my football pads on.

Oh man, I left my pads back in the desert.

I'd been carrying them for a bit, but in the chaos, I must have left them somewhere along the river. And just after they'd been broken in.

"You will let my friends walk," I say, staring hard at the old elf. "No more dragging. We're friends, not prisoners—"

I pause for a moment, deciding if I should try it. After a short mental deliberation, I give it a go.

"She is half demon, my other companion is half fairy. I order you, as high prince, to take us to your leader."

My face flushes at my own words. Possibly the cheesiest thing I've ever said in my whole life. But I'm amazed to discover that it works.

He watches me, his eyes widening, and he looks from me to Krista, then back again. His lips move through a silent set of words as he takes in what I said.

"The halflings from the prophecy—"

His surprised expression solidifies. He veils whatever emotion he has at learning our identities.

"Very well, when the toxin wears off, we will bring your friends to you," the older elf says.

He turns and walks away, our agreement hanging in the air between us as if it didn't even happen. What was he thinking? Does he believe who we are? Did Gobby lead us into some massive, terrible trap? I don't have time to worry about that right now. Instead, I check on Krista, whose face is contorted into a rage fest.

"Power down, Krista," I say, hoping my choice of words will at least lend me a half smile.

It doesn't.

She growls instead, raising both arms above her head until her bulging biceps appear like they'll rip her hoodie's sleeves. Her fierce black eyes regard me for a moment, and I'm sure she's going to slam her meaty fist into my face and knock me out, but she gnashes her teeth and nods. What happens next is nightmarish. Her thick body ripples, like those freaky, muscley dudes, and she shrinks speedily until she's the small redhead with baggy sweats.

"If they so much as glance at me wrong, I will kill them. And I'll tear your head off if you get in my way," she says, moving past me and bumping my shoulder with hers.

That went well.

It's not until we get moving that I'm able to count how many elves are in the group. I figured it had only been a half dozen or so, but as we walk, more and more meld out of the forest as if they had come from thin air.

My skin prickles at the thought of one of them stabbing me once more and numbing me out. I'm still frustrated my scales didn't block the attack, and I marvel at how I can feel broken when I didn't even have time to learn about this new ability.

We trudge on for an hour. I can't see the sun, and since I don't have a watch, I have no idea what time it is. I guess our travel time based on my inaccurate internal clock. To be honest, I've never had a skill for time. Krista walks next to me, glaring forward. I can hear her muttering something from time to time, but she does not appear to want to chat.

There are at least twenty elves surrounding us. Several are so near that I inch closer to Krista. Her arm brushes against mine. I expect it to elicit some bizarre response from her, now that I'm touching her, but she doesn't react. To be more accurate, her anger doesn't seem to change.

The forest thins out, and I exhale in relief. My arms prickle from all the foliage and plants rubbing against my skin. It's not that I don't like nature, but I have some allergies. Fall, in my opinion, is the worst time of the year. I peer down at my arm where a red rash resides. It itches like nuts.

"Okay, that was horrible," a ragged voice says to my right.

I spin in that direction, my breath catching. Krista turns, too, her hand coming to the side in an oversized grip. We both sigh in relief when we see Amir.

"My head is pounding like crazy. I couldn't do *anything*," he said. "I felt like a baby as they dragged me along."

I chuckle. Largely because if I don't laugh, I'm positive I'll fall over.

"It'll get better," I say. "My headache went away pretty fast."

He looks at me with a doubtful expression, then rolls his eyes. "Says the boy with the dragon blood. I don't expect my body to recover from poison the way yours does."

I frown. He's probably right, but I don't want to make him feel bad. I'm trying to be a good friend.

"I'm sorry for all this," I say. "I never told you about the dragon thing because . . ."

"I would assume you were an insane person?" he finishes.

I nod. "Something like that."

He laughs.

"Bro, I'd have told you to check into the loony bin. But that doesn't mean I'd stop being your friend. We've been best buds for way too long for me to drop you like that. Anyway, this is fine. It beats going to your games."

I grin at him, throwing a soft punch. He feigns pain, then tosses a punch of his own at my arm. The scales *do not* appear, thankfully. I'm sure they wouldn't feel great to punch with bare flesh.

After about another thirty minutes, Dad and Jared join us, both with grimaces on their face. Jared, even though he's half blooded like Krista and me, doesn't recover well from the toxin. I guess super healing isn't part of the fairy superpower package. I glance at the bandages on his chest. He winces from time to time. He's still healing from the deep wound. After a few pleasantries, we walk in silence, moving forward because that's where the elves seem to move.

Before I can ask how much longer our journey will be, an elf appears to my right, making me jump out of my skin.

"They are quite human," the elf says, gesturing toward Dad and Amir.

It's a new elf, or I *think* it's a new one, but I can't be sure. They are all blue and brooding. Kind of hard to tell the difference between them all. His black hair is tied back in a long ponytail running down his back. His irises are yellow like a cat's, but his pupils aren't slitted like one.

"Yes, I'm human," Dad replies. "And so is Amir."

The elf glares at them before turning to face the direction of our path.

"Humans not safe," he says, his voice low and measured.

I stagger. I didn't have to translate what he said to the others. He's speaking English. It's disjointed and kind of mumbled, but he just spoke English.

"So you *can* speak English," I say, crossing my arms.

He ignores my comment. "I learn human speak, little bit. Human no safe here. Get taken and imprisoned by dark races. Some say killed."

"How nice," Amir mutters. "Just what I want to hear."

Dad is staring hard at the elf. They lock eyes for a profoundly uncomfortable length of time before Dad speaks.

"Why do the dark races want humans so badly?"

The elf points a blue-skinned finger at me.

"Because of them. After blood pact, after halflings were made, the dark races—jealous. Wanting halflings of their own. I expect they take from anger. To punish," the elf says.

To say he was good at English would be an overstatement. I mean, he was doing pretty good, for an elf. I'm not exactly a language teacher, but he gets an A for saying things that are understandable.

"No matter, discuss with elf king. We here," the elf says.

Dad's next words die on his lips as the elf leads us into a clearing. The blaring sun above shines downward onto a wide, grassy space. Each long blade of grass points upward toward the blue sky, not moving a smidge. The stillness is so unnatural that I tilt my head to the side to look at it differently. When I do, the whole thing goes fuzzy, like I've just gone underwater. I blink, and it looks the same.

What's even more mind-numbing is the fact that I can feel a breeze. We're deep in the forest, but I can still sense a cool bit of wind blowing through the trunks and branches around us. Even the leaves rustle here and there. It feels amazing on the sweat that cakes my skin. But the grass is so still.

"Dude, that's freaky," Amir says. "Why isn't it moving?"

I shake my head at his brazen question, but to be honest, I'm glad he asked. I didn't want to sound stupid asking.

The elf fixes Amir with a disapproving expression. "Fool human. It's magic."

Amir nods, then gulps. "Oh, okay. Yeah, makes sense."

His voice sounds feeble next to a nine-foot-tall, muscled blue elf.

"Where are we?" I ask, looking up at him.

"The path to elf capital," he replies, looking at me like I'm a fool.

We all stare at the field.

It's at that moment when Jared speaks up.

"There's nothing there."

The elf closest to me grunts, then fixes Jared with a flat stare.

"I sense fairy blood in you. Can you not sense the magic of your heritage? Are you so lost from your family that you have forgotten this? Is human blood too strong?"

When he finishes, Jared looks ashamed. The secondhand embarrassment that emanates from him is so intense that I want to shrivel away myself, but when I take a moment to reflect on it, my chest burns. I don't know why, but I glance at Krista, and I see the same sentiment in her eyes.

We both turn toward the elf, opening our mouths to speak, but I let Krista. She wouldn't take it well if I spoke over her.

"You think we *chose* to be sent away from Qotan? You think we *wanted* to leave this place? None of us wanted this. None of us even knows anything about our so-called heritage or what that means. So you can shut your mouth," Krista snarls.

I squirm next to her as I note her body growing. Her arms get thicker and more purple. Whatever I was going to say would sound dumb after her tirade, so I just glare at the elf. I have no idea why I'm so protective over Jared. Perhaps it's because he saved Gobby.

The blood drains from my face.

Everything has been happening so fast. With my friends slowly coming to join us, I didn't think about the small goblin. Krista looks like she's about to tear off the elf's face. The other elves around us tense, holding up spears and bows in preparation to skewer her. But I can't think about that. I throw my hand out in front of her to stop her.

No one was expecting this, for they all pause, their gazes falling on me.

"Where is Gobby?" I ask with a measured tone.

With their previous talk about the dark races, I know inside that something bad has happened. The elf stares at me with a fuming expression.

"Gobby? I know this word not," he says.

This shouldn't annoy me, but it does.

"The goblin, where is he?"

The elf grins with understanding.

"Ah, the pet goblin. We take him to sacrifice to the forest. They like sacrifice, eat flesh of enemies freely," he says.

I don't think. Instead, I move my hand away from Krista and let the intensity of my anger burn bright. I stoke up the heat inside my chest, letting it flow to my palm where a flame explodes. The elf's expression goes from smugness to surprise to fear.

"You will not sacrifice Gobby," I say.

The tension in the air grows. The elves around us draw their weapons and point them at us. I feel Dad's back press up against mine. Jared put his back to mine, too. And Amir is on the other side of Krista, where I can't fully see him.

"Stop nonsense," the wizened elf says. "Halflings and elves should no fight. Bad for harmony. Weapons away, now."

There is a ripple of something in the air, like his words carry an enormous weight. It washes over me like the sigh of a massive beast, and I can't help but relax, my fire going out. Krista relaxes as well, her body shrinking back to her normal self. I'm glad to see that the effect reaches the elves, too, their drawn weapons tipping downward toward the ground.

When the wizened elf speaks next, I can tell his voice has changed. For one, his speech becomes more eloquent and smooth—and second, my friends seem confused.

"It is unwise for any light race to fight with the true heirs of their kingdom. You may be half humans, but your royal blood puts you higher than us," he explains. "We have a duty to get you to safety."

I did not expect to hear this after being drugged, dragged, and yelled at. At what point were they going to tell us about the "higher than them" thing? Here I was thinking we were swine, impure somehow for being half human, half—well, whatever we were.

"We will proceed; translate for your friends, then follow. Our time will grow short rapidly," he says.

To my utter shock, I watch as he steps out of the tree line toward the unmoving field of grass and disappears. There's no flash of light and no noise. He's just . . . gone.

Amir's mouth hangs open. "What in the—what just happened? Did that blue dude just disappear?"

"Either that or this is all just a dream," Jared says. It sounds almost hopeful, but we all know it's not.

I tell them what he said, but it's hard to focus as elves left and right move toward the strange open field, each disappearing as if they were never there at all. The one elf I'd almost burned to death glares at me, then steps forward. He's the last to disappear.

"I think," Dad says behind me, "this is some sort of test. If they genuinely expect you are royal-blooded, they must realize they can't hold you captive."

I grind my teeth. "But they have Gobby captive."

It drives me nuts that I haven't seen him still.

"Let's get a move on, then, or the blue idiots are going to leave us behind," Krista says rigidly before walking toward the field. As with the others, she's gone in the blink of an eye.

I feel my dad's hand on my shoulder, and he squeezes it.

"Gobby will be fine, I'm sure. Shall we?" He nods toward the wall right as Jared and Amir go through at the same time.

"Not much else to do," I say. "We can't go back."

With that, we walk toward the field.

AMIR LOSES HIS LATE-NIGHT SNACK

Okay, have you ever taken an ice bath? Great. Have you ever taken an ice bath that's invisible and about ten times colder?

That's what this felt like. I gasp as my whole body drops way too many degrees below what I'm guessing is healthy. It's so unpleasant that my throat closes up, and I can't breathe. The only fortunate thing about it is that it only lasts a few seconds.

Still, in those few seconds, I expect I know what death feels like.

Dad and I stumble out of the magical coldness, and I fall to my knees.

"That was—awful," he says, bending over and putting his hands on his thighs.

Amir lays on the ground next to me, breathing hard. Jared appears to have disappeared. I'm worried for a second until I notice a cat sitting next to Amir, licking its body frantically.

"Don't be so dramatic," Krista says, rolling her eyes. "It wasn't that bad."

Jared, the cat, grows rapidly until the large boy is perched on his toes, his face twisted in pain.

"Not all of us are immune to temperature changes like you," Jared complains. "I'm beginning to think I drew the short end of the stick with my heritage. Fairy blood is not as useful."

"No speak poorly of bloodline," the wizened elf says, appearing out of nowhere. "Light race blood is sacred, pure for all. Fairies made portal for us elves for protection."

His face scrunches in disgust, then he speaks again. "English is too unwieldy for my tongue. You will translate for your comrades," he says, looking directly at me. "You are a dragon blessed by nature."

The reminder doesn't please me. If I'd known my dragon heritage destined me for translation, maybe I'd have been less curious about coming here. I sit up straight, ready to convey whatever he is going to say to my friends when my mouth goes dry. The forest is gone. I spin, my eyes wide as I search for the thick trees and brush. There's a thicket far away to my right, but there is only a vast plain on the other side and behind me. Reflected sun from the blue ground makes me wince in pain.

No, not blue ground, a sea. It churns wildly as if being buffeted by a storm. Then I notice the wind, and my brain has all sorts of trouble catching up to the situation. We are very clearly not where we were a minute ago.

"Fairies have travel magic. As such, they created this portal, among others, to guide us to the borders of the forest and sea, where the regions of light races reach. Only those of elven blood can use this specific one," he says.

I scowl. "But we just came through it."

He glowers at me, unbothered by my comment. "With our permission. We are a day's journey from the elven city. On foot, it will take too long. You ride your beasts."

The elf gestures with his hand toward the blank air. I watch, my mouth ajar, not understanding what he means, when suddenly my vision is filled with red. It takes my mind a moment to register what they are, but a wash of jubilant happiness brings me to reality. The crelotins, all five of them, appear out of thin air. While I relay the information to my friends, three elves, two women, and a man bring the crelotins toward us, their hands wrapped firmly around the tentacles of the beasts. It seems odd to see these animals and not be terrified, but I'm actually relieved.

I move to the crelotin furthest from me, knowing which one is mine—or rather, the one I rode—and stroke the front of its snout. The rough exoskeleton catches at my fingertips. My friends do the same thing. As I stare into the beast's eyes, I know that it trusts me. It gives me conflicting feelings of rightness and wrongness.

"Now that you are bonded with the creatures, travel should be brief. Come," the elf says.

I turn toward him, then frown. "Where are your horses? Or, whatever you ride?"

The elf smiles, his shining white teeth bright in the sunlight.

"Elves have no need for mounts. Your crelotins will have plenty of challenge trying to keep up with us. Mount and follow."

After I convey the message to my friends, and after another moment of boosting Amir onto his mount, everyone is on their crelotin ready to go. Except for me.

"Where is the goblin?" I ask firmly.

The elf looks at me, surprised, but doesn't answer.

"I won't leave until you tell me that he's okay."

His eyes harden and his mouth presses thin, making his wrinkles smooth out along his chin and cheeks.

"Very well, look there," he says, pointing with his staff. I turn to see a group of leanly muscled elves, their blue skin taut and thick. They walk in a circle. Five of them hold their hands inward like they are carrying a casket, and my stomach sinks when I see it. They told me that Gobby was okay, but they've killed him. I know they must have because why else would they carry him like that?

When I catch a glimpse of the box, I realize it's not a casket at all, but more of a cage made from tree roots pressed close together. Glowing red eyes peek out at me, sad and rage-filled.

"Are you kidding me? What is wrong with you?" I shout, leaving the side of my crelotin and rushing over toward the elves. They all tense, four out of the five drawing wicked-looking daggers that glow with a strange light. I should be scared by this, but I'm not. If these elves are allies with me, they won't attack me, right?

My doubt must be apparent as I near them. One of the elves raises his weapon to strike me. I curse, digging my foot into the ground like a baseball player until I skid to a stop.

"Let him out of there!" I shout at them.

They stare at me, various shades of irises scrutinizing me. I gulp. If it came to a fight, I'd get pounded like a little kid. The four elves hold their weapons steady.

"Halt! What is the meaning of this?" the leader elf says. I keep my eyes on the group, particularly the one at the front. Movement next to me makes me flinch, but when I glance that way, I realize it's Dad. Similarly, someone comes to my left.

I'm floored when I see that it's Krista.

Is she standing *with* me?

I decide not to let that get to me because the shock of it might break my concentration.

"Gobby is a friend. He doesn't deserve to be in that cage. Let him out!" I say.

No one moves, which is unsurprising. They seem confused more than anything. I think for a moment my translation powers aren't working, but then they all start glancing at each other. The ancient elf comes up next to us. The sunlight shines right on his face from this angle, and I'm struck by how old he looks. His hands are curled and gnarly, cavernous wrinkles everywhere.

"The goblin cannot be released. It is the nature of his race, the blood in his veins. If we release him, he will attack. It is their way," he says with a measured expression.

"*Nature?* That little guy saved our lives. He's the very reason that the goblin army didn't catch us until the forest. Did you think of that?" I say, exasperated.

The elves still wear confused expressions. Either they don't understand my words or they think I'm a lunatic. After the day I've had, I expect the latter is more likely. Finally, after too long of a silence for my liking, the elf in front speaks. His eyes are a light red color, which makes me shiver at the oddity.

"What say you, Sage? Shall we kill the green pest to assuage our revenge?"

My jaw falls open.

"Don't you dare even think about it!"

I move forward without thinking, holding my palm open and conjuring fire. It blazes on my hand so hot that I can feel the oppressive heat on my cheeks and brow. I recall moments as a kid, sitting by the fire, the same heat teasing my flesh and making me curious what would happen if I stuck my hand inside. It seems strange now that I know nothing would have happened.

"Peace, young dragon. I have no desire to kill your pet goblin, but I cannot allow him to roam free. He will stay within the cage until our magic weavers can assess his mind," the sage responds.

I fume, the fire within me stoking as if I added loads of fuel to it.

"Yeah, no, that's not what we're doing. You are going to let him go before we keep moving."

My impetuousness may very well get us killed, but I'm adamant. Gobby does not deserve this treatment, not after helping us escape and using his magic to conceal us. Before I can continue to explain this, the elf in front of me swipes his weapon downward. It happens so fast that I don't have a chance to defend myself. Fortunately, the scales work this time, and the strange glowing blade smacks into my forehead, knocking me back a little. I stumble and put my free hand to my head. Fortunately, there's no blood.

I growl and throw my flaming hand outward, the fire washing over the elf and his bare skin. He howls in pain and jumps backward, his sword falling to the ground at my feet.

"I said *peace*," the sage commands. A wave of forced calmness rushes over me, and I shudder. I suddenly have the desire to hide behind someone and get away from the power.

"Trevil," the sage continues. "Tend to our brother. Dragon boy, you will desist from attacking those who saved you from certain demise. The goblin remains in his cage, and—"

I'm only half listening to this guy because, despite the artificial feelings that are being pressed into my mind, I'm still fuming. My brain, during this fit, has locked onto the fact that dragons are the highest rulers and that my mother is the high queen. Pushing my chest outward to make myself seem bigger than I actually am, I interrupt the sage.

"I command you, as the dragon high blood prince, to release the goblin."

The silence that follows is so piercing that I almost run away from the awkwardness. My comment seems like a long shot, and now that I've said the words, I can't stop the heat from rushing to my face. I think of all those kids I made fun of in school alongside my fellow football team members: the nerds, making fools of themselves with their cardboard swords and shields. Now I wonder if they are the smart ones. I wish I'd listened to them and learned about the lore of their stories and role-playing campaigns. I'm out of my league here. Amir had invited me more than once to join a campaign, but I often ended that idea with a derogatory statement. Shame from my past comments creeps in along with the uncomfortable silence.

Finally, the sage's angry expression melts away after he bores into my soul with those terrifyingly white irises.

"Very well," he says.

That is *not* the reaction I was expecting.

"You carry the blood of the Dragon Queen Ellistra, after all. This I cannot contest," he says, waving his staff so the elves surrounding the cage with Gobby back away.

"Wow, that actually worked," I whisper. It's supposed to be only to myself, but Dad hears me and nudges my arm. And unfortunately, the sage does, too. He spins toward me, his face full of something. It's not quite anger or annoyance, but something in the middle.

"You may be the high prince of this realm, but you won't be able to call on your bloodline for everything. In this, I concede, but do not trust that you can command us, especially not when we reach Terendrell."

At first, I'm not sure what that word means, and I tap the side of my head, trying to get my translator brain to tell me the English equivalent. When it doesn't, I connect the dots that it's the name of an elven city. Dad leans in next to me and speaks from the side of his mouth.

"What's happening? What did you do to them? They look furious," he asks.

Right. That was all in a different language. I relay it quickly for him, and he stifles a laugh.

"Now I understand why you said you couldn't believe that worked."

His shoulders bounce up and down in mirth, and this only makes me more embarrassed. Now my own dad thinks I'm ridiculous. I don't bother trying to be modest about it as I walk up to Gobby's cage and slam my hand down on the side. The plants are surprisingly strong and wet, as if they just grew out of nowhere and formed the box. This seems like a normal day activity for the elves. "Oh, let's just make a magic box of plants! Okay, boom, it's done." Flaring the heat in my palm, it bursts into flames and sears a hole in the top of the cage. Gobby cries out in fear, but I pull my hand away and wave it to get his attention.

His glowing deep red eyes fixate on me, and I nod, holding my hand out to him.

"You're free. Come out of there," I say.

A few of the elves gasp as they hear me talk to him. They just heard me speak Goblish. Gobby takes my hand, and I pull him out, once again surprised at his body's density. He's no lightweight.

"Thank you, Master. Your kindness is appreciated," he says, bowing.

I pull a disgusted face. "Gross, don't call me that. You're a friend. Just call me a friend."

Gobby's eyes widen, and he looks at the ground. "If you say so, friend."

By now, the rest of the elves have pulled away from us. Many of them have their weapons drawn as if this little guy were going to stab me in the heart. And yet, I feel completely at ease with him.

"Come, nightfall will be upon us faster than we think," the sage says. I nod, then gesture for Gobby to follow. I let him ride with me this time, apologizing with my mind to the crelotin. The beast sends a wave of annoyance and also pride at my decision to let the goblin ride with me. I get the sense that she wants to prove herself.

By the time I'm mounted, I glance over to the sage and raise my eyebrows.

"Follow, beasts, as you can. If you trail behind, do not despair. Follow our emotions in the distance," he says.

Then he disappears. I blink, looking around for him. I catch a glimpse of his robe flickering in the sunlight, but it's already a hundred yards away in a few seconds. Before I can even exclaim at how fast he's running, my crelotin jumps to motion, and I yelp, grasping for its tentacles to keep from falling off. Gobby lets out a cry of delight, the other crelotins following behind. Amir looks green, like he's about to lose the delicious plant-based meal of the previous night. Jared looks like he's having the time of his life. Naturally, when I think of him, he looks at me, knowing that he's on my mind. He throws his hands backward and enjoys the wind.

Of course someone who can probably turn *into* one of these things would be having a good time. Krista has the same disgruntled expression of determination on her face. She holds fast to the tentacles of her crelotin, and while I sense a bit of confidence in her, there is a little apprehension. Dad? He looks like a complete natural. He moves with the crelotin as if it were part of him. Years and years of breeding and training horses will do that to you.

I'm shocked that our mounts can move this quickly, and I wonder why Gobby never mentioned it. That thought is soon lost as we approach one of the elves. He looks determined, his arms jerking forward and backward as he presses over the wide-open plain. He doesn't seem to be breaking a sweat. Given that I know nothing about elves, except for what I've seen, I half expect them to be incapable of sweating. At that moment, I think I should probably learn more about them.

Probably unimportant.

Our breakneck speed continues for way longer than I expect, the plain covering most of the ground we move through. I steal glances at the tree line to my right and wonder what part of the forest we were in before we went through the strange portal. Though we are moving at a wild pace, I can still see the leaves blowing in the breeze. Animals dart in and out of the trunks moving in the same direction as us. A deer slips out, bounding across the wide, grassy plain parallel to my crelotin, but it soon falls back as my mount presses forward. As it disappears, a mountain lion or other kind of cat—I don't know what exactly—comes out of the forest and does the same thing.

I'm amazed, and I'm glad for something to watch other than the boring view of the plains and sea to my left. Trust me, I spend plenty of time watching that, but you can only stare at the shiny blue-green water for so long. We travel for hours when suddenly my crelotin slows so fast that I almost fly forward off its back. My body presses up against Gobby, who lets out a surprised grunt.

"Humans are heavier than they appear," he grumbles.

I mumble an apology, then look around to determine what's happening. My friends have all stopped as well. A scattering of blue-skinned elves walks in measured paces around us, and I'm filled with a wash of exhaustion and relief, emotions that come from my crelotin. I pat her back, saying something reassuring but knowing that she might not understand.

"My behind is raw," Gobby says gruffly, reaching to rub a spot on his lower back. I stifle a laugh, but that doesn't last long before I shift on the exoskeleton back and wince.

"Oh my," I say, leaning side to side, grunting in pain. "Me, too."

I hear retching to my right and turn to see that Amir has finally let go of the meager meal from last night. An elf materializes out of nowhere on the other side of my friend, and I jump. He says nothing but holds out his hand, the skin of his palms lighter blue than the rest of his body. There's something green there. It's a leaf of some sort.

"For sick. It helps," he says in English.

Amir coughs, wiping his mouth on his sleeve. He takes the leaf. "Okay—what do you want me—"

"Chew. Eat. Is simple," the elf says.

He watches Amir with a serious gaze, and when Amir doesn't do what he's told immediately, the elf's eyebrows shoot up. He waves his hands in front of him. It's not a gesture I'm familiar with, but at the same time, it gives distinct "hurry up" vibes.

"If this makes me throw up, I'm aiming it at you," Amir says.

The elf scrunches his nose, but it seems like it's because he doesn't understand Amir's words, not the idea of vomit hitting his face. After a long grimace, Amir pops the leaf in his mouth and chews it. He gags once. He works the leaf in his mouth before swallowing hard. All at once, his face relaxes, and he sighs, letting out a small chuckle.

"Well, I'll be. That actually worked!" he exclaims.

The elf nods, then walks away, not saying anything else.

"Gee, our company is enjoyable, isn't it?" Krista murmurs.

The irony of her, of all people, complaining about our companions is not lost on me.

Before I can say something snooty and off base about her not being fun to travel with either, Jared speaks up.

"I'm definitely flying the next leg," he says, wincing as he shifts on his mount's back. "Then Gobby can use my crelotin and give yours a break."

My crelotin impresses disappointment at the idea, but it's mingled with a measure of relief.

Amir spins on Jared, an expression of intrigue on his face.

"Okay, but was it like—hard to learn to fly? Or did you have to learn like a baby bird?"

I roll my eyes. My inquisitive friend is back, so I can't complain. Poor guy has had a rough go.

The two launch into a spirited conversation about Jared having to learn various things as different animals, but my attention soon drifts away. I'm distracted by an exchange of a couple of elves to my right. They steal glances at me, whispering something to each other. I can't tell what they are saying because they are too far away from me, but it seems shady. I spot a flicker of metal that looks like money pass between their hands.

They must be making a bet about me. Just David, your usual failure-of-a-dragon pulling on his bloodline to make commands. Too bad I can't defend myself against some toxic darts. Heat rushes into my chest and face, and I have to focus to keep my cool.

"Count to ten," Krista says next to me.

"What?" I say, turning toward her.

She's not looking at me but instead faces forward. Her jaw is hard, and she's obviously holding something back. Jared talked about her experiencing an unnecessary amount of rage by being a half demon, but I still wonder if that's an excuse for her to be a jerk and get away with it. Though, I have to say, she never looks happy. The few times I've seen her smile, they were never freeing smiles. Mostly vindictive, slightly amused smiles.

"Counting to ten helps me from losing myself to the anger. I can tell you're pissed. Before you go all living flame on them, count to ten," she says.

I fold my arms and shake my head.

"I'm not mad about anything. I'm just tired of riding this crelotin."

She scoffs. "Yeah, okay, dragon boy. Keep telling yourself that."

It bothers me that she can tell I'm angry, but I want to save face, so I shrug and don't continue the conversation. Concentrating on calming myself down, I face forward and try to act as aloof as she is.

"Fine, the next time I get angry, I'll give it a go," I say.

All the while, my mind starts counting down. Jared glances at me, his mouth pressed in a tight lip of hidden amusement, but I glare at him. I hate that he knows I'm lying. So much for trying to keep my cool.

"You aren't the only target of their ridicule, you know," Krista says. "They hate me. My demon blood is a problem for them."

I frown. She's still not looking at me, and that annoys me a bit.

"What are you talking about? They respect you because you can go all she-monster on them. I'm pretty sure you could hold your own against a few of them. Me? Not so much," I say.

This time, she laughs. My heart skips a beat, my eyes widening slightly. She flips her fiery-red hair over her shoulder, the sunlight catching in it as it waves in the wind. I'm both shocked and mesmerized by the sound of her laughter. It's an unnatural and entrancing thing.

"Dude, get your head out of your butt and look around," she says.

I do, and I know exactly what she means. The elves that were formerly talking about me now shoot angry glances at her every few moments. I scan the field around us and discover that many of the other elves are doing the same thing. Emanating hatred. They hate her.

"What's that about?" I ask.

She shrugs. "Demons were once aligned with the dark races."

My mouth falls open.

"Wait, are you *serious*? Your dad is a bad guy?" I pause to ensure that I'm getting her parentage right.

Her jaw stiffens. "*Was*. Krell, the king of the demon race. Big purple veins, red hair. You won't be able to miss him if you spot him."

I get where she gets her demon form from.

"I'm sorry," I say. It is a weak apology, but what the heck am I supposed to say to that?

She brushes it off. "I didn't get to choose my parentage, so I can't complain. Every time I get too angry about it, I lose control. Mom's been scared enough of me before, and I've broken a lot of things in my lifetime. Only once did I accidentally hurt her." There's a flash of pain in her eyes before it disappears. "I don't lose it anymore."

I frown, wondering what happened, but I'm not brave enough to ask. Based on the situations we've been in, I kind of don't believe her about the "I don't lose it anymore" part. But hey, she knows herself better than I do. I have so many questions about her, about demons, and about how they were made part of the light races, but my thoughts are interrupted as Dad's crelotin slides between Amir and me. He had pulled ahead a bit ago to talk to the sage elf, and the look on his face suggests that he has an update.

"We should arrive in a couple hours," he says. "I have to say, I'm glad the elves speak some amount of English. Hearing them speak their language is stressing me out. I never bothered learning their dialects, only dragon. Though I'm rusty with that."

I gape at him. "You *speak* dragon? Please tell me you are making that up."

He shakes his head before letting out a chuckle. "No, I learned it from your mother. She speaks English very well, but I learned her language to draw us closer."

"You have to be lying about that. Dragon isn't a language. What is it, a bunch of roars and growls?" I joke, turning to study Krista. I don't know why I do it. I guess it's because repeated traumatic experiences bond us, in a way. I'm not disappointed when she cracks a smile. She should do that more often.

"See? You can't understand—my letters—no—words when I speak," Dad says.

I furrow my brow.

"What? Why are you talking like that?" I say.

"Woah, Mr. Johnson, that was wild!" Amir says. His attention snaps to Dad so fast, and he looks amazed.

"Wait, what did I miss? You sounded like you forgot how to speak English," I say.

Dad bites his lip like he's holding back a laugh.

"I guess your translation powers don't let you hear what I said. I spoke Dragonese."

I groan. "Oh, come on! I find out my dad speaks some fantasy-land language, and I can't even *hear* him do it? This world is cruel."

Dad laughs, and Amir joins in. Gobby shakes his head in front of me, and I grasp his shoulder, asking him what's wrong. He speaks back over the laughter in his gravelly tone.

"Humans laugh too much. It's weird," he says.

This makes me bust up even more. A few of the elves keep glancing over at us, and I'm positive they think we are insane. I'll have to ask Jared if he has any idea what they are expecting, though more than likely their thoughts aren't in English, so he probably can't understand them.

An elf about thirty paces in front of me collapses suddenly, and my laughter dies. I furrow my brow, trying to understand why he fell over, when another elf ten paces away from him collapses too, a shaft of something protruding from her back.

Something half naked, buff, and very green materializes in the air in front of the elf who fell over.

THE DISAPPEARING ORCS

I don't have a chance to process what I'm seeing before I hear Dad shout a warning to me.

"David, get down!" he yells. I'm too focused on the green-skinned figure. He has the shape of a man—a muscular dude—but his teeth look all messed up. I could be wrong, but I'm pretty sure I only count four fingers on each hand. I don't stare much longer before a few more figures—green, shirtless, and also buff—appear out of nowhere scattered around in the field.

"David—"

The left side of my face meets the ground, cutting off Dad's words. When I hit the hard earth, I'm not prepared for the pain that lances up my cheekbone and through my arm. My left leg erupts in agony as something heavy crushes it.

The crelotin's body is on top of me. I feel a rush of panic press into my whole body, making me want to jump up and run away, but then it shifts to anger and frustration.

I groan, trying to cope with the beast's emotions as they flow through my mind. I know they aren't mine and that I should be feeling intense pain and confusion, but I'm being fed a different message from the beast. When the crelotin scrambles to its feet, my leg is ground into the earth and my vision swims. I wonder if I'll pass out and die from an orc's axe to the head, but the pain is over, a dull numbness left in my leg.

Things and people move around me at a rapid pace, but I can't see as well from where I am in the tall grass. Elves shout, and I hear Krista scream something before her voice gets quieter as if she were running away. Testing my leg, I try to lift it, but it falls back to the ground. The pain makes my vision blur. Something snags my arm, and I try to pull away. My fight instinct is ramping up as I open my hand, the flame already there.

"Stop! I won't hurt you! I will help!" the gravelly voice shouts.

I sigh in relief, knowing it's not one of the orcs coming to stab me to death. It's Gobby. He's tugging on my arm, trying to pull me up. His grip feels like a child attempting to tug their father up off the ground. That, but their dad is a ninety-year-old man who can't feel his leg anymore.

I let the fire go out in my hand and roll over to push hard against the earth. The moment I do, the pain from my leg washes over me once more and my vision spots.

I curse, turning to see my lifeless leg.

"I will use magic," Gobby says, then lifts his finger, placing it on my temple. His skin is a lot rougher than I thought it would be, like his fingertips are made of heavy, thick ridges of hard stone. He mutters something that my dragon blood apparently doesn't know how to translate. It sounds like "Rickter mortom cragletomp." The moment he finishes, a warm feeling pools in my head, and the pain vanishes from my leg.

"You can *heal*, and you kept that to yourself?" I say, lifting my leg.

He frowns, shaking his head. "Not healed. It's only temporary, I tricked your mind into— augh!"

An arrow hits the ground near us, and he yelps, pulling more vigorously on my arm until I'm standing. When I get my feet under me, I wobble a little, noting that my left leg feels weak, like I haven't exercised it for a very long time. My knee is bent at the wrong angle, and the sight of it turns my stomach.

It's probably better to look away.

Sounds of fighting echo in the waning daylight, elves thrusting their curved blades outward and slashing at the orcs.

I rack my brain to recall my last experience with orcs. They were some of the things that attacked us at the homecoming game back home.

This thought tugs at my gut, and I bend over at the strength of the pull. My chest constricts and tears well in my eyes. Shaking my head, I lift myself back up to see Gobby staring at me, hands fidgeting in front of him. The powerful tug disappears as quickly as it started, and I lock my jaw. I've never been homesick, but I wonder if that's what the sensation was. It's hard to get homesick when you never leave home. Vacations? Rarely. Sleepovers? Definitely not. Dad kept me close to the home base. For a good reason, don't get me wrong. Still, I do wonder if I've missed childhood to some degree.

"My spell will wear off soon. We must hurry to the trees to hide. The orcs are coming fast!" Gobby says, tugging on my arm and gesturing wildly to the tree line.

"No—I have to—fight them," I say, turning to watch as an elf slams the side of his blade into the face of a green man. I lick my lips, adrenaline coursing through me. Minor battles are being won and lost all over the place. Another arrow wizzes past my head, and I grunt, leaning back, the shooter narrowly missing me.

Scanning my surroundings, I see an orc draw a bowstring back, a black arrow fitted on the string. He's aiming at me and Gobby. I clench my teeth as he glares at me over his green hand, a crooked smile visible just beneath. I don't let him get his shot off. Instead, I summon a flame and throw it forward, like a football going long. It launches from my palm toward the orc, making him shriek as my death fireball comes at him. I miss so badly that I call into question my high school football career, but it manages to land about four feet from him. Then it explodes, flames engulfing the dried grass next to him. He releases the arrow, which flies far off to my left. He never gets to nock another arrow as an elf woman leaps upon him, a curved blade out and ready. She slices downward and he's dead in one blow.

"Where did they come from?" I ask Gobby.

The small goblin shivers, his hands covering the top of his head as he cowers in fear. "They are orcs, sent by Urothar, the k-k-king. I know not how they found us."

Urothar? Man, that guy drew the short end of the name stick, but at least I know who Gobby is talking about. The orc king. The very person who wants to capture me and the others. The bad guy. He's the one who needs to die in these fantasy books, right? I'm regretting telling Amir no every time he tried to get me to read those nerdy books with him.

Amir.

"Amir!" I shout.

Of all the people in this group, he's the least likely to battle with one of these orcs. He was standing right next to me when I got knocked over. I still don't know what knocked over my crelotin in the first place, but I can feel her off to my left. She's stamping her feet and sending out waves of intimidation toward the orcs. They cower in front of her, overcome by the emotions.

"Amir!"

I stop yelling when I spot him. His arms flail over his head as his crelotin spins in circles, kicking outward at the orcs. I grit my teeth and run toward him. My gait is uneven and feels wrong, but I don't have time to linger on it.

An orc with long black hair snags Amir's foot and drags him off of the mount. His scream reaches my ears as if I were standing right next to him. The orc lifts him off the ground by his arms and drags him away.

I don't think, I just act. Tossing a ball of flame outward, I smack the orc right in the chest. His chain mail shirt isn't affected, but the cloth shirt underneath lights on fire, and the creature howls in pain, swatting at the licking flames.

When I reach the orc, he is too distracted to notice. I bellow a fighting shout, channeling my inner offensive football player, and run my shoulder right into his sternum. My shoulder cracks, then dislocates. I feel I'm going to throw up, but I push past the pain as the orc sputters and tries to right itself.

I search around frantically for something to fight with, but there's only grass. The orc spins on me, grinning with his crooked and yellowing teeth. Two canines protrude upward a couple of inches. I turn on him and blast him with my flames, and he screams as he dies.

Energy flows from me, my legs threatening to buckle underneath me. I'm forced to shake my head to restore lucidity to my mind.

I bite my tongue, holding back the terror and fear of what I've just done. I'm not a violent person; I never have been. I've just killed an orc, and a pit forms in my stomach. I try to reason away the pit, telling myself they are a dark race and that it's okay. They're bad, right? And I'm defending my friends and family.

The pit doesn't go away.

"The spell isn't lasting! Be careful!" Gobby says. I didn't realize he'd followed me, and based on the way his whole body quivers, I suspect he regrets it.

"What do you mean?" I ask, but then it hits. My left leg goes numb with pain, and I gasp, collapsing to the ground. My vision swims yet again, then blurs. When I examine it, I notice the slight bend of my knee. It feels broken once more.

I spin on Gobby, expecting him to be holding a knife, ready to plunge it into my face after having lied to me about fixing my leg, but he simply stands there wringing his hands together.

"I told you, take care. My spell only tricks the brain. It hides pain. It doesn't heal you," he says.

I try to ask something else, but a hand on my arm pulls my attention away.

"Dave, what is going on?" Amir asks, his face pale.

"Ambush! We need to get to the trees!" I shout over the tumult.

Amir follows my finger, then nods. He pushes himself up to his feet and reaches out to the crelotin, which somehow still stands tall, regal, and unafraid.

"I can't get on it again!" Amir says, trying to mount. I frown, then turn to Gobby.

"Do it again," I command.

He shakes his head. "No. You are just a dragonling, and you might not recover if you push on a broken leg."

I don't have time for this. I grab him, snagging his shirt and raising him up. Despite his density I can still lift him.

"Do it *now!*" I say, my tone forcing fear into his eyes.

He mutters the thing again, pressing his finger to my temple, and the pain is gone in a flash. I sigh, then stand up, noting the weakness of my leg. Amir leads his mount forward; Gobby and I follow close behind. I'm hobbling like a wizened old man as the others fight. Real hero, aren't I?

In the distance, Krista shouts as she tugs on the head of an orc. He falls to the ground, unmoving. Another three come at her with spears and crude iron swords slashing. She bats them away, one of them losing his weapon. The other two hold fast, pressing Krista away with joined effort. She falls back, rage in her eyes, when someone else comes shouting from behind.

Dad rushes the remaining orcs, swinging one of his swords and slamming it into the helmet of an enemy. He's down in a second. Taking advantage of the break, Krista swings a fist, knocking another orc unconscious.

A gigantic eagle swoops in from somewhere above, snatching two orcs in its massive talons and flying upward. I can only assume it's Jared. My mouth gapes as I watch him fly high above, dragging the screaming creatures until he opens his talons. They fall, flailing and screaming. Loud thuds litter the earth. I wince, turning and hobbling after the other two. We reach the cover of the trees faster than I expect, my eyes taking mere seconds to adjust to the darkness within.

"Now what?" Amir says. I feel his arm press up against mine, shuddering. I want to put my arm around his shoulders and tell him it's all going to be all right, but I don't know that. Instead, I grab his hand and squeeze it.

"We'll figure this out, trust me," I say. "Let's move deeper so they can't see us. Let the others do their work."

Even as the words leave my mouth, I shake my head. The knowledge that the other half bloods and my dad are out there battling for their lives alongside the elves, and that I'm hiding in the forest, makes me want to kick a tree. So I do. My football cleat thumps against the nearest trunk. I regret the action as pain lances up my toes into my calf.

"Ohhhhhh!" I groan. The action somehow breaks Gobby's spell and the pain of my messed up leg rushes back in. I collapse against the tree that was the target of my ire.

"Dave! What happened?" Amir asks in a shaking voice.

I hold up my hand to stop him. He pauses, frowning. That's a good sign. His eyes are adjusting to the lack of light. It will be easier if we can both see in the dim. I figure my dragon blood enhances my eyes, so seeing in the dark isn't a problem for me.

"Just—being dumb," I grimace. I turn to Gobby. His eyes glow in the darkness, and I can't help but shudder. He looks like he's from a horror movie.

"I need—the pain gone—again," I say, panting.

Gobby's eyes flicker left and right, a clear sign of him shaking his head.

"No. If you ignore the pain too long you could cause lasting damage. It is a *mind* trick. I only *make* your mind think there's no pain, but the injury is still there," he says.

I know he has a point, so I grit my teeth and unfold my upper body from my legs.

"Fine, we still need to move," I say, hobbling forward.

I know I should probably jump on the crelotin—riding seems logical—but my instincts warn that it'll make me an easier target for an arrow. Staying low seems the best course for the moment.

My gait hasn't changed, but at least my mind understands *why* I'm hobbling now. I thought I had a broken leg, but it doesn't hurt as much as I expected. I send a prayer of thanks above, then focus on the task at hand. Amir pats the side of his crelotin, and the slapping sound against the hard exoskeleton is dampened by the thick brush and canopy above.

The fighting sounds fall away, but not completely. We stop when they are quiet enough to not feel like we'll become pincushions for arrows. Even though we're not far enough that we can't see some action, trees and brush veil most of the battle. What I *can* see feels like a flip book: figures dance in and out of view between the overlapping tree trunks. Thinking about it that way makes me chuckle.

Amir nudges me. "Have you gone insane? They're going to kill your dad and the others. What are you laughing about?"

I hadn't considered that . . .

I fix Amir with a hard stare. "They'll be fine." *They got trained as kids.*

I don't say the last part. Amir doesn't deserve the frustration. He doesn't deserve the angst or the regret. In all honesty, I'm not sure Dad deserves it either, but I can't help it. Since taking me from Qotan, he'd known all these years that I might have to come back and fight—or that we'd be attacked someday and I might need to defend myself. I'm breathing hard now. The thoughts rushing through my mind are inducing a stress response.

"Umm, Dave, can you *not* light the forest on fire?" Amir says.

I flinch, realizing that my hand is as hot as an iron. A flame engulfs it. The closest leaves to my small inferno have shriveled and curled in on themselves. I also smell burning fiber. I've singed my football pants. I curse and close my hand, the flame going out.

Gobby watches me. I can tell he's terrified. He may even be wondering when I'll decide that he's no longer of use and fry him. The thought is horrid, and the betrayal would be deep. I won't do that.

"Gobby, stop—"

He shakes his head, a murderous look in his eyes. I freeze, the rest of the sentence frozen in my vocal cords. That's when I hear the crunching. Branches and leaves crackle to our right. I squint, trying to decipher what might be there, but I see nothing. I hold as still as possible, Amir and his crelotin do, too. I doubt the crunching sounds are coming from a friendly source. Otherwise, they'd be calling our names.

"They came in here; I'm sure of it," I hear a deep voice say.

"How can you be sure? There's so many groamin' elves out there. It could have been any of them," a higher-pitched voice responds.

Orcs.

I wonder if this is a female orc. When my dragon mind doesn't translate "groamin'," I surmise that it is a curse or insult of some sort.

"Oh, close your jaws! One of 'em was pale skin, the other brown. Ain't no elves I've seen with that skin. They was carrying a goblin. Probably to skin and eat him," the first orc says.

My stomach twists at that thought, and I can't help but look down at Gobby. He's wrinkled all along his face and hands. His intense red eyes remain fixed on me, steady and unmoving. He holds both hands up, two of his fingers held upward, the other two pointed down. He's muttering something, and I strain my ears to hear.

"Cannot see, surrounding life, yet no strife, cannot see, cannot see," he mutters.

I wave my hand, trying to get him to be quiet in case they hear his words.

A branch snaps much closer this time. The male orc is within three feet of where we stand in the dark. They had lapsed into silence when I started focusing on Gobby. At first, I didn't know what the goblin was up to, but now I understand.

The male orc, his head bald and his face a pale green, stops about two feet from my face. He bares his yellowing teeth as he scans the area behind me with his gaze. Every time he passes my face, he doesn't lock on to it. It's as if he can't see me.

Gobby is weaving a spell of illusion to conceal us.

I fight the instrusive thought to reach up and slap the orc's face. His rough skin looks like tanned leather hide, and his irises are black, with pupils of a pale yellow. It's so backward that I find myself shaking my head to stop staring at him. The other orc steps up next to him, her skin the same color but her head full of black hair. It's braided into three thick strands that run down her back. She has the same yellow teeth, the bottom canines protruding upward over her upper lip.

One quick glance at their weapons is enough to know the danger we're in. They each have an iron sword strapped to their belts. The male is shirtless, his muscular chest and abs sporting swirling designs of a bluish tattoo. The art is a bit mesmerizing, but when he breathes out in my face, that feeling is gone.

It smells like the dude had raw fish and feces for his last meal. I hold back a gag as he continues talking to the female orc.

"They're not here, we're wasting our time. Let's get back to the fighting."

"Rugnug, that would let the half dragonling free. That's him, I'm sure of it. He's a right prize for Urothar," the female responds.

"Bagh, this is boring. I'm leaving," the male orc says. "If the Urothar wants the boy, then he can come get him himself."

The orc turns, his hand resting on the hilt of his weapon. After a moment, I think the female orc will walk forward and run right into me. She tilts her head, considering something. Then she waves both arms in a dismissive manner and saunters away. I let out my breath as slowly as possible, trying not to make a hissing sound. I manage it, but not without feeling like I'll pass out.

When they are about ten paces away, I try shifting my stance to watch where they go. Before I lose sight of them, however, I lean forward. That's when a branch cracks under my foot. My whole body responds with a quick shot of energy, and my head shoots up to look at them. They have both turned around, wicked grins on their faces.

I freeze, hoping that Gobby's illusion spell will keep us hidden, but there's something in their eyes that tells me they can see me now.

I don't think; I just act. Filling both hands with heat, I let flames erupt there. The female orc's smile fades, and she takes a step back. The other one, however, continues grinning before rushing toward me. Thrusting my hands forward, I stoke the fire within my chest, forcing it out through my hands in his direction. The fool runs right into the spouting flames, a scream ripping from his throat. I smell burning flesh and leather, and I grimace to ward off the nausea. When it clears, only a charred husk of a humanoid form remains.

I feel winded, like I just ran a mile and a half. Huffing, I lean over to catch my breath. I've never used so much power like that before. So much for being a fit football player.

"Cursed dragonling!" the female orc shouts at me before turning and rushing away. I think I should catch her and kill her the way I just did the other orc, but between the exhaustion of using my powers, and my leg, I know I don't have a chance. Still, I try to lob a fireball at her, missing completely. It slams into a tree and the trunk erupts into flames.

"We need to run," Amir says. "If they didn't know where we were now, they can just follow the flaming trees."

He's right. I ruined any chances of hiding, the burning tree a beacon for our enemies. I press my lips together and nod, turning away from the dead orc. My mind replays the event over and over in my head. The heat, the fire, the smell, the sound . . . it makes me want to curl up in a ball and hide away for the next week. I know I can't do that, though, not with Gobby and Amir to protect. I hear Krista shout from afar. I watch her tear apart another orc. It's a terrible scene, something from a grisly wartime movie. I turn away, head spinning.

"Come on," I say, hobbling away from the corpse.

The others follow, Amir still carting the crelotin by one of its tentacles. The forest would be beautiful if we weren't running for our lives. It's probably not smart to part from the others in our group, but I tell myself that we'll go back there when the fighting is done. I wonder how many of the elves see me as a coward right now, running and hiding in the forest with the human and the goblin. What a fitting dragon prince, they'll say. I tell myself it's all because of my leg, but part of me wonders if that's truly it or if I'm just a coward.

A fresh breeze carries through the trunks, a thick pine and musty smell wafting into my nostrils. I breathe deeply, letting the scent try and calm me. It doesn't work.

"How far should we go?" Amir asks.

"Just a bit farther," I say, but the pain in my leg is becoming unbearable. I collapse. I can tell that it's worse, and my leg pokes out at an even worse angle.

Gobby makes a clicking sound with his tongue. "I told you that you'd make it worse. My spell made you push too hard. You need rest and let your blood work on it."

I grimace. He's right, and I know he is, but I can't stay here in the field like a sitting duck while everyone fights. The orcs will find us and pounce on me like a cat.

"I'll be fine," I say, rubbing my leg and wincing.

"Dude, they messed your leg up," Amir says. "Don't dragons have like—super healing or something?"

I grunt. "I can, it just takes more time than we have."

Gobby frowns. His mouth is unusually large for something so small. The tips of his mouth bend downward so far that they reach his chin. I'm confident, and not the least bit encouraged, that he could eat my entire head in one bite. Gobby suddenly looks a lot less docile in my mind.

"Dragon blood heals quick. You just need a few hours," he says.

Amir's eyebrows furrow, and he looks at me, waiting for me to translate. I do, and he nods.

"I'm a lame, plain old human, aren't I?" he says, looking down at the soft, loamy ground beneath us.

I stand shakily and put my arm on his shoulder, joggling him.

"No, you aren't. I didn't ask to be born like this, and it doesn't make me any better than you."

This elicits a bouncing chuckle from him.

"You are insane, David. You can literally *throw fire*, and you tell me you aren't better. You can just shove that up your—"

An axe embeds itself in the trunk near my head. Amir jumps back with a terror-filled scream—one that I didn't think possible from the teen. He leans into his crelotin. I turn sharply, wincing as the sudden movement twinges my leg. Another axe comes spinning though the trees and slams into my chest. I grunt as I'm thrown back into the tree closest to me. The axe clatters to the side, my scale defense having just kept me from getting butchered. I try to ignore my leg as I stand up straight. Gobby mutters and waves his hand in the air, working his magic.

My lungs desperately draw in air, struggling from being winded by the heavy axe. I finally catch my breath, holding my gaze steady on the forest area where the axe came from. There, a half dozen figures meld out of the forest. A smaller orc, about my height and stature, walks forward casually, his face barely visible in the canopy-filtered sunlight. He sneers at me, and I can't help but step back. His appearance is humanlike, only with green skin and the same teeth poking up over his upper lip. He's clearly human—or at least part human. His arms aren't unnaturally long like the other orcs. His hair looks human, too, as do his eyes—though his irises are the same pale yellow. He wears a chain mail shirt and a metal helmet adorned with an insignia on the top. A grin flashes on his ruddy green face, and I shift on my feet.

"Seize them," he says calmly.

Orcs close in on us from all sides, melding from the foliage. I fling my hand outward, charring the hand of one with a spout of flames. The orc screams out in pain and stumbles backward, falling to the ground. Amir shouts something before his voice is muffled. Two orcs hold him captive.

The crelotin rears up, ready to fight, when an arrow comes from our side, piercing the creature in the shoulder above its foreleg. It screams, a wave of terror and pain coming from its head like some sort of radio broadcast. I feel it, and I know the others do, too. Orc and human alike, for we all stumble or wince, some holding their heads in shock. The crelotin disappears through the trees, and the feeling goes away.

Gobby, quicker to recover than the rest of us, lets out a growl and lunges forward, a knife appearing in his hand. My gut twists knowing he'd had a concealed weapon all this time. He dives toward the weird human-looking orc. The orc swipes one of his arms to the side, slamming Gobby hard on the face, and he crumples to the ground.

"No!" I shout.

I put both hands together and spread them out. A wave of flames flows out of my palms in a sideways arc, flying quickly and colliding with some orcs. They are thrown backward, the force of the power overcoming them while also lighting them aflame. My vision swims from the excess use of my power.

"You will desist with that corrupted flame, dragonling," the human-orc says. "You're only delaying the inevitable. My father sent me to capture you, and I will do it."

He draws a sword and advances on me. My hands become flames again, and I toss them forward at him. He slips side to side, moving at an impossible pace. No matter how hard I lob them, I can't seem to hit him. The other orcs who I had just knocked over watch as this orc approaches me. He's feet away, and before I can react, his sword comes right at me. It connects with my shoulder, heat pooling in the area as the dragon scales protect me. I don't get cut, but the blow still knocks me to my knees.

"That's it, you'll come with me now," the human-orc says. "Bind them!"

They tie thick ropes around my ankles and my arms. Amir and Gobby are being restrained, too. I struggle, pushing against the orcs who hold me. I call flames to my hands, burning a couple of them. They cry out in pain and shrink back, nursing their wounds.

"Enough of *that*!" the human-orc commands, rushing forward and smacking my face with the butt of his sword. My vision swims, and the forest turns into a murky set of darkened greens and browns. By the time things form into normal images, I'm tied tightly on all fronts. My head throbs, and for once, the knowledge that my scales protected me from cuts doesn't console me. Even though I know I won't bleed out, I still feel despair. Something slips over my head, a necklace of sorts, with something heavy on the end.

"There, that will keep the fire at bay," he says.

Sure enough, when I try to light my hands on fire, it doesn't work. My body feels electric with fear.

"What did you do to me?" I shout, fighting against the restraints.

"Silence! Urothar will be thrilled that his son finally succeeded," the human-orc says.

I forget about the fact that my flames aren't working for the moment. Wait. Didn't one of the orcs just say that the *king's name* was Urothar?

"You're half orc," I say. My voice is scratchy and vague, probably from the throbbing in my skull.

The human-orc smirks. "You think you are the only half blood in Qotan? There are more of us than you think. Though more so on the side of the disgusting light races. There's nothing special about you, even if your mother is Ellistra."

I laugh—a hysterical laugh—and the human-orc frowns, folding his bulky green arms.

"I'm glad I didn't get the short end of the stick for mystical parent. To think I might have looked like *you*," I say. It's a low blow, I know, but it hits the nail right on the head.

Christmas is a beautiful time, reds and greens adorning everything from our living room fireplace to the Christmas tree in our small-town square of Kentucky. It's all I can think about as the human-orc's face turns red in fury.

"You won't be so quick when my father has his way with you," he spits. "We go now. The human can be processed—the goblin, executed for treason."

Processed? What does that even mean? Before I can ask, or comment on the strange pitchy tone of the half orc's voice, two of the orcs surrounding us disappear. I blink, looking at the spots where they were moments before. I think back to the field where the orcs started appearing out of nowhere. Is that a power of theirs? Teleportation? I can't dwell on this too long before a few more of the orcs disappear.

"Sire, Urothar commanded that we bring *all* halflings. We can't leave until—"

"Silence! My father doesn't know their ability to fight. Even now I can feel our army dwindling, dying to the elves and the half demon. We'll take these three and get the others later," the half orc says. "*Now.*"

The orc bows, then reaches into his pocket, pulling out what looks like a stone. He mutters something and then disappears. The ones holding Amir and Gobby press similar stones to their faces, and my friends vanish before my eyes.

"No!" I shout, but I can't say much more as my headache explodes further in my temples. Heat seeps out of my cheek where the scales protect me from a sword blow to the face.

"Ah, the dragon's boon," he says. "It won't last forever, I'm afraid. I'll have to abuse you a bit more while I have the chance."

Another smack to the face. I groan, and my hurt leg throbs alongside my head.

"I'll handle this fool," he says. The orcs holding my arms on either side let go. They vanish after muttering to the strange red stones in their hands.

The human-orc grabs my hair and thrusts my head backward. It hurts, but it's hard to tell because it isn't worse than my throbbing head or smarting leg. He gets close to me, so close I can smell his breath, which smells like he ate a steak. I want to fry him the way I did earlier, but I can feel the heavy stone on my chest drawing my power away. I'm relieved the scale protection isn't broken, too.

"You are the prize I've waited my whole life for," he snarls.

My stubbornness takes over, and I spit in his face. He recoils, roaring in anger, then smacks my face again. I fall to the ground in a heap, the ropes cutting into my arms and legs. Just then, I feel the heavy necklace slip off my neck from the force of my fall.

I can feel the heat returning to my chest. Something forceful rolls me onto my back, and I stare up at the half orc, now alone after all the other orcs have vanished. I could fry him right now, burn the ropes away and kill him, but I wait. They took Amir and Gobby. I'm guessing he's about to do the same thing to me, so I hold back.

"Father will finally give me my birthright—the reward I deserve," he says. His voice makes my skin crawl, and it takes everything in me to keep from lighting my hands up. Instead, I watch as he lifts a stone from his pocket—the same red one the other orcs used. He kneels down on my chest, his weight crushing the breath out of me. I open my mouth, gasping for air. He grins, then drops the stone into my mouth. It falls to the back of my throat, causing me to choke. He mutters the strange word, and the forest and the half orc disappear.

WE KNOCK OUT THE ENEMY

I feel like I'm on one of those spinning rides at a carnival. You know, the ones where you stand up against the wall inside this giant drum thing and the centrifugal force makes you stick to it? That's exactly what's happening to me. And rather than being unable to see outside of the ride, everything is swirling colors. I'm also doused with the same chilling cold from the elves' portal. Together, the two experiences make it a whole different kind of torture. My stomach seizes like I'm about to lose what little contents are in there.

All at once, everything stops, and I fall forward, unable to catch myself from the ropes binding me. A jarring force rockets through me as I collide with the hard ground. I close my eyes, letting the vertigo and spinning sensation slow down. Once I'm able to think straight, I charge my hands with fire, burning the ropes from my body with ease. I'm glad that necklace thing that suppressed my powers fell off.

It only takes a moment for me to recover enough to push myself upward. The moment I do, I gag, coughing the stone out of my mouth. It thuds to the ground, and I shuffle away from it. My throat is raw, but at this point, I'm just grateful for the air.

The first thing I notice is Gobby and Amir laying on the ground next to me. They are still bound, so I move quickly, untying them as fast as my fingers will work.

Amir groans and holds his head. I spot a small pile of vomit-colored goo next to his face. I swallow hard, shuddering as my own stomach offers to send everything back up. To prevent this from happening, I focus on my surroundings. We've landed in another forested place, though the trees are sparser here. There are fewer tall pines and more deciduous, yellow-leafed trees. I spot movement to my right and spin that direction. An orc comes out from around a tree.

I don't hesitate. My hand erupts in flames, and I throw a fireball before he can even register what's happening. He screams in pain, the fire washing over the front of his body and searing his skin.

Pressing forward, I throw my fist, flaming once again, into his face. It connects with a dull thud, and he whirls in place, falling to the ground. I wince as pain lances through my fingers. Two more orcs come running, probably from hearing their friend scream. Bending my knees, adrenaline rushing through me, I light both hands on fire and prepare to throw them forward. Before I can, however, one of the orcs throws a knife at me. I gasp, trying to stand and jump out of the way. It's moving too fast, though, and it slams into my chest.

It bounces off my jersey like it ran into a hard rock wall, tearing a gash in the fabric. I groan, knowing that Coach is going to be pissed when he sees what I've done. Red scales cover the skin of my chest, and I send a word of thanks to my mother for being a dragon.

When the elves knocked me out with their toxin, I was afraid that my scales were broken—or that whatever defense mechanism made them work had expired. The fact that it hasn't gives me a burst of new confidence.

A female orc throws another knife, this one bouncing off my face. Even though it doesn't pierce me, the force of it still smarts. I shout and throw a ball of flame at her. She says something I can't make out—probably a curse of some kind—then eats dirt, falling to the ground.

The other orc's face contorts into something that makes him appear constipated. He has darker green skin than the female, and pure white incisors. He leaps forward, a sword appearing out of nowhere, and slashes at me. He moves fast. I have no training in sword combat, so I end up taking it right on the shoulder.

Thank the scales, yet again.

Even though it doesn't cut my arm off, the sword's blow shoves me hard to the side. That's definitely going to leave a bruise.

I stumble away, holding my shoulder and trying to gain footing, but the orc is bearing down on me relentlessly. He raises his sword above his head, ready to slice downward into my face, then he blinks. He looks around, appearing confused. My heart races, but I cock my head, trying to understand why he stopped. Finally, I understand. Gobby is waving his hands in a circular pattern, his lips muttering something over and over.

He's hiding us—concealing us from the orc.

I close my fist, summoning the flames once more. I focus on scaling up my hand, hoping to give it more oomph for when I slam the orc's ugly face. The red scales respond. Grinning, I throw my fist outward, connecting with his jaw. It gives way under my knuckles, and it hurts a lot less than when I smashed the girl orc's face. He collapses unconscious, his braided black hair smoldering where it caught fire.

I breathe out, looking around for other opponents. There are none.

"Good timing, Gobby," I say, moving to my friend and holding out a hand. He smiles, his sharpened teeth gleaming in the descending sunlight.

"It's an illusion. It is not that amazing," he says. His face changes, and so does the skin around his cheeks. It's taking on a bluish hue.

Oh. He's blushing. I guess that means his blood is—wow, okay, too much for me to process right now.

"I—hate—spinning," Amir groans from the ground at my feet. I can't help but laugh as I reach down and hoist him up. The first time, and the last time really, that I witnessed Amir spinning was on a carousel about five years ago. A local carnival came every year, and with it, they brought rides and other amusement. We'd begged our parents to let us ride the merry-go-round, and they finally relented.

Let's just say that the kiddie ride ended up being a nightmare. I didn't realize it was possible for a human to vomit that much.

"If it makes you feel any better, I got pretty sick myself," I say.

"Nope, still feel like a pile of garbage. Thanks for the try though," he says, his voice muffled by the arm he presses against his lips. I slap him a few times on the back to encourage him—a very football team gesture—and the expression he gives me suggests that he wants me to stop.

Raising my eyebrows apologetically, I turn to examine our surroundings once more. It's hotter here than it was in the thick of the forest. Sweat beads on my forehead and runs down my back. There's also the sound of running water. It burbles in the distance, and all it does is make my mouth excessively dry. Parting my lips, I run my parched tongue across my lower lip, the flesh catching there without the wetness. Through the sparser trees, I can see that it's flat all around us. Even though the trunks are thin and spread out, the leaves and branches expand outward, covering much of the sky and the horizon.

Still, the fact that there are no mountains near us means we had to have teleported far.

I freeze, my mouth falling open. The others. When I made the move to hide in the forest away from the fighting, I had no idea that we'd be transported away. Dad's going to worry.

"Where are we?" Amir asks, voicing the question we are all thinking.

Gobby grunts. "We are in the light land still. We're not close to any dark races."

I wonder how he knows. I decide that doubting the only native to this place would be idiotic.

"Any idea exactly *where*?" I ask.

Gobby widens his eyes. He doesn't know.

We all turn on our heels at the sound of crackling branches. With the recent appearance of the orcs, and the attack of the elves, my mind immediately thinks of all sorts of ridiculousness. Images of strange creatures flow through my brain. One of them distinctly looks like a dragon, black with glowing red eyes and flames jutting out of its mouth. What I see is far less imposing, but that's not comforting.

The half orc who shoved the stone into my mouth to send me here stands about twenty paces away. I don't think. My hands come up to my face, flames engulfing them. He scowls at me, then draws a wicked-looking sword. It's made from some type of blue metal. Gobby mutters next to me, and the air starts to ripple around us, as if the world were bending inward and being sucked into a hidden pinpoint.

Our enemy snarls and flicks his free hand. Something blue shoots through the air, and I hear a sickening squelch down at my hip level. Gobby shouts in pain, the rippling air stopping immediately. A small knife hilt protrudes from his shoulder, blue blood spurting and dripping down his brown clothes. He falls to his knees as my eyes widen. Heat flares up inside of me, and I advance on the human-orc.

He grins evilly at the injured goblin. "Stay out of this, traitor!"

I let out an inhuman growl, something closer to a savage man pretending to be a jungle cat. Grateful that my rapid healing mended my injury, my powerful legs propel me forward, and I spread out my hands, flames flowing continuously as if being stoked by massive bellows. The forest darkens around me as my eyes pick up on the blazing light from the torrent of flames. When I finally release them, Amir curses behind me—probably from the intensity of the heat.

The half orc is no more. I'm sure of it.

But I'm wrong. When the flames clear, he's jumped back a half dozen paces, clearly out of the firing line of my ability. And he's grinning. I grit my teeth, preparing to launch more flames in his direction, but he pulls out a necklace, a glowing red amulet at the end. I recognize it as the one that fell off my neck before this.

It's the thing that takes away my abilities. My stomach clenches. I can't let that thing get anywhere near me.

"If I hadn't had to search for *this*, I might have followed after you sooner," he says, glaring at me.

"Amir! Take care of Gobby," I shout before rushing forward.

I'm not sure I've ever thought about fighting before this whole Qotan debacle. Dad always told me that a peaceful approach is sufficient. That idea now sounds like the dumbest piece of advice anyone could give. If Dad had given me weapons and trained me to be a fighter, maybe I'd have more of a chance. At least I have some defensive instincts.

I remember reading a phrase somewhere—possibly in a movie or something; it doesn't matter where it came from—but it was along the lines of the element of surprise and being the first to attack. In any case, it's what I do. Bullheaded? Very much so. Stupid? Kind of, yeah.

The half orc holds his stance, the metallic-blue sword held in front of him at the ready. He stays perfectly calm, his stoic expression annoying me and making me want to wring his neck. When I'm five feet away, I let my outstretched hands blaze to life. Swiping sideways with one of my flaming fists seems like a good first play.

Wrong again.

The human-orc, while still grinning, sidesteps my attack and smacks me on the back with the flat of his sword. I gasp at the sharpness of the blow, but the heat that is left behind tells me the scales came in time to prevent me from being cut in half.

"Those scales are tiresome, aren't they?" he says, flicking his wrist again to pound me on the shoulder.

I groan, shuffling away on the sparsely grassed ground. This action is followed up quickly with another strike to the head, which snaps my neck to the side, the world turning sideways. I collapse to the ground, brain foggy and head pounding. Amir is shouting something, but I curse him in my mind. Of all the times for Amir to try to step up and do something, this is not a good one. I try to tell him to run, but all that comes out is a muffled croak.

My face flushes. A new burst of strength, birthed from the ashes of my shame, fills my entire being. I don't give up easily. Pressing my hands to the dirt, I take a couple seconds to ground myself and prepare to lash out at the orc again. Finally, I push upward, the force of my trajectory landing me on my feet. My arms are somehow stronger. Must be something in the air, I guess.

The orc advances on Amir. I should probably take advantage of his distraction with Amir and rush him from behind, but something tells me that won't work.

"Hey, ugly!" I shout. He spins, forgetting my friend and locking me with a burning stare. Amir stands there frozen, hands clenching to the side. Kudos to him for not running away.

"You dare insult the son of the high Orc King Urothar?" he says with a measured tone.

"Yeah, I think I do dare, you green piece of—"

I don't have time to finish my sentence before he lunges at me with his sword. The tip almost pierces my chest, but I jump back, imagining that I'm playing a game of dodgeball. This should be easy. There's only one "ball," and it's in the hands of the Wicked Witch of the West in orc form. The thought makes me bite my lips, holding back a laugh.

He lunges at me once more, and I barely spin out of that one. The problem is that this maneuver puts me facing the opposite direction with my back exposed. He takes advantage of this and slams the sword into my back. I wince at the pain but manage to turn around only to get another smack in the face. The ground meets my view a lot quicker this time.

"I am Gulran, the orc prince, bred to kill the dragon halfling and all the other traitors of Qotan," he says from above me.

Okay, he's speaking nonsense. If my mind wasn't already spinning and throbbing, I might be able to come up with a retort, but I can't. I groan and push one hand downward to flip onto my back. It's only at this point that I realize my leg doesn't hurt. While I'm grateful, I can't help but grit my teeth and wonder why it waited until *now* to heal rapidly.

Gulran. Nice to learn his name. So, he's not merely "human-orc" anymore. He stands over me, his blue sword raised high.

"Shall we see if your foolish mother's blessing is enough to protect from the full strength of an orc's thrust?"

I'm dead. I know that for sure. All those years living on earth, barely knowing anything about my heritage, and I finally set foot in Qotan only to get killed. The tip of the sword comes down so fast that his hands become a blur. I close my eyes, waiting for the final blow to pierce my chest and send me out of this life. But it doesn't come. I don't feel the pain. Is dying this easy? I assumed it would hurt more.

Abruptly heavy grunts ring out. I peek open an eye. The sword tip hovers an inch above my chest. Interestingly, the scales haven't grown there—I can tell because my skin isn't heated. Gulran's sword quivers in his hand as if there is some force holding him back.

"Argh!" he shouts, then his sword flies upward, slipping from his grip and landing tip down in the earth. Hatred burns in his eyes as he stands over me. He growls, raises his foot, and slams it into my gut. The scales appear this time, but pain still lances up into my chest.

He raises his foot to kick me again, but I spot a flash of green. Gulran bellows in surprise, stumbling away from me. At first, I have no idea why he decided not to kick me to death, then I see the small form of Gobby plastered to his face.

"Get off me, you traitorous fool! You'll answer for this crime!" he says, both hands trying to pry the little being from his head. He finally manages to push Gobby away, causing the small goblin to bounce to the ground with a few soft grunts. His arm hangs limply to the side.

"My father's magic stayed my sword to spare your life today, but only because of the pact. He needs your blood—*yours*, and the other disgusting half-breeds! If it wasn't for you, I wouldn't be half human. *You* and your kind are the reason I live this tortured life."

The despair in his tone confuses me. Did he just blame me for being born?

"What—what are you saying?" I ask.

This doesn't make sense. How could it be *my* fault that he is the way he is? Plus, he's not *that* ugly. He looks like a human with green skin and small walrus teeth. Okay, yeah, he looks a little ugly.

Gulran pulls a strange face before blinking a few times. I furrow my brow, wondering what's wrong.

"You—because of your heritage—the stake on Qotan—magic," Gulran says before his eyes roll back in his head and he falls forward on his face.

All is silent. Not even a single leaf rustles around me, and my whole body tingles at how weird it sounds. There should be a breeze. Still days like this are so rare. It's like I'm in a bubble or something. I lay there, my breath coming out in ragged waves. Gobby grunts, and I lift my head to see Amir watching the orc warily.

"Is he dead? Just like that?" Amir asks.

"I have no idea," I say.

"Not dead," Gobby says. "I poisoned him."

He holds up the knife he's pulled out. In the filtered light, I can see the edges are covered in a yellow substance.

The clever little dude. He latched onto the orc's face to poison him the same way we were the day before. It's a bit concerning that he's smuggled that along with us the whole time, but I try not to worry about it. I'm impressed that he was able to hide it from the elves more than anything. They had stripped him of weapons, hadn't they?

"I'm guessing the goblin's clicking grumbles mean something to *you*," Amir says sarcastically.

I laugh, stopping when it makes my head throb again.

"He says he poisoned him," I say.

Amir frowns and takes a step back from the unconscious orc. He shivers, then eyes Gobby.

"He's not going to poison *you*. Chill," I say, but I wonder if it's true. Gobby is one of the dark races. He could turn on us at any moment. I've seen enough movies to recognize that it happens, but I can't worry too much about it. He just saved my hide yet again. He could have poisoned *me*, but he didn't.

I look around the sparse trees, hoping to see some indication of where we can go, but nothing is apparent. Nothing moves, and nothing makes a sound. It seems like there should be the rustle of some leaves, but the stillness is eerie.

"Well, should we . . . um, kill him or something?" Amir says.

I freeze, looking down at the unconscious boy. I don't want to kill him, though part of me says we should. My eyes wander over to the charred remains of the other orcs whom I torched, and my stomach seizes. I almost gag at the sight of them now that the adrenaline has fled my body. Forcing myself to look away, I fix my gaze back on Amir and shake my head.

"I can't. He's just a kid like us. He didn't choose his parentage," I say. "Let's just get out of here."

I look at Gobby, wondering if he's disappointed in what I've said, but he has no expression.

"I will veil our path. He won't be able to follow us," he says.

Amir groans. "Oh, we're going to regret leaving him. But yeah, I'm not going to stab the guy—thing, or whatever—while he's down."

"We aren't going to leave him," I say, gesturing toward his limp form. "We'll tie him up and drag him where we go. Maybe we can get some information from him—"

As if in response to my words, Gulran's body shimmers where he lays. I flinch, putting my arms up in defense, but it's of no use. His body wavers once more before it disappears completely.

"Okay, that was weird," Amir says, shivering.

"That's what you both looked like when they teleported you away with those stones. He must have had another one on his person," I say, gritting my teeth.

"At least we don't have to worry about him attacking us anymore," Amir says.

I nod, then scan the forest. "So, where do we go?"

Amir shrugs, then looks at the goblin. Gobby gives his wide-eye shrug, and I'm at a loss for words. Everything looks the same: thin trunks with yellow leaves expanding every which way from the winding branches. I wiggle my fingers, my hands hanging down limply at my sides. Dad is out there somewhere, battling orcs. He could be dead. Krista and Jared, they could be dead, too, and we were sent who knows how far away from them.

"Gobby, are you sure you don't recognize where we are? You've lived here your whole life. Can't you tell us where to go?"

The goblin scowls at me. He waves both hands in the air.

"No idea. Somewhere in the light race region. There are no trees like this in our regions. Goblins aren't allowed here," he says with a waver in his voice.

I have the sudden urge to punch one of the trees next to me, but I refrain. Getting lost in the woods is not something I've prepared for. Dad and I have gone on camping trips, and I know basic navigation, but that's with a compass, a map, and known landmarks. I'm in a fantasy world with strange creatures and no knowledge of the terrain. I don't even know if the sun moves the same way.

No matter how hard I strain my eyes, I can't see too far into the trees even though a lot of them are spaced out. The sky is clear, but the trees are too high for me to see more than slivers here or there. If only flying had been something I inherited from my dragon heritage.

Then again, I'm not sure I'd want to sprout huge red wings in addition to my scales. I'm enough of a freak of nature as it is.

A thought comes to me, and I smile despite our situation. My hands shake from the revelation.

"We can climb the trees to get a better view. Hopefully we'll spot something that will be useful. Like buildings, or a mountain, or something we can move toward," I say.

Amir's eyebrows shoot up and he looks impressed. "Okay, that's actually a good idea. Wow, Dave, that's my job. You are supposed to be the dumb jock. I'm supposed to do all the thinking for you."

This joke isn't new. I think it's because he wants me to be the TV show stereotypical football jock with zero drive for school. My motivation isn't *zero*; it's just lower than normal. Only a few of the guys on the team fit the "not caring" bill. Still, I throw a punch at him, my fist thudding on his upper arm. He winces, then tosses one back.

"So you or me?" I say.

He laughs. "There's no way I'm climbing one of those trees. There are no handholds."

I smile knowingly. I didn't expect him to volunteer for the job. Gobby watches me with his glowing red eyes, a curious expression on his face. I translate for him. It's ridiculous saying the same thing repeatedly—apparently speaking different languages depending on who I'm looking at—but I'll suffer through it.

Climbing has always been my thing, so it was more of a joke to ask Amir. He appreciated the jibe. I can tell. In any case, with my lean muscle, my lightweight body is relatively easy for my arms to lift. Rope climbing has always come easy to me, and now that I'm in Qotan, I can't help but wonder if my dragon blood has anything to do with that.

I pick the tree nearest me because it has a strange-looking knot in it. I approach the narrow trunk. It doesn't have much for me to hold on to, but that doesn't worry me. Crouching low, I launch myself upward with my powerful legs and wrap them around the trunk. Shimmying up the tree doesn't take long, but when I reach the first set of high, spindly branches, the tree starts to shake wildly. I grip one of the branches with white knuckles, panic rising in me. There hasn't been one lick of a breeze, yet the moment I start climbing a good fifteen feet above ground, it picks up?

But I don't feel any wind on my face . . .

My hair isn't moving around my head. Despite the waving trunk and rustling leaves, the tree next to me is as still as ever.

Gobby shouts at me, but I can't hear him over the rustling. My jaw locks tight as I consider my options. So far, the tree isn't moving enough to throw me off, but I can't descend easily with the narrow trunk swaying. I resolve that it's better to move upward, hoping that whatever it is will stop. Peeling one of my hands from the branch, I reach up higher to grab the next one. The moment I do, the tree sways so much that I'm almost flung down.

My free hand flies to the side, momentum yanking it in that direction. The ground and sky switch continuously as the tree bends from left to right—the sky becoming the ground, and the ground becoming the sky. My stomach tightens as my fear of heights is triggered. Normally, trees aren't quite high enough to terrify me, but in this moment, I'm terrified.

I have no idea how I hold on. The palm gripping the branch is raw already. Grasping wildly for anything, the back of my hand slams into a branch. I wince, grateful for the spreading warmth of the scales. Hopefully that means I won't bruise. The tree swings in the other direction, and I flip my hand so my palm slams into another narrow branch. It connects, and I hold on, nausea building in my gut. I taste bile on my tongue, and my throat burns something awful. If I were to throw up now, it would not only be a mess, but it would make holding on for dear life impossible.

Why is this the only tree moving? The impossibility of this burns in my thoughts as a reminder that I'm in Qotan. This is role-playing in real life.

"Tree!" I shout as loud as I can. "*Tree, will—you—just—stop!*"

Nothing happens. My hands are slipping, getting weaker with each side swing. I close my eyes when I realize my vision is making me sick. I'm reminded of Amir's visit to the NASA headquarters. He told me he got to go on the spinning simulator. You know, the one that makes everyone throw up? This isn't exactly like that, but it sure feels like it. The sky and ground should not be changing so much. For a moment, I wonder if it would be best to let go and be thrown to the ground. My scales would protect me. But what if they malfunction like they did when the elves captured me and made my body all numb?

So, I do the only logical thing left. I light my hands on fire.

A screech echoes so loud that it makes my ears ring. The waving increases, and I let my hand blaze. Finally, the motion comes to a stop.

Don't kill me! Don't do that! My life is worth more than a wretched human's and an ugly goblin's.

My breath comes in ragged waves, and my heart thuds like I've just run a marathon. Tingling fills my hands. The vibrations from the rocking tree have nearly numbed them. I blink, unsure of what's happening.

"Where are you?" I ask the disembodied voice. Amir calls up to me curiously, wondering who I'm talking to, but I ignore him.

The tree. The tree, that's who I am. And you almost killed me for no reason at all.

Great. I'm talking to a tree.

A thought wedges into my mind. I remember hearing stories of trees that turned into women. Was that mythology? Or some other fantasy nonsense Amir told me about? He was often rambling about various things from his books even though I told him I didn't care about any of it. I *so* wished I'd listened when he wouldn't stop talking.

"No reason? You were trying to toss me to the ground! What else was I supposed to do?" I growl.

The tree shivers. Not enough to knock me off, but enough to indicate that it's outside of normality. That, and the air is as still as the air in my high school classrooms. Smells better though.

What manner of human are you that can do that with fire—oh! Another shiver. *Dragon! I sense the blood of a dragon in you. I'm ever so sorry—*

The tree continues to give me a string of apologies, some of which don't make sense to me. Something about knocking leaves off limbs and uprooting feet. Regardless, I have to turn off my brain so I don't get overwhelmed by the flood of ideas. The tree is starting to sound like Amir with his book monologue. I lift my hand and thump it on a branch.

"That's great and all, but I need to get up higher to look around. I need to see if there's anything close by—a place for us to go."

The tree sputters to a stop with another rustle of its branches. I figure that it doesn't have much else to do gesturewise, considering it's a tree.

Close? Why, yes, there's a little settlement not far from here. See there.

A branch close to my head goes from rigid to fluid, like a wriggling snake. Tingling runs down my spine, and I have the sudden urge to jump to the ground despite the damage it might do to my body. Before

I can react, the branch shoots down and wraps around my waist. I scream out, gripping the solid wood with white-knuckled hands.

If you please, I'm only attempting to help. I will not let harm come to you. Not now that I know you are a friend.

It takes an immense amount of concentration, but finally, I relinquish my grip on the branch. I'm lifted into the thick of the leaves and branches. My vision becomes a wash of yellow and tan-brown, and I have to keep myself from panicking as I'm almost suffocated by the thickness. Once I'm over the top, my breath catches in my throat. For miles and miles all around, there is a sea of colors. Yellow, red, green, and brown trees of similar heights span out as far as I can see. Deep-colored mountains disturb the horizon in the distance, thick clouds ringing the high peaks as if they had an intimate relationship with the stone. Here, a breeze rustles my hair, and I can't help but suck in the sharp freshness of it.

How does the air not rustle the trees below? I soon forget that thought as I'm hit with the pungent and familiar scent of smoke. A billowing column of gray shoots into the sky not too far from where we are. The place it's coming from is sparser than here, and if I squint hard enough, I can see the top of a structure of some sort.

See there, it's a fairy encampment. Should be a good place for you to visit, I should say.

"It's not far," I say. I make a mental note of what direction the smoke is coming from, then peer down. Vertigo washes over me, and I am forced to focus on a leaf that's close to my face not to pass out. My fear of heights activates as I realize I have a hold on absolutely nothing. I grip the branch around my waist so hard that my knuckles ache.

I'm unsure why the tree doesn't put me down there, but it doesn't. I stay up in the air, squirming inside the hold of the branch.

"Umm—can you put me down now? I think I know the way."

Oh, right. Well, it isn't far off, but I'll send a message to the fairies there to retrieve you.

A branch near me ripples—like what happened when this one snagged me—but instead of hitting me, it slaps the tree next to it. The ripples pass through it as if it were the wave performed by a raucous audience at a basketball game.

I open my mouth to protest. I want to say that if "retrieving us" is anything like this, then I don't want any of it, but I rush rapidly toward the ground instead. My voice gets caught as my stomach launches upward into my chest. It's like a horrible kind of roller coaster, with the only security being a thick restraint around your waist. As the ground approaches, I close my eyes, waiting for the impact.

When it doesn't come, I peek open my eyes. My feet touch the ground lightly, and I breathe out in relief.

"Am I crazy, or did that tree snatch you up like an elephant's trunk?" Amir says, standing a little off and watching the tree warily.

"Not imagining it. We've fully entered psycho land," I say.

Gobby narrows his eyes. I shake my head, not bothering to translate it. He wouldn't understand anyway—though, I do wonder what his reaction would be if he saw a car or Amir's cellphone.

I relay the information about the settlement nearby and the message the tree sent. No sooner have I finished telling them when a strange popping noise sounds near my head. Pressure shoots through my ears, and I gasp. It's the same sensation you get when you are descending altitude and your ears regulate.

Amir and Gobby both clasp their ears, wincing in turn.

"So sorry for being so rude. I wanted to get here as fast as possible," a tiny voice says near my ear.

I turn, chest tight from the intrusion of yet another disembodied voice. Color fills my vision, but it's all blurred. Blinking, I try to get my eyes to adjust to the scene. My body reacts as if there were a bug hovering right in front of my face. I can hear the buzzing of the insect wings and the tingling sensation of something closeby. I swat at the bug.

"I say! Do you often treat your saviors so rudely? And to think that I came to save you from the horrid dark races preying on humans," the voice says.

The thing flying in front of my face moves away from me, and my mouth falls open. A small woman hovers in the air. When I say small woman, I'm not being derogatory. She is literally the size of my palm. Frowning, I peer at Amir and Gobby.

"The trees told me of a human who needs protection, but I was not aware there were two. Where is your dragon escort? That was relayed as a part of the message, I do believe."

I squint to inspect her more closely. The minuscule woman has a beautifully brown complexion with thick, wavy raven-black hair extending to her shoulders. A blur of wings flashes behind her back. She wears a light blue gown reminding me of the sky. The sleeves are ruffled from shoulder to wrist, and she also has tiny black dress shoes.

"Um . . . am I dreaming right now?" I ask.

I don't remember falling from the tree, but now that I see this small bug-woman, I'm seriously questioning my consciousness.

"Where's Peter?" Amir asks. Everyone's eyes snap to him. The woman looks both confused and annoyed at the same time.

"I beg your pardon. I know no person by the name Peter. What a strange assumption," she replies.

It's kind of embarrassing how long it takes me to understand Amir's joke. My cheeks puff out as I suppress a laugh. I haven't seen *Peter Pan* in so long I'd forgotten about it.

"We're in Qotan, not Neverland," I say, smirking.

The fairy eyes me critically. She folds her arms and turns to the side, making a show of tapping her tiny foot in the air. Watching her do this is a little disorienting.

"Very astute, boy," she says, looking me up and down. She turns her gaze to Amir and purses her minuscule lips. "My dear, what strange clothing. Where did you commission it? Far southwest with the mountain dwarfs? Or perhaps these are gnome made. Quite silly they are at making clothing."

Her eyes slip to Gobby, and my ears are filled with a shrieking sound so high that I clap my hands over them. The sound doesn't last long before the fairy woman pulls out a small stick. My feet leave the ground in a rush, and I shoot upward in the air. At the same time, Gobby goes flying backward and slams into a tree, his glowing red eyes narrowing in pain. He stays there, pinned by some invisible force.

"What the—" Amir exclaims, but his voice is strangled by the strange lift upward.

"Goblin! How did you venture this far amongst your enemies? In all my years, I've never seen a single goblin so close to us. Oh, the queen will be cross when she finds out that the dark races are near."

"He's not an enemy! He's a friend of mine," I say.

The fairy appears even more confused.

"You consort with goblins, human? Do you not know where he must be taking you?" she replies. "To be sacrificed to the orc king, no less. Are you so willing to accept that fate?"

I can't help but swing my feet. The ground is at least four feet below me. It feels wrong to be hovering without anything solid beneath. Vines curve their way under the soft ground, thick roots grappling other thinner roots to create a network that is something of a beauty. I'm not sure how I didn't notice it before. It's mesmerizing.

"Look at me," the fairy commands. "Why are you consorting with this goblin?"

My brain snaps back to the situation, and I stutter, trying to gather my thoughts. "F—f—friend, he—is one."

"Oh, nonsense, that can't be. Goblins are the least friendly of the dark races," she says, glaring at Gobby. "I should kill you right here, but I fear I don't have the heart to do so. The queen will have to decide what to do with—"

"Don't kill," I say.

What has gotten into my brain? I can't figure out why I can't form a cohesive thought. Amir stares off in the distance, apparently so in shock—or maybe just tired—that he can't even register the conversation.

The fairy presses her lips into a thin line, scrutinizing me once more.

"You believe this creature to be a friend? I cannot fathom how that could be. Show me why you believe."

I furrow my brow. Show her what? It's not like I have videos and pictures of us hanging out and being saved by Gobby. I don't have the chance to ask for clarification on what she means before my mind starts flowing through the memories of how I met Gobby, how I named him, and why we are here.

The woman lets out a long breath.

"You are the dragon heir, is that correct?"

The look in her eyes tells me she doesn't believe me. At this point, I'm tired of games. I light both of my palms on fire.

"Yes, I see what you are," she scrutinizes me all over again. "I must say, you are far less than what we hoped for and expected. Where is your sword?"

I open my mouth, but she cuts me off.

"None. Can't fight with one, can you? I see. That's a shame. A bow?"

Once again, she shakes her head, not even letting me start to answer her.

"Your friend is equally useless—oh!"

Her exclamation makes me jump, and I follow her gaze to where Gobby is being held. Only he's not there. I bite my tongue, not wanting to tell her that he probably put up an illusion we can't see through.

"Illusory magic is quite inconvenient. Goblin, or Gobby"—she pauses and gives me a look of disdain—"come out at once."

Her energy and quick responses are making me dizzy. How did she know his name is Gobby? I didn't tell her that. She's acting like Jared did when he was—

"Oh. You can—" I begin.

"Read your mind? Yes. And I know about your friends. We'll find them soon enough, but first, where is that little—"

At this point, I cut her off. "He won't come out unless you promise to leave him alone."

I don't know this for sure. I can't read minds, but it seems like a good gamble. Seeing how small this fairy is, it's impossible to think that one of them could be Jared's mother. Jared is a tall, broad beast of a teenager, and this woman could be flicked ten feet with a good blow of my pointer finger. I quell the thought, worrying that she heard it and it'll offend her. She may be small, but she's proven trouble enough with her magic. It's only been a few moments since the fairy lifted me and Amir off the ground.

"Tut-tut, I will not harm him. Gobby, I swear to let you be," she says, then looks at me pointedly. "And stop dwelling on my size. I can make myself your size as easily as you could blink."

I peer around expectantly, but Gobby doesn't come out. I speak out loud, hoping that thinking about Gobby will be enough for my words to be translated. The fairy jumps when she hears me speaking, then smiles slightly.

"I say, you are truly dragon-blooded. No other being, human or not, without the translation gift, could speak to him," she says.

Gobby finally materializes a few paces to the left. He holds a sizable rock as if he were making ready to throw it at the fairy. She laughs heartily.

"Oh dear, did you think that you could best me with a rock?" she says.

The rock glows a little before flinging out of his hand. The fairy eyes the blue blood that is trickling down from Gobby's shoulder.

"Besides, you're injured. Best get that taken care of."

Gobby glares at her but winces and holds his injured shoulder. I start to tell her to put me down, but I'm descending before I can. As soon as my feet hit the ground, I rush over to Gobby, inspecting the wound.

"Ugh, that looks bad, buddy," I say, grabbing the bottom hem of my jersey. I wince, dreading what I must do, but tug heavily on it until it rips. The shirt is long enough that my stomach isn't exposed, but only just. I wrap it tightly against his wound, trying not to shiver as the blue blood covers my palm.

"Do you heal quickly?" I ask, but I know the answer before he speaks.

"No, it will take time," he responds.

The fairy sighs behind me, and I turn to glare at her.

"Now that that's settled, let's get somewhere more comfortable. Dragon, you'll have to vouch for the goblin at the settlement. If he so much as lays a hand on someone, it'll be your head, no matter who your mother is. And my name is Rolinda, your escort," she says.

"Our escort? How are you going to—"

The world melts away into spinning colors.

PASSING THROUGH THE TRAITORS' TEST

I could go my whole life without ever experiencing teleportation again. You'd think I would be used to it by now, having been through it twice before. That is nowhere close to true. My stomach clenches so hard that it hurts, and bile rises to my throat, but everything stops spinning as quickly as it started. I gasp, bending over and putting my hands on my knees. I'm still suspended in the air, though, so it causes me to rotate head over heels as if I'm in a no-gravity zone.

Amir retches yet again.

Rolinda scowls at him, as if his bodily reaction to spinning is about the rudest thing anyone could do. She stares at Gobby. One of her small hands is outstretched toward him, and he's squirming, his skin glowing ever so slightly.

"If you try anything, Gobby, be assured that your life will be forfeit before you can make it ten paces."

He glares at her but doesn't say anything.

"Now that we are here, let me change into a form more comfortable for you human folk," she says. A bright but steady glow emits from her feet and hands, spreading up her legs and arms. I wince at the intensity of the display. I shield my eyes, and a flash of orange lights the area.

When it ends, a human-sized version of the same fairy stands before us.

"Let's put you down," Rolinda says, waving her hand and letting me down slowly. Amir descends at the same time and sighs in relief, though he has to shuffle away from his recent vomit. It was mostly dry gagging, considering we've had little to eat or drink since his last purge. Poor guy.

"The goblin will have to stay here, I'm afraid. We can't have an enemy tromping through our home. The ruckus that would cause would be unimaginable," the fairy says.

I shake my head, trying to get the lightheadedness out of my brain.

"I already told you, Gobby won't do anything. He's with me, and I trust him."

Rolinda turns back to me, puckering her lips. "It's not me that's the problem. Try getting the whole population of the settlement to believe you. They'll have him strung up on a vine before you could even try to explain it to them."

I grit my teeth. She's adamant about this. Whatever war is going on between the light and dark races, the elves' reaction set a precedent for what Gobby would experience.

"Can't he just hide himself? With an illusion or something?" Amir suggests.

I grin, clapping my hand on my forehead.

"Amir, that's genius! Why didn't I think of that?"

He grins evilly. "Dumb jock, remember?"

Rolling my eyes, I translate for Gobby. His already plastered frown deepens, but he nods in understanding.

At this point, Rolinda has moved on, her large blue skirt skimming the ground. I can still see her wings, now human-sized. They flap wildly, and it looks even more strange than when she was fairy-sized. It's hard to tell if she is hovering or walking.

Gobby concentrates, then holds up his finger and snaps. A wave of gray mist coalesces around him momentarily, and when it clears, Gobby is gone. He's been replaced by a labrador. His blond fur is fresh and shiny, like what I would imagine a show dog to look like. I gape at him for a moment.

"Wow," Amir says in a breathy tone. "That's wild. I can't even tell he's a little green dude."

I nod in agreement before pointing ahead at Rolinda. "She's going to leave us behind if we don't hurry."

We rush to follow, and when we finally catch up, the fairy is going on and on about how the settlement was formed and disguised from unwanted eyes. Then why did I see smoke from above? When I bring this up, she shushes me and says that could be answered later. I have the distinct impression she won't remember.

We soon arrive at a thicket of different types of plants and trees, and my eyes land on a new face. He wears a hardened expression, deep brown eyes set back in recessed sockets. He has long brown hair that cascades down his powerful chest, and two small braids at the corners of his forehead. He holds an axe up and glares at me from under bushy eyebrows. I spot another that looks like him, only with slightly redder-brown hair and different facial features. They look fierce. They also appear like they've had a really bad day.

Oddly, they are also slightly more than half my height.

"No need to be so cross, Huron. They aren't intruders," Rolinda says, but she eyes Gobby.

"Sure, and me mum has three eyes, she does. That dog looks trouble enough. Also, we don't need more humans mugging up our home," the small man says.

"While I am inclined to agree, I have searched the halfling's head and know that the *dog* means us no harm. And there is only one human among them. Now, be a good dwarf and let them through," she says.

Her vouching for us apparently doesn't mean much, for the dwarves don't move.

"Not human? What do yeh mean by tha'? Theys both look human t' me."

Huron bends forward, glaring up at my face.

"Dragon," I say, pointing a finger at myself.

His eyes widen. "Dragon. As in—"

I nod and he clears his throat, stepping backward.

I engage the first dwarf in an uncomfortable stare, and after some more nervous sputtering from them, they relent.

"Roit—erm, be on yer way, then," he says, waving a hand past him.

He turns and gestures through an archway made from winding branches. I want to inspect the archway. From my peripheral vision, I can see it's incredibly well-crafted, but I don't want to stop staring into the dwarf's eyes. Even though I have no idea what their culture is, this seems like a battle of wills.

A tug on my arm pulls my attention away, and I glower at Amir.

"Did you seriously have a staring contest with that dwarf?" he asks, a dubious expression on his face.

I beam at him. "I would have kept it up if you hadn't pulled me away."

Amir shakes his head. "That dude looked like he was about to slice your head straight off. If they are anything like the dwarves in my books, I'm pretty sure he could do it."

I laugh but stop quickly when I notice how serious Amir is.

Now I feel like I have a target on my back. The center of my spine itches as I imagine one of the dwarves burying their axe inside. This whole experience seems more and more like a joke as time goes on—but it's far from a joke.

"Oh dear, it seems you're bothering the locals," Rolinda says as she leads us forward.

I gawk at the scene. I was sure that I'd seen smoke from the top of that talking tree, but that didn't make sense. There I'd only been able to spot trees with narrow trunks and yellow leaves, but here, the trees have thick broad trunks and span upward at least a hundred feet. How could I have missed trees *this* big?

Roped bridges with wooden planks litter the airspace above, leading from one large tree trunk to another. Wooden planked pathways lead to more wooden platforms secured to the sides of the trees. Squat wooden buildings sit against each of the trunks, and people—or creatures—hang out between them. And a gigantic bonfire blazes in the center of the buildings and trees. There's a decent bustling of people, too.

But most of them are definitely not people. I spot a few elves, at least ten feet tall, their blue skin as well as their height making them stand out. More dwarves, male and female, stalk through the crowds with cross looks on their faces. Each has bushy eyebrows and wears some version of leather clothing. While the men wear pants and vests, most of them with bare chests and arms, the women wear stiff-looking leather dresses. Flickers of light shoot between travelers. There are more fairies than I can keep track of. Rolinda made it sound like this was a small settlement, but the sheer number of living things moving about dissuades me from that idea.

Something bumps into my leg, and I yelp, pulling it away. Past trauma from being attacked by playful dogs locks my arms in place, and I almost fall over in fear. I'm not scared of dogs, per se, but when a few big ones come at me, I'm reminded of my childhood. The neighbor's friendly labs and rottweiler had leapt on me, knocking me over in a fit of playful growling and slobber. I was five, and at the time, they were twice my size.

Fortunately, this isn't a group of dogs.

Or maybe *not* fortunately.

"Beg your pardon, do watch where you are traveling for the sake of your smaller residents," it says.

I blink quickly, trying to understand what I'm seeing. It's a little man—but when I say little, I mean he only comes up to the middle of my shin. He's bald and carries a little umbrella over one shoulder. A woman of equal size and proportions hangs off his outstretched arm, and three kids follow behind.

"Are you going to stand there and say nothing? My—my—no wonder we abandoned the human realm all those years ago," the man says. Then he says something I can't understand to the kids behind him.

They cheer and swarm my shoes, bouncing to and fro. I can hardly feel them there, but before I know it, they are gone, hustling off to another part of the settlement.

"Oh dear, you've gained the ire of the brownies. I fear you'll regret that for your whole visit to Qotan," Rolinda says. "Follow me. We don't have far to go. Mind your shoes."

She says this without looking back at me. Amir and I both glance down at our feet. The laces of our shoes have been untied and retied together in a complex knot.

"Come on!" I complain, kneeling to fiddle with it.

"I can't believe they exist," Amir whispers, bending down to fix his as well. "Brownies in stories always do stuff like this. They were reportedly a huge problem in the UK for years. All of a sudden, sightings and mischief just stopped."

The small brownie father gives me a critical gaze before stalking off. Amir and I take a decent time to untie them; Amir is slightly faster to my disappointment.

Rolinda stops and turns slowly. "Yes, well, they are one of the only races to have lived among humans. Fairies did, for a time, but the whole environment of human nature and your realm became far too toxic for us mythical races. Now we melt away when we set foot there."

She humphs lightly, spins back around, and keeps moving. The way she said our environment became toxic feels like an insult. I don't litter or anything. I even volunteer with the football team for service projects to clean up garbage. I'm not a toxic human—or at least I don't think I am.

"But the dark races *can* live there, right?" I say with apprehension, remembering how we were attacked on the football field. The same tug wrenches my gut, homesickness plaguing me once again. I force the sensation away and focus forward on the fairy.

Rolinda stops, causing more than one grumbled response from passersby. A set of fairies in their small form, one glowing red and another purple, flit around her, making annoyed gestures. A dwarf woman, her large-busted chest practically falling out of her leather gown, glares at our guide, but steps around her.

"Why would you ask that?" she says, looking at me with large eyes.

My hands fiddle in front of my body. This woman fairy is rather terrifying. She stares at me with hard eyes, and I want to shrink away and hide somewhere until she forgets about me. Her eyes, filled with intense intrigue, soon soften and go wide.

"Oh dear! You were attacked on *earth* by the dark races? That can't be!" she exclaims, delicate hands flying to a mouth wide like an O. "But how did they not melt to nothing?"

Joy, she's poking around in my mind yet again. At least it saves time in communication.

I assume she is referring to the black tar. It makes sense that they wouldn't call it tar. Without pavement or cars, they'd have no need for it.

"I'm not sure," I say, looking at Amir. I'm about to translate when Rolinda speaks up again.

"I'm speaking English, halfling. That is why your human friend can understand. Spare me the time and answer my question from before."

I bite the side of my cheek, trying to keep a blush out of my complexion. I really dislike that they can read minds.

"I'm not sure. I already told you," I say. "All I know is that some held these stones that glowed red. They threw one of them, and we ended up here. Well, not *here*, but in the desert near goblins."

Rolinda gasps, her hand covering her upper chest. "I say! You survived an attack of goblins? You are more formidable than I expected."

Gee. Thanks for that one.

"You're quite welcome," she replies to my thoughts.

Another twinge of intense annoyance.

"Do you know what the stones were?" I ask, intentionally thinking of one in as much detail as I can.

Rolinda's face flickers with something. Is that fear? She hides it quickly and purses her lips.

"I have no idea. But blessed day that it sent the halfling heir of the dragon realm to Qotan, with a human friend, no less," she adds. "But the others with you, where are they now?"

I open my mouth to answer, but she waves her hand.

"Oh, you were separated in battle; I very much hope they are all right."

I furrow my brow, wondering if I should call her out on her hidden fear, but I decide against it. It's not worth it. Based on my experience with her, she probably won't react to me calling her a liar.

She shoots me a glare and turns away, continuing. And now she just heard me call her a liar.

The fairy moves off at a measured pace. I grunt, yanking off my shoes and going in my socks. There's no way I'm getting through that brownie knot anytime soon.

We follow her a short way, Gobby padding along as the dog. Soon, we arrive at an incredible building. It's large and wide, spanning between a dozen trees, the trunks plunging into the roof at various intervals. The whole thing appears to be made of vines, most brown and dirty, but some fresh and green. Flowers and unopened buds form all over the vines and roots, peppering the top with multiple colors and adornments. Birds flutter their wings, landing and picking at the large colored petals.

This building looks like it came straight out of a fantasy book. I catch a whiff of the flowers that bloom on the roof, bringing me back to memories of camping and mountain biking with Dad back on earth.

The thought makes my stomach clench, so I abandon it. Dad will be okay. I'm sure of it. I found out the man's a fighter only days ago, but I cling to the memory of him fighting fiercely. It gives me hope that he's not dead.

"This is the settlement gathering building for welcoming all visitors," Rolinda says in a jubilant tone, her wings giving another flit. "All guests are welcome, I suppose."

The expression she gives the disguised Gobby carries more than discomfort. She looks like a cross teacher, ready to pounce on a disobedient teen before ordering them to detention. Only, I'm pretty sure a fairy with magic will do more than put Gobby in detention. Without thinking, I move in front of him, putting both hands behind my back and grinning widely.

"It looks amazing! I appreciate the hospitality," I say with a knowing tone.

Rolinda's eyes move lazily from where Gobby hides to my face. She smiles the most fake smile I've ever seen in my life. Her body spins around, and she holds up her hands. The wall before us is a mess of vines hanging down limply, most of them thick and gnarly. The vines shift of their own accord, responding to the fairy's gesture. Immediately behind this sits a wooden door that looks like it hasn't been opened in ages.

I clear my throat, staring at it. "It looks like you haven't had visitors in a little while."

She stares at me flatly. "I'm sure I don't know what you mean. This door is used regularly enough. We had a group of humans here only six months ago. That's recent."

I nod, raising my eyebrows so I don't let on that "six months ago" is *not* an encouraging thing to hear. It makes the door look more imposing. What if those visitors are now rotting in the forest? I come up with that on my own, fear worming its way into my chest. Based on the surprised and outlandish looks we are getting from the creatures mulling about, I don't get the sense that they are used to visitors.

We stand there awkwardly, then Amir and I exchange a glance. He asks me with his raised eyebrows what we're supposed to do, and I shrug.

"Well, get on in there. What are you waiting for?" the fairy says.

"Oh, you want us to go through that door by ourselves. We thought, because of your—um—magic and whatnot, that you would need to open it," I say.

She giggles like a little girl. It sounds unnatural coming from a grown woman. I plaster a smile on my face.

"Okay, so we just go through. Anything else we need to know?" I ask.

The fairy shakes her head, lifting herself up to her tiptoes and winking at me. "Merely go on inside. This is the traitors' test, you see. Those unknown to our settlement must first enter the traitors' test. It's only a trifle."

My heart thuds quickly, the implications of the name flying through my mind.

"But we aren't traitors, so why do we have to go through that door?" Amir asks.

I'm grateful he did because I'm still processing what's going on. Not only am I overwhelmed at the sight of so many strange races, but I feel like a failure. If I am truly half dragon—and the heir to the high kingdom of all light races—shouldn't I already be aware of these practices? Of course, it's not my fault, but the way Rolinda looks at me expectantly weighs on me.

"Then you have nothing to worry about," she chimes. "It's an ancient tradition upheld by the fairy race in most Qotan settlements. All magic of dark means will be stripped, as well as any protective wards or spells. There's no need for them here. They can be re-enchanted upon leaving the building."

"Fair enough. I guess I'll go—"

I'm about to offer to go first, but I pause when I catch sight of two bright eyes staring at me from a dozen yards away. It's one of the most terrifying creatures I've ever seen. He's a man, but his whole body, chest, arms, legs, and head are *massive*—like two to three times that of a normal human. His eyes bulge from their sockets, and scarier than any of that is the dark purple skin and veins that cord up his arms and neck into his face. Spiraled black horns poke through his red hair, too.

He looks angry. Not like "I stubbed my toe and it hurt" type of angry but like "You killed my family, and I will exact revenge on you" type of angry. A coldness creeps up my limbs like my hand is slowly being slipped into an icy lake. His eyes bore into me, and I clench my fists, ready to summon fire to protect myself. Then he does a curious thing. He flashes a dangerous grin at me and holds up his hands. Darkness forms in the space directly around him as if the light were being sucked out of the air. In a moment, the cloud of darkness is gone, and so is he.

I gulp. Images of him appearing out of nowhere to chop me to pieces flow through my mind.

"Amir, you go first. I'll stick out here to make sure everyone is safe." I try not to think of Gobby and his disguise. None of the fairies around me react, so they must not be reading my thoughts.

My friend pales and swallows hard. "Okay. You sure? Cause I think a half dragon with a scale-skin shield is better equipped to deal with booby traps."

Rolinda frowns. "With what? I've never heard of such things. Traps, there are none, but certainly none of the booby variety, whatever that is. I must say English is an odd language."

She clicks her tongue at us.

"Ah, those are booby traps. My, my, don't think of such dark practices. Those are unbecoming of light races," she scolds, waving a finger at Amir.

He huffs, clearly unimpressed by her mind reading.

The whole situation is both comical and terrifying, so I just laugh at the interaction and gesture to Amir. He sighs before walking up to the decrepit door. It droops from its hinges, and I wonder if Amir opening it will make the whole thing fall off. My friend grips the metal handle and pulls outward.

"What the—" I whisper.

Behind the old door is a flood of something strange. It's like a waterfall, only mostly translucent—save for patches of color that writhe within the falling substance.

"The removal magic, as you can see. It's harmless," Rolinda says.

Amir grunts and eyes me critically. I catch his gaze, but only briefly. I'm too busy checking the spot where the huge man stared at us by the edge of the settlement. At length, Amir gets the courage, and with muttered prayers to some deity, he walks through the flowing, colorful water. It doesn't move as he walks under it. The sight is so unnatural that I shiver. My back tingles. I swear we are being watched by something malicious. There's a gathering of small glittering fairies, dwarves, and elves standing a bit off, but they appear harmless. They whisper to each other excitedly, watching us as if we were the next best thing on TV.

"Okay, Gobby, um, dog who's well-trained," I say. "Go on."

I sound like an idiot, but I can't outright say he's a goblin.

A few of the fairies gasp, making twittering sounds of shock. I've flubbed up. They read my mind and recognize who he is. Before it becomes more of a problem, the dog next to me barks, then saunters to the door. He hesitates for a moment before continuing through. A burst of light blinds me. It's completely soundless, like I've lost all my hearing and gone to a firework show.

My eyes flutter open to black sunspots. The waterfall remains unchanged.

Rolinda clicks her tongue. "We'll see if he survived that one. Deceitful green leech."

I round on her. "You *killed* him? What's wrong with you?"

I'm shouting. My palm heats up, and I sense fire right on the edge of being summoned. I refrain, however, and glare at the fairy.

"You knew it would hurt him!"

She shifts her head side to side, a wide grin on her white teeth. "Oh, of course, he used illusory magic already. Good luck! Either go through that door or you leave the settlement. You decide."

And with that, she disappears, a flash of light the only warning sign. I eye the normal door far to my left, which has a decently steady flow of people going in and out. Could I make it if I ran? Would I get in trouble? I'm technically a half mythical creature, so maybe I wouldn't get caught.

I don't know where *that* door leads. Of course, I don't know where this one goes either, but at least I know *who* is through this one. Knowing Gobby could be hurt, I square my shoulders, glare at the spot where the huge disappearing man once was, then stalk forward. I instinctively close my eyes, waiting for the wash of cold, but it doesn't come. Instead of the sensation of walking through a waterfall, it's like I'm walking through flames. I gasp. The heat washes over me so intensely that I almost fall forward. Pins and needles explode over every inch of me, and when I'm finally through the strange magic, my whole body is covered in red scales.

I emerge into a darkened hallway. The walls appear to be made of thick, packed earth. It's wet and damp inside, but my nose perks up at the scent. It reminds me of those summer days out with the horses after a rainstorm or working in the garden with Dad. The thought of my dad slams into me like a ton of bricks, and the intense tugging sensation returns to my stomach. I'm homesick all over again, and it sucks.

Orbs of floating lights glow at the top of the hallway, which is only a few feet above my head. Suddenly I feel claustrophobic and want to duck down, afraid that if I stand up too tall, I'll hit my head and cause the whole ceiling to come crashing down on me. My skin is still hot from the magic waterfall, and I worry that my hands will burst into flame and cause chaos in this narrow hallway. Breathing deeply, I focus on one of the orbs, the green light pulsing slightly. I frown, looking closer. As I do, I note that it's not a floating orb at all. It's a plant that's growing from the dirt. It's a large bulbous thing, a healthy green, and about the size of my balled-up fist. And the glow is coming from beneath the green surface.

"David! Help Gobby!"

Amir's voice clicks something in my brain, and I peer down at my feet. Amir appears unscathed in the dim light, but Gobby is lying unconscious.

"What happened?" I shout, leaning down and shuffling over to his prostrate form.

"I don't know! After I went through the door, nothing happened. I turned around and waited for you, but he came next. He flopped down on the ground and hasn't moved since," Amir says, biting his lip. "I can't tell if he's breathing—but CPR—on him—I don't think—"

I growl and lean down to press my lips against Gobby's mouth. My brain almost makes me recoil at the sensation. His skin is rough and hard, like I'm putting my lips to an ancient tree with thick, gnarly bark. Even though I manage to keep the contact, I can't stop a shiver from going through me. I puff the air into his mouth and lean back. Cursing, I realize I forgot to tilt his head back. After that, I lean in and try again. This time, the air enters his body, but it expands down lower than I would expect.

Of course, goblin anatomy is different. Still, the air went in, so I put my hands on his chest and press. It doesn't feel right. I'm panicking now, my limbs shaking to no end, but I keep trying.

"There is no use—" a deep and clear tone says from in front of us.

I jump to my feet, my hand blazing to life. Light flickers across the face of a man—no, a *demon*—who stares at me. Based on the sound of his voice, I guess the demon is male, but my demon experience is too limited to be sure. He's large and broad, so much so that his shoulders and back press against the ceiling of the narrow hall. His neck is stooped so that his head is at a ninety-degree angle. His eyes are pure black, and his purple skin is ribbed and full of deeper purple veins. The black horns coming from his skull are straight and point forward. They are shaped like a bull's.

He's clearly the same race as the person I spotted outside. He wears the strangest formal attire. The cut looks something like a tuxedo, except underneath the coat he isn't wearing anything, and the coat itself has no collar. It makes me think of pajamas but fancy. His bare chest shows thick muscles and more streaming veins.

"He is a goblin, and he's been marked as a traitor," the demon says.

"What did you do to him?" I say through gritted teeth. The fear imposed by the hulking creature flows through my limbs, but that's not what's making me shake. It's the anger from seeing my fallen friend. They did this to him, and I have a suspicion that Rolinda knew all along what would happen when Gobby went through the door.

"He is not dead. Calm yourself," he says. He puts up his hand and closes it sharply. The lights from the plant bulbs on the walls go dark, then zoom through the air and into his palm. My flame's light does the same, plunging us into darkness. I flinch. I can still feel the heat of my fire, but it's like all the light was absorbed completely. Having no choice, I let my fire go out. The eerie, glowing waterfall from behind me is still lit, but I can hardly make out the huge man through the dim. My skin has returned to its normal state. I kind of wish it didn't. Not if I have to fight this dude.

"Follow me," he says.

Frowning, I lean down to Gobby.

"Carry the goblin and follow me," the man instructs. I hear an intense shuffling sound, followed by grunting.

"Can you at least put the lights back on?" I ask.

Our guide grunts, his deep voice reverberating down the hallway. Suddenly the plant bulb lights come back on, and my eyelids flutter, trying to deal with the brightness. I spot the guy halfway through turning around in the narrow hall. He looks less than pleased, but he's holding his hand outward as if he let the captive light free.

"Thanks—" I say awkwardly.

He nods, his body still halfway turned, then continues to grunt and shuffle. Dirt falls from the ceiling of the hallway in droves. Small rocks embedded in the underground tunnel ceiling also rain down, pattering on the earthy ground. The whole process is extremely strange to watch. I wonder how he managed to make it down here in the first place. After a few minutes of grunting and shifting, he finally faces the other direction.

"Follow," I hear his deep tone order, but it's muffled by his body. He starts shambling down the narrow way slowly.

Amir and I exchange a glance but say nothing else. I don't like this arrangement, but I also don't like the idea of going back through the light waterfall. Bending over, I manage to get the unconscious goblin under my shoulder and stand up. I grunt when his back hits the ceiling, and I have to stoop so that he doesn't drag against the top of the hallway.

I'm relieved when the top extends upward to give us more space. Our strange guide ahead can now stand up as well. The floor transitions to a detailed tile of many colors, like a mosaic of plants and other animal life. The walls turn from earth to hard gray stone. The light plants, however, don't end. They continue to illuminate the way for us until we enter a larger hall, this one bustling with creatures. This must be the main entrance.

Our guide turns to the side suddenly, and I notice a small fairy floating in the air. Through the blue glow, I recognize Rolinda's face, contorted in a disgusted expression. She hovers away from the large purple-veined demon.

"You made it through in one piece—most of you, that is," Rolinda's liquid tone says. "Poor dear. Seems he could not pass the traitors' test. It's a shame. Thank you, demon, for bringing them through."

Her words confirm my assessment of the man. He looks similar to what Krista looks like when she goes all massive, except her skin remains the pale of her humanity. My stomach twists. They could be in trouble. My mind takes a left turn as Rolinda grimaces once more at the demon. Why is she appalled by him? There's a history there I'll have to uncover.

"Come this way. Ferona is most interested in meeting you," Rolinda says.

Amir and I shift closer together as we pass the demon. He doesn't make any moves toward us, but my skin prickles, my brain imagining him swiping outward and knocking us down with a quick blow. He doesn't, fortunately. Walking through the bustling creatures, fairies, elves, dwarves, and other things is much more difficult than I expect—especially with a practically dead goblin on my shoulder. Eventually, Gobby turns enough heads and causes many yelps of fright that it causes a bit of a commotion, clearing a path for us through the chaos.

Finally, we reach a set of double doors made from red wood.

"Ferona will speak to you here, in private," she says.

So many questions flicker through my mind, but I have to ask first about the hulking man.

"Who is that? Why is he here if you don't like him?"

I can make out Rolinda's tiny face through the blue glow of her aura. She looks confused before her expression brightens. "Oh, that is the defense of this building. I'm sure you gathered he's a demon. Nasty fellows they are. Never get on the wrong side of one. They'll make sure you never have the chance again."

She turns her nose up in disgust, and I can only think of Krista. Another image forms in my head, and I swallow hard. The man who watched me outside is another demon. Images of his smug face and fiery-red hair stab my mind. How is he connected to this? I'm even more uneasy now that I recognize who—or *what*—he is.

"It's a shame the dragons allowed the demons to join the light races. They've tainted us. Them and the sirens. Nasty shame, it is," Rolinda murmurs.

I want to ask another question, but the double doors open of their own accord. My stomach clenches, and I sense Amir sidling closer to me, shifting so he's behind me. I feel even more guilty for dragging him into this place, but there's nothing I can do about it now. My shoulder aches from Gobby's weight. I'm hoping I can set him down soon.

"Enter," a regal woman's voice sounds from inside.

Taking a deep breath, we walk forward through the doorway.

I MEET JARED'S FAMILY

I'm assaulted with the scent of flowers—and when I say assaulted, I mean it's so strong that my nostrils burn, and I practically cough up a lung. I know it's not just me because Amir hacks loudly, too. On top of that, it's so bright that I'm forced to squint to prevent myself from going blind. The air feels cool and fresh, and warbling water sounds off to my right. Blinking the brightness out of my eyes, I manage to get them to focus on my surroundings.

And it's a whole lot of color.

Flowers of various shapes, sizes, and shades adorn the entire floor. The room is basically one massive field of flowers. There's a pattern to how they all grow, but I can't quite decipher it.

Rolinda sighs behind me. I didn't realize she planned to come in with us. She made it sound like she had other things to do. I guess "private" doesn't mean without her being here. Or maybe that's just her personality. She's already given off the "I'm a snooty teenager, and I can do what I want" type of vibes.

"I love this room so much. It's where we grow all the flowers we need for the medicinal concoctions. Need to sleep better at night? Try the little pink ones there. Need relief from intense pain? Those purple ones with the yellow innards. How about if you want to feel more energized? Then—"

"Rolinda, now is not the time to educate these guests on the practicality of our fields," the booming female voice sounds from all around us.

My chest tightens and I hold my hand out just in case I need to flame someone in the face.

Rolinda's tiny face flushes, and she looks down at the ground. Her wings are a blur as they keep her upright in the air, but there isn't any sound matched to the movement. Shouldn't they sound like hummingbirds or something?

"Yes, my liege," she says.

Amir and I exchange glances. His eyebrows are arched up high and his chest rises and falls rapidly. He's either very excited or extremely nervous. I assume it's the former because he starts muttering things to himself, his hands a flurry of motion. He's entered one of his geek modes. It's best to let him be.

"Are these truly the humans we've been notified of?" the disembodied voice asks. "They look more disheveled than I would have thought."

I frown, inspecting my person to see what she means. And yeah, I see it. My white football pants have stains all over. They look like I found them in a dumpster. My football jersey is ripped in too many places to count, and my cleats look like they've never had a proper sole in their lives. Based on all the things we've experienced in the last few days, it shouldn't be surprising that I look homeless. With a quick sniff of my chest, I pull a face. I smell like death incarnate. Amir looks the same, only his jeans are in decent condition. His backpack hangs from one strap on his shoulder. It is ripped down the center, papers exposed to the air. I don't know how he managed to keep it with him after all we've been through.

"Yes, my liege, and this one"—Rolinda gestures to me broadly with one of her minuscule hands—"has the blood of a dragon. Ellistra's brood."

Ellistra. I've heard my mother's name before, but hearing it come from a living fairy feels so much more important. The very person I've wanted to meet my whole life. Even after a few days in this insane place I've come no closer to meeting her than I had before.

"I see," the high-pitched woman's voice bellows, "and I see the goblin failed the traitors' test. It's probably for the best. No friend to Urothar is welcome here. Now, how about I slip into a better form for our conversation."

A rush of wind comes from nowhere, tugging on the upright flowers and making them dance to and fro. I can feel it on my cheeks, my sweaty brow, and my back. The scent is the most amazing and fresh thing I've ever had the pleasure of enjoying—an exaggeration, of course, but I'm going to bask in it shamelessly. The wind picks up flower petals in droves. It's like the huge flower patch offered itself up to the wind. I clench my hands and watch as thousands of petals come together, forming into a massive shape of something.

Standing before us is a large woman made entirely of flower petals. She has a slightly more rump shape than Rolinda.

The movement and wind die down as quickly as it had started, and then I hear the voice again. Only this time, the flower-petal woman's mouth moves along with the words.

"Now that's better, for you at least. It probably felt like you were talking to a ghost."

I nod but don't know what else to say. I'm too busy staring at the fairy made from the flower petals. She's at least a foot taller than me, with her hair pulled up in a bun and half-moon spectacles perched on the tip of her nose. She looks motherly, and I have the strange urge to hug her, which makes me flush. Flower petal wings flap lazily behind the flower fairy's back. Despite being made entirely of flora, I can see a resemblance to Jared. It's both striking and strangely vague, so much so that I can't describe it.

"I am Ferona, queen of the fairies of Qotan. Let me have a good look at you," the fairy queen says. "My goodness, you look worse for wear. What did you have to go through to make it here?"

The question is straightforward, but I find myself unable to answer. What *have* we had to go through? It's been weeks since we came here, hasn't it? No, that can't be, the game was just days ago.

"Um—we were sent to the middle of a desert first, and then we were captured by goblins . . ." I pause, then turn my head to look at Gobby, who is still on my shoulder. My mind goes blank.

Ferona raises eyebrows made from a bright set of yellow daffodils. The daffodils make up her long hair as well. My guess is that she's a blonde. That would explain Jared's hair coloring.

"And then?" she urges me on.

I blink slowly. What has gotten into me? It's like I can't speak properly, like something is trying to overtake my brain. I could probably lay down and go to sleep right here. I'm exhausted, and the intoxicating smell of the flowers is lulling me, calling me to slumber. I shake my head to try and wake up. Gobby's weight drags me down. Given the lack of threat and the fact that I might pass out in exhaustion, I gently lay the unconscious goblin in the bed of flowers at our feet.

The queen purses her lips, then clicks her tongue. "Let's try something else. Simply recount your journey in your mind. I'll be watching."

So I do.

I think about how we tromped through the desert on foot, drinking from the strangely clear and cold river until we were captured by the goblins. I think of how I learned about my scale protection and what happened with Gobby. I think about the crelotin and how strange it was riding them. My heart pangs at the thought of my mount. She wasn't really *mine*, but the way we shared emotions all the time made her feel that way. Next, I recall being captured and taken by the elves. It feels like a blur. Then, I think of my leg and how there is no longer pain. My dragon blood finally healed it. It was about time. Then, there was Gulran, the red glowing stone, and—

"No need to continue. I believe I understand what happened until now. My dear, to think that the orc king's own kin tried to send you to your demise is quite overwhelming. If he had captured you, I fear everything would be lost. How fortunate for you to have been delivered so close to this settlement."

Questions flow through my mind so quickly and overwhelmingly that I slip to my knees, the soft petals cushioning my fall. Some of the more colorful petals smear their color on the white fabric of my football pants, but at this point, I don't care. They're already so grungy, and they smell like trash. The thought makes me grimace and look up at the queen. Rolinda giggles and makes a show of covering her nose.

I really hate the mind reading thing.

"Please don't fret, young dragon halfling. I've met with many adventurers over my lifespan, and believe it or not, I have smelled far worse than you. My senses are a bit dulled in this projection though. Still, we'd best get you and your friend cleaned up."

Her pupils shift over to Amir. Is that derision in her eyes? Or simply surprise that he's not Jared or Krista—the other halflings.

"I must say, it is fortunate that your human did not wind up missing. It's a dangerous time to be human in Qotan. We will outfit your young friend and ensure that he is properly transported to one of the grand gates to earth. Only two remain open as of late," she says.

I clear my throat. "So there *are* gates to earth? Where are they? How can we get to them?"

I had no reason not to believe my dad's assurances that the gates existed, but it's much easier to trust someone from here with this information.

My mind is frantic. This confirmation gives me a burst of hope and energy. Maybe we can get home easier than I thought.

"I fear one of them is within the orc's territory. The other still functioning is within your own kingdom, young dragon prince. There was once a portal in each of the major kingdoms, but they have degraded over time."

I hate being called dragon prince. I'm not able to keep the grimace off my face, but she must not notice or doesn't care because she continues talking.

"The dragon's portal is the one you must reach. Through it, we can send this boy home," she says.

I slap my chest enthusiastically. "The others will be relieved to leave."

The fairy queen inspects me. I have a distinct feeling—like a tickle in my mind—and I realize she's sifting through my thoughts. Shaking my head to deal with the sensation, I clear my mind of all thoughts. It must have worked because the flower-petal queen crinkles her brow.

"There is no need to remove your thoughts. I mean you no harm," she says. "Who are your other companions?"

My mouth falls open. "You don't know? I would have thought—"

"No need for that. I am the monarch of a major kingdom within Qotan. I can't be aware of all the entrants to Qotan. If I could, that would help us reduce unnecessary contact with humans."

There was the hard tone again, the slight derision. This is all so overwhelming. So, in my mind, I show her images of Krista, Jared, and my dad.

The queen's eyes widen. "My son! So, he has ventured to our homeland."

Her form shifts and ripples as she moves so close to me that I can feel the tingly sensation of her presence. My instinct, and my personal bubble of space, pressures me to shove her away. I suspect any attempt to do so wouldn't have an effect. She's a collection of flower petals, after all.

"My dear boy, he's so grown!" Her expression turns grave. "It does not bode well that you three are here. That's one half of the required souls for the prophecy. If Urothar manages to get a hold of you, that would be devastating. But I see your mother's ward is protecting you well."

I don't know what to say next, so I choose to focus on what she said last.

"My mother's ward. What does that mean?"

She smiles broadly, then holds up her hand. A vine shoots upward out of nowhere and flings at me like a whip held by some invisible hand. I gasp, my mind becoming alert, but I can't move fast enough. The spiked vine wraps around my arm. But I don't feel any sharp pains, only warmth. Red scales cover my wrist where the vine resides. I try to pull away, and fortunately, there is no resistance. The vine listens to me.

"*That* ward. As a dragon kin, you can call on the scales at will, but Ellistra blessed you with protection from your enemies until you could come home. When you face her once again, the spell will be broken. I placed a similar ward on Jared, though not as strong."

Enemies. That would explain why the scales didn't activate against the elves. I frown, watching the scales slowly disappear from my arm.

She waves a hand in the air. "Yes, you are correct about the elves being your friends; that is *perhaps* why they did not work. My attack wasn't anything less than serious, which is why they worked just now. I trust your mother's ward wholeheartedly, hence my reaction. Think naught of it."

Her eyes go all misty, and she looks off in the distance. "Indulge me, dragon prince, and think of my son."

Even though I feel like a really weird familial third wheel, I do take the time to think of Jared.

I think about how he shifted into animals to save me back on earth. I think about his plunge into the river with Amir, their eyes flying open and their mouths gasping at the intense cold. I think of how he was willing to sacrifice himself to get us free and to save Gobby.

"How wonderful of a boy he is. And with my hair, no less," she says, clasping two hands together as a thank-you. "And the redheaded girl. Krell's own offspring."

"That is Krista. The half demon."

She nods slowly. She already knows this, having read my mind, but I still felt the need to introduce her. "Three of the six, all in one place. It must be coming true."

Ferona speaks in a measured tone, her voice going low as she thinks about Krista. There's the same anger I spotted earlier in Rolinda's face. A history. Something that does not bode well for my friend. Okay, Krista isn't technically my friend, but I don't know how else to think of her. My chest aches with longing to see my dad again, to know if he's alive. My mind latches onto the fact that she mentioned "six," but I don't have time to think about it before the queen continues.

"They are safe," Ferona says. "My informants in the elf kingdom told me that Ilvinar—the elf king—sent an envoy to fetch them hours ago. They should be safe there."

I breathe a sigh of relief.

"Pardon me, ma'am, or fairy—queen, person," I stumble on the words, not sure how to address her.

"Call me Ferona. You are the high prince, after all."

"Sure, okay. Ferona, what is this prophecy you are talking about? What does it have to do with us?"

Amir grunts next to me.

"And why are humans so endangered?" Amir cuts in, his voice cracking slightly.

Ferona holds up a finger made of purple and pink flowers. "One at a time. Humans, as of late, have been going missing left and right. When we discovered this, we evacuated as many to the human realm as possible."

"And you think I might go missing, too?" Amir asks, his voice full of emotion.

Her lips—made of a bundle of roses—purse, which makes her look almost comical. She stands up tall, her wispy wings flapping behind her back in a mesmerizing rhythm. I marvel once again at the detail of the flowers. Each wing is crafted with exquisite intricacy.

Glancing over at Rolinda, I wonder how to scale this version of the fairy queen is. When I first heard that Jared was her son, I almost laughed out loud. That kid is huge. To me, it's inconceivable that he could come from something as small as a fairy. But I didn't consider their human forms.

"I fear you will be taken, yes," she replies. "It is a wonder that you have not been captured yet. To think that three of the royal heirs could have fallen into the orc king's hands.... All would have been lost."

She's speaking like it's a well-known fact. Yet, I wasn't aware of the other kid's existence until days ago. Jared and Krista clearly knew about me. They knew I existed, and somehow, they managed to find me. Why did I get the short end of the stick?

"You keep talking about more of us. Are there other half humans? I mean, I met the orc king's son earlier," I say offhandedly.

You would have thought I said the most offensive thing in the world. Rolinda gasps and puts her hand to her tiny chest, and Ferona's mouth opens like a fish, her brows raising high on her forehead.

"You don't know?" she says.

"Don't know *what*? What's going on? Why would the orc king want us so badly?" I ask.

Aside from the fact that he wants to take over Qotan, I have a feeling in my gut that there is something else going on with us half bloods.

"Rolinda, please seal the door if you will," the queen says quietly.

The tiny blue fairy flits away from us, her wings still soundless. Her glowing form grows less distinct and more into an orb of blue light. My stomach drops as the room takes on a solemn tone. I have the feeling I'm about to hear some bad news. I flinch away instinctively. I want to hide somewhere. Anywhere. There's something foreboding about this conversation.

"The human should leave," Ferona says. She also eyes Gobby's limp body. "And this should never fall on the ears of one from the dark races."

My jaw stiffens. Does she really think she can kick my friends out? Gobby's unconscious, and I'm pretty sure that—unless dark races can spy while they are out cold—he's not a risk. And there's no way that she's going to kick Amir out of here. With humans apparently going missing all the time, I can't let him out of my sight.

I ball my hands into fists at my sides, a burst of confidence and adrenaline entering me. It's hard to say if I'm crazy or if I'm playing a part, but I feel princely. Focusing on that, I stare the queen down.

"David, I care not for your worries, but they must leave. I insist—" Ferona says, replying to my unspoken thoughts.

"No, they stay," I say through clenched teeth.

She glowers at me. "I am the queen of this kingdom, and therefore have all the rule and say. They will leave our presence while we discuss this, or—"

"No," I say again. "If you force them to leave, then I go with them. Whatever you have to say can be trusted with Amir. Gobby is unconscious; he won't hear a thing."

The queen narrows her eyes.

"If the human boy should fall into the wrong hands, this could put you and Qotan at risk," she warns.

I shrug. "I'm already in enough danger as it is. Amir stays."

I glare at her hard, trying to sound authoritative. I'm not entirely sure how the politics work in Qotan, but I'm part of the high kingdom over the light races, so that must mean something. Sure, I'm probably not higher than a literal queen, but I try my luck.

And it plays out. Though based on the look in her eyes, I'm pretty sure she's considering ending me with her fairy powers.

"Very well," she concedes. "The prophecy, then."

That does sound foreboding.

"Nearly forty years ago, the royals of the light races, and our new allies"— she says this with so much contempt that I assume she's talking about the demons—"sought the guidance of the seer dragon. Each race had soothsayers, those who claim to perceive the future. We wanted to know how to defeat the orc king and the races of the dark. The answer was not what we hoped it would be. We expected a weapon or a strategy. Something that would ensure the defeat of the growing opposition."

I lean forward on my feet, enthralled by her story, knowing inside that it's going to end with me. I hate that I know it, but the twisting of my gut tells me I'm about to find out why I'm here.

"In this, we were frustrated, for he spoke of an ancient law. Something lost to generations of light race heritage. It spoke of an agreement between humans and mythical races. The agreement gave the races the power to push back the darkness. Little did we know the former agreement had been broken and such protective power lost. The soothsayer dragon spoke of six half bloods—half human, half mythical race—as a ratification of the former magical agreement."

She looks solemn now, her flowered brows and lips turning downward. I breathe hard, and my heart beats so heavily that I think it might stop from exhaustion. Amir's hand reaches out and grasps mine. He senses it, too. Oddly enough, I wish Gobby was awake. What she is going to say isn't good.

"'That by the lives of six half bloods, the magic will be released. By their blood sacrifice, the agreement will be made whole.'"

There it is. My breath catches in my throat. Tears form in the fairy queen's eyes, but she keeps her face stoic. A tear, represented by a single rose petal, slips down her cheek. So that's it. They need six of us halflings . . . to *sacrifice.*

Amir squeezes my hand. It doesn't make me feel much better.

"Are you *serious*?" I ask, my voice tense. "You created half human children so that you could *kill us*?"

She looks pained. "Daviron—"

"Don't call me that! That's not my name! My mother may have called me that when I was born, but I'm not some prince. I'm just a confused football teen thrown into this stupid world for no reason other than to die!" I shout.

I know I'm acting like a child, but my ears are ringing, and all I hear is roaring in them. My palms are hot, and I squeeze my hands tighter. Amir yelps, letting go of me. I realize it's because they're burning up and on the brink of flames.

"I am sorry, David," Ferona says. "We didn't want you to find out this way. But there is a connection between you all. After the prophecy, only six of the monarchs were able to conceive with humans. None of the others did. We took that as fulfillment of the word. None of us had the heart to sacrifice you then, so we sent you away to the human realm with your human parents. Until you came of age and could understand your role—"

Rage rushes through me, and my hands explode in fire. The flames are so big that they climb up my arms, singeing my football jersey and licking at my cheeks. I should probably care about my jersey, but I don't. I'm angry, like *really* angry. At my dumb mom. At this dumb fairy queen. At Qotan. I just wanted to live a normal life, and I was doing a dang good job of it until the attack on the football field. It happened after Jared and Krista showed up. There's no way that was a coincidence.

"What does 'coming of age' even mean? I'm a sixteen-year-old. Is that old enough for you to slit our throats?" I say tersely.

She shakes her head. "Twenty, that was the plan. It was always the plan. But you were found and brought early to Qotan. There is no hiding you any longer."

Movement to my right pulls my attention that way, and I see Rolinda shift in a bright flash to her human form. She looks pained, her hands clasped before her. There's something in her gaze, something that breaks me. It's sadness . . . no, despair. I turn back to the queen.

She wears the same emotion. My anger diffuses slightly, the flames lowering to a smolder. A patch of flowers are singed in a ring around me, stopping just before the spot where I deposited Gobby. I almost fried him alive.

They don't *want* to kill us. They feel stuck. Probably as stuck as I feel.

"There isn't any other way?" I ask, my mouth trembling. I bite my lip, hard. The pain of it sends a shock through my brain to bring a bit of lucidity through the intense emotion.

"We don't believe so. These past sixteen years we've been trying to find another way, but there is none," she says.

I square my shoulders, trying not to lose my temper again or burst into embarrassing tears. "Fine. Where are the others? Besides me, Krista, and Jared."

She seems taken aback by this question, as if she expected my outburst to last longer before I came along.

"We do not know. They were lost to us at the same time you three were taken from earth. I knew somewhat where my lover was to take Joiron, but the others are simply hidden. There was a system devised to be able to find you, but I am not present to describe nor bestow said device upon you. Suffice it to say, the other three must be found."

Joiron must be Jared's fairy name. I wonder if he knows it. No one has mentioned it up to this point.

I narrow my eyes. "You mean, you have no idea where they are? I find that hard to believe, considering you can just read everyone's thoughts."

She shakes her head. "My abilities are only usable on those near me or in my projection. I was not there at the time the other children were taken. Though I sense you do not believe me, there is little I can do about it. If I *did* know, I would direct you to them."

My head is spinning. I crack my neck, trying not to let it take over my mind. Despite my efforts, I feel lightheaded. Thoughts of passing out dance in my mind, but I press them away. So many questions rush through me. I grab hold of one that is burning brighter than the others.

"How did the goblins and orcs come to earth? I thought they couldn't set foot there without melting?" I feel like I'm talking about a witch getting hit with a bucket of water.

"I do not know. Any race, dark or light, cannot set foot in the human realm, not anymore. It's become too corrupt of a world. I'm not certain how they survived long enough to send you here. But I fear they will soon find the other three royal halflings. They are not in Qotan. I know because our searching devices cannot see them."

I still don't understand what she means by "searching devices," but she did say she'd get to that later, so I push it away. My legs feel like they will soon come out from under me, but I grit my teeth and force them straight.

"And the other halflings? Who are they?" I ask.

"I do not know, fully. We agreed not to share much information about our kin until the time that you were all twenty years of age. All I know is which of the races succeeded in bearing a half human heir. You three, plus that of the elves, the dwarves, and the sirens."

The tone of her voice changes on the last one, like she's trying to hold back contempt. She doesn't try hard enough. I log a mental note to discover what she had against sirens. I'm not familiar with a lot of fantasy creatures, but I think those are the ones that sing to sailors, taking advantage of them to eat them. Okay, now I feel sick.

"I do not know where they are on earth—or what their traits or names are." She sighs. "But now that you three are together, I fear we must gather the others, lest they fall into the hands of the dark races. If they can go to earth, the others are at risk. You must find them."

She says this last part while staring directly at me. It feels like she's staring into my soul. In the whole of my regular life, I did not see myself becoming a real-life "quester" like Amir reads about. None of it seems fair. I just want to play football and go to college. Who knows? I might have been able to find a girl and settle down someday. That doesn't sound like it's going to be possible anymore. Something burns in my blood. This is my duty. My responsibility.

"I'll find them," I say with conviction. I look to Amir. "We need to get back to earth. You shouldn't be here, not with humans going missing."

Amir looks offended. "You're seriously going to kick me out of this party? I've *literally* been living my life vicariously through fantasy books. And I find out my friend is a *half dragon* and has a quest to find other half-blooded teens. You really think I'm going to sit by the side? No way, man."

He raises an eyebrow at me, and I can't help but laugh. He sees this as an adventure and not a terrifying life experience. We've almost died multiple times, but he is apparently unworried. I decide not to argue with him. In the end, if we find a way to earth, I'll leave him whether he likes it or not. My chest constricts at that thought. It's kind of a betrayal, but I can't let him die for no reason.

Rolinda eyes me knowingly, a slight tug on her lips. The look on her face shows me she agrees with my unspoken plan. I shoot her a glare that warns her against telling Amir anything.

"Okay, fine, but we still need to get back to earth," I say, looking back at the queen. "The gate, where is it exactly?"

She smiles. "We merely need to get you to your own home, Daviron—David. Your mother manages the gate to earth. As of late, it's been used to usher humans home. I doubt she will enjoy sending you back to earth. You're safer in Qotan, after all. However, it is imperative that you return to your realm; she will understand that even if it takes her time to come around. I will help you get to the portal. But first"—she concentrates on me—"you need new apparel and a bath."

Rolinda grunts. She's holding her nose and waving the air around as if she were in the sewer. I can't stop the heat that creeps through my cheeks.

"Yes, a bath, indeed. I'll have them drawn," the fairy says to the queen.

"And new clothing. Something more appropriate for this world. And get this young prince a weapon. Your fire may have protected you thus far, but there are more dangers that can't be burned to death."

I swallow, grateful I haven't met any of those yet.

"Passage to your allies will be provided after such. Farewell, dragon prince. Find the others, protect my son. Bring him home to me," she says.

I nod, unsure if I want that responsibility. Somehow I care more for Jared, now that I've met his mother. Thoughts of Krista dance in my mind, and heat flares in my chest. I press that away. I don't have time for whatever that complicated feeling is.

"I will," I reply.

She nods, then raises her hands high in the air. With a whoosh, her form disintegrates into flowers, greenery, and petals all fluttering to the ground. I'm assaulted with the intense floral smell from before. Just like that, the queen is gone.

"Come, dragon prince. I'll show you to your room for the night," Rolinda says.

I furrow my brow. "I don't think we have time to stay. Aren't we supposed to meet up with the others?"

Rolinda giggles. "No, it's much too late to travel. The night is dangerous, especially for humans."

She gives Amir a withering look, and he shrinks back, apparently unhappy with the attention.

"I'm to quarter you for the evening; by morning you will meet with your friends, and we will make our way to your palace."

Her words give me a sinking feeling. *My* palace? That does *not* sound right. I feel homesick again. All I want is to see my dad so I know he's okay. I want to see Jared, and strangely, part of me wants to see Krista. A tight feeling pulls at my gut, and I wince. It's not painful, but it's powerful, as if I'm about to have a bad bowel movement. I know it's connected to my homesickness, so I press thoughts of Kentucky to the back of my mind.

"Follow me, young sirs. You need your rest," Rolinda chimes.

I reach down to lift Gobby back up, wincing as I anticipate his weight returning to my shoulders.

"Oh, leave him. We'll take care of him for the night," Rolinda says, waving a hand.

I sit up and flash her an angry look. I don't even have to say the words.

"No harm will befall him. I swear on Ferona's life," she says, holding up a hand like she's making an oath.

"You better be telling the truth or I have a fireball with your name on it," I say, raising my eyebrows.

She purses her lips, but doesn't respond. Instead, she turns and leads us out of the room.

Amir huffs at the interaction. "Anything will be better than sleeping on a crelotin's back."

AN UNEXPECTED
COMPANION

When they said they were going to let us stay overnight, I didn't know we would be treated like kings. I stare at myself in a full-length mirror hanging on the wooden wall next to my bed. Adjusting my leather belt, I bite my lip. I feel like a fool. As I inspect my clothing, Amir's role-playing friends come to mind.

A beam of sunlight shines through the window at my back and splays a network of leaves and branches on the wall next to the mirror. Waking up this morning had been a lot easier than I expected. Turns out, when you have the natural call of animals in the bright and early morning, it's hard to sleep through it.

I've been spoiled by my suburban life. Who knew?

I stare at myself, the loose white shirt somewhat baggy on my frame. It doesn't look right, but I don't have anything else to put on. These are the only clothes Rolinda left for me. I slept in them last night. Was I supposed to? Probably not. But I was so tired that when I took the bath they'd drawn for me, I'd dressed and just passed out. The four-poster bed, with a dark wood frame, is austere and grand, making me feel like royalty.

I'm wearing somewhat formfitting pants. I think they call them breeches? I don't know. A bundle of gray fabric lays at my feet. It's a cloak they say is good for traveling, particularly in the cold. The boots fit me perfectly. In fact, everything seems to fit me perfectly. When I asked about that last night, Rolinda laughed and said that brownies don't need anything other than a quick glance to make clothing and shoes to size.

"Well, dragon boy, today is the day you face your mom," I say to my reflection.

This makes me sick to think about. An image of my mother flashes through my mind, and I grimace. It's not that I don't *want* to see her—but I kind of don't want to see her. Nothing like sidling up to my long-lost mother who sent me away to "protect me" but at the same time has plans to sacrifice me and five other teenagers.

Yeah, I'm not all that excited.

I sigh again, looking at the small wooden desk that sits next to the mirror on the back wall. A sword lays there, sheathed in a beautifully crafted and intricately designed scabbard of a deep brown leather. Feeling awkward at Rolinda's insistence that I have a weapon, I grasp the case and put it to my side. It is not as heavy as I thought it would be, but it's clearly a real sword.

After struggling with it for a few minutes, I finally get it situated. The person in the mirror is definitely *not* me. He's way too good-look-ing. His piercing blue eyes stare at me, a slight smile on his face.

I shake my head and look away. I don't like it, but I'll suffer through it if it means I'll get to my mother's palace safely. My football jersey, still stained from my travels, is folded nicely on the bed. I threw the pants and cleats away. I don't want to have to buy new ones and break them in, but the others were too far gone. In reality, Coach could get me a new jersey, but I'm attached to this one and don't want to let it go.

If I ever get to play football again. My throat tightens up and I clear it, trying to ward off the newfound truth of my life.

A soft knock raps on my door, and I flinch.

"Yes?" I ask.

A pause. "It is Rolinda. Are you suitably covered so that I may enter?"

I blush. The thought of a grown woman fairy seeing me without clothes mortifies me. It's not like I'm unaccustomed to being seen that way—I'm on the football team for crying out loud—but there are no girls on the team.

"Yes, I'm wearing clothes. Come on in," I say, staring back at my reflection.

The wooden door pushes open. Two large men are standing behind the slighter form of the blue fairy. When I say large, I don't mean tall. One of them is a dwarf about two heads shorter than me, but with arms so thick, they look like tree trunks. I recognize him as the dwarf from the day before. The other stands a few heads taller than me, has blue skin, and is shirtless. His abs and strong chest practically stare me in the face.

Rolinda squeals in delight and clasps her hands together. "My, my, those brownies outdid themselves. You look like a proper prince."

I grunt, my face growing a little hot. While my mind wants me to retort with something gristly and rude, I resort to something more polite.

"Thanks . . . I guess. I don't think clothes will make me feel any more princely than I do right now," I murmur. "That is to say, not in the slightest."

Rolinda laughs again, the sound mesmerizing. "You would be surprised what a fresh set of clothing can do for royalty. We don't dress up that way because we feel like it."

I start, my eyes finding hers. "Oh, you're royalty?"

She smiles at me, her deep brown eyes drawing me in like melting hot fudge. I shiver when I realize I'm wooing over a fairy. How lame can I get? It takes a lot of effort to tear my gaze away from her, but I do. I stare at the imposing elf behind her instead. All twitterpated feelings are gone in an instant because the elf looks like he'll crush me.

"Yes, I am the niece of the queen. My mother is her sister, though she's no longer living," Rolinda says.

There's a somber tone in her words. There's a story there. I'm not familiar with fairies and their life expectancy, but based on conversations with Amir, I don't get the sense they die often.

"Huh, so that would make Jared—"

"My cousin, yes," she replies.

I snap my attention toward her, and I'm lost in those eyes all over again. Her dark complexion, matched with those irises, makes me want to fall to my knees and give her anything she wants. Her smile deepens, like she knows she's doing something diabolical.

More pounding on my door makes me jump yet again. It sounds like there is an army outside wanting to kill me. It's rhythmic, so I guess it can't be something completely feral, given that it sounds like a sentient person. Whatever trance Rolinda holds me in breaks, and I call out to the door, my voice cracking like a prepubescent teenager.

"Come in!"

The door opens slowly, but no light filters through it. It's blocked completely by a large figure with purple veins protruding all across his arms and face. His pure black eyes peer at me, and his expression is blank. It's the same demon from before. My breath catches in my throat, and I tense, prepping to defend myself. He notices my reaction, and it seems to make him sad.

Not what I expected.

"It is time for you to leave. Your human friend and the goblin are waiting for you below," he says, his voice impossibly low, so much so that it vibrates my chest cavity with each word.

"Okay." It's all I can manage to say with this beast standing before me.

For a moment, no one moves, then Rolinda gestures wildly with her hands, indicating to the demon that he should leave. He grunts, then turns and shambles down the dirt hallway. Each light he passes dims so deeply that it almost goes dark, pulsing back to life as he moves away.

"Demons are so unpleasant," Rolinda says, crinkling her nose. "I still don't know why they were allowed to ally with the light races. No matter how hard they try, they'll never be one of us."

That's a harsh comment, but then again, I don't know too much about demons. Krista doesn't strike me as the best example of one either. Her temper gets *way* out of hand far too easily. I wonder how the demon who just walked away manages to keep his anger at bay.

Maybe he doesn't.

I remind myself that Krista wasn't my only experience with a demon. I saw that huge figure outside this building before I went through the traitors' test. He looked very similar to the demon here, only bigger and with flaming-red hair. I shiver, hoping I don't encounter him in a less ideal circumstance.

I don't feel safe following him—not alone at least. In an effort to ward off the discomfort, I ask a genuine question to banish the awkwardness of the demon interrupting us.

"Why do you say that? He seems nice enough."

No, he really doesn't. I'm just trying to make small talk.

She frowns, then looks after him.

"No need to worry; I am coming with you. *He* is one of the more pleasant demons. I would not say he's nice, but he's mostly kind. You should see him when he gets a sharp word from Ferona or any of the other patron fairies of this settlement. Yet, it's a wonder none of our buildings are smashed to pieces. It takes him ages to calm down. Normally, we send him into the forest to gather more wood. He's surprisingly productive when he's angry," Rolinda says.

These words are not encouraging, and I want to follow after him even less than I did before. I gaze down the dirt hallway, considering the thick roots that run through the floor and guessing how easily I could navigate them if the demon were to attack. I'm relatively nimble, sure, but these roots are thick and uneven. The apprehension is clear in my mind, and Rolinda chuckles lightly.

"I may dislike demons, but I can attest that Kroniv will not harm you. He's been a loyalist to the dragon queen, your mother, for many years. Plus, he can be more pleasant than you think if you get to know him," she says.

I nod, but I'm not thinking about that anymore. My mind is on the redheaded demon from the day before. A thought pops into my head, and I have to ask.

"Can demons, um, change their hair color? Like, with their powers?" I ask.

Rolinda stares at me, blinks twice, then holds her hand up to stifle a laugh.

"No, not at all, why would you ask something like that?" Her laughter comes out in stronger waves now.

I shrug. "Never mind. I just don't know much about them. That's all."

Suddenly I don't want her to come along. I don't need someone ridiculing me about what I don't know about the races in Qotan. Twisting my heels on the hard packed earth, I face the tunnel and stalk out. To my surprise, and now discomfort, Rolinda flits next to me in her fairy form.

"I do not mean to jest. You'll learn all you need to in time," she says.

My mouth stays glued shut. I wish I could keep her out of my head.

I'm surprised to catch up to the hulking demon. He did say to follow him, but I'd stalled long enough that I'd thought he would have made it farther. The moment the two of us are behind him, he picks up the pace, each of his heavy footfalls pounding the dirt floor. We lapse into silence for the next few minutes as he leads me through a couple winding tunnels and into the main hallway. As with the day prior, it's bustling with various creatures and animals. I pause, staring with wide eyes as a skunk walks by me. It looks in my direction, then sticks its tongue out at me.

Rolinda giggles.

"The skunk says that you really shouldn't stare," she says.

I bite the inside of my cheek. "You can read the skunk's thoughts?"

She raises her eyebrows. "Of course I can. Sure, I can't speak all the languages that I hear, supposing their thoughts are in words. Many beings just think in images. That skunk, for example, *did* think in images."

"Then, how did you know I offended him?"

She smiles wryly. "Well, he thought about you staring at him for a good while, then he imagined spraying you in the face. I put the rest together."

The floor changes from dirt to a patterned white mosaic tile walkway and opens up to about four times the width of the smaller tunnel we came from. Everyone seems so focused as they walk about, greeting each other in strange languages. A brownie couple, one that looks strikingly similar to the one I'd seen the day before, stalks up to me and smiles.

"Well, once again the brownies were able to fit the perfect clothing for an esteemed figure. You look quite the part, I must say," the squat man says.

Even though I'm used to compliments, it still feels strange. I didn't do any of the work. All I did was stand there while they mentally collected "measurements."

I can't complain. Every bit of the new clothing I wear is very comfortable. The boots fit me perfectly, and the material they used is tough, but it also melds to my feet. Based on the strong smell, it's fresh leather.

"Thank you for making them for me," I say.

He takes his little bowler hat off his head, showing he's almost bald except for the white-lined patch along the sides and back of his skull. His wife smirks at my compliment and smiles at me again.

"It's all in a day's work. Them's strong bits, to be sure. They'll keep you right safe as much as they can. Exceptin' you probably don't need much of that with your heritage," he says, then gives me a knowing look and walks away.

I frown as I watch them leave. Did word really travel *that* fast about who I am? I didn't talk to anyone. And Amir wouldn't either. The only person who could have—

I turn to Rolinda, my jaw locked.

She gives me a falsely innocent smile, then answers the question floating in my head.

"Don't be too cross with me. I only told my friend Hilda. She's known to keep secrets for hundreds of years."

Her smile deepens, and she stalks off after the hulking demon. He doesn't pause for me, but I can see that he's slowed his pace. As I trudge on, more and more creatures eye me—some are obvious, others try to keep it more discreet. I don't know why I'm so frustrated that more people know who I am. It's not like I was told to keep it a secret, but the attention seems like it could be dangerous.

The crowd thins out as we exit the tunnel and enter a tall and grand dome-like room. The ceiling is at least fifty feet above us and is made of the same dirt as the rest of the walls. Although, it's covered with thousands of the glowing green plants. Lights from within their membranes pulsate slowly, giving the illusion of green stars high above. My mouth falls open as I stare at them, taking it all in.

The floor is still made of intricate tile, but there appears to be some type of swirling, colorful design. Without the ability to see it from above, I can't tell what it's depicting, but I wonder if it's figures of some kind.

"Dave!" a familiar voice calls. My limbs flood with relief and I see Amir standing not too far off. Gobby lies on the hard ground still completely lifeless. I feel sick seeing him like that, but I trust the fairy queen's words that he's not dead, just in a coma of sorts.

Amir has changed clothes, wearing a similar outfit to my own. He still holds his backpack. He's clutching it so tightly that his knuckles are white. I raise an eyebrow, and he gives me a look that says he'll talk to me about it later. His expression brightens, and he gestures to his clothes.

"I feel like I'm living my DnD character. They even gave me a sword!"

He uses his free hand and pulls the sword free. The silver blade glints in the lights from above. The handle and end of his sword are plain. Well-kept, I can see that, but plain. I glance down at mine. A giant red ruby is set into the metal. The hems of my clothing glint as well, some precious-metal type thread woven into the fabric of the shirt and cloak. It's not something I noticed before, but with Amir here, I can see they made my clothing richer.

Some people would probably eat up this attention, but I hate it. I don't care if I have princely blood in me. I'm not a stronger or more capable warrior. Jared and Krista are. They should be revered more than me.

The doubt I harbor in my mind eats at my chest, and I push it away, plastering a false smile on my face.

"And I bet you don't smell like a bag of crap anymore," I say, elbowing him in the arm.

"Like you were much better yourself! You smelled like you'd played fifty football games without even looking at water," he jibes.

I shake my head and elbow him once more. We laugh together, almost as if this were a completely normal day after school in Kentucky. Then Amir's eyes fall on the demon, and his face melts away.

"Augh!" he screams, stumbling on a sizable rock on the edge of the pathway. Before he can tumble to the ground, the demon's arm shoots out and catches him in his descent. His hand is so large that I can see his fingers on one side of Amir and his thumb extended to the other side. It's so unnerving that I have to look away.

"He's going to kill me!" Amir shouts. "Help me! It's—"

"I will not kill you," the demon says, his low voice washing over me. His dark eyes linger on Amir before they dart to me, then to the goblin.

Rolinda clears her throat. "Yes, well, not today at least. Demons are known for their brutality, but you have been made quite docile, haven't you?"

The demon tenses, and I swear his eyes start to glow. His muscles pulse and bulge, growing as if he'd just lifted a ton of sets at the gym.

He glares at the fairy, and she glares back. I feel like I'm witnessing contention that has spanned eternity. The demon finally backs down, looking at me.

"We can't wait. It's time to go," he says in his deep tone.

Rolinda clicks her tongue and then sighs. "It is a pity. I would so love to learn more about the human world. It seems so delightfully boring," she says before eyeing Amir. "But your friends are most likely in the meeting area already."

"These will bring you to the right location. As I said before, we cannot have the teleportation magic pointed into any main cities. That is and always will be too big of a risk. We the fairies have set up a number of locations throughout Qotan. Most of them are activated by a location-specific spell or a stone. For this, you'll use the stones."

Her tinny voice sounds so strange. With a loud pop, a wave of blue smoke covers her, and then she's a full-size woman. She holds out her hand and says something odd. A set of three stones appears, hovering in the air. These are around the same size, like a few marbles meshed together, and they are cut to be smooth. A burst of blue glowing light emits from inside.

"These will take you to a spot close to Ellistra's palace. If I'm correct, your friends will already be there," she explains. "Don't touch them until you are ready to go."

As she holds out her hand, the stones float toward us and hover just before me, Amir, and the demon. I stare once again at the demon's strange attire. He's wearing what I would consider a gentleman's suit, like something a peaky blinder would wear. It's complete with a vest and pants. Everything on his person is stark black.

I gape at the large being. "You mean *he's* coming with us?"

Rolinda nods. She seems pleased, like she's excited to pawn him off on us. "Well, you need someone to protect you, don't you?"

As much as I want to protest, I close my mouth tight. Sure, I can do some amount of damage with my flames, but I'm no fighter. The flashing memory of my previous encounters with orcs enters my mind, and I suppress a sigh. My chest pangs with regret at the knowledge that, once again, I was shortchanged when it comes to the fighting thing. Still, I stand up straight and put my hand on the handle of my sword, feeling the need to remain dignified.

Rolinda raises an eyebrow, apparently expecting me to argue with her. I don't have any talking points. I'm not fit to defend anyone, so I figure we'll take him. As if we had a choice.

"Fine," is all I say. "But what about Gobby?"

I nod to the unconscious goblin lying on the ground.

Rolinda grimaces. "You still insist on bringing him with you? He should wake when you leave this place. The magic suppressing him should lift once he's out of our way. You can always leave him. I'm sure Queen Ferona would be happy to dispose of him for you."

I glare at her. "If you suggest that again, I'll be happy to dispose of *you*."

Her eyes dart to my face and her jaw hardens, but she doesn't retort. I narrow my eyes and command my brain not to let my face redden. My comment sounds childish, and to be honest, I'm not feeling extremely confident in myself. But I won't budge. Gobby saved my life, and I'll keep saving his. I don't know my mother at all, save for the weird magical message she sent me, but I can't help but wonder what she'll think of the goblin. Does she hate the dark races as much as the fairies do? Will she threaten to take Gobby and put him in a dungeon?

I force my mind to go blank. This is something I don't think I'm ready to tackle yet. Besides, I will know soon enough how she's going to react.

"One of you will have to hold on to him. He shouldn't need a stone himself," she assures me. Her tone suggests she is not happy about this.

I nod, then move to pick up the goblin. A massive hand presses on my shoulder, holding me back. I flinch, feeling how heavy it is and how close the purple veins are to my skin. His refrigerator-cold flesh chills me even through my clothes.

Licking my lips, I remind myself he probably won't kill me. They wouldn't let him rip my head off.

"I will carry him. No need to tire yourself." His deep tone rumbles through my chest.

A few fairies and elves passing by stop and stare at him for a moment before moving on. My guess is they felt his voice vibrating their skulls as well.

"Okay, yeah sure," I say, but I don't feel okay about it. This is one of those moments I would rather argue with him and carry Gobby myself, but I fully recognize my inability to contend physically with the beast. Without saying anything else, he takes one step closer to the goblin and scoops him up in his massive palm. The image of a kid holding a toy flashes in my head. Seeing the small goblin up against the massive demon only exacerbates his size.

We stand there amidst the bustling creatures. They all stare at me. My eyes dart to each of them in turn, stopping for a ridiculously short amount of time on the demon because he still weirds me out. I clear my throat.

"Right, yeah, you want me to give the go-ahead. No problem," I say, feigning confidence. My dragon blood does not make me a natural leader even though that seems to be what they think. Rather than argue that point, I just shrug and count. "One. Two. Thr—"

Halfway through saying the third number, I snag the glowing stone out of the air. An icy chill instantly slips through my arm and chest, filling my whole body with an intense cold. The bustling underground building melds into a wash of color that's smudged and hard to distinguish. Rolinda's face combines with the melding world, and she looks . . . hostile somehow. My stomach seizes as the world spins. The color scheme shifts to a more natural set of hues—greens, browns, and grays with a blue overhead ceiling. And then all at once, the spinning stops.

I gasp and stumble forward, somehow managing to keep my feet. Amir is not so lucky. He pitches forward, cursing as his hands slam into hard stone. Even the demon staggers. Gravity pulls me backward, and after blinking my eyes, I realize it's because we are on a steep hill. My eyes track upward as I follow the ground until it becomes a solid stone wall towering up as far as I can see. The massive mountain looms above us. We've been transported a good ways up the steep incline of the mountainside. A sea of green foliage and flitting birds spread outward from the bottom of the hill. Another part of the same forest we were in before, no doubt. A grunt from above me pulls my attention there. To my relief, Gobby is waking up.

"What—happening—augh! Demon!"

He shouts when his face comes within inches of the veined visage of the demon. He flails around, kicking his legs and arms until the demon relents and puts him down. He scrambles backward, his arms and legs quivering. Unfortunately for him, he scrambles *down* the hill and loses his balance. I shout a warning just as the small green creature rolls backward, beginning a long tumble down the hill. A blur of black shifts next to me. The demon has stopped Gobby from going too far, his massive left hand holding the goblin in place.

I gape at him. How can he move so quickly for his size? But I look away, hearing Amir retching on the ground.

"For once—!" he gasps. "Can we *please* choose a method of teleporting that is not so spin-ney?"

That makes what, the fourth time he's vomited since we came here? Dude can't catch a break.

I laugh, not because I think it's funny but because my mind is overwhelmed, and I don't know how else to cope with it. Fortunately, Amir doesn't hear me—or he doesn't care about my reaction. Holding out a hand to him, he takes it, and I lift him up. Just then, a strong breeze whips across my body, tugging at my thick cloak, the clasp straining at my neck. I hold my hand there in a childlike panic to keep it from flying away.

"Where are we anyway?" Amir asks, wiping his mouth on his sleeve.

"I have no idea," I reply.

We both look at the demon. He says nothing.

"I guess . . ." I pause, looking up at the clouds veiling the top of the mountain peak. "This must be where the dragons live."

And my mom, I think, my neck tightening up in nervousness.

"David!"

A new voice sounds from behind me. I freeze, hoping it's not my imagination. When I turn, I see a group of tall blue-skinned elves dressed in leather battle armor. A few hold massive bows on their backs, while the others carry weapons like swords and knives. One of them looks familiar. It's the same elf who expressed disdain for the goblins when they first saved us. It's not him I'm looking at though.

Around them stands an array of horses, all without saddles, and a few of the now familiar and larger crelotins. My eyes glaze over one of the creatures and a strong sense of comfort and happiness swells within me. This is the exact crelotin I left when the orcs teleported the three of us away. It's odd feeling comfort from such a terrifying creature. Somehow, though, she's become mine, in a way.

I look away when I see my dad rushing forward with his arms open.

"Dad!" I cry, pressing forward.

You know those cheesy movies where the two people run in slow motion toward each other, and then they embrace? I'm embarrassed to say that this is exactly like one of those movies. Except that I stumble more than once on the ragged and rocky mountainside. Still, I manage to make it to Dad and grab him in the manliest, most football-like hug you've ever seen. He gets some good slaps on the back as well.

Dad hugs me back, then pushes me gently away, looking at my face. "I thought you were gone, son. When you disappeared in the forest, I was kicking myself for not teaching you how to defend yourself." He pauses, taking in my clothing, his eyes lingering on the sword strapped at my waist. "But I was relieved to hear you were okay."

I nod, but I'm too overwhelmed to say anything. It's only been less than a day since we were separated, but any amount of time worrying about a dead family member wears on you.

"I'm fine. I'm glad you are okay," I say finally.

Wherever they went, they have new clothes like what we've been given. Dad looks like he came right out of one of Amir's fantasy books, complete with a side sword and a shirt of chain mail. I gape at him. Seeing him like this seems so strange when I know his profession is working on a horse farm. Jared stalks out from the ring of elves, a grin on his face. He's wearing the same type of garb, although he has a bow and quiver of arrows slung across his back. A long hunting knife is secured at his waist, too. He comes up and holds out his hand, which I take, expecting a handshake, but he pulls me in for an awkward hug. I pat his back, and he pulls away, unabashed.

"Looking good, dragon prince," he says, then winks at me. "The elf king filled us in on all the particulars that you got. You really missed out on seeing their kingdom. That place is wild."

"Sheesh, Mr. Johnson, you're looking good," Amir says, coming to my side and putting his arm over my shoulder.

Dad laughs. "I haven't worn clothes like this since I left Qotan with you almost seventeen years ago. I didn't realize I missed it until I put these on last night."

I hear Gobby complaining about a "huge purple-veined brute" to my left. Dad hears the muttering and looks in that direction, starting at the sight of the massive demon. His hand grips the handle of his sword, but he smiles after a moment.

"Your guard, I take it?" he says.

The demon nods but doesn't say or do anything else.

"Demons haven't changed much, I see," Dad notes. "Not a man—or demon—of many words are you?"

The demon grunts. "There is no point in speaking much. Anything I have to say will be written off by any other race. We're here for nothing but our strength."

I gape at him. This is the most I've heard the demon say since I first encountered him. He stares over my dad and fixes his attention on something there.

Following his gaze, my eyes land on a mess of red hair.

THE KING'S ERRAND

My mouth goes dry as I stare at the piercing green eyes of Krista. Her mouth is turned down as if she's not happy with what she sees. At first, I think she's glaring at me, but then I see she's looking past me at the demon. What is going through her head? She looks like she's ready to tear something in half—but then again, she always looks like that. For some reason, I'm a little annoyed she isn't looking at me. She doesn't seem relieved to see me.

Now I feel even more stupid. A strong breeze buffets my clothing, the fabric tugging on my arms and legs as if nature wants to pull me off my feet. I turn my face to the wind, looking over the thick forest below. Dark clouds are growing rapidly. It could be my imagination, but I swear I smell the potent scent of rain saturating the ground. A shiver slips through me as I take in the glorious scent. It serves as the perfect distraction, and my annoyance melts away.

Krista folds her arms, her brows crinkled together as she continues to stare at Kroniv. This time, I smile and give a small wave in her direction. It feels too forced. I'm shocked when her eyes flicker to me. She gives a half smile.

Suddenly the red-haired terror makes my heart skip a beat. I clear my throat and make my way over to her, thrusting my hand out. My mind screams, "You're being embarrassing," but I press the thought away. Who cares? I'm not trying to impress this girl. She's not my type. It's the red hair. Jared grins, and I tell him mentally to shove it in his dark place. His smile falters.

Krista keeps her arms folded and glowers at me. "I see you didn't get killed. Did your friend keep you alive?"

She nods toward Amir with her head, and my mouth falls open. Does she really think Amir could have done anything to protect me? The smirk glued to her face indicates she's joking. A flare of something inside—embarrassment, or possibly more annoyance—makes my face flush. I pretend I don't feel it.

"Oh yes, he whipped out his cell phone and played his horrible 70s playlist. That scared everything away," I say sarcastically.

Krista laughs at that. I blink a few times, staring at her.

"Did you just . . . make that sound? Surely that didn't come from the demon girl's mouth," I joke.

I don't know why I said that. It's rude and will probably make her go all purple-veined and rage-y. Instead, her half smile spreads to the other side of her mouth, and she lets out a light chuckle.

"Very clever, dragon boy. Don't get used to hearing it. The only people who've heard me laugh are dead now," she comments, her smile lingering for a moment before it falls away. She stares at me flatly.

I laugh lightly, but it doesn't last long when I see how serious she is.

"Wait. You're joking right?"

She winks at me, then points behind me. Gobby is there, shaking like a leaf. His short green form quivers as he clings to Amir's pant leg. I can't tell if he's cold or terrified. Based on how his eyes continue to bounce between the elves and Kroniv, I'm guessing it's the latter. Jared looks back and forth from Gobby to me, then walks over to Krista, throwing his beefy arm over her shoulder. I'm shocked she doesn't push it off or yell at him to stop touching her.

I can't help but wonder what she'd do if I tried that. Holding my breath, I sweep that thought aside. The last thing I need is to start getting fond of the girl who could literally punch a hole through my face. Jared's eyes twinkle, and I curse him once again with my thoughts.

"I guess we'd better get a move on," Krista suggests, finally shrugging Jared's arm off her shoulder.

"Which direction are we supposed to go?" I ask, turning around to gaze once again at the tall peaks of the mountain.

Thick white clouds that previously hugged the jagged mountain peaks have moved to the side, revealing the outline of the top. It's so high up. I can't see many details, but at least my view isn't blocked by anything.

"I can fly up and see if there's a path that we can follow," Jared suggests.

I nod. "Yeah, that would be great."

He steps away from Krista, readying himself to transform.

"No need to fly," a deep and commanding voice sounds. It's the elf from before. He stands with his chest puffed out. I can't tell if it's because he's trying to declare his dominance over the rest of us, or if that's just how he stands. I note that the other elves stand in a similar fashion. It's likely just their culture.

"I have been to Ellistra's kingdom before; the path is forward. It will lead to a way that moves forward and backward, repeated until the top," he says.

"Okay?" I say. "So we just walk on?"

The elf nods. "We must make haste. I sense a storm on the wind."

At this, Dad speaks up. "It wouldn't hurt to have Jared fly up and make sure there is no army or bandits ready to ambush us ahead." He dips his head to the tall Samoan as if giving him permission.

Jared gazes up at the sky. He looks troubled. His brow furrows as if he sensed something foreboding. Then his face sprouts black feathers. I've seen him transform before, but in the past, it was either too fast or I was too distracted to get a good look. His new clothing melds inward with his body as he shrinks into a deep black crow. Even though the transformation is kind of creepy, Jared's intelligent gaze stares back at me. Before I can tell him to be careful, the bird chirps loudly, then flies off. I watch him until his path crosses with the sun high above us.

"We might as well keep moving while we wait. It's unlikely that we'll run into trouble before Jared will see it," Dad suggests.

"Wise words. We move," the elf says. He stands with his bare shoulders pressed backward, his powerful chest pushing out. His pitch-black hair flows free over his blue skin. There's a kink in his hair, as if he recently had it in a ponytail. "I will go first with half of my entourage. The halflings and humans behind me, and the demon will stand in the rear." The elf regards Kroniv with a dark expression before addressing me. "Does this plan suit you, High Prince?"

My mind goes into a panic. I open my mouth to respond, but my tongue feels like it's been tied. Stuttering, I try to find the words to say the plan sounds fine. Krista nudges me with her elbow. We lock eyes, and she gives me a look that says, "Well, are you just going to stand there?"

"Yes, that's a good plan," I finally say, feeling awkward. I don't know why, but putting my hand on my sword grounds me, making me feel better.

"So be it," the elf replies. He issues a set of commands in a lilting language that I only hear for a moment before my magic translates the words to English. He puts most of the ranged weapons at the rear, save for one: a thin elf woman as tall as the imposing elf leader. Her leather vest and shorts leave a lot of bare blue skin showing, but she doesn't seem bothered by this. The irises of her eyes are silver, and her hair, also black like the other elf, is tied up in a messy bun. Her longbow extends past her shoulders and down to her legs.

"Man, I'm totally geeking out right now. We are literally being bodyguarded by *elves*," Amir murmurs to me.

I smile at his comment. It's the perfect distraction from the awkwardness of me having to approve of the plan. How can I possibly be the highest-ranking person in this group? I'm just a high school kid. Biting my lip, my hand moves unconsciously to the built-in pouch in my pants where I've stuffed my beat-up jersey. I'm certain if I make it back to Kentucky, Coach won't let me wear this one on the field, but it doesn't feel right to leave it behind.

If—I really wish I could say "When."

Something firm snags my elbow, and my chest tightens. My other hand clenches in preparation to throw it into whoever is holding me.

Krista chuckles. "A little on edge, are we?"

The fact that it's her should make me feel better, considering her past anger infractions. But it doesn't. As much as I don't want to look into her face, I can't help it. I let my eyes wander there. I never noticed how pale her skin is, but now that I've seen both a normal demon and her in her demon form, I realize how light her complexion is. There is no way that she and Jared could ever be considered blood relatives. Of course, I know they aren't, but I recall seeing them back at school and trying to make out how they could be related. Their human parents, even if they were married, couldn't have produced these two.

That seems like so long ago. Thoughts of my football team and high school, along with memories of seeing Krista and Jared, rush into me like a ton of bricks. I feel that familiar tug in my gut, but this time it's so strong that I almost double over. Instead, I hold it back, a heavy grunt coming from my mouth. Krista frowns at my reaction.

"Are you okay? I didn't even punch you or anything," she says.

I nod but can't say anything else. The feeling soon dissipates, and I unclench my jaw.

"Sorry, I'm getting weird—" I pause, choosing my next words carefully. The last thing I need is this girl to think I'm weak for missing home. "I'm just feeling some homesickness. That's all. It makes my stomach seize up."

There's something in her eyes, as if she knows what I mean. Her mouth parts slightly, and I think she might agree with me or say that she knows how I feel. Instead, her mouth shuts tight, and she presses her lips into a thin line.

"Anyway," I say, changing the subject as quickly as possible. "What did you want?"

Okay, that sounded way harsher than I meant it to be.

She smirks at me as if she's impressed with my impertinence. Her head moves closer to mine, and my face flushes, my chest burning. I think of my girlfriend back in Kentucky, and how, despite us becoming a "thing" recently, *she* doesn't make me feel this way. Guilt fills me, but I suppress it, holding my ground even though I want to back away. I can almost feel the coolness of her body as Krista presses close to me.

Her icy skin seems *so much* less strange when she's in demon form.

"I have something for you," she says. "From the elf king. He told me to give it to you *privately*."

Not what I expected. While I'm glad that she didn't move in for a kiss or to whisper something intimate, I still feel the tension in my chest.

"Okay?" I say.

She raises her red eyebrows.

"Oh, you want to give it to me now, and you can't," I say, putting the pieces together.

Wow, I really am an idiot. It took me altogether way too long to figure out what she was saying. She gives a closed mouth smile, keeping her eyebrows raised and then moves away. Another strong gust of wind tears at my clothing. This gust is so strong that I have to turn my head so I can breathe. My feet wobble on the tilted earth, but I hold my footing. The dark clouds over the trees are moving closer. I bet the elves are not going to be happy about waiting.

Clearing my throat, I turn to the lead elf.

"My friends and I need to talk privately for a minute," I say.

He turns and regards me with a critical gaze, his shoulders pulled back. His pecs are more imposing than his hard eyes. I feel self-conscious about how small my muscles are. It's dumb, but the guy is ripped. He's the elf equivalent to a gym rat.

"There is no time for that. You speak must be right here," he suggests in his broken English.

Krista growls quietly to my side. She folds her arms and gives me a pointed look. I'm guessing she wants me to abuse my station. Just then, Jared flaps back into our party, the bird growing and expanding back into the tall and broad Samoan.

"Why did we stop moving?" he asks. "There's nothing but rocks and a pathway ahead."

I send terse thoughts to him about the situation, and his mouth tightens. He nods an apology, falling silent. I turn back to the elf.

"Well, yeah, not gonna happen. Give us just a minute," I say, gesturing to Jared, Amir, and Gobby to follow me.

"Not the goblin," Krista's voice hisses in my ear, so close that it tickles my back.

I glare at her. "Why not? What is this secret thing you want to give me?"

She sighs and throws her head back, pulling her delicate hand through her hairline. My heart skips a beat.

Before she can give me a reason, I point not so subtly at the elves. "I'm not going to leave him with them. I know they'll gut him before we get back. Besides, he can't understand what you are saying anyway, so why does it matter?"

Her eyes still smolder, but she shakes her head and waves her hand dismissively. She turns and heads off toward a massive boulder perched on the steep mountainside. Jared and Amir catch up to me, both giving me quizzical looks.

I sigh. "Not sure what her problem is. She says she has something for me."

Jared's eyes light up and he nods. "Yeah you're going to want to hear this."

Once again, I wish I could read minds like him.

Amir looks confused but says nothing as Jared takes him by the arm and pulls him toward the boulder. Gobby comes up to me and stares at me with his unblinking and glowing red eyes.

"My friends have to give me something, and I don't want you alone with the elves," I say, feeling the magic work in my words.

His eyes widen, and he moves toward the boulder with the rest of us.

"Hey, Dave, what's up?" Dad says, coming to stand next to me.

"Krista apparently has something for me. She said it's supposed to be private." I feel embarrassed that I didn't think of Dad. It's not that I don't trust him; I was just so focused on the other half-blooded kids, Amir, and Gobby. He doesn't look offended.

"I'd better stay here and keep an eye on these ones. I don't get the sense they're enjoying each other's company," he says, nodding to the odd group.

The group of elves have created a loose circle around Kroniv. Even though they're conversing with themselves and not threatening the demon, the furtive glances toward the massive purple-veined creature speak to the elves' uneasiness.

"Just fill me in later on what they give you, okay?" he says.

I nod, and he trots back to the group, his hand on his sword. Seeing him move so easily on the sloped mountain while holding a weapon reminds me of all the secrets he kept from me. How could he live in Qotan for so long and not talk about it? I knew he'd been here, and I knew a little bit about this place, but he has to have so many stories. Making a mental note to ask him about this later, I turn into another bout of wind and clench my muscles to stay afoot.

The trek to the boulder is only a few seconds, but with the wind and how big the rock is, I know we'll have privacy. I step around the massive stone, which is at least twice my height—if not more. The wind dies down significantly, and I can't help but sigh when it does.

Krista, Jared, and Amir stand with their backs to the boulder, their gazes locked on Gobby. He's inspecting a stone on the ground with two of his fingers. With a quick motion, he picks one up, holds it close to his eye, then bites it like he's searching for gold.

"What is this 'thing' you want to give me?" I inquire, looking to Krista and pumping my fingers with air quotes.

She leans back against the stone, her cloak fluttering to the ground behind her. Even though we're out of most of the wind, her hair flaps at the tips from the breeze. She regards me with a look I can't even try to interpret, then reaches into a pouch at her waist. Her hand comes out, and I find myself marveling at how her skin feels cold to the touch.

It's so pale that it makes me think of a vampire. My face flushes again. Forcing my eyes away from her hand, I instead focus on the thing in her grip.

"It's a rock," I say, confused.

It's smooth and gray and cut into a round shape about the size of a pocket watch. Dad has a collection of pocket watches at our house. It's one of the weird things he likes to collect for no reason at all.

Krista flips the rock over. It's separated into six sections with hard grooves, like someone carved them in. A single symbol resides in the center of each "pie" section, but they mean nothing to me. A bronze dial sits in the middle of the rock pointing to one of the sections.

Krista laughs, then tosses it to me. "Yeah, it's a rock. That's exactly what I said when the elf king gave them to us."

Knowing she said the same thing to the elf monarch makes me feel a little strange. To think that I could have similar thoughts to this easily angered half demon girl . . . it's not comforting. She flashes another smile at me, deep and mischievous, and I look away before my heart thumps itself into oblivion.

I catch the rock and heat bursts through my palm. A gasp escapes my mouth, and it falls to the ground, bouncing twice before it comes to a stop. Krista smirks.

"It's not going to hurt you," she says.

"Right, yeah, okay," I say, but my confidence is shot. I scoop up the rock, wincing at the intense warmth inside. It's not *hot*, but it's close enough that my danger sense is acting up. "What is it?"

Jared steps in now. "A way to find the others."

Understanding showers over me. "The others—"

"The other half-blooded rulers," he says eagerly.

My mouth falls open, my mind searching for a response. I can't think of anything. Jared gives me a pitied look as if he's listening to my thoughts and thinks it's adorable. This makes me even more embarrassed, so I look at Krista. This doesn't make me feel better.

"How? Why?" I ask.

Krista presses her shoulder blades against the boulder to come out of her lounging position.

"There's a message for you from the king himself," she says. "It'll be easier if you hear it from him."

She points to the spindle on the compass-like stone, and I frown.

"Just grab that. The old dude put something in it—a message for you."

I swallow hard, my senses sharpening as nerves skitter across my whole body. This isn't the first time I've gotten a message from a person in Qotan. I definitely *did not* appreciate the feeling of being transported somewhere else. Why couldn't he have written a note? Were all the kings and queens of Qotan so complicated? The air suddenly feels a lot cooler, and the smell of the forest wafts through the wind more potently. My heart pounds loudly in my ears, and I can't hold still.

"We don't have all day, dragon boy. Get on with it," Krista urges.

I glare at her, but she's right. The elves are probably chomping at the bit to get moving. With one last tentative sigh, I slip my thumb over the bronze spindle. My senses dampen all at once, the sight of my friends on the boulder melting to black. The sound of the wind disappears, leaving me in near perfect silence. The smells of the forest shift into something more floral. As the colors form into images around me, so does every other sensation. It's humid and very warm. I'm deep in some tropical forest. Multicolored foliage, flowers, bushes, and tall trees surround me on every side. There's no breeze—just still, muggy air. Chittering animals and singing birds echo each other's calls, creating a cacophony of sound.

A snapping branch pulls my attention to the left. A small furry animal—something I can't identify, but it looks similar to a squirrel—burrows a hole into the soft ground. Its long tail disappears into the recesses of the earth.

"I am sorry for the circumstances of this message," a man says, his voice somewhere between deep- and high-pitched. I spin in the direction of the sound and come face-to-face with a tall elf. His skin, blue like the other elves I've seen, is tight on his face, tugging at his mouth and eyes in an upturned fashion. He gives off an aura of prestige, youth, and strength, but his eyes betray his age. There's no wrinkles to be found, but I swear I can see all the pain and struggles of centuries behind his pale purple irises. His chest is almost bare, save for a strap of leather with intricate adornments of dyed wood. A wooden crown sits on his head, his long black hair woven upward into it as if it were growing into the wood itself.

"I would've liked to have contacted you from within the throne room of Terendrell, but some things are best left secret even to those closest to us. This message is for you alone."

Two elves stand behind him, backs straight and expressions hard. I can't help but glance at them. One is another imposing and angry-looking male elf, the other I recognize as the same elf woman with the bow who stands on the other side of the boulder.

"There is little time," the elf king says. "By now, your friends have met you on the way to your mother's city. By now, they've handed you the single most important thing you can have as one of the six heirs to the Qotan thrones."

He holds up his hand, the compass-like stone in his palm. "When each of the royal halflings was born, I extracted a piece of you, a bit of your lifeblood. It's *this* that Urothar wants, your collective blood, and it's with this that I can pass on some of our elven magic."

I move forward cautiously. As far as I know, this is just a memory, like a message on a phone's voicemail, only with video. Sure enough, as I stalk closer to him, the elven king doesn't register it. If he can see me in this weird memory, he doesn't indicate so. His words echo, and I feel the tingle of the translation magic tickling my mind. He's not speaking English.

"You must not fall into the hands of Urothar. If you do, all is lost. Your friends have indicated that the dark races discovered a path to earth, a path that doesn't mean their certain death. It's imperative that you find my daughter," the king says. "Find her and bring her to me so I can be with her once more. I've infused each seeking stone with your blood and the other royal halflings'. I saved these stones for the six heirs, for whoever could first find me. I hoped it would be my daughter, but you will do."

His eyes grow somber, tears welling there. His hands form into tight fists, making his muscled arms flex and his physique sharpen. I'm totally intimidated. This guy looks fierce.

"Find her, please. Bring my kin back to me," he says, his words thickly accented. This last part is in English, not his elven language.

Then the message melts away like chocolate on a hot sidewalk in the summer.

When I come back to the present, I see that no one has moved. How long was I watching the message? The searching feels heavy in my hand, as if it carries the worries of many people. Each symbol affixed to the stone—six in total—is unique, but I can't tell what they mean. Rather than numbers or images, each is a combination of lines, both jagged and straight, as well as circles.

"Did he show you how these worked, then?" I say absently, holding it up for Krista and Jared.

Krista presses her lips thin and eyes Gobby and Amir.

"He did, but I'm not going to show you unless you make them go," she says.

I roll my eyes and thrust the stone toward her face. She's too far away for me to invade her space, but she gets the message.

"The elf king"—I have forgotten what his actual name is—"gave us a way to find the others, and you haven't even bothered giving them a try?"

"Woah, woah, woah! He gave you a way to find the others? As in, the other half dragons?" Amir sputters.

Krista glare lands on Amir. "Not all of us are half dragons, you dolt."

Amir doesn't seem affected by her comment. "So why haven't you tried it yet?"

"We have, but three of them do nothing. My guess is those are the ones still in the human realm," she says, holding out her compass stone.

Amir reaches out and tries to take the one from Krista's hand, but she pulls her arm away. "It wouldn't work for you anyway. Plus, the symbols don't make sense. Which one is for who?"

Rather than answer her, I lift my hand to the spindle, which is currently pointing at a set of parallel diagonal lines with a small circle above and below. I turn it slightly to land on the next pie slice. This one has a complex array of diagonal lines. A brilliant trail of white light bursts from the compass and moves in a ribbonlike fashion toward Krista. At this point, I've already seen so many strange things that this doesn't feel unnatural at all. The light dances on her chest and face like it's moving with the wind. I turn the spindle back to the other one and it goes dark again.

"Real subtle, isn't it?" Amir says. "Shouldn't be a problem when you walk around earth with those little puppies, huh?"

Jared scoffs. "I don't think they care about subtlety."

I'm pretty sure I don't need to fill in the blanks as to why that's not a good thing. We can't travel all over earth with a rock that emits light. Gobby's unwavering glowing red eyes watch the stone in my hand, and I suddenly wonder if it was a good idea to bring him along. But I press that thought away. I vouched for him. I will stick by it.

A flash of movement to my left makes me jump. I throw my hand outward. A jet of flames explodes from me, and I hear a yelp.

"Dave! It's just me! Can you calm down with the fire?" Dad says, exasperated.

I grimace. "Sorry! I'm a little on edge."

My flames die out as he pokes his head around the side of the boulder. He glances at the rock in my hand, then inspects all our faces and nods. Apparently, he doesn't seem to care about knowing what it does.

"The elves assure me we need to leave," he says.

I exchange glances with the other kids. Why am I not surprised they are aching to move? Slipping the stone into the pouch inside my pants, I gesture for my friends to follow.

"All right. Let's do it," I say.

I stalk out from the boulder and head to one of the crelotins standing at the back of the crowd.

WE STUMBLE INTO A DRAGONLESS DRAGON CITY

The sun dips low over the forested horizon as the crelotin bumps under me. I try to move along with the mount to reduce the saddle soreness, but I know I'm still going to feel it. It seems like there should be saddles on these creatures. Despite having spotted a fair number of them since being in Qotan, I've not seen one saddle.

My eyes droop periodically. I'm tired. Queen Ferona told me this portal would take us close to the dragon city, but we've been riding for hours on the side of this massive mountain range. Dark clouds flash and sputter behind us, but they aren't catching up. It's like they are keeping a safe distance from us on purpose, which I try not to let psyche me out. All in all, it's better than looking down.

See, I'm terrified of heights. *Terrified.*

I blush, and Jared clears his throat at the same time. I glare at him, wondering if he hears thoughts on a general broadcast or if he's intentionally listening to me. I'd rather not know, to be honest.

The path has changed drastically since we started. We'd been skirting the lower part of the mountain at first, the peaks staring down at us from above like protective guardians. But now, the path points upward quickly, and we are on a set of steep switchbacks.

My eyes start to hurt from how hard I'm staring at the ground. I'm intentionally not looking at how high up we are. One slip up would mean the end of my life. My heart thuds in my chest at the thought.

"The crelotins are well adept at keeping you safe. They are among the smartest breeds of companion animals in Qotan. I know not how you managed to procure these ones, but they are already proving loyal to you," the stern female elf says to me.

She is clearly trying to make me feel better, but it's not helping. I just stare and stare until my eyes are dry and in pain. That's when things go wrong . . .

Amir whistles softly. "That is incredible. I don't think I've ever seen anything so beautiful before."

I try so hard to remind myself how terrified I am of heights, but his comment makes me too curious, so I look up. I can't help it.

The scene before me is incredible. I can see the glimmering of the distant sea on the other side of the forest. Flitting animals and birds shoot up out of the trees, either to catch food or to fly for pleasure. The trees, mostly a wash of green and brown, sport multicolored flowers and buds. They light the forest below. My enjoyment lasts approximately two seconds before my eyes land on the cliff at my side.

My heart enters my throat and my stomach falls to my feet. Everything goes blurry as my breathing hitches. I barely feel myself falling forward when Krista's strong hands grip my cloak, and the choking feeling of the clasp on my neck brings me back to reality. The scream which tears through the mountainside doesn't feel like mine. But it is.

"What is wrong with you?" Krista shouts at me. "Are you trying to get yourself killed?"

Her stern tone aides in pulling me back to the present, but I'm still fuzzy. Her hand is huge, and it's full of purple veins. Her expanded wrist continues up her shirt, which is now ripped up to her elbow. Her swollen arm presses out on the fabric. I'm grateful she was riding right behind me. Maybe she saved me because she's starting to like me, but that thought terrifies me.

More blurs, and then somehow Amir is suddenly there, his hands on either side of my face. His features come into focus. "Breathe, Dave. Don't look to your left, just look at me."

Nausea riddles my insides as I listen to his instructions. This isn't the first time he's had to bail me out of a height's situation. Suddenly I'm on the ground facing the mountain. I don't even remember getting off my crelotin. Amir is still right in front of me.

"I'm fine," I try to assure him.

He shakes his head.

"Sheesh, Dave, you know you can't look off mountains like that. You could have just taken my word for the beauty or given us time to get away from the cliff," he scolds.

The elves, while bothered by the delay, allow me to sit and get my wits about me before getting back on my crelotin. This is a delicate process for me, given that I have to do it while keeping my gaze away from the edge. Even though I know the drop-off is there, not seeing it helps with my fear.

"You are the son of a dragon royal line. Can anyone else not see the intense irony of the fact that he's terrified of heights?" Krista says. "You'd be a worthless dragon."

Her tone is hard. Is that because she had to call on her demon side to save me? I glance at her slight form. Her now exposed forearm looks like a toothpick, and I'm sure her bicep looks the same.

Gobby is riding with Amir now, since everyone deemed it unsafe for anyone to ride with me lest I fall off the mountainside.

I sit up straight on my mount, trying to hold on to what dignity I have left. There isn't much. We ride in perfect silence now, and I'm too afraid to look at anyone else. I keep my gaze high, watching the clouds and sky. Fortunately for me, we're traveling far enough away from the edge that I can look out at the scenery without vertigo taking over.

"We will arrive soon," the lead elf calls back from the head of the group.

I suspect they all thought we'd run into trouble, hence why we have so much protection, but we've run into no one else. My gut tells me that's not a good thing, but no one says it aloud. The only communication from anyone is quiet conversations I can't hear. Dad rides up front with the elves, his back straight and his hand on his sword. The elves travel on foot, seemingly unbothered by the distance or the uphill road. What are these guys made of anyway?

"There are no dragons in skies," the female elf says. "This is trouble. Why do they not fly? Where are sentries to warn of danger?"

Krista grunts, and I look at her for the first time since the incident. The moment I do, the embarrassment I feel from her saving me hits me like a massive wave. I gulp, trying to keep my expression in check. Her green eyes fix onto mine, and though the hardness never leaves her gaze, she doesn't seem to be making fun of me.

"Are dragons known for flying around for no reason?" The disdain in her tone is a little off-putting.

The lead elf glares at her. "Those with wings belong in the skies. Demons like you belong in dark. No use in coming to light."

His disjointed English only adds to the bitterness of his tone. Whatever history this elf has with demons feels deep and complicated.

Krista's jaw hardens, the purple veins slipping up the side of her neck and into her cheek. She doesn't transform into her terrifying demon form; I can tell she's holding back. The elves continue to watch Kroniv from their peripheral vision. It's obvious how they don't want to be anywhere near him.

"How much longer until we're there? I can fly up to see how close we might be if you want," Jared suggests. It's obvious he's attempting to change the subject to alleviate the arguing. He seems like the peacemaker type.

The lead elf grunts loudly. "No need. I see the city. Just there."

He nods his head forward in the direction we are traveling. The path continues into a thick patch of clouds. Gray and white fog obscures my ability to see. I squint, trying to get my senses to pick up on what I might be missing.

Large boulders make up most of the scenery to the right of the path, and there's loose rocks and rubble to the left before the drop off. Bits of plants and greenery poke up here and there, but the tall pines don't start until further up the mountain. The peaks to our right are a lot smaller than they were when we left. In fact, I can make out the details of some trees near the top. That is, before more clouds amass from the wind, covering them up from my view.

The wind isn't strong here. During the trek, gusts of wind buffeted us now and then. But it seems so calm now. I wonder if that storm is almost upon us? When I look behind me, the dark clouds stay at the same distance. Weird.

"Only elves can see through the illusion before us. Magic veils Dranith," the elf says.

My mind tingles at the word. It's a word I'd forgotten from our conversation days ago. The whole time we've been traveling, it seems like people have been avoiding saying the city name—like if they said it, a secret would be ruined.

Gobby clears his throat, and I turn to him, raising an eyebrow.

"There is a bad illusion ahead. I can see through it with my magic. It should be stronger," he says.

Amir narrows his eyes at the goblin sitting on the crelotin in front of him, then he looks at me questioningly.

"He says he can see through the illusion, too," I translate, leaving out his opinion.

Krista, without looking toward Gobby, speaks up. "What's the point of an illusion if dark races can see through it?"

It's a good question, and one I hadn't thought of.

"Only elves and those strong with illusory magic can," the elf says. "This creature should not be here. He knows too much."

I sigh, putting my hand to my temple. Everyone is still so upset about Gobby being here, but they need to chill. He's not going to betray us. Regardless, I relay his words to the rest of the group.

Gobby doesn't seem to notice the biting comments, but then again, he probably can't understand them. No one decides to elaborate on the thought, and no one suggests we throw him off the mountain. My guess is my presence is what protects him.

Even though I know most of these elves don't respect me, on account of how they've treated me since we were first rescued, they still steal glances at me. Something like fear flickers in their eyes. I can't help but look at the back of Dad's head and wonder why he didn't bother telling me dragons were *high* rulers of Qotan back in the human realm. I had to find out I'm high ranking by being thrust into a magical world.

I shiver at the thought. This awards me a glance from Krista, and I press my lips together.

"I will proceed to dispel the magics that protect Dranith from your eyes. With it are protections no creature can survive without the resolve to do so," the leading elf says. I watch him with a measured gaze, remembering that one of the elves called him Parlequin earlier. I log that in my memory, figuring it's probably rude to just think of him as the head elf forever.

My mind tingles with the translation magic. I'm coming to understand when someone is not speaking in English more often now, partially because he spoke way too eloquently just now—but also, hearing it feels different.

The tall, muscled elf gestures to a few of his companions, and the four of them head off into the thick white clouds.

"I guess they'll come back?" Krista says.

"They're going to dispel the magic. I guess it's unwise to venture into whatever protections they've put in place over the city," Jared translates for me.

I blush. It's still so strange to know that Jared can pluck the language from my head. It's like he's stealing my only useful ability and therefore my usefulness. I shoot him a grateful look despite this thought.

A soft groan comes out of Amir's mouth, and I raise an eyebrow at him.

"I kind of wish I could see what traps they put in place. Like, would someone get thrown off the side of the mountain? Or would they turn to stone?" He folds his arms and scowls.

Krista stares at him with her mouth open before putting a hand to her forehead. "You're insane, kid. Were you just planning to run inside and test it yourself?"

Amir narrows his eyes. "Uh, no, that's why we have the extras."

He gestures to Krista, whose expression hardens. Amir wiggles his eyebrows at her, then grins goofily.

I can tell Krista wants to say something biting back to him, but she doesn't. Instead, she locks her jaw. I spot purple veins growing up her neck and her skin swells on her fingers. Having her ability influenced by anger seems rough. She mentioned how uncontrollable she can become when she's angry, but I've only ever seen her go all demon in battles. Something's eating at her right now though.

As if in response to my thoughts, her eyes meet mine, and she shoves her head to the side, a gesture for me to follow. With a tug on her crelotin's tentacles, the mount shambles off about ten paces away from the others. I follow with my crelotin—only, mine responds to my thoughts. I'm getting more used to riding on the beast now. She feels familiar, like a long-lost family member or a best friend.

When I get closer to Krista, she's not looking at me. Instead, she's staring over my shoulder. I shift uncomfortably on my mount, which suddenly feels like a rock underneath me now that I'm alone with her. Her fire-red hair is tied back in a thick and poofy ponytail, like the brush of a broom. I knew another girl with hair like that in middle school who was bullied for her looks. The idea of Krista being bullied makes me stifle a smile. At the same time, my eyes fall on her freckled cheeks and her green eyes. My breath catches, and I find myself unable to look away. She really is . . . good-looking, in a strange way.

Her eyes snap from over my shoulder back to me, and I jump, looking away abruptly.

"Jared's going to stay over there. He can hear our conversation through my thoughts. I'll just relay what you say to him. That way, the elves won't get too suspicious," she says.

"Oh. Yeah, that makes sense."

Why does she care so much about being suspicious? Her tone suggests she doesn't trust our company, but that doesn't make sense. She was just in the elven realm and didn't get killed. Wasn't that enough evidence that they don't want to hurt us?

"I'm just going to get to the point," she says, glaring at me.

I'm left wondering what I did to make her mad. The purple veins have slipped back under the neck of her leather vest and cloth shirt.

My eyes wander down as I inadvertently search for them. I stop, swallowing hard when I realize my eyes have drifted a bit too low. Either she doesn't notice or doesn't care. I suspect it's the latter.

"Have you felt anything weird since you've been here?" she asks.

I frown. "Uh—well, I've been teleported all over the place, which feels like a frigid ice bath. I walked through a curtain of light that I thought would flay me alive, and um . . . I had my leg snapped in half."

Okay, I probably don't need to be so facetious. I can tell she doesn't appreciate it, but what did she expect? I've never been to this place, and Dad didn't prepare me for it, so I'm feeling a bit vindictive. Her face falls a little, her mouth a thin line pointed downward, but she doesn't appear angry. Honestly, I should feel grateful I'm not dead yet, considering my inexperience.

"That sounds like a story," she says, furrowing her brow. "But it's not what I meant."

She pauses, clearly considering her next words. During the quiet, I feel compelled to move my leg to make sure it's healed even though there hasn't been pain there in a while. My dragon blood healing me is incredible. It's probably why I've never been truly injured my whole life. During football, I'd taken plenty of bad hits. One time I swore I felt my collarbone snap, and it hurt bad. The next day, I was completely fine. These musings over my football injuries bring thoughts of Kentucky—of home. I can almost smell my bedroom and feel the carpet beneath my feet. The intense tugging rips at my stomach again, and I gasp, leaning forward on my crelotin.

Krista tenses, one of her arms expanding rapidly to become a beast of a thing.

"Are you okay? What happened?" She scans the area around us.

"I'm fine," I say quickly, afraid of what would happen if she grew to her demon size. Would she punch my face through? *Could she* punch my face in? I have no doubt she could. "Sometimes when I think of home, I get this weird pain in my stomach. It's just—homesickness."

I say the last part with reservation, afraid of her ridicule. Her eyes widen, and she relaxes suddenly.

"That's what I mean!" she hisses, glancing over my shoulder. "I don't think it's homesickness. I've been homesick before. My parents left me in the forest for a week to practice survival skills once when I was twelve. I was homesick then; this is something different."

Wow, did she just admit she's been homesick before? Why was I so embarrassed? Her words hit me, and I gape at her.

"Your parents *left you in the forest for a week*?" I say in shock.

She waves my reaction away.

"Story for another time. This is not homesickness. It feels like something else. It's unnatural but feels important. Jared has felt it before, too. We talked about it last night. What does it mean, do you think?"

I reflect on the feeling I had moments before. It was like I was being pulled somewhere by an invisible hand. Before I can gather my thoughts, Parlequin's voice sounds.

"The magic is gone. We proceed," he says in his simple English. "But be wary, something is amiss."

Krista gives me a withering look, clearly disappointed I didn't come up with my answer before leading her mount back to the others. As she turns, she whispers to me. "Keep that between us. It seems important. I don't know why, but it might have to do with our heritage."

Heritage. It's a word I've not thought of much. I'm relatively sure most teenagers don't talk about their ancestors a ton, at least not beyond grandparents and aunts and uncles. It's even less interesting for me. Dad never told me about Mom's family, for obvious reasons. "Hey, your grandma breathes fire!" It never went beyond Mom. He also never told me about his family or where he grew up. Have I always wondered? Yes. But it seemed like one of those topics you just didn't breach. As it is, I feel like a heritage-less teenager.

Shaking my head to come back to reality, I look up, and my breath is taken away. The thick white clouds have disappeared from our path replaced by tall columns of marbled stone that shoot high up in the air. Tiered buildings, massive and blocky, made from the same material, go upward hundreds of feet. The rocky dirt path converts to a marbled brick road that extends steeply upward through the buildings. It's the most incredible thing I've ever seen. That's not particularly difficult, considering I've lived a sheltered life.

Parlequin and the elves who accompany him stop the rest of the group. I pull my crelotin up to Dad's, and we give each other wary looks. There's something I can't decipher in his gaze. Is that regret?

"No dragons. Know not why," the elf says. "When we wall came, no guard meet us. This don't bode well."

Dad grimaces. "There should always be sentinel dragons. Those set to watch the way. I haven't lived here for at least seventeen years, but that was always the way."

I slowly turn my gaze toward the city. Despite its grandeur, there's cracks along the marbled columns in numerous places. Vines of thick leaves grow up the sides, probably contributing to the broken parts. Even from afar I can tell it's not pristine—at least not the way I would imagine it should be. My stomach drops as I think about what this could mean.

"We have traveled far, but we may need return, and—"

Parlequin's words are cut off when another elf shouts a warning. Movement flashes before my eyes, and all I see is black. I feel Krista's hand on my bicep, and I jump, shooting her a glance. She's not watching me though. She's looking up at something above Dranith. This all happens so quickly that it takes me a moment to realize that Kroniv has stepped in front of me. Am I in danger? He's treating himself like a human wall. I'm not sure if this makes me feel better or worse. What could put the huge demon on edge?

"A dragon comes," the female elf says evenly.

Her voice is sharp and clear, not quite high but not quite low. It's so mesmerizing that I don't process her words properly right away.

"Dr—dragon?" I stutter finally, but no one hears me.

Sounds of shuffling and clinking echo on the boulders to our right as the elves prepare themselves for battle. Krista pulls one of her great swords from her back, the bicep of her wielding arm bulking up to account for the weight. It's both disgusting and fascinating. Even Dad has drawn his sword.

I hear the swooping of massive wings, and I shudder. That is a sound I've only ever heard in movies about giant birds—or heck, even dragons. It's surreal to hear it with my own ears in real life.

Gently I place my palm on the arm of the demon in front of me and shove against him, pointedly ignoring the icy chill. He doesn't move right away, but he feels my touch. His black eyes turn toward me, regarding me with an emotionless gaze. Even though it lasts only a second, I hate every part of it. Still, he gets my message and shifts to the side.

Crunching gravel reaches my ears from his massive footfalls. My eyes are assaulted by two things at once: first, the marble of Dranith, and second, the scaly blue dragon that zooms in our direction. Dual horns protrude from its narrow head, curving upward in parallel Ss. Scaled blue skin stretches over every part of the beast except for the webbing between its wing tendons, which is a lighter shade. Yellow eyes bore into my soul as the massive creature, which is at least the size of two school buses, lands on the ground before us. It sends a wave of dirt and dust that presses me backward on my mount. I half expect it to snap outward and eat me in one bite, but it doesn't. At least a hundred sharp teeth poke up and down, covering the bottom and top lip—if dragons even have lips.

Pressure builds up in my head so suddenly that my hand shoves up to my forehead. It feels like something is trying to burrow inside. After a painstaking second, I let it in. Immediately, a deep and rich voice rumbles through my mind.

Who approaches Dranith during such a time? Who are you to disturb the peace of Queen Ellistra?

Hearing this, along with the massive creature in front of me, is about the most terrifying thing I've ever experienced in my life. Intrusive thoughts such as "What it would feel like to be bitten by all those teeth?" and "How fast could this dragon kill me?" flow through my mind. I'm shaking, and I want nothing more than to get away from it. How could I possibly be related to a dragon like this?

"We come in peace, to deliver with safe passage the heirs to the light kingdoms of Qotan," Parlequin says.

The dragon makes a huffing sound, then takes a few steps back, the ground rumbling with each clawed foot. Another blast of strong wind, coming from seemingly nowhere, buffets me, and I scramble to grab on to one of my crelotin's tentacles. A wave of uneasiness flows through the connection I have with the beast. Given that I'm feeling that same way already, it only adds to my apprehension. My heart thuds in my ears. After the wind dies down, I look up to see that the dragon's wings have settled to its sides.

Parlequin has crouched into a lower position, likely to keep from being blown off his feet. The elves at his sides have adorned similar crouches.

Peace has long since left the city of Dranith. The orc king has swept many of my brothers and sisters from their homeland, the deep voice rumbles in my mind.

Everyone shifts and shuffles around me, an understandable reaction to the news. My mouth hangs open, and Krista nudges me from the side. My face reddens, and I snap it shut. Marbled monoliths and buildings loom over us, empty and dead, looking almost like a giant ghost town. I've never seen a ghost town in person, just in documentaries, but even those were creepy enough.

"What has become of the queen?" Parlequin inquires. "Has she gone the way of the spirits?"

Tingling rushes into my mind, and I know the elf has shifted into his Elvish language. Krista's grumpy look confirms it even more. I find Jared and raise my eyebrows. He nods at me to let me know that he understands. At least he can help me recall anything we might need to relay later.

She is within the palace, protected by her most trusted guards. Come, let us enter as equals, lest she strike you down with her fury thinking you are the enemy, the voice says, pressing in on my mind.

What happens next is altogether insane. I shouldn't be surprised, given that I've witnessed a similar thing when my mother shifted, but the giant dragon rears up on its hind legs and throws its wings out wide. Its skin glows a subtle blue, matching the hue of its scales, then it starts to shrink inward. Amir gasps from somewhere behind me and says something about how crazy this is. Within moments, the dragon's snout shrinks, turning into human features. His hands and face turn a fleshy tan color, and his body melds into a set of dark leather armor and chain mail, a bloodred cloak at his neck. His hair is blue, cropped short on the sides and long in the center. It's peaked upward like a mountaintop. It looks a bit comical. His eyes are the same yellow, and it looks creepy beyond all measure.

"I am Aurin, keeper of the throne and chief protector of Dranith and Queen Ellistra. Come, she would have words with you," he says.

His piercing yellow eyes pan over us. He pauses once on Kroniv, and I feel the same level of contempt from him that I gathered from Rolinda. For some reason, this makes me angry. The demon is terrifying and hulking, yet I feel I can trust him. Will I regret that later? Probably. His eyes stop on something over my shoulder and he pauses, his expression hardening. He holds up his hand, and fire erupts in his palm.

"You have a dark race among you," he says, pointing with his free hand. "Has he corrupted thy thoughts toward the dragonkind?"

"No!" I find myself saying loudly, even before I'm fully comfortable saying anything.

Aurin's eyes dart to me. "Who speaketh to the chief protector so freely? What human art thou which—"

His eyes widen suddenly, and his anger dissipates. "Dragon blood," he whispers, only audible because of his deep tone and how it stands out stark against the lighter weather sounds. It's as if he's forgotten about Gobby. He walks toward me steadily. I don't like the way he's staring at me. Even though it's probably stupid, I hold up my hand and summon a ball of fire. His mouth twitches, and he stops.

"My, my, a dragon-blooded human, indeed. Intermingling of humans and dragonkind was banned almost twenty years ago due to the prophecy. Ellistra must pass judgment on your parents, whoever they be, for breaking the law," he says.

Dad tenses and pulls his crelotin in front of me. Kroniv has repositioned himself opposite Dad, blocking me as well.

"He *is* Ellistra's son, heir to the dragon kingdom," Dad says, holding his sword tightly.

Aurin's eyes widen, then he shakes his head. He regards me critically, looking at my dad. "It cannot be. Is this truly Daviron? Son and heir of Ellistra? And you, his human father?"

"I am. We've returned to help save Qotan," he says.

A grin tugs at both edges of the dragon's mouth. "A joyous day. We must celebrate! But first, a confirmation."

Without warning, blue wings erupt from the man's back, and he leaps upward above us all. He flings his hand toward me, the bluish flames careening at my face. I gasp and try to counteract with my own ball of fire, but mine flies off course wildly into the air. His flames slam into my head, heat washing over me and my crelotin. Heat flares through my body, but at the same time, I'm not in pain. Instead, my skin is warmed and tingly. I gasp, terror taking over my instincts. My hands shake, but I pull them up to see they are covered in red scales. I'm not hurt.

My crelotin lets out a wail and shifts side to side. Its red exoskeleton is singed all along its neck and back. Anger flares inside me, and I call another ball of flame.

"You hurt my mount, you idiot!" I say before throwing my own fire at him.

The dragon easily dodges it, flapping his wings until he lands on the stoney ground once more. He bows his head, speaking softly in my mind. *I must apologize. I meant no harm to your beast. He will be mended by our healing kin once we enter. My liege, I am sorry for doubting your heritage, but your mother's boon still rests upon your brow. You were protected.*

I'm still angry, but I bite my tongue. Then I let an altogether unexpected thing come out of my mouth. "Stop with this stupidity. Take me to my mother!"

Where did these words come from? I sound so commanding.

He looks up at me, apology in his expression, then he turns and saunters casually down the pathway toward the city wall, shifting back into his human form. Parlequin and his companions follow after. Kroniv goes next, then Dad, me, and Krista—Amir and Jared behind us. I feel the scales retract, my skin cooling to a normal level.

"Dude, that guy just fried you! That was awesome!" Amir exclaims. "That was hotter than the fire at that Japanese restaurant we went to last year."

How like him to think that was cool. I don't care who this dragon thinks he is. What if I'd not scaled over? What a lunatic. I think back to when the elves captured us and how my scales didn't work. I'd assumed it was because they were friends, and they'd said as much, but this guy's attack was blocked. Maybe mom's ward is more robust than I thought, knowing fatal attacks from nonfatal ones. How great of her chief guard to give me a fatal blow.

As he walks ahead of us, I realize something looks off.

His clothing. It's not like what I wear, or what any of the elves do. It looks familiar somehow, like I've seen it before. Looking down at my clothes, I scoff. Most of my chest is bare. Singed sleeves and a hem is all that's left of my top. My pants are gone along my thigh and knees, his spell destroying my clothing. I grit my teeth and squeeze my hands tight. I'm pretty sure I've never been this exposed before.

The ground steepens as we near the entrance to the grand city. Aurin passes through and continues walking. Parlequin and his guards follow, then Kroniv. As they do, I look more closely at Aurin and his bloodred cloak. There's a symbol etched on the back of it. It looks like a ring of spikes, curved around each other. My stomach drops and dread fills me. The last time I saw that was when we were attacked by the orcs.

My eyes widen, and I gasp. "Something's wrong! Everyone be care—"

Red-cloaked figures spring from the darkness behind the walls and fall on the elves, who engage them in battle. Dad pulls his sword free and attacks the closest enemy, a green-skinned orc with massive arms. I reach for my own sword but can't manage to pull it free. Something massive slams into my crelotin and knocks me from the top of it. I land hard on the stones, but I feel my scales heat up my skin to protect me. It still hurts.

Rough hands grasp for my arms, and no matter how hard I thrash, I can't shake them off. Sounds of shouting and clashing metal ring in my ears. My head whips from side to side, causing everything to be a blur of motion.

"Put him out!" a grumbled voice sounds in my ear.

Something soft presses against my mouth and nose, and I panic, drawing in air with ragged gasps. A warming pricks my mind, and before I can hold my breath, I collapse into darkness.

THE TRAITOR AND THE REVELATION

My head hurts. It's the first sensation that comes before any of my other senses. It's a biting pain. My brain feels like it's at a rock concert.

I'm not a morning person. My whole life Dad has struggled to get me out of bed. The only thing that prompts me to class on time is knowing that too many infractions would get me kicked off the football team. Despite my head throbbing, these thoughts tug at my gut, which serves to pull me closer to full consciousness.

A sensation presses at my eardrums, and after a moment of focusing, I can tell it's laughing and clinking, like I'm in a loud bar. I'm not old enough for bars. Even if I were old enough, I can't imagine I'd spend much time in one. Trying to pry my eyes open, I stop the moment bright light invades my vision.

Did I fall asleep at school in the lunchroom? Did someone knock me out on the football field? My mind is so muddled that I can't keep anything straight. Maybe during the homecoming game, I got slammed in the head. That would make the most sense.

The image of a green face and toothy grin with long bottom incisors materializes in my head, and the football theory dissipates.

Qotan. I'm not on the field or at school. Marbled columns fill my mind, a blue dragon with a scheming smile and twinkling eyes. His deep voice rumbles in my memory, bidding us to follow.

My eyes snap open, and my senses flood me so quickly that my brain threatens to shut down. I suck in a breath and start gasping. I'm sure I wasn't drowning, but for some reason, I feel like I wasn't breathing for the past few minutes. Burned spots flicker in my vision as I stare upward at lights flooding down on me. The subtle laughing and eating sounds explode in my ears, raising into a decibel level that makes me want to clap my hands over my ears. When I try, I can't. My hands are restrained. Panic sets in then.

I scream, the sound a bit weak as I attempt to take it all in. Some of the noise around me quiets. Averting my eyes, I see the blood-red-cloaked backs of two orcs. The back of their heads are full of matted and oily black hair. One has a thick ponytail that runs down his back, and the other has close-cropped hair that's been spiked upward.

The room I'm in is long and relatively narrow. White and gray marbled columns, much like the ones we saw when we first entered the dragon city, line the room on both sides. A single long table sits at the center and faces of all kinds stare at me. They are grotesque visages, twisted into sneers. Most I recognize as orcs or goblins, the smaller creatures barely reaching above the top of the table to peer at me with their glowing red eyes. There are other creatures too—ones I don't recognize but look terrifying in their own way. Some are massive with blue skin and empty eyes. Their crooked teeth are exposed and their tongues loll to the side. At one point, I spot a shadowlike creature, but I can't focus on it for too long before I feel hands on my arms. The hands drag me to my feet, and I wince as my head gives one massive throb.

"Hey! Watch it!" I cry, turning toward a set of orcs. Adrenaline fills me, and I explode in flames, the red-hot fire spreading from my hands up my arms. The cloth of my new shirt—or what's left of it after the dragon blasted most of it to bits—burns away, exposing my pale forearms. They release me, dancing away with curses and other things my translation sense can't understand.

I spin, preparing to fight my way out, but when I pull my arms apart too far, they snap against thick chains that weigh my wrists down. Metal cuts into my skin, and I marvel at how I didn't notice them before.

"Silence in the court!" a gravely baritone shouts. It echoes throughout the austere room, all the creatures falling silent. "Put your fire away, dragonling, lest you do something you regret."

My eyes find the owner of the voice, and I freeze. A tall orc, shirtless and muscled like a gym rat, sits on a massive throne at the head of the room. He's raised up high enough that I can see him over the two orcs that stand before me. These both now point jagged daggers at me. I feel the urge to throw the flames at them, to burn them to a crisp like I did the orcs back in the forest, but something stops me.

Struggling sounds . . .

I step back, taking a quick glance to see what the noise is. Everything slows down. Amir's deep brown eyes stare at me, wide and terrified. Something breaks in me, and I pause. He's never looked so scared before. What I see next chills my skin. I look past Amir to see Parlequin on the floor, beaten and bloodied. Dad sits next to him with his arms tied behind his back and a dead look in his eyes. Blood drips from a gash in his hairline, making him look grisly. An orc stands over each of them, swords pointed at vital parts of their bodies.

"Your flames can't stop them all at once, dragonling. Put them out," the orc leader says in a commanding tone. "Or make your choice. Who lives? And who dies?"

Deflated, I let my flames snuff out. Dad turns to look at me, an apologetic grimace in his eyes. This makes me feel guilty. His burden of protecting me is visible in his entire countenance. When they ambushed us earlier, they knocked me over like it was nothing. My flames could have done something, but in that moment, *I* failed *him*.

But he thinks he's let me down.

Terrified to do so, but knowing I have to check, I turn to the other side. Krista and Gobby are both tied up in a similar fashion. Thick braces of metal secure Krista, who is in her demon form. Her massive purple-veined arms and neck are held by chains. Twisted twin horns point upward from the top of her forehead. Five orcs stand around her holding on to the chains as she fights and struggles against them. One orc holds a cage with a raven inside, spikes poking *inward* toward the animal as if it will fight its way out. The bird's beady black eyes fix on me. Jared. The spikes are so he can't shift back into human form or something larger. Technically, he could shrink to something smaller, but he must have a reason he hasn't tried that yet. Most likely because we are vastly outnumbered.

A wave of nausea overcomes me.

On the other side of Jared, the elf woman sits with misty eyes, bruises on her head and cheeks, her arms tied behind her back. All the other elves and Kroniv are nowhere to be seen. While I hope they made it out, I have a suspicion they are dead.

My resolve is on the brink of shattering to pieces. My hands shake, and I force myself to look up at the large orc on the throne. The chair is made of the same marbled stone, but it's huge, way too huge for any humanoid creature. Even the orc doesn't fill out the seat. He simply sits perched on the edge, the back extending at least twenty feet over his head and the sides at least eight feet away.

"So, my plan worked after all," he says, glowering down at me. "When I sent my minions to fetch you and the other halflings from your wretched realm, I did not expect you to walk right into my hands. Then again, I didn't expect to take Dranith so soon."

The orc's hair is long and dark brown, arranged in four thick braids that extend from his hairline and disappear behind his back. He has metal cuffs on his wrists made from some dark metal. They're studded with various jewels. A skirt of some sort is his only piece of clothing. It extends down his legs, which I assume are just as beefy as the rest of him. He doesn't skip leg day, that's for sure. Even his feet are bare with yellow nails, long and brittle.

He stands, his frame upward of six feet tall. His eyes pan over the group, pausing on me, Krista, and Jared.

"And now I've captured three of the necessary half-breeds to get exactly what I want," he says. My tingling mind warns me that he's not speaking English. For once, I kind of wish my ears were only hearing the unfamiliar sounds of the Orcish language. At least then I could focus on getting out of this mess. I glance at Krista, who's glaring at Urothar.

Closing my eyes, I think a message to Jared, telling him to try to find a way out of this. My eyes snap open when I feel the presence of something right in front of me.

Urothar stands inches away, his bare green chest so close that I could probably bite him. While that's somewhat tempting, I have no desire to know what orc flesh tastes like. It's enough to make my stomach turn.

He stares down at me, his irises so dark that they blend into his pupils. His breath, hot and sticky, flows into my face, and I can't help but gag. It smells like rotting meat and mold.

Urothar laughs. It's a booming sound that echoes in the now quiet room.

With a strong swipe, he smashes his fist into the side of my head. Tingling erupts in the area, the scales cropping up to block the blow, but my neck still flings to the side, aggravating my already pounding head. I groan. He's grinning at me, crooked teeth affixed between his sharp canines.

"Those scales will be an issue, but we'll get there in a moment," he says, then turns away from me sharply. When he speaks again, I know he's switched to English. "I must show what happens to those who don't hear me."

His feet thud on the stone floor as he walks past the others and stops in front of Gobby.

"What happens to those who betray. Bad choice, goblin."

Urothar's hand shoots outward quickly. He grabs Gobby by the throat and lifts him off the ground. Gobby's eyes bulge, and he thrashes side to side.

"Stop!" I shout, my words coming out in Orcish. "He didn't do anything to you!"

I start to say my normal explanation of "He saved me, we can trust him," but I stop myself. That's exactly the point. He helped us despite the other dark races. I think back to the traitors' test and how those very decisions landed him in a coma for hours on end. Gobby's face pales as his breathing cuts off.

"Stop! You'll kill him!" I say desperately, tugging on my restraints.

Urothar looks slowly in my direction.

"No," he says flatly. Then, he slams a fist into Gobby's stomach, causing the small goblin to flip over, his back bending too far. I hear a sickening snap as something breaks. Gobby goes still. Frantically I summon flames and throw them in Urothar's direction, hoping to char him like I did his minions. In my panic, I miss the mark entirely.

Anger flashes in his eyes. He lets Gobby fall in a heap. To my relief, his chest is moving. He's not dead. He just needs to heal. I can fix this. I can get him help, and it'll be fine.

"You used fire," Urothar growls. "Bad move."

He nods toward the elf woman captive and snaps his fingers.

The orc holding the elf woman stabs his sword through her shoulder. She cries out in pain but doesn't fight back. Her restraints keep her from trying.

"No!" I shout again, but I let my flames go out.

It could be Krista next, or Amir, or Dad. There's nothing I can do.

"What do you want from me?" I ask desperately.

He grins at the question.

"Your life, in the end," he says. "I need you and the other tainted halflings. Your human blood is weak, vulnerable. But the prophecy says sacrifice you, and I will gain power. That is what I want. But first, we deal with pesky protection."

He snaps his fingers again, and I hear shuffles behind the massive throne. Two orcs—one I recognize as the half orc son of the king—come around the marbled stone dragging a woman. Her long brown hair is tied back with golden bands, and her blue eyes loll to the side with her head. She wears a regal gown of red with a chain mail vest, but her hands and feet are bare. The scabbard at her side is empty as well. Her expression is dull and distant, but she is beautiful.

It's my mother.

I recognize her the moment I see her, but my mind can't comprehend how she's here, how she's restrained. In the vision she'd left for me, she was a great dragon, massive and red. She could blow flames and likely bite these orcs in half. I notice a thick metal collar around her neck, a single symbol glowing in the center. My eyes tear up.

"Ellistra!" Dad shouts. He growls and pulls against his restraints to no avail. "What have you done to her? I'll kill you for this!"

I've never seen Dad lose his composure like this. His protective reaction at seeing her stings me. There's a longing in his eyes. He loves her . . .

Stoking the flames on my arms, I throw them outward, blasting the orcs around me. They scream as they are engulfed by the heat. My whole chest flares with the most intense heat I've ever felt. I stare at Urothar. His mouth is turned upward with a look of amusement. I'd like nothing better than to wipe that grin off his face.

Abruptly, something hard hits the back of my head.

The world goes black momentarily, and I'm barely aware of the ground slamming into my whole body. Pain erupts in multiple places on my chest, wrists, and knees. I feel cold. Blinking to try to get some lucidity back into my mind, I allow my vision to go from intensely blurry to sharper. The lights above me are even more oppressive than they were when I first woke up.

I hear Urothar's voice before I see him. "Well done, my son. Perhaps your human heritage isn't going to ruin you completely. It's good to know that the spell of warding has been broken."

Someone's voice is muffled through a gag, or maybe a hand. I turn my head, wincing as my head throbs. A rough green hand is pressed over Dad's mouth as he tries to shout. Blood drips on the ground next to me; I can smell the metallic scent. Feeling sick, I try to press myself upward, only to fail and fall back down.

"It's a shame that your mother only put the warding in place until you met each other in person. One look, and that was it. I can do whatever I want to you now," Urothar says to me, his voice dropped low so that the others can't hear. This makes it doubly creepy.

"What—do—you want—from me?" I manage to gasp out.

He laughs, the booming sounds making me close my eyes to suffer the throbbing of my head.

"For the sacrifice, you fool," he says, turning his back to me and walking away. His long toenails click on the ground. It's all I can hear in the quiet of the room. Dad has fallen silent. Tears are flowing down his cheeks. I've failed him. He's going to watch me die.

"Do the rest of us a favor, you ugly potato face, and speak in English! Unless you want to keep going on your date with David!" Krista shouts.

Despite the pain radiating through me, I laugh. It's purely desperation at this point, but I can't help it. This seems to throw Urothar into a frenzy. He spins on his heels and rushes toward her. He throws his fist into her gut, making her grunt and double over.

"Quiet! You are nothing but sludge! The light races need nothing of you. I should kill you now," he says, slipping a large dagger from his belt. The blade is black with veins of glowing red. My breath catches, and I expect him to thrust it into her chest, but he doesn't. Krista laughs.

"You can't, can you? You need all six of us before you can kill us," she says.

I blink, trying to take in what she just said. It must be correct because the orc king glares at her, then punches her in the face. Her head snaps to the side, but she keeps grinning. Jared flaps wildly in his cage next to her, chirping and chittering.

With a huff, Urothar turns and walks back to his throne. I'm still on my stomach, but I press my palms into the marble and lift my chest up. Everything spins as my head flows with blood, but I persevere, moving to a sitting position. Thoughts fire through me so quickly that I can't keep track of them all. My scales didn't protect me. I'm vulnerable again, all because I set eyes on my mother. Ferona told me the ward would only last until then. They could kill us, right here and now, but they won't because of the prophecy. I can't believe I didn't put that together until Krista said it. We have more leverage than I thought. It's not a lot of leverage, but we can make it work.

I summon a ball of flame in my hand and point it toward Krista. I shift to my knees and try to hold it steady even though my hand is shaking like a leaf.

"Let us go, or I'll kill her. Your sacrifice would be ruined then," I say.

Krista's mouth twitches upward, the purple veins moving with it. She's probably fuming inside. Or maybe she approves of this plan.

Urothar glares at me, but he doesn't seem troubled.

"You will not do it. You are weak. I see it in your eyes. False threats will do you no good before me, dragonling. Save time and put that away," he chides.

My jaw hardens, and I move the flames closer to her. She doesn't even flinch, though I'm sure it hurts to have fire so close to her skin.

"Gulran, stop the dragonling," Urothar says.

There's a flash of movement to my right, and something blunt and hard hits me between the shoulder blades. There is no heat and no scales. I pitch forward yet again, barely getting my hand in front of me before my face slams into the stone.

"Thank you, son. Watch him closely," Urothar says. "I may not be able to kill you, but I can deal with another problem."

He snaps his fingers, and his half orc son moves out from behind me. I look up to see Urothar pointing. By the time I make the connection that he's pointing at Gobby, it's too late. During the exchange, Gobby had woken up, gasping in pain. The small creature's eyes are wide, glowing red with fear as the orc prince holds him up by his shirt and thrusts a black sword through his chest.

"*NO!*" I scream, the sound tearing from my throat.

Gobby's blue blood sickens me, but I hardly notice, instead watching the light fade from his eyes. Any hope I harbored to save him—to heal him—is gone. It's only seconds before the prince throws him to the ground. Tears pour down my cheeks. I feel powerless, so weak that I can't even defend my friends. Knowing Urothar will kill anyone with ease makes me realize the danger Amir, my dad, and the others are in. I must obey anything he says.

"Now that *that* problem is done with, give me the stone," Urothar says, holding out a massive hand.

"I—what?" I stammer. I can't understand what he's saying. Gobby's dead. I didn't know the goblin well, but after all he'd done for me—I can't—I can't focus on anything else. He helped me understand their magic.

Now his blood seeps into the stone floor. I swallow hard, my hands quivering.

"Give me the stone," he repeats.

Rough hands grab me and hold me down. It's not difficult; I'm not putting up any more fights. Not now. They search me until Gulran finds where I've stored the searching stone.

"Here, Father," he says, his tone less gravelly than his father's, but I can still hear the resemblance. He tosses it to his father, who catches it with ease, staring at it with a greedy expression.

"The key to finding the others. Thank you for bringing this to me. Now I can locate the other halfings and bring them here to die with you."

My stomach falls. The elf king gave those to us, telling us to keep them safe, and now I've managed to lose mine in less than a day. Urothar turns the dial, frowning when nothing happens.

"What is the meaning of this?" he murmurs, growing softly. "Why does it not work?"

A bit of satisfaction stirs in me. It only works when one of us three touches it. Even Dad couldn't make it work, and he and I share blood.

"You need *their* blood to work it, Urothar. That is another reason you must let them live," a new voice sounds from behind me.

My skin chills. Not because I'm scared of the new person coming, but because I recognize the voice. I've heard it before. The *day* before, in fact.

From a doorway to the side of the narrow and marbled room strides a woman wearing an elegant gown of blue with glowing gossamer embellishments.

Queen Ferona.

22

I FIND THE ANSWER INSIDE

My blood boils. After only seconds of staring at the fairy queen, I clench my hands so hard that they ache. My nails bite into the skin, knuckles glowing white. I don't know how long Jared had flapped inside his cage during these exchanges, but I notice he's unmoving now, a light whimper coming from him. He's shifted into a small fox-like animal, still well within the cage limits, but capable of a new sound.

The fairy queen regards me with a look of contempt, then gazes at Jared.

"I see my offspring has trouble with his emotions. That, plus his tainted magical abilities. I have no doubt he'd be best sacrificed after all," she says.

Her hair is pinned up in a tight bun, so blonde that it practically glows against the bright, flaming lights all around us. Her piercing blue eyes look electric as she stares at Jared with a slight smile on her face. Little wrinkles about her eyes and mouth add years to her age, making her look something like mid-forties. Given that I have exactly one experience with seeing a fairy, I don't know why it surprises me. Probably because all the fairies I've seen in movies and books always look like little girls. They sound like them, too.

Krista growls to my right. Her body has swollen larger than I've seen before, her eyes pure black as her demon blood pours through her emotions.

"*You!*" she shouts. "*You* would betray your son? What is wrong with you? After all the messages you sent to him, after all the things you did for us, why now?"

I glance at fox Jared, and even though I don't know animal emotions, it's clear what he's feeling as he stares at the ground. He never seemed like an inflammatory person and seeing his reaction right now validates that. Krista probably does most of that work for him. For once, I'm pleased by her disposition. Someone needs to say the hard things.

Ferona purses her lips, tilting her half-moon spectacles downward to glare at Krista over the top.

"My reasons are my own, but since you're not going anywhere," she says, looking back to me, "I have nothing to hide."

She gestures behind her to where the two orcs hold my dazed mother.

"The dragons are no longer fit to rule over us." She sniffs. "They have been blinded by the wiles of the humans and their realm. They freely opened the portal, allowing humans to *pass through* without any regard for the safety of Qotan. It was imperative that we seized control from her and her brood for the benefit of all in this land."

I grit my teeth, pulling on the chains that bind my hands and my feet.

"What is so wrong with humans? What are they doing to you?" I say, feeling cheeky and brave.

She stares at me flatly. "They are weakening the magic of Qotan. It's no wonder as to how it will happen. Don't you see? Their own realm is devoid of such magic. They've leeched it away for their own greed and power. They'll do the same here if they're left to live."

She eyes Amir and my father, her lip curling upward and her eyes narrowing.

The queen turns her head to look at Urothar on the throne. He's still staring at me, his teeth bared ever so slightly, like he's waiting for me to get close enough that he could take a bite out of my flesh. This makes my stomach turn, and I avert my eyes even though I can still feel his on me. As I do, I notice a marking on Ferona's neck. It's a swooping symbol that seems vaguely familiar. It's glowing the same subtle white as the one on my mother's restraint around her neck. My mind whirrs into activity. The same symbol is on the goblins, orcs, and massive trolls.

"I could not take Dranith alone. The armies of the fairies are few, and most are no match for the flames of a dragon mouth," Ferona says. "But the orcs are strong. They and theirs have been battling us endlessly without giving up for hundreds of years. In them is strength. The answer was right in front of me. I'd spoken an oath with the other light races to lock away whatever power lies in the prophecy with human blood."

She looks disgusted as she glares in Jared's direction. "Little did I know that my blood, and my magic, would be tainted by that wretched human. Do you not see it? Shape-shifting is not a fairy's magic. That is the taint of his islander blood."

Ferona's expression is pure hatred, and her face flushes in her anger.

"That mutt of a boy carries precious royal fairy blood, and he's ruined it all."

"Wow, you're mother of the year," I say sarcastically.

Her eyes flash with something, and it seems like she's about to zap me with her fairy powers, but she doesn't. Instead, she smiles at me, then lifts a finger to her neck.

"Your words mean nothing to me, dragon boy, for your voice will be silenced soon enough. You'll swear your fealty to the orc king, as I and many of my kind have, or we'll start killing your friends one by one."

She lifts a delicate finger and taps her neck where the glowing symbol pulses.

"The magic of the orcs is quite incredible, I must say. To dominate the will and mind of one has so many applications. If only it wasn't bound by the limitation of the agreement of the bearer," she says. "Thanks to my craftsmen, and their knowledge gained from the elves, we can use his domination magic without consent."

I follow the queen's gaze to where my mother stands with her eyes glazed over. The symbol makes sense now. It's how they are holding her at bay. Even though I don't know the finer details of how she was captured, I surmise that she trusted Queen Ferona, and that was her downfall.

"I will never consent to that," I say darkly. "Your magic won't work on me."

It's a bold claim, and I have no idea if it's true. My legs shake, my fate suddenly feeling inevitable. Still, I hold my hard gaze and lock my jaw. They won't have the satisfaction of seeing me panic. There has to be a way out of this situation. Turning left, I see the crumpled corpse of Gobby, and a fresh wave of fear and anger washes over me. Even though we're surrounded, I know I can't give up. My mother is right there, and my father is in silent tears to my right. I stoke the heat in my chest, and my arms burst into flames once more.

There's no need for any of that, dear. Ferona's voice echoes in my head. I gasp as a sharp stabbing shoots through my skull. My flames go out instantly. What just happened?

"As you may well know, dragonling, fairies have the power to enter your mind. Not only can I hear every thought you have, but I can enter inside and commune with you. This is how I will ensure your compliance," she says coolly.

A door opens loudly behind her, and an orc stalks in carrying three metal collars similar to the one strapped on my mother. I can't help but look at her helplessly, crying out in my mind for her to wake up and help us. Nothing happens. There's no way out of this. Ferona walks smoothly over to the basket and lifts one of them, eyeing it.

"Such beautiful craftsmanship, I must say," she says.

Krista spits on the ground. "You have terrible taste in fashion, then. How about you try one of those on yourself?"

Ferona ignores her comment, instead turning slowly to face me.

"For years, I've lived under the protection and weakness of your mother. For years, I've suffered in silence, knowing that Qotan was being led to ruin. Now I have three of the six prophesied halflings and the means to find the others."

She holds her hand backward, and the orc king tosses the compass-like stone to her. He misses his toss, but somehow it is caught midair by an invisible force and directed to her palm.

"Biding my time was worth it. It became all too perfect when my son stumbled on you, dragonling. I had plans to send the orc's minions to retrieve him and the demonling when he heard your thoughts," she says, throwing Krista a condescending look. "I don't think it could have worked out any better for me. I knew the moment my son laid eyes on you that you were Ellistra's son. Your internal light burns so bright."

Jared shifts from a fox into a dog, though the whimpering doesn't stop.

Krista stops struggling against her restraints. She's now staring at Jared.

"Oh yes, when I left a message to my infant son in a magic stone, I left a piece of me. It was with this piece that I could find you, track your every move. I could hear his thoughts until he learned to put up a mental barrier. Still, I could see everything. It's a shame you left the stone back in the human realm when you were transported here. It would have made finding you so much easier."

She holds up the collar to the basket and lets it fall inside with a loud metallic clink. Lifting her hand with the searching stone, she stares at it with a hunger that chills me. Small bits of shuffling echo in the almost silent room, and I almost forget that there are other creatures here watching the whole scene. It's incredible that they've managed to stay so silent. They watch us, their eyes full of wonder, fear, and anger. Even though they don't have normal human features, I know how they feel. I'm reminded of the crelotin and how they interact with emotions.

Echoing footsteps pull my attention back to the monologuing queen. I've stopped listening. My brain is shutting down because I'm so overwhelmed. I want to lay down and sleep. Maybe I'll wake up to find that this has all been an incredibly vivid dream. If I could throw a massive flame at her, maybe I could—

"Remember, dragonling," Ferona says. "I can read your every thought. Before you can stoke a big enough flame, I'll have it suppressed."

Krista roars next to me, pulling against her chains so hard that the orcs holding her pitch forward, falling on their faces. She rushes Ferona, dragging the surprised orcs with her. Ferona's face twists into fear rapidly, and she backs away. Krista grabs a handful of her gossamer gown and yanks her forward. The fabric rips, and Ferona yelps, almost falling on her back before her wispy wings flutter and keep her afloat. It takes four more orcs slamming their shoulders into Krista to hold her back, but they manage to secure her.

"Well—I—now you see," she says, clearly flustered, "why demons should never have been allowed into the light race treaties. Now they have the enmity of the dark races as well. You all deserve to die."

Ferona stares daggers at Krista, and honestly, it's a look that I would expect from Krista herself.

"Your blood will be drained soon, demonling, along with you other half-breed mutts," Ferona spits. Heat in my chest flares hot, and I almost light myself on fire, but Ferona whips her free hand out and points it at me, shaking her head. I pause, but I'm still fuming.

"Speaking of," she says, closing the distance between us, her feet still hovering above the stone ground. "I need to borrow some of that."

She holds up a finger, painted blue fingernails reflecting the bright lights above. With a swipe of her hand, my cheek starts stinging, hot liquid dripping down. The scales do nothing to protect me. Even though they told me the ward was broken when I saw my mother, part of me still hoped it would react.

The traitor queen presses the stone against my cheek until a drop lands on the surface. The moment it touches, a light flares from the center and beams out along the spindle. It's pointing directly at Krista.

"That should last us some time, I think," she says, withdrawing the stone from me. "Magic runs deep within our blood, even yours. Humans have their own uses, which is where I found the key to your realm."

I glare at her back, imagining so many ways to fry her to death. Knowing she is hearing every thought I have gives me satisfaction. Still, she doesn't give any indication that she's listening. One image—her body engulfed in my flames until she's blackened—plays in my mind. I want her to see it, to know what I will do to her for what they did to Gobby and my friends.

Ferona stares with wonder at the stone and twists the spindle until it moves to another section. This one points at Jared. With another turn, the light disappears. She frowns, looking at me.

"What did you do? Did you break it?" she says, glaring at me.

In truth, I have no idea, but I play it off, grinning at her. "Yes. I tampered with it to make sure you could never find the others."

She glowers. "A lie. What is the truth, boy? Don't waste my time with your words. Your mind will reveal all."

The truth of the stone starts to seep into my mind, but I rush to fill my thoughts with anything else. Images of killing her, plans for breaking free and saving us, memories of Gobby dying on the stones—anything to induce strong emotion, to block out the truth.

"Stop with these meaningless thoughts! Give me what I need!" she shouts, clenching her hand.

She's only targeting my mind. Why isn't she seeking the thoughts of Jared? Or Krista? They know just as much information as I do. Technically, Amir was there, too, when we tested the stone.

I freeze, panic rising inside. Ferona grins evilly.

"I'll answer the question you asked in your mind, dragonling. That is, these two have guarded their minds against me. Their parents have taught them well. It takes years of practice to block one's mind from a fairy. But you and your human friend . . ."

She stares at him. Shaking, I pull on my chains and start to shout. "He doesn't know anything! Listen to me!"

A punch hits me in the gut, and I gasp, doubling over in pain. By the time I've recovered, the fairy queen is beaming.

"The stone need only enter the human realm to find them. Thank you, human," she says, eyeing Amir.

His eyes widen. He's breathing hard, and his face pales. I've never seen him so terrified. The confident and smart Amir from before is long gone. He has unwillingly given Ferona the information, and I put him in danger by dragging him here.

"Humans are so weak. It's the sole reason they leech every bit of life and power from everything around them. Yet, you aren't completely useless. As servants, you have merit. And your blood has special properties." She moves to Amir, slipping the searching stone somewhere in the folds of her dress. I look for where it might have gone but can't see it anywhere.

She grabs Amir's chin and upper arm, lifting him from the floor.

"Fairy portal magic is powerful, but there is one place we can never go. Until recently, it was a limitation that drove me mad," she says, lifting a finger. "But it's the blood of a human that solved that mystery for me."

A rumbling growl comes from the throne behind her, the orc king shifting on the massive throne. "Get on with this, Fairy Queen. I didn't employ you to talk us to death!"

Ferona winces, then bares her teeth, keeping herself turned away from her new ally. It's subtle, but I can see she's shaking ever so slightly. There is something wrong with her. After seeming so confident and strong, she's acting like she's scared of the orc king. I glare at her brand, the one on her neck, and eye my mother, still standing in a trance. If I could get to my mother and pull off that collar, then—

Don't waste your time, or mine, Ferona presses into my mind. I grit my teeth against the pain that comes with the words.

"They must understand my breakthrough discovery. They must *know* why they have no hope of saving themselves or their fellow halflings!" Ferona screams at the orc king, then she fixes her eyes on Amir. "Let me take some of that blood—"

"Leave the boy alone!" Dad shouts.

I jump at his words. His face looks calm and serene, but there is hatred behind his brown eyes. He had fallen silent for so long staring at my mother that I didn't know he had that much in him.

Ferona releases Amir's shirt, leaving him standing again on the marbled ground. He's still quivering like a leaf.

"It would be so much more poetic to take the blood of the very sire who created the mutt-bred dragonling," she says, hovering over to my dad. She holds out her hand, gripping a roughly cut dark stone. It looks exactly like the stone the orc's son threw at me earlier, though this one doesn't glow. Without hesitation, she places all five nails of her fingers against Dad's cheek. He stares at her, resolve written in every part of his posture. Ferona shouts, pulling her hand back and slashing Dad across the face. He gasps in pain as streak lines of blood appear on his cheek. She presses the strange stone against his skin, and it absorbs much of the seeping blood. The rock starts to glow a steady red.

"And now you see," she says, holding it up, "how we can bridge the gap between the races of Qotan and the human realm. With this stone, we can transport our kind there and preserve them until they find the others. We simply need copious amounts of human blood. It's good you brought these to us. We haven't been able to capture many humans lately. We'll need to take every drop of life from them to fill our stones. Of course, once we are through, we can just pluck some mortals from your world and create more stones for us."

My skin chills. Tears well up in my eyes. Amir is sobbing now that he hears what his fate will be. Ever since arriving in Qotan, we've been told about disappearing humans and about how it's not safe for them. And now we know why . . .

"Human blood has a draw to its home. The blood of our races reacts the same. It's what I used to infuse the very stones that brought *you* here."

My stomach turns. That means she had to drain the blood of . . . . I shudder to think of who she sacrificed for those stones. I think back to that day when the small goblin threw the stone at my feet and sent us here. If only I had dodged the stone, or if I had been trained to fight better . . . maybe we would still be on earth. Maybe I would have played the homecoming game and we would have won. The familiar homesickness tugging returns to my gut, so strong that I gasp in shock.

Ferona doesn't seem to notice. Instead, she's gaping at the stone in wonder.

Human blood has a draw to its home.

Her words echo in my mind. Tingling enters my head and travels down my arms and legs. It's a simple idea, but it feels right. I focus on my bedroom, on laying down in my bed and smelling my kitchen. The tugging intensifies. Could it possibly be?

Krista said she'd felt similar tugs when she thought of home. She said it wasn't homesickness, but something else. It felt like . . . magic.

I snap my attention to Krista. She doesn't struggle against her restraints anymore. Her eyes catch mine and I raise my eyebrows. Did she just make the same connection? Did she come to the same wild conclusion that I did? It's possible I'm insane, that what I've thought of isn't true, but I have to try. Fixing my gaze on Jared the dog, I imagine sending my thoughts to him. I'm unsure if he's listening to my mind, but I hope he is at this moment. He looks at me, then I see him nod. It's the confirmation I need.

"Such beautiful light, made by the life liquid of such an inferior race, but—"

She pauses, her face going slack. Spinning toward me, a look of terror washes over her face. She's heard my thoughts *and* my idea.

Knowing I don't have time to wait, I explode in flames. The orcs holding my chains gasp and jump away from me. I've never burned so hot in my life, and I stoke that, leaping forward at the fairy queen. A scream rips out of her mouth as I shove my hands toward her dress, lighting it on fire in multiple places. She tumbles to the ground, and I leave her there, spinning toward Amir. I put out my flames and jump forward, my hand gripping his wrist.

"Come on!" I shout, pulling on his arm and reaching out for my dad.

"David!" Dad calls.

When I turn to look at him, he's being dragged away.

I grip Amir's arm and try to pull him with me, but I meet resistance. The orc holding his chains is pulling back. Two more orcs appear out of nowhere and grab me. When I try to create more flames, I feel Ferona blocking it mentally. Cursing, I turn toward Jared.

His cage is empty. My mind reels. It must have worked.

"Krista!" I shout. "Think of home!"

As the orcs grab me more forcefully now, I twist, trying to knock them off, but I don't have the strength to get out of their grips. We struggle, and all the while I keep hold of Amir's wrist, squeezing him like a lifeline. My eyes lock on Dad, his face solemn and bloody. He looks sad, like he regrets something. I desperately want to reach him so I can take his hand to pull him along, but he's too far away.

He mouths the words "I love you," and my heart shatters. It's too late. I'm going to miss my chance. With every bit of me, I think of home. I focus on school, on my classes, my house—on the football team.

The tugging rips at my stomach, and I grunt in shock. An icy chill leaks from my mind all over my body. I feel it leave me where I'm in contact with the orcs and with Amir, seeping through the connection. Everything around me starts to blur as if I'm spinning. Dad's face melts away. I try to scream, but no sounds come out. Suddenly I'm falling through the air, everything going black. It lasts only seconds before my feet hit something firm, and I'm assaulted with sounds and lights.

A car horn blares in my ears, making me freeze, eyes wide. Bright headlights blind me, and more cars start honking. I cover my ears, turning to see that Amir has passed out on the road.

The *road*.

My heart thuds. Tall buildings surround us. Billboards flash advertisements about musicals and other products. Hundreds of people—actual humans—move about busy sidewalks as if they didn't know what was going on. A few stop to gawk at the commotion in the road.

Strong hands try to pull me to the side. One of the orcs that grabbed me before I thought of home is here. Its face is twisted in fear as it wails and screams, tearing at my clothing as if desperate for help. To my horror, I watch as its face melts like butter, its skin turning black. I recoil, stomach roiling. Within seconds, its body and clothing melt into a puddle of black ooze.

I stumble away, almost tripping on Amir's limp form.

"David!" Jared calls.

So much is happening around me. People have started shouting at me to move. Jared's there in an instant, lifting Amir with his powerful arms. I gather his feet, and we struggle to the sidewalk.

"It worked! I can't believe it worked!" I gasp, sitting down on the cement.

Jared looks worried, and my stomach drops. Krista hasn't come yet. My eyes widen, and I turn to the street, hoping to see her soon.

"Come on, come on, come on," I whisper.

The air in the road warps suddenly, twisting and writhing like water swirling down a drain. Then a form appears out of nowhere. Krista's massive purple-veined body lands hard on the pavement, causing more ruckus on the road. Her steeped horns protrude upward in a terrifying display. I stumble toward her and grab her beefy forearm. It's freezing cold to the touch. A shiver rockets down my back, but I ignore it despite how unnatural it feels. Pulling as hard as I can, I manage to get her attention. Pure black eyes stare at me, furrowed and full of anger.

Shouts of fury change to shouts of fear as people witness Krista's form. I know we have to get out of sight as soon as possible.

"Jared! Grab Amir and let's move!" I yell as Krista finally takes to my tugging and stumbles off the road.

Jared slings Amir over his shoulder, and we rush to the closest alley we can find. It's not completely empty. A few homeless men sleep against the brick wall a dozen yards away. We stay in the dark, waiting. No one follows, which completely shocks me. Then again, we didn't do anything illegal.

Once we catch our breath, Krista has shrunk to her normal size. Her hands clench firmly at her sides, and I can see the anger still running through her. Without warning, she slams her fist into the brick wall. No mark is left there, further evidence that she doesn't have her strength without being in demon form.

She leaves flesh and a trail of blood on the bricks. When she moves her hand, I see her mangled skin and knuckles.

"Jared, your mom is a piece of work," she says, still glaring at the wall.

Jared looks crestfallen, but he doesn't argue.

"I can't believe it. The first time I meet my mom, and—" He curses and slumps against the wall with his free shoulder.

My breaths come in ragged waves. We made it out. Before they could control our minds, we made it out. The tugging in my gut was my human blood pulling me home. The realization that I had a way home all this time strikes me heavy and hard. I bite my lip, leaning against the wall and sliding down it.

The only image I have burned in my mind is the desperate look in my dad's eyes as I left him there to die.

I can't stop the tears from falling, and I don't care to try.

THE SEARCH BEGINS

I sit on the cloth seats of Jared's and Krista's van. Their dad, Bob, drives silently down the road. My chin rests on my elbow, which I have propped up on the window so I can watch the landscape go by. We've been driving for a few days now, heading west. This may be the first time I've ever gone on a long road trip and not been terribly bored.

Okay, it's the first time I've been on a road trip. Dad and I spent a long time in Kentucky, with no ventures outside for vacations.

Thoughts of Dad make my chest constrict. I want to sink into my mind and live there in memory for the rest of my life. Unfortunately, I don't have that luxury.

It's been two weeks since we managed to teleport ourselves out of Qotan. No one knows how we teleported to New York when we left Qotan, but I have a suspicion that Qotan is overlaid with earth. Because we had traveled far via fairy teleportation in Qotan, we had traveled far in the human realm. It's a shame that my first and only time in New York was after almost being killed by a traitorous queen.

I peer at Jared in the front seat. He looks sullen. Ever since he found out about his mother, he's not been the same. I let out a small chuckle. Here I am making assumptions about how different he is when I literally met him less than a month ago. Going to a different realm and almost dying a few times has a way of knitting people together.

Amir snores in the seat next to me. He's been sleeping for most of the ride, and I honestly can't figure out how he can do it.

Jared's and Krista's parents flew to our rescue a couple days after we made it to New York. While we waited for them, we had to hole up in coffee shops for as long as we could until they kicked us out. We had no money, and we were dressed like a troupe of fantasy role-players. Honestly, I'm shocked I wasn't embarrassed about it. I earned those clothes, though it was probably good we didn't have our weapons. Police would have been undoubtedly hailed.

We've been moving about ever since. I want to go home to Kentucky, to sleep in my own bed, but I can't. Jared told his parents about his mother's stone—the one she spied with—and they promptly destroyed it before coming to get us. Even with that, we can't go back. The fairy queen knows where we were found, and now we know she has the means to send the orc king's forces to get us again.

Even Amir's life is at risk in that place.

The thought they will likely use my dad's blood to do it boils *my* blood. I finger the hem of my jeans, trying not to let tears fall again.

Krista turns around in the seat right in front of me.

"Are we still moving in the right direction?" she asks.

I sigh, reaching into my pocket to pull out one of the stones. Even though Ferona took one, we still have the two gifted to Jared and Krista. It turns out they are not specific to a person; we just need one of us to hold it for the magic to work. The bronze spindle points to a tree symbol with a half-moon hovering above it. None of us know what the symbol means, but we tested it and discovered that it's not the three of us. We ruled those lines out quickly and then picked a random one.

A beam of white light comes out of the spindle, pointing to the front right of the car.

"Yup. It hasn't moved completely north yet," I say.

She nods, then regards me with a soft expression. She's been a lot more pensive since we got back from Qotan, and I have to say, I'm not sure I'm all right with it. I was just getting used to her angry and belligerent personality.

"We'll have to stop soon and stretch our legs. I could use a spar session," she says.

I give her a soft half smile and nod. "Yeah, that would be good."

After seeing how terribly I handled myself in battle, Krista has made it her personal goal to train me to be a warrior. The trunk is filled with weapons: swords, shields, spears—whatever we could fit into the cargo space. I can only imagine what a policeman's reaction would be if they pulled us over and found an arsenal of outdated weaponry.

Amir stirs suddenly and bolts upright. "Are we there yet?" he says groggily.

"Nah, man, you can go back to sleep," I say.

He nods, then slumps back against his pillow. I smile despite the circumstances. Bringing him with us is probably a dumb idea, but they've seen his face. Ferona knows he's with us, and we don't want him going home. He could put his parents and little sister in danger. Instead, we had to call them and say that he, including myself and my dad, are under protective services. We made something up about witnessing a crime and how we need to leave Kentucky for some time.

To say that his mother was upset about his perfect attendance record being messed up would be an understatement. Still, I think they are more relieved to know he is safe. We were gone for days in Qotan. And unlike other "portal fantasy" stories I've read, time did *not* stop here.

That thought tears me up. Dad has been in Qotan for two weeks without us now. There is no way he's still alive. My throat closes up, and I choke back a sob. Jared peers back at me. I know he's listening to my thoughts. I say something snarky about privacy and how he should leave me alone in my mind, and he frowns, turning away. He means well, I know he does, but one of the first things I need to master is blocking my thoughts from people like him.

It's possible. Krista and her parents can do it. Until then, I have to suffer knowing that he can hear my every thought.

The van pulls up a hill, the landscape out my window tilting with the steepness of the incline. There's nothing to see while driving in this place. I almost wish there was something to watch, not because I'm bored, but because I don't like being left alone with my mind.

I sit up and hold my hand in front of me. Focusing on the skin, I imagine it warming up. Not *heating* up, just warming. The tingling sensation I became all too familiar with in Qotan prickles the back of my hand, and red scales form. Energy seeps from my chest, but at a slow rate. There's no explanation for how I know that energy is being pulled from me, I can just tell. If I hold the scales for too long, I'll tucker myself out.

Pressing the feeling up my arm and into my palm, the scales spread. Even though the ward my mother placed on me is gone, I still have the protection. In addition to sparring, I've been practicing this. As soon as I can control it fully, I'll be able to last in battle a lot longer.

"Looks like we're coming up on a town here soon. We'll stop and grab some food. Maybe stay for the night," Bob says from the driver's seat.

"You kids doing okay back there?" Stacey, Krista's mom, calls back.

"Could use more snacks, I'll admit," Jared says, holding up a few empty wrappers.

Stacey laughs. "Teenage boys eat way too much. I can't believe you haven't eaten us out of house and home. That, plus Krista's demonic appetite. We're lucky we aren't poor."

Krista rolls her eyes and leans against the back of her seat. "As long as you keep me from transforming into my demonic form, then I'll eat like the skinny girl I am. Keep David away and we're all good."

I narrow my eyes and kick the back of her seat playfully. She feigns anger, baring her teeth at me, and we all burst into laughter. We have moments like this here and there. They're the only thing keeping me sane.

Find the other three. That's the only plan we have. What we do from there, we have no idea. The stone resting on my lap instills a drive within me, within *us*, to protect the others. Now that Ferona has the other searching stone, I know she'll be trying to find the other half bloods. I can only hope that we can get there faster.

"Let's try not to make a scene here. I'm sure there are warrants out for our arrest with what happened in the last town," Bob says lightly.

Krista scoffs. "That cashier deserved it. The coupon we had was still valid, and he was being a jerk. Besides, they can buy a new cash register."

She had lost her temper and, with swollen arms, she had smashed it to pieces.

"Yeah, well, let's try not to make a scene here. We'll need to stay at a hotel or something. I have some work to do before we move on," he says.

Both Krista's and Jared's parents work from home. They do something with computers, building stuff for tech companies. None of it makes sense to me, but they are loaded. At least, more loaded than we ever were. They've worked on and off during the trip, but I don't mind. It allowed us to rest from the long car rides every couple days.

We fall silent as the van slides past a sign that says, "Welcome to Sutherland."

A few people mill about on the sides of the road, but it's mostly empty. I lean back against the window and let my thoughts take over again. There's no telling what will happen from here, but I feel a drive to save them—the other kids. Whether it's my royal dragon blood, or simply motivation to avenge my father's death, I know we have to save them.

I can only hope we will all be ready when the orc king comes calling again.

Loved it? Hated it? Let other people know what you thought by leaving a review! This would help me out in so many ways and I would appreciate it so much.

ALSO BY DAN KENNER

Books by Dan

www.dankenner.com

Epic Fantasy

Shielded: A Prequel to The Lightbearer Chronicles - Get the Ebook
FREE at www.dankenner.com/free

Awakened: The Lightbearer Chronicles Book One

Transformed: The Lightbearer Chronicles Book Two

Ascended: The Lightbearer Chronicles Book Three

Young Adult

Sunfire

Middle Grade

The Search for Silence

A Voice in The Noise

The Thundering Echo

About the Author

Dan lives in rural Idaho where he happily lives with his wife, six children and numerous goats, chickens and a cat named Wilma. Aside from writing, which he'd happily do full time, Dan spends most of his time outside in the homestead he built with his wife. When he's not writing, he spends his time with his nose in a fantasy or sci-fi book.

You can connect with me at https://www.dankenner.com

ACKNOWLEDGEMENT

I have a lot of peoeple to thank for this process. First off, thanks to my wonderful wife who, despite not being a huge fan of fantasy and sci-fi, always supports my crazy stories and offers to read and give feedback on them. Thanks to my amazing kids for loving to read and constantly begging for me to keep writing and keep creating adventures for them to enjoy.

I want to thank my Father in Heaven, above all, for giving me a mind that can create and a drive to bring clean and fun stories to families that they can trust. We live by stories and we thrive by them, and I am grateful He helps me to think of them, create them, and bring them to readers.

Thanks to Danielle Harrington for being an incredible editor. I've been through a number of editors and am thrilled to have the opportunity to work with her. Additionally, I want to thank Meghan Hoesch for her skills in copy editing. May you both be blessed for eternity for knowing how to fix my garbled jumble of words. I'm sure you'll be able to help me with my messy writing again.

Thanks to my mother for always being willing to read the first versions and tell me they are good. Whether you believe they are or not, your positivity helps immensely.